"DON'T TOUCH THAT RING!"

Max's yell came too late. The stranger had already seized the ring and pulled it free. A blaze of electric white winked out from the ring. The floor shook, things fell off the shelves, even the heavy desk jumped up and hopped a foot back as the light fogged out vision like a sudden thick cloud.

Max staggered back against the desk, fighting to stay on his feet as a black funnel spun out of the ring. He grabbed control of his confinement spell, fed it a shot of his power, and squeezed. The spell turned bright blue and tightened on the ring. The tube of inflowing black began to narrow. Max gritted his teeth and fed his spell again. The vortex was now the height of the room, surrounded by expanding shock spheres bursting like bubbles, silver and orange and blue. And in the midst of it something physical was taking shape. There was little doubt what that was, or rather, who. The form of the trapped Death was coming through!

CATASTROPHE'S SPELL

Mayer Alan Brenner

DAW BOOKS, INC.
DONALD A. WOLLHEIM, PUBLISHER

1633 Broadway, New York, NY 10019

For Sandy

Copyright © 1989 by Mayer Alan Brenner.

All Rights Reserved.

Cover art by Walter Velez.

DAW Book Collectors No. 787

First Printing, July, 1989

1   2   3   4   5   6   7   8   9

PRINTED IN THE US.A.

ACKNOWLEDGMENTS

If writing represents the disciplined exercise of personality through talent, I owe more thanks than can adequately be stated to those who have helped shape both the personality and the discipline. In particular, my thanks go to Arthur Byron Cover, for his unrelenting emphasis on the setting of high sights, his encouragement tempered by cogent criticism, and not least of all for quoting Faulkner's dictum on action as character at a critical time. Thanks also to Jeffrey P. Semel and Frank Zajaczkowski, to Joshua Bilmes and the Scott Meredith Literary Agency, and to Sheila Gilbert, my editor at DAW. Finally, my most personal thanks must go to my immediate family—my brothers, Sunny and Matt, my parents, Esther and Harry, and, of course, my wife Sandy. I hope you're all aboard for the next one.

TABLE OF CONTENTS

1 MAX ON THE ROAD   9
2 THE CREEPING SWORD   19
3 THE GREAT KARLINI'S PROBLEM   43
4 SHÀA OUT OF PRACTICE   60
5 SHOP TALK   75
6 THE CREEPING SWORD STALKS AGAIN   91
7 SHAA CONVERSES   108
8 SCIENTIFIC INTERLUDE   122
9 WHAT I DIDN'T KNOW   129
10 SHAA AND MONT GO BOATING   158
11 THE CURSE OF THE CREEPING SWORD   170
12 SHAA AND MONT GO TO JAIL   186
13 MAX DROPS IN   196
14 MONT SOLOS   210
15 BIG TROUBLE   219
16 THE DEN OF OSKIN YAHLEI   232
17 COUNTERPLOTS AND COUNTERSPELLS   244
18 REPERCUSSIONS   260
19 THE CASTLE OF DEATH   277
20 THE DANCE OF DEATH   293
21 BACK AT THE BILIOUS GNOME   313

1
MAX ON THE ROAD

The air was thick and the heat oppressive. Outside the flap of canvas that covered the doorway, a vast range of beige desert overlaid by a scattering of scrub ran to the horizon. The line of dust raised by the approach of the caravan hung motionless in the air, stretching south from the oasis into a cluster of low hills. Max dropped the flap, turned, and descended the short flight of steps, his eyes still smarting from the desert sun. Each stair had the solidity of rough board, reassuring after the sands of the past few days, except for the bottom one, which yielded under Max's foot in a very unstairlike fashion. He rocked back and squinted down. The stair shifted in the gloom and became a man dressed in loose dark clothes and sprawled out on the floor, burbling pleasantly but stuporously. By the look of him, he might be burbling still when the caravan passed through the next time, heading south again at the end of its run. That probably meant the local rotgut was either very tasty or very dangerous. Max stepped across the man and proceeded across the room.

At the other end of the room was a bar, on which Max rested an elbow. The room itself was a natural gully in the rock next to the oasis, covered over with a heavy canvas tent. Cables ran from eyebolts driven into the rocks up to timbers that supported the canvas roof.

Another caravan had been parked at the oasis when Max's had arrived, but most of its crew had not been in evidence. They were certainly missing no longer. Gently reeling forms were propped in chairs and on tables, or piled in low mounds on the rock floor. An arm-wrestling match was in progress at one side, deep in the shifting green haze from a half-dozen guttering candles. The bartender emerged from a shadow behind the counter and pushed a mug at Max. "You know any good ruins around here?" Max said to him.

A hefty growl from the other end of the bar drowned out any reply. The man behind the growl, Max discovered as he turned to eye him, was about seven feet tall, and was waving a trestle table over his head with one massively corded arm.

"You want another drink?" Max asked. "I'll buy you another drink."

The guy growled and hefted the table. "Okay," Max said, "no drink." It was just as well, as the bartender had managed to conveniently disappear from sight. Behind the bar counter, framed by several large boulders, was a cave containing stacks of large kegs. The upper lip of the cave formed a narrow ledge overhead. Dangling in front of the ledge over the bar was a line of additional kegs, lashed together in threes and suspended by cables from pulleys. The cables ran down to a rack of marlinspikes in the rock at the end of the bar, just on the other side of the counter from Max. The giant swung the table again and took a bead on Max.

"Don't be ridiculous," Max said. "It's too hot for this kind of nonsense." The man reared up with the table. "All right," Max said, "have it your way." Max leaned over the counter, selected one cable, grasped it firmly with his right hand, and sharply cocked his right wrist. A blade sprang out of his sleeve below his palm and slashed the rope. Max rose swiftly into the air as a trio of lashed kegs at the other end of the bar equally swiftly descended. The kegs struck the waving table, the table overbalanced as its wielder lost his grip, and with one loud *thud* and a trio of lesser thumps the table slammed into the giant's head and the kegs again hit the table. All collapsed in a clatter and small cloud of dust. A final two shards fell to the floor, there was a moment of silence, and then the unmistakable sound of a contented snore arose from deep within the heap.

Max swung onto the ledge over the bar and seated himself. He sipped at his drink, which he had retained in his left hand, and slid the knife back into its spring-loaded sheath. "Fortunately for you," he directed his words down at the pile of wreckage, "it's much too hot to get involved in serious exertion." In another week at the outside the caravan would be clear of the desert, he thought, and then it was a straight shot across river and the the plains to Drest Klaaver, where at last report Shaa was hiding out. He was looking forward to seeing Shaa again.

The bartender had reemerged from his hiding-place. "So what about the ruins?" Max called down.

"Ruins?" the man said, looking out at the room. "Whaddaya need more ruins, what you did to me here isn't good enough?"

For a change, Max was not actually on the run, which is to say that he didn't think anyone in particular was after him. Of course, his perception (which happened to be wrong) did not materially change the situation. He still had a pursuer, and later that night the pursuer caught up with him.

The large moon was up, along with some of the small fast ones. Max dangled his legs over the tail-board of the rear wagon, watching ground pass in the pale light. A large shaggy form loped around the wagon and hoisted itself up next to Max. "I still say you should have hacked him into little pieces," it said. "If you could have waited for me, *I* would have hacked him into little pieces."

"All the time with you, Svin, it's fight, fight, fight, hack, hack, hack," Max replied. "I'm not going to say that philosophy may not be superior in the long run, and it certainly has the virtue of simplicity, but by the same token—"

"It is the course of honor, the only true course for a warrior born," Svin said with a note of finality.

"That's fine as far as it goes," Max responded, "but not all of us are warriors born. Some of us subscribe to the concept of old age instead."

Svin thought that over. A shadow passed over the large moon—three circling dwarf buzzards, moonlight shimmering on their feathers. The smallest one swooped down to have a look at them, its ten-foot wingspan draping a darker black over the rocks. "Look at that thing," Max said. "It's got plenty of body to feed, but it manages fine without a lot of hacking and slashing. I don't know how much of a goal in life *it* has, but seems to get by pretty well on a more passive lifestyle."

". . . Where *do* you think it finds enough to eat?" Svin, perhaps because of his northern metabolism honed in the icy wastes, was perpetually hungry.

"There's always carrion around somewhere, if you know where to look for it."

Svin shook his head. "Carrion, Max, is for lesser beings. We will die in battle, as a man should, and go triumphantly to meet the gods."

Max, who *had* met some of the gods, had not been impressed. "Watch out for remarks like that, Svin, you never know who's listening."

"Fah!" Svin said. "What does it matter if—" Max heard a muffled "clunk" next to him. Svin began to raise one hand to his head, then fell over backward into the cart. A heavily thatched arrow with a flat blunt head dropped into his lap. Max pushed off the tailgate and landed silently behind a rock. The wagons began to clatter and jangle away down the path.

A low voice buried in a reedy gargle came from the same direction as the arrow. "Honor have addressing I Maximillian, Vaguely Disreputable?"

Max raised himself slightly and squinted over the rock. Back there in the gloom, he thought he could make out two glowing orange sparks, spaced at the right separation for eyes. "You're Haddo," he said.

"Haddo am I. Serve I Great Karlini. You come?"

Karlini? "Yes, I'll come," Max said. "Of course, I'll come. Just let me get my stuff." He got up and sprinted after the wagons.

Svin was breathing, and a large lump was forming on his forehead just over his nose. Max shook him, without noticeable effect, then rolled him into a more secure position deeper inside the wagon. Shaking his own head, Max found his two packs, slipped the larger one onto his back, and jumped to the ground. The caravan moved away behind him. The pair of orange eyes approached.

"You were a little rough on poor Svin,there," Max said, handing Haddo his arrow.

"Situation's nature was unsure I."

"Yes, well, I suppose they don't make barbarians like they used to, either."

"Considerate you are," Haddo said, indicating the arrow, which then disappeared inside a sleeve. The glowing orange spots (which Max, for want of a better explanation, *assumed* were eyes) floated in the opening of a hooded black cloak. The moonlight failed to penetrate the opening, and, in fact, seemed to make little impression on the surface of the cloak either. "Thanks I give."

Haddo glided off into the desert to the west. Max followed. "Nice bit of shooting, though, Haddo."

"Trained well, I."

"So how is everything, Haddo?"

"Problems. Always are problems."

"Are you going to tell me what's up, or do I have to wiggle your tongue myself?"

"To wiggle, first must find," said the featureless black hood. "Karlini will tell."

"Where *is* Karlini?"

"Days by foot. Trackless are wastes."

Max sighed. More time stomping through the desert. "In the old days, they had machines, Haddo, machines that could have—"

"Old days gone. Matter not. Still now, things not bad."

"I wouldn't exactly call walking for days through trackless wastes 'not bad.' "

Haddo sounded smug. "Said I only distance by foot. Did not say by foot we go. Brought I bird."

They reached the bird before dawn. In the false light, Max and Haddo climbed yet another hard-packed rise, watching for more of the thorny succulents that had already snagged the strap off one of Max's packs. At the bottom of the downslope below the rise was a dark rounded sand dune. Haddo scampered down the slope and whistled a low trilling whistle. The dune stirred and rose. It was the bird.

Only major cities and other big-time operators usually kept the big buzzards, which might mean that Karlini had come up substantially in life since Max had seen him last. The buzzards ate a lot, but not being especially concerned about what they ate, each one could serve quite adequately as a refuse disposal department. Among the species of giant birds, they were also about the dumbest. No one needed much intelligence from a bird, of course, but it was helpful if the bird had the attention span to remember what its current task was. The buzzards were particularly known for getting distracted during official state visits or large pageants and unexpectedly taking off for their ancestral breeding grounds, usually bearing with them several surprised dignitaries. In fact, Farthrax the Munificent had been crowned Emperor after returning, the better part of a year later, from the mountains where the breeding went on. He had always refused to talk about it, but the general amazement over his return was enough to cement his reputation as a favorite of the gods.

"Is this thing safe?" Max asked.

"Through trackless wastes rather walk you?" Haddo said. He resumed whispering in the bird's ear slit. Max grabbed a dangling strap and climbed aboard. Haddo scratched behind a feather, patted the bird on the side of the head, and came back. Max helped him swing into the saddle in front of him, forward on the body between the wing roots. The bird stood, hopped up and down tentatively a few times, flared its neck feathers, and subsided back down onto the ground.

"Nothing say you," Haddo muttered. He screeched at the bird. The bird screeched back, then lurched to its feet. Max checked the belt holding him in the saddle. The buzzard fanned its wings, broke into a run, strode up the ridge, and hopped into the air.

The sun rose as the bird circled, gliding and gradually gaining altitude. Thermals and whirling dust devils sprouted from the desert floor. The bird began to move in earnest, gaining speed with precise flicks of its wingtips, spiraling up one thermal and launching itself across the desert to the next.

Around noon a line of craggy hills appeared in the northwest, and later in the afternoon they were over them. The hills were as barren as the desert, but the exposed rocks displayed colorful strata of red and purple and bright yellow. The shadows lengthened and the colors of the rock had begun to glow with deeper hues when Max suddenly thought he smelled damp salt. "Haddo," Max said.

"Not bother," Haddo said. "Complex is landing procedure." A salt lake grew underneath, tucked into the folds of the hills, silent and smooth in the still air. The buzzard banked around a peak and headed for an island. The island was covered with buildings—no, a castle.

Max took a closer look. The castle was not *on* an

island, the castle *was* the island. Walls and towers dropped smoothly into the lake, and the upper part of one ring of crenelations protruded from the water like a reef of stepping stones, the top of each rectangular block barely awash. The bird circled once around the central cluster of towers, gauging the air currents, then abruptly nosed over and dived. It pulled up just above a flagpole, sideslipped onto a walled field, ran a few steps, and settled to the ground.

Max helped Haddo down and followed him to the front of the bird, feeling as though the flagstones of the courtyard were executing sharp banks beneath his feet. Haddo whistled something at the bird, letting Max scratch under its neck. After a moment, Max gingerly straightened. "Okay, Haddo," he said. "Thanks for the flight. Now what about Karlini?"

Haddo gave a final remark to the bird. "Here wait," he said to Max, and staggered off through a doorway. Someone passed him coming out, the someone wrinkling his nose fastidiously.

"Wroclaw!" Max said. "Nice to see you again."

"Very good to see *you*, sir." Wroclaw was gaunt, with olive-drab green skin and bones of not quite human proportions. His ancestors had been conjured, one way or another, but that wasn't something usually discussed in polite company. "Are you fit, sir?"

"That remains to be seen. I suspect it depends on what Karlini wants out of me."

Wroclaw coughed discreetly. "Very good, sir. Will you see the master now?"

"I hope so, Wroclaw, I really do."

"Ahem, yes, sir. Will you follow me, please?" Crossing the doorway, Max's hair crackled with static and he caught a whiff of ozone. Inside the corridor, though, the air was much cooler and the tang of salt much less apparent.

"Do you know what I'm doing here, Wroclaw?" Max said.

Wroclaw rounded a corner and came to a stop at the

entrance to a cramped circular staircase. "Any idea I might possess," Wroclaw said, "would undoubtedly be less than the complete truth. The master is, as always, the best person with whom to raise the matter."

A raven cawed faintly six times, somewhere off in another wing. "Oh, goodness," Wroclaw said. "Time for dinner already. Please wait here, sir, the master will be along shortly. I must see to the cook."

"Very well, Wroclaw." Max leaned on a stone windowsill across the staircase and watched shadows creep up the hills. One hill had gone into total eclipse by the time a figure bounded down the stairs toward him, running one hand through its hair. "The Great Karlini, I presume," Max said, "and if you don't tell me what's up very quickly I'll turn you into a carp and eat you, raw."

"Oh, good, Max, it is you," said the Great Karlini, pushing hair out of his eyes. "Haddo's certainly faithful, but his eyesight isn't quite perfect and we're never too sure what he'll bring back."

"That robe needs to be washed."

Karlini looked down and started, apparently noticing a cluster of fresh stains for the first time. "Good old Max," he said. "How do I manage without you?"

"That depends on what you've gotten yourself into this time."

Karlini dropped an arm across Max's shoulders and led him down the stairs. "So, Max, how have you been?"

Max stopped. "That's it," he said. "I'm leaving."

"Max, now don't—"

Max crossed his arms. "Look, Karlini, you get me dragged all the way out here, ruining a perfectly good caravan trip, and then you won't tell me why. Haddo won't talk, Wroclaw won't talk, you won't talk. You know what that says to me? What that says to me is that you want me to do something that probably involves human sacrifice, and I bet we both know who's the relevant human."

Karlini sat down next to him on the stair. "Don't glower at me like that, Max. It's not that bad, but it *is* a long story. Actually, it's not *that* long a story, but it's sort of—"

"Karlini."

"All right, all right. You noticed the castle?"

"Yeah. Nice castle."

"Well . . . it's okay."

"So, what's wrong with it? It have rats? Things?"

"It's not what it has," Karlini said, "it's what it does. It moves."

"Moves."

"Not like earthquakes, I mean, or settling ground. I mean you wake up in the morning and the whole castle is planted somewhere else. It's been here for almost two weeks, but before that, it was bounce, bounce, bounce. Just enough time to figure out where we were, and then, poof!, another hemisphere. We spent six days somewhere around the North Pole; almost froze solid. I'm just waiting for this thing to head for the open ocean."

"I assume we'll get to the real point when you tell me why you can't get rid of the place."

Karlini looked at Max suspiciously. "You sure you haven't heard about this before?" Max shook his head, no. Karlini sighed. "Well, that's the problem all right. It won't *let* me get rid of it. I can't even walk out the door."

2
THE CREEPING SWORD

At the same time Haddo was flying Max toward Karlini's castle I was sitting at my desk minding my own business, the major thought in my mind being whether I'd be able to afford to eat after the day after tomorrow. There was no way I could have known about Max and Haddo at that point, of course, but I wouldn't have cared anyway since I'd never *heard* of Haddo or Karlini or Max. Food was the issue, and realizing it was already past the middle of the day and that I hadn't had a customer in a week, I was wondering how hungry I'd have to get before I'd be walking the streets looking for odd jobs as a manual laborer. Then someone knocked on the door. I put the half-drained flask in a drawer and said, "Come in."

A woman entered. "My husband has been kidnapped," she said.

She told me that her husband had a large warehouse on the docks and a fleet of barges on the river. He hadn't come home the previous night. According to her, he had always come home before. A note had appeared under the door in the morning. She passed it over to me.

Payment of 20,000 gold zalous will cause the re-

19

turn of Edrik Skargool. He is not hurt, yet search
will cause death. More instructions will forthcome.

The Creeping Sword

"Huh," I said. The style was stilted, making me think
of someone who was trying to sound educated without
the benefit of actually having an education. On the
other hand, the words were spelled right and the pen-
manship was neat. Still, I didn't have to look too
closely to find the really unusual detail. The medium
was a sheet of burnished copper, and the words had
apparently been etched into it with fire.

"Do you have any idea who this Creeping Sword
is?" I asked.

"Certainly not, of course not," she said. "That's
your job, isn't it?"

I made a noncommittal sort of hrrumphy sound and
let her start talking again. She had gone to the police,
such as they were. With the current political situation,
the police weren't about to investigate anything, unless it came as a command from the Guard. She had
gone to the Guard. The Guard was having too much
fun enforcing martial law to worry about another kidnapping. The only kidnappings they were interested in
were the ones they were doing themselves. I hoped for
his sake they hadn't picked up Skargool. I wasn't
about to fight the Guard for him, even if she paid me
a lot, and I didn't think anyone else would be prepared to either. "Will you find him?" she asked.

"I'll do my best," I said, "under the circumstances.
That's my job."

She made an unhappy face at me. Sometimes that
was a good tactic—I'm a man, and like any man I'll
turn gooey under the right circumstances—but it wasn't
going to work on me this time. I didn't like her. "If
I'm willing to pay you good money and give you my
trust," she said, "I would expect that you would at
least be willing to guarantee—"

I had been leaning back in my chair. Now I let the chair fall forward so the two front legs hit the floor with a sharp "thud," and pointed a finger at her for further emphasis. "Look, lady," I said. "Roosing Oolvaya is a big city. There must be fifty thousand people here. Any day of the week a bunch of them disappear and never get found. Now we're sitting with a dead Venerance, the son who probably knocked him off is in charge, and mercenaries are running around the streets controlling the rest of the normal Guard. You think that doesn't make things worse? It makes things a lot worse. People are getting rounded up, people are getting executed, and people are getting kicked into the sewers just for being in the wrong place. Not criminals, not only political folks, just people, you understand that? In this kind of situation, a lot of old grudges find themselves getting settled, a lot of nastiness pops up. It's a real rough time."

"But," she said, still pouting, "but what should I do, then?"

"If you hire me, I'll find your husband. If he's findable. *Are* you hiring me?"

"Yes, yes, of course I am, even if—"

"Then get ready to pay this Sword person."

"But 20,000 zalous! How could I—"

"I'll get you the money back if I can."

"But can't you bargain with—"

"You might reflect," I said, "on the fact that money can generally take more wear and tear than husbands can."

She shut up. I asked questions, but none of the answers were helpful. There were no disgruntled employees. The list of business enemies was short; she said her husband had a reputation as a straight dealer. They had no children.

"Who gets everything if he dies?" I said.

"Why, I'm not sure. I don't really know."

I had sent off a messenger earlier, and he returned with Turbot. Turbot was in more or less the same line of work as me, whatever that was, and we used each other as backup when things were going on. He was glad to have something to do that might pay. So was I. As the wife was leaving in Turbot's custody, she paused and looked back.

"Will you find him?" she repeated.

"Yeah, I'll find him," I said. I strapped on my sword and headed for Skargool's warehouse.

Skargool Cargo was a hulking two-story building with heavy timber walls attached to its own wharf. The manager was a hulking man named Kardu Chog. He wasn't attached to a wharf, but one finger bore a ring with a stone the size of a rowboat.

"Me, I was first mate on the first barge Skargool ever sailed," Chog said expansively around a vile cigar. Tobacco leaves were one of the things Skargool imported, shipped up the river from the south. "First mate, aye, and crew, too. The two of us, like brothers." He waved at the humidor on his desk, offered me a cigar. I shook my head. He shrugged and took a massive pull on his own cigar, a line of solid ash advancing toward his mouth. "Skargool and me, we go way back."

"What about his wife?" I said.

"What do you mean," he said slowly, "about his wife?"

"His wife. How long does *she* go back?"

Chog leaned back in his chair and squinted up through the smoke. "Mind you now, I don't really know her, but she's been around now for, oh, five years, six. Why do you want to know?"

"Just asking questions," I said. "Part of the job."

I poked around, asking more questions of the workmen. From all accounts, Edrik Skargool was indeed that rare thing, a rich boss well liked by his employees. Another relevant fact also came to light: Skargool walked home daily, along the same route.

I left the warehouse, crossed the street, and entered

the dive on the other side; step out on any street around the wharves and there was bound to be a bar within arm's reach. When my drink came, I laid an ool next to it. "The Skargool place," I said.

"Yeah?" said the bartender.

"Anybody seem interested in it?" I spun another ool in the air.

The bartender licked his lip and thought, then shook his head sadly, eying the ool on the counter. I pushed it toward him. "Let me know," I said, and told him how to find me.

I worked my way along. From the feel of the kidnap note this thing had been a job worked out in advance, not a bit of random work popped on the spur of the moment. The Creeping Sword, whoever or whatever he was or they were, would have hung around getting a handle on Skargool's movements, and might still be keeping an eye on things. Maybe somebody had noticed something. It wasn't a real good bet. The waterfront was always filled with transients, and with the number of out-of-town fighters bolstering the Guard things were bound to be worse, but maybe one of the regulars had an eye open. If nothing else, the Creeping Sword might hear I was asking questions and come after me. Coming out of the fourth bar, I felt a bump and tug at my side. Attached to the touch was an arm. I grabbed it as the kid tried to twist away. He was somebody I knew.

"How's business, Glinko?"

Glinko looked up at my face and turned white. "It's you," he said.

I shook him up and down a few times. "Yeah, Glinko, it's me. You're losing your touch. You're also turning into an idiot."

"I didn't know it was you," he whined plaintively.

"Save it. Maybe you can do something for me."

A look of calculation appeared. I shook him again, then opened my hand and dropped him. The street was muddy. The streets were always muddy. "You didn't have to do that," he said.

"You didn't have to try to pick my purse, either. Fortunately for you, I generally take the long view." I showed him an ool.

Glinko stopped trying to clean himself off. The coin interested him. Coins always interested him. Coins interest most of us. "Who cares about mud anyway," he said. "What do you need?"

"The Creeping Sword," I said.

"The who?"

"That's what I want to know. This Sword kidnapped a businessman."

"Skargool?" Glinko said.

"Yeah, that's right. Tell me about it."

"You going to give me that?" he asked, meaning the ool.

"You going to give me a reason to?"

He glanced around the street, then slipped around the corner of the bar into a narrow alley. The street had only been about three times the width of the alley, but on the other hand except for us the alley was empty. "I know Skargool," Glinko said in a low voice, "I know most of the guys down here. That's what I do, keep an eye out." Glinko was a spotter for one of the thief-gangs. "Skargool's a right guy, pays good, he's good to the workers, you know? Half the guys around here want to work for him. Then a couple of weeks ago a lot of bad talk started. A ship of his was late, see, and all of a sudden there's talk like Skargool might have sold the crew to the slavers. That's how it started. Last I saw him was two days ago. He was walking home. He didn't look good. He looked real depressed. Now today he's missing, it's all around the street."

"Okay." I gave him the ool. He said he'd nose around for me and check in later. He went back to the street, and I slipped out the other end of the alley.

I tried a few more bars without much more luck and ended up at the Grumpy Gullet. Civil unrest or no, Slipron was there, at his usual table in the back. I handed him the kidnap note Skargool's wife had given me.

Slipron screwed a lens into one eye, Oolvayan glass in a bone housing, and scrutinized the engraving, rubbing the copper plate between two fingers. Then he tapped the plate with a fingernail and swiveled the lens up at me. "It's worthless, of course, excepting perhaps only the metal itself."

Slipron being the best fence in Roosing Oolvaya, his comment meant he could move the thing for a profit and was willing to bargain, but selling it was not what I had in mind at the moment. I told him so.

"Ah," Slipron said. "Well. This engraving is not professional work." He rested a finger across the inscribed words and closed his eyes. The letters around his finger swam briefly. He brought the plate up to his face and sniffed. "A firepen. Definitely a firepen."

The tapster was passing with a tray of foaming mugs, and I snagged a full one for Slipron. He handed me back the ransom note. "I know of Edrik Skargool, and I consider him a good man," Slipron said. "I also note the line of this letter that reads, 'Search will cause death.'"

"They're talking about search by sorcery," I said. If an antisearch spell had been set up around Skargool, any finder probe keyed to him would set up feedback in the protector field, feedback that might be enough to fry him. Whether the Creeping Sword had the facility or the money to get a spell like that was another matter. I thought it was a bluff. Even if it was a bluff and a sorcerous search might find Skargool, hiring a magician to run a decent search would cost a lot more than my own time. If it wasn't a bluff, and the magician wasn't good enough to avoid or neutralize the no-search field, that would be it for Skargool.

Of course, I wouldn't hire a magician. I wouldn't even go near magic unless it grabbed me by the neck and forced my nose into it. Magic is more trouble than

it's worth. It messes up everybody's life. It had messed
up my own life enough in the past to give me more of
an education than I'd ever wanted. No, all this case
needed was legwork, and legwork I know.

"What if this message isn't referring to sorcery?"
Slipron said. "What if they don't care what kind of
search it is, and they spot you looking for him?"

"Give me a little credit," I said. "This is my job,
and I know what I'm doing. I know how to be careful."

Slipron looked doubtful. A chair scraped next to us,
and a gust of garlic announced the arrival of Gag the
Hairless. The name dated back to an incident where
the bladder of gas Gag had been using to blow open
the strongbox on board a barge had blown up in his
hand instead. His hair had grown back in around the
flashburn scars, but a name is a name. "The word's
out you're looking for a snatcher," Gag said.

"Sure," I said, "why not? Have you got one?"

"Who knows?" Gag said. "This town's so crowded
you can't keep anybody straight."

I tossed him an ool. Fortunately for me, Skargool's
wife was paying expenses. Gag flagged the barmaid.
The barmaid brought him a bottle, which Gag upended, wiping green froth off his mustache. He burped,
and said, "Okay, now," leaning forward on one elbow. "A guy hears lots of things. You don't always
know what to think, you know what I mean? This guy
Skargool, one day you hear one thing, then you hear
something else. One day everybody wants to work for
him, the next day you hear he's flogging his crews."

Slipron, whose attention had apparently wandered
off to another part of the room, looked back at Gag.
"Flogging?"

"Yeah, flogging," Gag said, "I mean like with whips.
All these years he's shipping grain, oats, like, and then
all of a sudden they say there's always been loot underneath. Treasure, I mean, gold, jewels, real loot.
Buried under the oats, all these years. I mean, I've got
nothing against oats, I've got to eat, too, but oats isn't
the same thing as loot."

"That's an interesting story, Gag," I said. "Now work the Creeping Sword into it."

"What's that?" Gag said.

"That's what I'd like to know. You find it out and it's worth money."

"How's about a, whatta you call it, a retainer?"

"I'll pay," I said, "when I have something to pay for. Don't push your luck. You hear lots of stuff, Gag, and that's good. Find out who started the talking about Skargool."

Gag scowled and drained the bottle. I had been keeping an eye on the rest of the room, watching for someone else, and now he came in, heading straight for a small table in the back of the place in a corner mostly in shadow. I rose and went over. A steaming casserole was already present on the table, and the guy was digging into it by the time I crossed the room.

I pulled up a chair across from him. "I want to talk to your boss," I said.

He didn't bother to look up; I was sure he'd spotted me on my way over. He didn't miss much, that's why he had the job he had. "Are you on a case," the man said, swallowing a mouthful off his knife, "or you just looking for some action?"

"It's a case."

He grunted, pulled a piece of fish out of the casserole, squinted at it, and threw it over his shoulder where it stuck to the wall. "We may have a job, too. Interested in some honest work for a change?" He laughed a coarse harsh laugh.

"Depends on the work," I said.

"Sure it does," he said. "Somebody'll come by your place."

"Right," I said. The table I'd shared with Gag and Slipron was empty, so I headed for the door. I was almost there when it crashed open propelled by a pair of lances and a rabble of tough-looking men wearing the armbands of the Guard.

"All right, you goons," the corporal shouted as he

raised a truncheon, "this place is closed! Move out to the street and— "

The place erupted. I ducked as a small table flew over my shoulder directly toward the corporal, plunged my fist into an eye, and shook my left leg loose from a set of sharp teeth. As I shoved a hand with a knife out of my way something crashed into my back and knocked me to the floor next to the wall. Sticking close by the wall, I dodged and crawled forward and climbed through a broken shutter onto the street. A knot of fighting guys spilled through the door to my left. The three Guard mercenaries watching the front of the building turned to deal with them, and I limped away from the bar, down the street, and around the first corner. My back was throbbing, but I figured that was part of the job; maybe I'd sock Skargool's wife for some extra expense money when I hit her with the final bill. I rinsed my face in a trough and walked away from the wharves into the city.

My office was over a laundry in the Ghoul's Quarter near the wall on the south side. The clapboard sign with its open staring eye creaked gently in the breeze from the river. A man was waiting outside my door. "You are examining the disappearance of Mr. Edrik Skargool?" he said.

"What's it to you if I am?" I said, unlocking the door. He followed me into the office.

"I represent the Oolvaan Mutual Insurance Carriers."

Oh, no, I thought. "Insurance?"

"Yes, indeed. Mr. Skargool has a substantial policy, amounting to perhaps 140,000 zalous."

I lowered myself gingerly into my chair. "Bonded insurance?"

"Yes, of course, bonded. Certainly."

Insurance, dammit, insurance. This was real trouble. I'd never worked an insurance case before, and I didn't want to start now. Look at it this way, a lawyer who'd once shared a bottle with me had explained things. When you can ride for an hour and get to a new place where there's a totally new set of laws and jurisdiction, when people disappear without a trace all the time, either because they're dead or just because they want to disappear, when you want to buy insurance in one city and know it'll be recognized someplace else, you've got to have one key thing. You've got to have some widespread authority nobody's going to argue with.

Insurance was a contract with one of the gods.

The tweedy man crossed his legs. "Unfortunately, our organization is understaffed and," (he gave a delicate cough) "chronically overworked, so it is our policy to rely on local assistance for claims investigation whenever possible."

"Now wait a minute," I said. "Let's clear up a few things here. I'm—"

"I apologize if I have not made myself clear." With his faded tweed cloak and his slack pale face, he could have been any nameless functionary buried in a bureaucracy's coattails. His voice, though, had the uncompromising tone of someone who always got his way, on his own terms. Even if he wasn't dangerous himself, he had big-time friends. "Whenever an investigation is in progress," he told me, "we employ its findings."

"Whadda you mean, 'we employ'? In this business, you employ, you pay."

"This is not *your* business, this is *our* business." He flashed a smile; at least that's probably what he thought it was. "Consider our business practice a tax on your business practice. You may also consider it a licensing test. We expect any investigator to comply with our own standards for proof-of-claim."

"Standards?" I said. "What do you mean, your standards? I know my job like—"

"Then you will have no problem, will you? A causal chain or other validator of legitimacy must be demonstrated. Cases of fraud or collusion are punishable, either on the part of the beneficiary or the investigator."

I'd never seen one of these policies, of course, but that wasn't going to be any excuse. If you got noticed by the gods, I'd always heard that the best thing to do was keep your mouth shut and do whatever they wanted, and hope they'd forget about you when they were finished. But what would it take me to get finished? "What if this, ah, 'investigator' can't come up with a definite solution? Sometimes *nobody* can tie up all the pieces, no matter how good they are."

"Ah," he said, "hmm. Indeterminate cases are not desirable. With proper validation and under special circumstances, they may be, hurrumph, reluctantly accepted. Quite reluctantly."

"Okay," I said, "I've got no choice. I realize it, I'm not an idiot. What kind of insurance does Skargool have, anyway?"

"Life," he said, "of course."

"Don't you have ways of knowing whether he's still alive?"

He turned up one corner of his mouth in what might have been another try at a smile, or maybe just a nervous tic. "Omnipotence is not one of our patron's virtues. These things take time and energy, and attention." He got to his feet.

"Just one more question," I said.

"Yes?"

"Who took out the insurance, and when?"

He gave me the tic again. "The wife, of course. One month ago."

"Right," I said. "How will I get in touch with you?"

"I will be in touch with you. Good day." The door closed behind him. I opened the desk drawer and took out the flask with the better stuff, then decided to just hit my head against the wall for a while. I turned around, and behind me the door creaked open again.

"What now?" I said, but this time the man was different. With a shapeless cap pulled low enough over his face to rest on the bridge of his nose, and a generally squat frame, the guy looked a lot like a giant toad. "Da time ta see da boose is now," he said.

"Yeah," I said, "da boose." I put the flask back and followed him out the door.

We wound around local streets, heading generally back toward the docks, and finally entered a shuttered house where we descended to the basement. Beneath an old rug was an iron grate. The guy rolled up the edge of the rug, being careful not to disturb a slender thread that ran from one frayed corner off into the darkness. Then he turned his back, did something behind him in the gloom, and waited. Running water gurgled below the grate, gradually growing fainter. Finally the grate clanged and squeaked open. The edge of a ladder was revealed, leading down into the sewer.

A concealed mechanism drained the last swirls of water away as we reached the base of the ladder. One section of the facing stone wall had opened, revealing a crawlway. Bending low, I followed the guy into the wall, through several ascending turns thick with sewer slime and algae, and up out of the garbage into a small torchlit anteroom. Three other exits led down through the floor or into the walls in a similar manner to the one we'd entered through. Four men got up from a table and pushed me against the wall. One of them took my sword and frisked me, two others kept their hands on their swords, and the final one nervously slapped a large cudgel against his palm. They didn't find anything; I knew better than that. The thugs moved aside and one grunted, tilting his head in the direction of a wall tapestry. I moved the tapestry aside and went through the concealed door behind it.

The new room had walnut wall panels, a bookcase filled with leather-bound volumes, and a large desk with a man seated next to it. The man was wearing a dressing gown embroidered with dragons and other zoo fodder and had on his nose a pair of spectacles, through which he was studying a ledger. He looked mild-mannered enough, and he could be, but generally he wasn't; this wasn't the first time we'd met. He looked up at me, over the top of the spectacles, and said, "Sit down. What's on your mind?"

"It's not a what," I said, sitting. "It's a who. Edrik Skargool. Somebody kidnapped him, but it doesn't sound like you."

"Hah," he said. "The kid has a lip." He leafed through his book, alternately watching me over his glasses and glancing down into the book. "Skargool. Here he is." The boss read for a moment. "He's rich, yeah, but it's mostly property, not a lot of cash. He pays his protection dues regular, no trouble there. Kidnap rating's low, so you're right, hah, why should I take him out? Stupid. Whoever did it, stupid. Some people got no business sense." His eyes looked up at me again. "Like to know your own ratings, hah?"

"I'm sure it would cost me more than I've got to find out. I'm sure you know that, too."

"Hah," he said noncommittally.

"Anyway, that's beside the point," I said. "The one thing I do need is this. You have anything on somebody called The Creeping Sword?"

"The what? Creeping Sword? You got to be kidding. What idiot kind of name is that?"

I passed him the kidnap note.

"Creeps," he said, studying it. "Some punk. Punks all over the place. Whole damn town is crawlin' with punks." He threw the note back at me. Then, for good measure, he grabbed his ledger and threw it across the room. It was big, and heavy for a book, and made a loud thud against the stone wall. The guards from the room outside the tapestry suddenly appeared and began to drag me out of my chair. "Civil wars," the boss yelled, glowering at his thugs. "I hate 'em. Bad for business. Lousy for everybody. What?"

I had been gargling at him, hoping he would remember me before the boys actually started carving. The boss stared at me for a second, then said, "Forget about him, boys, he's all right. Put him down, boys."

They dropped me back across the chair and filed

out. I sat up, worked my shoulder around a bit, and steadied my breathing. "Thanks," I said.

"Yeah," he replied. "I've got a job you can help with. You know Kriglag?"

"I've heard of him, never met him." Kriglag ran the wharf rackets.

"He's a dope. He thinks he's gonna work with this new Venerance, what's-his-name, cooperate with all these damn foreign mercenaries, end up fencing their loot maybe, I don't know what-all. Maybe he's a big enough idiot to work with somebody called a Creeping Sword."

"I'm listening."

"I'm gonna take him out," the boss said. "I'm gonna take him out tonight. You want to be in?"

"Yeah," I said, "I do. Thanks."

"You're with Netoo." He jerked his head at the tapestry. I went through it and told the boys I was with Netoo. I followed the one with the cudgel through another tapestry and down a hall.

There were thirty of us, more or less, divided in four teams. I strolled around the assembly room, asking my usual questions, until we moved out.

Night had fallen by the time the first two teams sloshed off into the sewers; sometimes I think more activity and commerce in Roosing Oolvaya takes place in the sewers than overhead in the streets. Nevertheless, the bunch of us under Netoo headed into the streets with the sorcerer. She was up in the front, next to Netoo, helices of fine blue lines making gloves around her gesturing hands as she walked. The blue shapes left a slowly fading trail behind her in the air.

The clamor of some riot a neighborhood or so to the north came intermittently to us. There was no sign of the Guard, though, and I wondered if the boss had managed to convince somebody to concentrate on other areas for the evening. A tendril of river fog curled around a building ahead of us and up our street. We entered the fog, and Netoo stopped the team to confer with the magician.

The magician gestured a few times, almost lost from my view in the fog, cocked her head to listen to nothing, and nodded. Netoo motioned us on. We crept one block, exiting and then reentering the fog, turned right, and moved down an alley. Netoo touched the shoulder of a man holding a bow. The man fitted an arrow and shot. The arrow turned into a shadow and disappeared into the mist. This was followed half-a-second later by a soft clunk and rattle, and then the thunk of a falling body. The magician nodded again and whispered to Netoo. "Around the next corner," Netoo said. "The house with hanging plants. All ready? Okay, go."

We spread out and padded quickly around the corner. Shadows dark against the light mist flitted over the rooftops from other directions. They hit the roof as we hit the front.

Steel abruptly clashed. I paused to let my teammates engage, then charged through the crowd and hit the door shoulder-first. The door burst open onto a courtyard where other forms already struggled. I charged through them, too, aiming for the inner door. Shouts of "No mercy for traitors!" and "Death to the usurper!"—our attempt to disguise our origin by implicating local malcontents—came from behind, above, and below, indicating that the sewer teams had reappeared as had the roof squad. I hit the inner door and it sprang open. A robed functionary scuttled by, looking frantically around. I grabbed him by the collar and said, "The Creeping Sword."

"I know nothing," the man said, trying to faint, and I hit him over the head with the flat of my sword.

It went like that for a while. Then I found Kriglag.

Taken totally unprepared and with all his escape routes cut off, Kriglag was trying to make the best of a hopeless situation. He was drunk. I wedged myself into the closet with him and dragged him to his feet. Jugs rolled off his chest and shattered on the floor. "Kriglag!" I said.

"Hwazigah?" he said, eyelids sagging.

"The Creeping Sword, Kriglag, The Creeping Sword," I said, yelling it into his ear.

"He's a bad, a bad guy," he said, and started to snore.

I shook him. Then I broke the neck off a jug he'd apparently missed in the confusion and poured the contents over his head. Kriglag opened his eyes and said, "Wha?"

I put the tip of my sword where his crossed eyes could focus on it. "The Creeping Sword, Kriglag."

"Gemmy outa here."

"Tell me about the Creeping Sword."

"You get me outa here first."

I slapped him across the jaw. "Tell me why I should bother," I said.

Kriglag's head was clearing. "Creeping Sword, yeah. This guy from upriver someplace. Had this idea. He'd make cash and a good-guy image at the same time, snatching rich rats."

Maybe his head wasn't that clear after all. "Rich rats?"

"Rich scum." Kriglag paused to cough for breath. "Guys with lots of dough who got it by being scum. People nobody would miss, be glad to see them go."

"So he came to you. What did you tell him?"

"I'm no fool," Kriglag said. "I told him, try it out. If it worked, maybe I'd take him on."

"Where did he go?"

"I dunno. He was going to come back when he had results."

"Anybody else know about it?"

Kriglag smirked and breathed a foul breath in my face. "My partner," he said.

I lay the edge of the sword along his throat. "Who?"

Kriglag kept smirking. "Get me out of here or you'll never know."

I hesitated. Then, with a chorus of "No collaboration!" a bunch of my new friends burst into the room

behind us. Kriglag looked over my shoulder at them,
glanced back at me, and lunged toward my blade. I
couldn't believe a survivor type like Kriglag would go
so far as to impale himself, but just in case I pulled the
sword out of his reach. "You're a sap," he yelled at
me as they dragged him away.

I spent a few minutes with his ledgers. Kriglag kept
lousy records. Still, I was able to tell that he'd done a
lot of business moving hot goods, goods that had started
out in warehouses on the wharf. I couldn't find out
which warehouses, but I made a list of the stuff. One
of Netoo's people arrived to take charge of the books,
so I wiped off my sword and went home.

A messenger woke me in the middle of the night
with a note from Turbot.

New message received. Ransom drop tonight.

Turbot, always maniacally terse, apparently had things
under control. I went back to sleep.

I spent the next morning running down the list of
business rivals Skargool's wife had given me. None of
them had anything bad to say about him, and none of
them seemed to have anything to hide. None of them
had missed any of the hot warehouse goods Kriglag
had entered in his ledger books, either. It wasn't until
I was finishing up with the fourth name on my list that
I suddenly wised up. I asked the guy for his own
rundown of Skargool's competitors.

The names he gave weren't on my list.

Their stories were even more interesting than the
ones from the list Skargool's wife had provided. They
knew Skargool better. They knew him well enough to
know he'd been getting upset. He'd found out someone was stealing from his stocks. And he'd gotten
suspicious about his wife's fidelity.

They couldn't understand how Skargool had suddenly picked up these rumors about flogging, and sla-

vers, and being a general taskmaster. They all liked him, and they were his competitors in a notoriously cutthroat field. According to them, he was honest to a fault and underworked his employees, if anything.

Then I wasted a few hours talking to firepen dealers.

The firepen had been a fad item a few seasons ago. After the initial enthusiasm, people realized that the pens wore out much too fast to be of real use, and in any case weren't good for anything besides graffiti. They would write on walls, metal, pavement, indeed, on anything but paper and parchment; paper and parchment they ignited. Flashy but impractical, and occasionally downright dangerous. The type of thing some upriver yokel might think was pretty hot stuff.

One minor sorcerer was still making the things, selling some out of the stall in front of his home and a few others to local merchants. Demand had settled down to a couple dozen pens a month, so he was able to tell me quickly where each one of them had gone. The second merchant he sent me to was a hit.

"This bumpkin kid with pimples and a big rusty sword," the woman said. Displayed on a table in her stall were an array of neatly stacked fresh fish and assorted geegaws in baskets. "Thought he was heaven's gift itself. Maybe he was, back home, with them country girls." She sneered at me and tried to sell me a fish.

The guy had bought the pen three days before, which fit. I went back to the wharves to hunt up Glinko. When I found him, I wished I hadn't looked. He'd been fished out from the ebb spot behind a piling under a wharf. Somebody had gotten his fingers around Glinko's throat. The marks of the fingers remained, and something sharp on one of the fingers had torn open his carotid.

As I gazed down at Glinko, I became aware of another man gazing down next to me. It was the representative of the Oolvaan Mutual Insurance company. "You are making progress?" he asked.

"Absolutely," I said to Glinko. "Lots of progress."

"Will we have to pay on the claim?"

"Without knowing the exact terms of Skargool's policy, I don't know. You might."

"When will I know?"

"Tonight," I said, "sounds like a good bet."

He inclined his head at me and stepped away. Since I was already in the area, I stopped in to see Chog, the manager at Skargool Cargo. The man with the boat-sized, sharp-jeweled ring.

"Had some trouble, I see," I said to him. One of his eyes was red and purple and swollen shut, and his knuckles were scraped raw.

"Trouble with the Guard," said Chog. "Hounding me, they were, mercenaries hounding me, me with a reputation in this city."

"Right. Mrs. Skargool got another note this morning, did you hear?"

"Good news, that must be good news. My friend's return must be near. The two of us, Skargool and me, like brothers."

"So you said," I said. "I'm going to make the ransom drop tonight."

"I must know the outcome as soon as possible."

"As long as you mention it, you can hear it direct. Drop by Skargool's house tonight around midnight."

"Midnight. I will surely be there." Chog smiled.

I went to Skargool's myself and settled accounts with his wife. She was holding up remarkably well under the strain, tried flirting with me again and everything. I took Turbot aside and discussed things with him, and then he took his sword and left.

I had never seen that morning's note, so I examined it to pass the time. It was firepen on copper again. When I compared it to the first one, though, the script was slightly different. I showed it to Mrs. Skargool.

"You ever see this handwriting before?" I asked her.

She held it close to her face and studied it carefully, then looked up at me, her clear blue eyes wide and guileless. "No, no, I'm certain I've never seen this before," she said. "Is it important?"

"Not really," I said.

At dusk, a messenger arrived with the last note. The messenger didn't know anything. He'd just been handed the note and an oolmite coin, on a street corner, and he scurried off quickly into the dark without asking for a tip. The note read:

> *Pack the money in two sacks. At eight, the detective will take the sacks and walk to the corner of the Boulevard of the Fifth Great Flood and Brewer Street. He will come alone.*

The intersection was in a shabby section of the wharf district. We prepared the loot, and at eight I left the house.

Tacked to a wall at Fifth Great and Brewer was a folded cloth. Inside the cloth was another copper plate. The inscription told me to go the Haalsen Traders wharf, which was about a three-minute walk away. At the wharf, yet another note instructed me to go down a ladder and put the sacks into a dinghy moored at the base. I figured it was about time for that; twenty thousand zalous could get pretty heavy. The note also suggested I wait at the bottom of the ladder for the next half-hour or so. I put the bags in the boat, a cable tied to the boat drew tight and pulled the boat away into the shadows under the wharf next door, and I cooled my heels for a time. When I decided I'd rested long enough I climbed the ladder and went back to Skargool's house.

As soon as I walked through the door Skargool's wife pounced. I'd had trouble dragging a useful word out of her for two days, and now she'd finally decided to talk.

"Did you give them the money? Where's the money

now, didn't you get it back? Where's my husband? What—"

"Shut up," I told her. "I only want to say the whole thing once, and I'm not going to say it until everybody's here."

"Where's my husband?"

"I don't think he's coming."

She started to snarl and spit at me, but at this point I didn't care. I knew her too well by now, not that there was that much to know. Kardu Chog the manager arrived, followed shortly after by Turbot. He gave me a very slight nod and sat down by the door.

"Now will you tell me—" said Skargool's wife.

"Not yet," I said. "That's not everybody."

The wife and Chog both started. "What are you talking about?" Chog said.

"We're waiting for somebody else."

Mrs. Skargool looked around nervously at everything and everybody except Chog.

Exactly at midnight, there was a knock on the door. It was the guy from the insurance company.

I stood up and started to talk. "Skargool's dead," I said, mostly addressing his wife. "He was probably dead before you came to see me. Skargool was kidnapped by The Creeping Sword, but that's about all anybody's told me that's been true.

"Chog, here, was the silent partner of Kriglag—"

Chog made a sudden lunge out of the couch.

"Stay," the insurance agent said.

Chog stayed. His hand had frozen in the air, on the way into his opposite sleeve, and one foot was raised. I nodded at Turbot. He went and pulled a long knife out of Chog's sleeve, then pushed him back onto the sofa. Chog was breathing, and his eyes were darting frantically, but otherwise he didn't move at all. Turbot sat down, too.

"Kriglag ran the wharves," I continued, "and one of the things he ran was hot merchandise. A lot of the merchandise was stuff that Chog stole from his own warehouse. Skargool's warehouse, really, but Chog was running it. Since Chog kept the records and Skargool trusted him, it took a while for Skargool to catch on.

"By the time he did, Chog had another plan. Kriglag had told him about The Creeping Sword. The Sword was an idiot kid from upriver someplace, and he had this idiot idea. He would kidnap a businessman who was both rich and nasty to his employees, but not so nasty that someone wouldn't be willing to pay the ransom. I guess the Sword wanted to become some kind of a folk hero, kidnapping only people who deserved it. If his victims didn't show up again, either, nobody was supposed to be too upset. After all, they were bad people, right?

"All Chog had to do was run around spreading stories about how rich and how terrible Skargool was, and then wait for the Sword to bite. I don't know exactly how long it took, but he was right on the mark. The Sword bit.

"The thing was, Chog was following Skargool, too, and when the Sword picked up Skargool, Chog followed the Sword. After the Sword wrote his first kidnap note, Chog came in and got rid of them both.

"That was it for The Creeping Sword, and that was it for Skargool. That's about it for the case, too." I waited until I could see the look of relief appear on the face of Skargool's wife. That's how much I didn't like her. "Except for one thing," I said to her, "the insurance. That was dumb, real dumb, taking out the policy yourself. I don't know whether you love Chog or he loves you, or whether he made you think he does or you made him think you do, and I don't care. I don't even care if you deliberately set me up so I'd figure out about Chog and the Sword and think that was the whole story. What I do care about was the other thing on your husband's mind, finding out that you and Chog were playing around behind his back, and probably figuring out the other reason he'd never noticed Chog stealing from him. You, keeping his attention distracted. It wasn't just Chog, it was you too. Both of you conspired to kill Skargool and get the insurance and the business."

She had frozen, like Chog, when I mentioned the insurance. The insurance man hadn't bothered to interrupt, he'd just pointed a finger at her. I turned to him.

"Satisfied?" I said.

"Eminently," he said. He pointed a finger at Chog and then at Skargool's wife. Balls of flame materialized and consumed them. Then his form lit up in a quick flash followed by a column of billowing smoke. When vision returned a few seconds later he was gone, apparently dematerialized into the vapor. I think only I noticed the catch on the front door as it snapped shut, and the small puff of cold outside air. That was all right with me; I figure every profession's entitled to a little extra mystery.

"Who was *that?*" Turbot asked.

"Either a magician working for the insurance company," I said, "or some god, slumming." Hopefully he wasn't a god, and if he was I hoped I'd done well enough by him so now he'd leave me alone. As it turned out later, I'd done *too* well for my own good, but I still didn't think I'd had a choice. Turbot and I split the ransom money, which he'd stashed outside after he'd recovered it from Chog's hiding place (which he'd found when he'd tailed him from the pickup point earlier), and went home.

It had been a lousy case. I'd sort of liked Glinko. I thought I would have liked Skargool, too.

3
THE GREAT KARLINI'S PROBLEM

Wroclaw began clearing the dishes. "Thunda-tenchon dropped by the house about a year ago," said Ronibet, Karlini's wife. "Stayed for a month eating up all our food, but we did manage to get some good work out of him. I think he went off and gave a presentation on our results at a meeting down on the coast. 'Manifold Processing in Stabilization of Third-Order Matrices,' isn't that what we called it, dear?"

"Huh?" said Karlini. He had spent the meal alternately muttering to himself and staring darkly off at the walls. It was uncharacteristic behavior for Karlini, who Max often thought was the most manic talker he'd ever met. Karlini's gaze wandered off again.

"I haven't gone to a conference in years," Max said, wiping the remains of a fruit rind from his clean-shaven lip. His tunic, which he had loosened for comfort, was open at the neck, revealing a small amulet covered with jewels and a delicate filigree of microscopic runes. "Haven't wanted to waste the time. Nobody ever says anything significant at those things anyway; any good stuff they always want to save for themselves. Not that I blame them, mind you."

Wroclaw appeared again with a cigar box. Karlini stirred and reached for it but, at a sharp glance from

Ronibet, slumped back into his chair. Max took a cigar, bit the tip off, stuck the other end in his mouth, and, waving off Wroclaw's long flaming match, snapped two fingers in front of the cigar. The end of the cigar sparked red and a small cloud of smoke arose.

"Always showing off, aren't you," Ronibet said.

Max turned his hand over, revealing a miniature striking pad and flint affixed to the end of his thumb and third finger. Max grinned at her, then slipped the device off and returned it to a pocket. "So how's that animalcule stuff you were up to?"

"It's coming along nicely," Ronibet said. "Remember my theory of cells, where all living matter can be subdivided into other microscopic living units down to a certain level? It's now clear that the theory is substantiated. Not only that, I think I've identified the food-to-magic conversion organelles you postulated."

Max puffed thoughtfully on the cigar. "That's good work," he said, "better than good. Extremely important work. If you can figure out exactly how magical essence gets produced down inside these cells of yours, then the Big Plan becomes more than just a mad pipe dream."

"You and your Big Plan," Karlini muttered. "As long as I've known you, there's always been the Big Plan. And what good has it ever done you? What good has it done any of us? Just a lot of fool dreaming, that's all it is. We'll never be rid of the gods, there's no use even talking about it."

"What's eating the Great one?" Max said to Roni. "I thought he wanted to quit being dominated as much as any of us. Don't I remember him going on and on about getting his free will back?"

"I've changed my mind," Karlini said. "There's no such thing as free will. If it's not the gods it'll be something else. Politics, economic forces, bad weather, even the science you love so much, Max. There's always some force running your life."

"Yeah, fine then," Max said. "The force that's running my life at the moment is *you,* you idiot, so there. You planning to tell me what I'm doing here and why you're in such a crabby mood or am I supposed to keep dragging it out of you chunk by chunk?"

"He's right, dear," Roni said. "Knowing Max, I think he's been very patient with you."

"Yeah, that's me," Max said, "the very soul of patience. So tell me about this curse, already. You can't leave the castle, you said. Does that mean the invisible wall of molasses, the endless maze, the—"

"His heart stopped," Ronibet said.

Max looked at her, looked at Karlini, uncrossed his arms and leaned forward, then sank back in his chair. "Hmm," he said. Max examined his cigar absently, stuck it back in his mouth. A large cloud of smoke rose. Max watched it waft upward and coalesce into a compact ball. "Your heart, you say. You walked out the door and keeled over?"

"That's about the size of it, Max." Karlini agreed.

"Now *that,*" Max said, staring at the smoke ball as it rolled along the ceiling, "is very interesting indeed. A spell or a curse, I wonder. I assume you had your life-protectives running? Of course. Could this thing have keyed off them?"

"I thought of that," Karlini said. "I haven't just been sitting around here doing nothing. I've come up with a lot of possibilities, and none of them have been any help at all."

"Don't get testy again," Max said. "I was just thinking out loud. You brought me here so I could figure out a way to get you out of this. You don't have to get sharp with me. Why don't you go back to the beginning and give me the whole story." He raised an eyebrow and eyed Karlini.

Karlini ran a hand through his hair and absently ruffled it further. Ronibet looked at him and sighed. "All right, Max," said Karlini, staring off at a line of brightly colored pennons dangling from the mezzanine balcony. "This is how it started. We're sitting at home, the place by the ocean, you remember it. It was a nice morning, clear sky, no portents, nothing. So we're having breakfast outside on the terrace for a change, when all of a sudden a whirlwind starts to blow up. I reached for the napkins—"

"Stick to the facts," Max said.

"Huh?" said Karlini.

"You've never reached for a napkin in your life."

Karlini looked over at Ronibet. "This is supposed to be a friend?" he said.

"Yes, dear, and not just any friend, one of your very best friends. That's why you're going to ask him to risk his life for you, and why he's going to do it."

Max grabbed his cigar out of his mouth. "Now just a second here—"

"Wait for the whole story first, Max," Roni said.

"Yeah," Max said, after a moment. "All right. Karlini?"

"Okay. Roni went for the napkins, and . . . where was I?"

"The gong," Ronibet said.

"Right, okay," Karlini said. "So we're looking off the terrace into this whirlwind, which seems to be centered about half a mile from the house in the middle of the coastal plain. The wind is pretty fierce where we're sitting, but because of the dust and flying grass and shrubs we can tell that the thing is even more intense at the center, so intense that it's even starting to form a funnel. Then, all of a sudden, the sky rings."

"The sky?" Max said.

"Yes, that's right, like it's a solid metal dome, and someone's just hit it with a rod about ten miles long. Dull metallic boom, just massive, the sky reverberates, the house, the ground, us, *everything*—like an earthquake with sound. All the dishes bounce off the table. I'm barely able to stay on my feet, but my insides feel like goo in an eggbeater. And then, right in the middle of the whirlwind, this castle starts to materialize."

"*This* castle," Roni said.

"Giant bolts of lightning are running up and down the wall of the funnel cloud. As we watch, each lightning spark begins to light a ghostly image of a castle. At first all it looks like is an image, a mirage or some strange optical effect, since it's transparent and parts of the castle don't appear to be there at all. The lightning keeps flashing, and as the image of the castle gets more distinct, we can see that it's rotating slowly in the same direction as the funnel, hanging in midair a couple hundred feet off the ground. An especially sharp bolt strikes on the far side of the image, and before the flash has faded the castle starts to solidify in earnest and drop down toward the ground at the same time. The wind starts to die. The castle drops faster, still turning, and hits the ground. There's a tremor and the earth jumps all over the place, about what you'd expect if a small mountain suddenly appeared and fell in the backyard, one last bolt of lightning strikes one of the towers, and then the lightning's gone. The castle digs itself into the ground like a corkscrew, slows, and stops. The funnel pulls up into the air, the wind dying, and all of a sudden it's gone, too. Everything's quiet and peaceful just like it was about thirty seconds before. The only difference is that now there's this castle sitting in the middle of the plain, chunks of dirt torn up all around it, what's left of a grove of trees sticking out from under the right side, and a small dissipating cloud turning slowly overhead.

"We figured we'd better check it out.

"I ran some scans on the castle from the house, but as far as I could tell, it was inert. Given the nature of the manifestation we'd just seen, that was certainly a surprising result, but it held up. From everything I could find out, the castle was nothing more than a large pile of rocks and mortar. Roni wanted to leave it alone at that point, but I wasn't comfortable with this new castle just sitting there, looming away, not explaining itself at all. The obvious thought, of course, was that the owner was about to come out and conquer the neighborhood, or that maybe somebody might have stolen it and dumped the evidence on us with the owner probably in pursuit. Things looking the way they did, I thought it would be safest to investigate further and at least try to figure out what we were dealing with.

"I picked out some equipment—"

"He emptied out half the lab and piled all the stuff on poor Haddo," Roni put in.

"—some *relevant* equipment, just things I thought we might need, and we strolled over.

"A lot of the castle is underwater at the moment, so you couldn't get the full impact on your way in, Max, but this place is *big*. Seen up close, right from the base, it just hung there in the sky, massive and craggy, all these towers and battlements and hulking escarpments holding who the hell knew what kind of nastiness. Black stone, and gray, scarcely a touch of color in the whole place except for some lichens and moss on the walls. The thing was absolutely silent. Not a sound. It was the kind of quiet you hear in the forest, when some creature has just chased most everything out, and anybody who's left is just holding their breath and trying not to move, hoping the thing doesn't notice them and goes away. But every test I ran, even standing next to it, was negative. As far as I could tell, the castle had never been near a spell in its life.

"The castle was cold, though, cold enough so frost was condensing on the walls and the air was chilly just from standing next to it. There hadn't been any snow or ice on it when it arrived, so I made the tentative assumption that whatever process had landed it there had also sucked the heat out. Now, I'm not sure that's the whole truth, but I don't know if it matters.

"We decided to take a walk around and see if there was anything different about the back. There was no obvious way in on our side, you see, and I wasn't going up a sixty-foot sheer rock wall unless I had to. If the ground had been perfectly flat, a brisk stroll around the castle back to the place we'd started would have taken about twenty minutes, maybe a half hour. Of course, as I've said, the terrain was really a mess from the castle trying to screw itself into the ground. Right up next to the wall the earth dropped down ten to twenty feet, making a small gully or earthen moat. Cracks and pits and snaky crevasses ran all over the place, and mounds and rough hills were piled up between them. The smell of churned dirt hung everywhere.

"The castle wasn't exactly quiet, either, as it turned out. As we clambered along, every so often we'd hear the castle give a creak or a rasp or a giant groan as it settled, and the ground would quiver a bit. The thing that was starting to worry me more than anything else was the idea that the castle had just decided to drop in for a visit and was getting ready to take off again, probably with the same wind and storm and devastation it had arrived with. As it turned out, of course, I was right, but it wasn't imminent at that point.

"Finally, on the side of the castle facing away from our house, we found something helpful. The rock base the castle was resting on looked like the top of a mountain that had been sheared away. Parts of it had been filled in or built up with additional rock, but the area we were facing was just solid cliff. About thirty feet up, where the cliff seemed to end and the rock wall began, was a gateway. A roadbed extended out from this gate over our heads. Since we were looking from underneath, we could see a set of strong buttresses springing from the cliff wall to support the bottom of this roadbed. Where the buttresses ended, about ten feet out from the wall, the roadbed also ended in a jagged ripped edge; the rest of the span had apparently been torn away. Backing up for a better look, we spotted a portcullis in the gate, partly raised. It looked like an entrance, sure enough, but it was still thirty feet up. By the time we had finished our walk around the castle, though, it was apparent that that was the best-looking way in.

"I didn't want to use any active magic around the castle, at least until I had a better idea of what was going on, so that meant anything dramatic like levitation was out. We all know how much energy levitation takes, too, and I didn't want to incapacitate myself for a week just to get into a position where the trouble might really start. Instead, Haddo managed to get an arrow with a trailing line up through the portcullis. We pulled through a rope and I climbed up the wall.

"The place still looked deserted from the top of the roadbed. Beyond the metal spikes of the portcullis, the road made an abrupt turn to the right and rapidly ascended, so my view of the inside was limited. I could see a few burned-out torches set in sockets in the walls, and a niche for a guard station, but that was about it. Roni thought it was a perfect setup for a trap, and, frankly, I thought so, too. I ran a few more probes. Again, nothing. I checked the portcullis and the gateway itself. Nothing. I even pushed a mirror through the entrance to inspect the inside surfaces of the gateway. Nothing, nothing, nothing. So I went in. And, of course," Karlini said, holding his head and looking disgusted, "there was something, and it got me."

He took a drink of water.

"I walked through the entrance and the most powerful field spell I've ever felt jumped out of nowhere and grabbed me. I still don't know where it came from, but whoever set it up had power to burn, power that would have put any of us in a coma for a year. Roni told me they saw a burst of light, mostly reds and purples. All I know is that my aura suddenly went visible. Whenever I've looked at it, its manifestation is a solid shell standing about a foot out from my body. The shell has a slightly fuzzy edge, and the space is filled with blocks of shifting color. Since I'd restored my personal defenses before starting out, I should have seen an unbroken surface with a dull metallic, slightly reflective sheen. Instead, when this field hit the aura surface the aura *rippled*, irregular patches all over the place turned yellow and started to glow, and then these glowing yellow patches began to peel up, like scales lifting off the skin of a snake. It looked like I was molting, if you can believe that. Small globules of writhing tendrils darted in through the gaps under these scales and spread out. The tendrils shot around like flying worms, diving through the floating blocks of aura and down into my skin. I could feel my consciousness being cataloged." Karlini shuddered. "It wasn't fun. It was like having each piece of my mind turned into a fingernail and drawn slowly down a long slate wall.

"Did I mention that I couldn't move? Well, I couldn't. I tried to fight back, of course, not that that was any help; every defense, counter-spell, or neutralizer I thought of was squelched before it could even form. The thing had clamped such a lock on me, it was all I could do to even think. Not that much time had elapsed—less than a second or two external—but you know how time seems to play tricks when you're in that type of situation.

"Still, there was something strange about it, I mean something even stranger. I was aware that something was missing; not from me, from *it*. You know how, even under the strongest attack, you always get some glimpse of the consciousness on the other end? Backscatter, or whatever? Well, this time there was nothing. It absolutely felt like there was nobody on the other end, nobody there at all.

"Okay, somebody had left a monitor trap, fine, you run into them all the time. But we all know they have tradeoffs. The bigger they are, the more difficult it is to hide them. The more powerful they are, the more it takes out of you to create them. And the more powerful they are, generally speaking, the more powerful you have to be to be able to charge them up.

"So there I was, caught in the most powerful thing of its kind I'd ever felt, wondering who could have built it—and having the sinking feeling they were on the way to see what had set it off.

"But they weren't."

Karlini took another drink of water.

"Instead, the tendrils started to get shimmery, fall in on themselves, and go out, and patches of the field started to relax. I staggered, all the parts of my body jerking in different directions, and then I just fell down. The tendrils that were left slid off into the flagstones. I felt the rest of the field float away and dissipate. By this time, my aura was the shabbiest thing you've ever seen, tatters and holes and rips all through it, and probably as a result I didn't have the energy to try to restore it. An aura may not *be* the person, as Iskendarian claimed, but at the very least it's certainly a reflection of the person's state. I felt like my aura looked. All I could do was lie there and breathe for a moment.

"Then I heard a noise out on the roadbed on the other side of the portcullis. Roni, disregarding my explicit instructions, had come up the rope after me. I opened my mouth to tell her to stay away, but before I could say a word she was over the edge of the drop and heading for the entrance. Of course, I shouldn't have worried. Roni's one of the smartest people I know. She stopped outside the gate."

"Well, he didn't look quite ready to die," Roni said, "at least not at that second, so I didn't want to take the chance that running after him would call down the same attack on me."

"I made myself roll over and went for the exit," Karlini said. "I suppose you could say I made it. My body made it, anyway. Just as I crossed the plane of the portcullis I felt a terrible pain in my chest, like it was being crushed by a giant foot. I started to pass out. Roni grabbed me as I collapsed—"

"He was also turning a bright blue color," she said.

"I guess I was just a dead weight, and that weight pulled both of us over, and we fell back inside the gateway.

"Two things happened, or rather one thing happened and one thing didn't. The thing that happened was that the pain in my chest went away. The other thing was that nothing happened to Roni. Nothing attacked. The monitor spell didn't appear."

"It wasn't a permanent guardian," Max said, "it was a one-shot."

"Right," said Karlini, "and I'd sprung it.

"We sat there for a while. When I could stand again, we started to explore the place to see if there was any other way out. We didn't find anything. The spell that had snagged me was the only trap we could see, but that spell had bound me to the airspace of the castle. Whenever I tried to leave, my heart stopped. It wasn't only through that first doorway, it was flying, climbing over the wall, teleporting, every possible way of getting away that I could think of. Obviously, I wasn't supposed to leave. 'Wasn't, isn't the word. I'm *still* not supposed to leave."

"However you had entered the castle," Max said, "I suspect you would have activated the monitor. It didn't care *where* you came in, it only cared that someone *had* come in."

"I think you're right, Max, I figured the same thing. I also think the monitor was looking for the right kind of person, somebody with the right level of magical expertise. That's the reason for all that intensive scanning and probing I went through; it was checking me out to see if I was qualified. I suspect that especially because of what happened later."

"I had a feeling there was more," Max said.

Karlini squinted at him. "Of course, there's more. Roni and the rest could come and go at will, but I was stuck in here. The next thing I knew, they had all decided to move in with me. They trucked over all the laboratory equipment and most of the library, and a whole pile of other stuff. The castle had plenty of food, so we weren't about to starve. It also had some inhabitants of its own, like the big bird you rode in on.

What it didn't seem to have was a clue to what was going on.

"Then on the third day I was upstairs in one of the towers, searching an area I hadn't visited before. I had been climbing a circular staircase that wound around the core of the tower, with rooms on each level opening off a landing. Most of the rooms were locked behind thick wood doors, and I hadn't run across the keys yet, so mostly I'd been slogging up the stairs, looking for secret passages and suchlike. I was thinking about sitting down to rest for a moment when I came around the corner to the next landing, high up in the tower. The door off the landing was hanging open. I mean it wasn't merely open, it was *hanging* there, dangling at an angle from the top hinge, scorched and gouged and pretty well bashed in. All the surfaces in that area were scorched as well—wall, ceilings, and floor. An outline of burnt soot against one wall still kept the form of a tapestry that had been flash-fried. I—"

"Was there a smell?" Max said.

"Yes, there was, it was a burnt odor, but the smell wasn't fresh; say at least a week or two old. Anyway, through the broken door was an office. As I climbed past the door, I suddenly realized that I had gotten sleepy, very sleepy, in fact so sleepy that I felt my eyelids dropping closed and found myself starting to snore. Without even knowing it I must have fallen to the floor, because that's where I was later, but that wasn't on my mind at that moment since I had slipped smoothly into a dream.

"I was in that same office, working on . . . something, I don't know what. A wide window to my right overlooked the lower works of the castle and a mountain landscape. Even though I didn't get a good look out, I could tell that the mountains stretched much higher than the elevation of the tower. There were snowcaps at the upper levels. Something was on my mind, again I'm not sure what, and I decided to take a walk to think about it. I pushed back my chair and went to the door.

"The door was locked, but there was no lock apparent, and no doorknob, doorpull, or lever. Instead, I raised my right hand and touched my palm to the surface of the door. Aural colors appeared around my hand and rippled out over the door. The image of the door wavered, as though there had been a layer of thick clear liquid lying on the surface and plunging my hand into it had disturbed it. It didn't seem that the substance of the door itself was rippling, it was more like tossing a stone into a pond. You can tell that the bottom of the pond isn't really moving, but you're getting a refractive effect from the waves in the water. Anyway, this ripple pattern spread rapidly out over the surface of the door. When the pattern reached the wall, the door swung open.

"I walked out onto the landing. Again, it was the same scorched landing I had just crossed while I was awake. The difference was that now, in the dream, it was intact—no soot, no fire, no damage of any kind. A colorful tapestry showing some kind of political conclave hung on one wall where I had seen just its burnt outline a moment before. As I walked out the door, though, a bright glint on the floor caught my attention. I bent down to look. The glint was from a clear faceted jewel set in a unfamiliar gold ring. My mind was still distracted by whatever I had been thinking about, so before I quite knew what I was doing, I was reaching for the ring. Suddenly my mind clicked in. I realized that ring had no business being there, just sitting on the floor, and I had better not touch it, but my hand kept going. The ring was pulling it in.

"I was frozen in position, bent over on the floor, fighting my own hand. My hand slowed, but I was already too late My forefinger touched the ring.

"Sheets of lightning crashed out of the ring and danced along my body. The jewel was like a pinpoint slashed out of the sun. I felt—how do I describe it?—I felt like my aura was being drained down my forefinger and into the ring. More lightning came out, followed by balls of fire. My perception was strange, distorted, I was stretching out and being compressed and wrapped around, the world was getting vaguer and more distant, and then—snap!—the world was gone. And I woke up.''

Karlini took a drink of water, let his head flop back, and gazed up at the ceiling. Max, with a vacant look on his face, stared at a spot over Karlini's head, his lips pursed. Then he took the final few puffs on his cigar. Roni drummed her fingers on the table.

"Let me give you my analysis," Max said finally, "and you tell me if it matches up. Whoever the true master of this castle is, he set up a pretty involved anti-theft system, which you sprung part of. I assume that this . . . well, call him a person, even though he probably wasn't . . . this *person* figured he might be attacked or kidnapped, even in his own castle. In fact, that's what happened. Your dream was no dream, it was a replay. This person's enemy had left that ring as a trap. The ring sucked in the guy's aura and whatever aura-bound powers he had, and his consciousness, too. Sounds like a pretty interesting ring, when you think about it . . . especially since the ring isn't around now, I assume. Whoever set the trap transported the ring into the tower from some other place and then recalled it when it had done its job.''

"Why couldn't they have physically dropped the ring there?" Roni said. "Why spend the energy for a transport?''

"Even if you could get into a place like this in the first place, would you want to stroll up and plant a booby trap right under your victim's nose? No," Max said, "if it was me I'd spend the extra power and be glad of it. I'd rather not be anywhere in the vicinity. Anyway, the ring went off, but somehow the castle master managed to leave a record of his last perceptions in that tower. He meant for this record to be triggered by the next person to enter the area. Probably not just any next person, either, I'd bet, but rather the person who had set off the other alarm.

"Both the dream and the monitor and the whole moving castle itself are part of the alarm system. If the master really was attacked and subdued, the castle would take off, and would keep going until it had found the right kind of person to get him loose, or to conduct the revenge if it was too late. The castle was also going to make damn sure that the person it had chosen didn't leave until the rescue had been arranged."

"Yes, but, Max," Roni said, "the person who'd been trapped by the alarm couldn't leave the castle to do the rescue."

Max took a small bite out of the stub of his cigar and munched reflectively on it. "Well, Roni, that's the major detail I don't like. The castle master goes to all this trouble to trap somebody who's supposed to rescue him, then makes sure that rescuer can't leave the castle. There's a couple of possibilities. One, the master figured the rescue could be done without the rescuer having to leave the castle. I assume if that was possible, Karlini would have already thought of something. Right?"

"It can't be done." Karlini said. "At least, if it can I haven't figured out how."

"Right. The second possibility is that the person trapped in the castle was supposed to get somebody else to actually do the rescuing."

Karlini sighed. "Right, Max. That's the way we figured it. The person in the castle is a hostage. That's me. I'm supposed to pull in favors, or hock myself, or sell whatever treasure I have to get this guy rescued."

"Or," said Max, "you're supposed to call in your friends."

"How many magicians do you know of who have those kind of friends?" Roni said, with a touch of sarcasm.

"Aha," Max said, "now that is exactly the point

that concerns me the most." He rose and started pacing around the table. "If I were thinking about groups of magic-users, well, of course, there's the different confederations and specialty guilds. Everybody knows their members aren't what anyone would call *cordial* to each other, they're more backbiting societies than anything else. There's a few small teams and partnerships you run across now and then, but . . . why was your doorstep the first place this castle showed up?"

Karlini shifted uncomfortably in his chair. "Well, it wasn't really the *first* place—"

"Other stops aren't the point if nobody sprang the trap, and you know it. It sounds like a setup. It sounds like a setup to reel in our gang, find out who we all really are, and then—"

"Max, ever since I've known you you've been seeing plots—"

"Yeah, I'm still alive, too, and—"

"But there's never *been* a plot—"

"What about the—"

"Max, shut up," Roni said. "You, too, dear." She waited, staring back and forth at the two of them. "That's better. Now, Max, Karlini's trapped here. You know the only way we can think of to get him out— rescue the owner of this castle. Karlini's hunted down the ring. It's in Roosing Oolvaya. Somebody has to go get it, and you've got the best chance of any friend we could find. Will you do it?"

Max had stopped with his back to the table and his hands clasped behind him. "I'm the best one? Not Haalsen Groot? Krinkly Louise? Boorgonga? Hell, what about Shaa? I was on my way to see him. I know where he is."

"You're it, Max," Karlini said, not looking at him either. "Groot's settled down with his importing business. Louise is down south someplace. Boorgonga might be in hibernation for all I could find out. And you can't honestly tell me you'd wish this on Shaa."

"You know this guy in the ring is probably a god. You know what that says about whoever trapped him."

"We know, Max," Roni said.

"You know what the gods think of me."

'Max," Karlini said, "give me another plan, any plan. Tell me who to hire. Let's cook up some real zapper of a spell, scare up an army, dammit, I don't know, come up with something else, anything."

Silence fell, lengthened. Then Max turned around.

"One try," Max said. "That's all we get. And we all know damn well who's the best choice to try it. I'll do it. Of course I'll do it. But that doesn't mean I have to like it." He took the dead stub of cigar out of his mouth, looked at it, and scowled. The dark butt shimmered and began to glow, turned white, a painful white, and exploded. The stemware rattled. Sparks and tiny flaming embers drifted down. Max jammed his hands into his pockets, still scowling as he watched the sparks go out. "Aargh," he groaned disgustedly. "All my life I work to learn more, pick up some tricks, get more competent. All so I can end up in messes like this."

"All so you can help out your friend when he's in a jam," said Roni. "What else would you do with all that competence?"

"Yeah, right. I guess it's too late to complain. I just hope this thing isn't going to involve undead. I *hate* undead."

Roni and Karlini looked at each other. "Uh, Max?" Karlini said.

4
SHAA OUT OF PRACTICE

Zalzyn Shaa fled east, having left Drest Klaaver just ahead of the squad bearing orders for his arrest on a charge of practicing medicine without a license. Shaa's skills as a physician were not in question. His license, however, had been issued by the preceding government, which had left power abruptly and without advance notice. Shaa had been relaxing in his lodgings at the back of his consulting room, his feet up on an ottoman, browsing through a recent case digest from the Imperial Conclave of Physicians, when the former Chief of Police had arrived to request his services. The former Chief of Police had made this request by the simple expedient of launching himself through a window from the street, demolishing Shaa's coatrack, and collapsing onto the rug, bleeding profusely and (Shaa quickly determined) in a fairly terminal fashion. Shaa, estimating the consequences of being associated, in even such a circumstantial manner, with the losing side in a power grab, had quickly liquidated his practice, packing his tools and light valuables on the former Chief of Police's horse, which he appropriated in lieu of other payment for his services. He rode swiftly through the Bridegroom Gate at the west end of the city, made a wide detour through the northern agricultural district, and headed east for the river.

Pursuit, as Shaa had expected, was not significant, the new government undoubtedly having better ways to squander its resources than bringing down minor players, especially those with the bad taste not to present themselves neatly for incarceration. Shaa wasn't too upset about his strategic departure. He had discovered early in his apprenticeship that medicine, exercised with wholeminded diligence and without a leavening of other projects, was boring. As a result, Shaa's professional history tended toward bouts of medical practice interspersed with abrupt career shifts. He had been established in Drest Klaaver for almost two years, which for him amounted to stagnation. It had been time for a change, he reflected, and a new taste of the open road.

The road was clear and the surrounding ground cultivated and gently rolling, and it was spring to boot. The air was filled with the smell of young grass, turned earth, and the occasional cow. Small towns and hamlets came and went. Shaa rode patiently, doing calisthenics in the mornings and working out with his rapier at noon. By the time Roosing Oolvaya and the mist of the river appeared on the horizon, Shaa felt ready for them.

Some of the peasants and townspeople Shaa had spoken to as he neared the city had told him rumors of growing unrest and political instability. The tales hadn't bothered him much. Roosing Oolvaya was always in a state of unrest, and instability was something of a local custom. Still, as the sprawling district that had overgrown and then surrounded the city walls grew nearer, it became apparent that actual checkpoints had been set up, and patrols were on the roads. Smoke from several fires hung in oily nets above the city.

A permanent bazaar of tents and stalls and cut-rate stableyards for caravans lined the shoulders of the major west road, but no structures intruded on the roadbed itself. There was traffic in both directions. Farmers and their carts predominated, but a trickle of refugees headed outward as well. Shaa watched faces as the former Chief of Police's horse ambled on. Amid the soil-rooted and weather-gouged stolidity of the farmers and the city-honed craftiness of the residents was a mixture of hues, creases, shapes, and statures from places farther afield; all human, but not without their human share of diversity. The cosmopolitan air was certainly not unusual in a district given over to itinerants and traders, quick deals and quick fights, but the typically boisterous and surging character of the place was subdued. A general feeling of wariness lay atop everyone's features.

Well, Shaa thought, *that is fine with me.* Whenever something broke, one kind of person left and another kind of person showed up. He had been each, at one time or another. At the moment he felt like the type that showed up. Of course, he was out of practice.

He reached the western gate and the militia on duty waved him through. Shaa found a stable a short distance inside and left off the horse, shouldering the saddlebags, and walked on, checking his bearings and reassuring himself that he could still get around in the city. There had been no recent floods, so there was little danger of civic renewal having substantially changed things. The next block—ah. He turned into an alley. The alley, scarcely wide enough for a large person, narrowed further, the protruding second-story balconies drooping to within head-cracking range. The alley wound to the right, and then suddenly after an abrupt twist to the left it terminated at a closet-sized cul-de-sac surrounded by blank three-story walls. Several ferns protruded from the dusty ground. Shaa parted the leaves, revealing a grating. He wrestled the grating to one side and stretched an arm down into the shaft, feeling along the facing stones. The first stone was solid, and the second, but the third stone tingled suddenly against his hand and wobbled under his touch. Excellent, it was still keyed to him. He pulled the now-loose stone free, exposing a recess in the wall. Ah, Shaa thought again. Quite satisfying.

Rummaging through the saddlebags, Shaa selected a
sack of supplies and a pile of assorted implements,
which he had secreted about his person. The saddlebags fit neatly into the gap in the grating shaft. He slid
the stone into its slot and the grating into its frame and
started back along the alley. Two twists before the exit
to the street, Shaa heard a muffled thud from around
the bend in front of him, like that of a head encoun-
tering a low-hanging balcony, followed by a whispered
but scathing curse. Letting his cloak fall back, Shaa
reached across his body and grasped the hilt of the
rapier on his hip. A young man in a red and yellow
tunic stepped around the corner, rubbing his forehead
with one hand and waving a long blade with the other.

"Yes?" Shaa said.

The man looked up, startled, his eyes snapped to
Shaa's shoulder, where Shaa was now *not* carrying his
saddlebags, his eyes narrowed as a look of avarice
appeared on his face, and he turned the point of his
blade toward Shaa. Shaa brought his own point up as
he lunged. For an instant, Shaa visualized his blade
puncturing the right ventricle and severing the descending aorta, but he decided to be lenient. He was,
after all, a physician, and that did involve certain
oaths and a particular underlying philosophy. The man
beat ineffectually as Shaa's sword punched through his
right bicep and neatly withdrew. The bravo staggered
back against the wall, his own blade dropping from his
fingers and his other hand clasping his wound, and he
sank slowly to the ground. His mouth made an open
astonished circle. Shaa stepped over his legs and continued toward the exit.

As Shaa reentered the street, a small pack of dogs
appeared going the other way, back into the alley.
"Ah," Shaa said again, inclining his head pleasantly at
them. "My compliments." The last dog nodded back,
and Shaa strolled off into the city.

The old part of Roosing Oolvaya was a cramped
place, constrained by the shapes of the city walls and

the crabbed windings of the narrow streets. Even in the bazaars and business districts the crowds were sparse. People looked over their shoulders and walked lightly, keeping watch for mercenaries, the militia, and the Guard. Some stores were closed, with boards thrown up and rudely nailed across doors and shattered windows, while other stores and buildings had been sacked and burned. Smashed merchandise lay trampled on the cobblestones.

Several times Shaa encountered bands of armed men marching freely through the streets. They wore armbands showing an unfamiliar rune that looked, to Shaa, roughly like a flaming purple pretzel. Shaa was not accosted, though some of the troopers eyed him expectantly and fingered their swords. It was still early in the afternoon, the day was pleasant, and tempers were comparatively mild, so it appeared that the different forces were not yet spoiling for trouble.

Shaa wandered in a roughly eastward direction, listening for news as he went. Finally he found himself on a street that took a sharp zig and unexpectedly opened onto the Boulevard of the Fifth Great Flood. The Boulevard, much wider and in a much livelier state than the other streets, was the center of the waterfront entertainment district. Muggy breezes from the docks and wharves five blocks east rolled in sluggish currents toward the rest of the city. Sailors off the river barges rolled in along with them. Shaa stepped around three mariners snoring in a happy pile at the intersection and ambled down the Boulevard.

Most of the entertainers had removed themselves from the street, although a number leaned from second-story windows, surveying the traffic and making an occasional proposition. Shaa checked them over with a professional eye. He had spent time on the Boulevard. Aside from his long-standing fondness for the Fifth Great Flood, he had once combined a part-time job as Waterfront Health Inspector and Tariff-Collector with a fairly lucrative smuggling racket.

During the course of Shaa's walk, curfew notices
had begun appearing around the city. Shaa, along with
most of the population, had no intention of actually
staying indoors, but he decided he might as well put
his feet up for a bit and see if the world would provide
anything interesting for free. Shaa made house calls,
and he didn't see why the world should be less particular. He ran through his memories of the local inns.
The Wyvern's Fodder had been his favorite in Roosing
Oolvaya, but it was near the north wall, at least a
half-hour's walk away. Hmm . . . he had once spent
productive time at—what was that place?

As it turned out, the place was the Bilious Gnome,
and it was only two blocks north. The inn was embedded in the ground floor of a three-story building constructed in the classic Roosing Oolvaya style. The
lower two floors were relatively utilitarian, with prominent hardwood beams meeting at right angles to frame
and support the whitewashed facade. The upper floor,
though, was a general riot of overhanging, protruding,
and rippling timbers zigzagging and colliding in clever
patterns, leaving the overall impression of a trestle
bridge filled with patches of plaster. Egg-shaped and
squared-off windows of different sizes occupied the
larger spaces between the timbers. Because of the
haphazard layout of the beams, all the windows for
each story were not on the same level. In fact, the
curving windows with their rippling glass seemed to
bounce and bound all up and down the walls. Although the views from some of the lower windows on
each story could only be appreciated when you were
lying on the floor, conversely affording passersby in
the street a sight of the feet and legs within, Shaa
thought the net effect was rather artistic, at least when
the street was wide enough to stand back and appreciate it. Unfortunately, the streets rarely *were* that wide,
with the characteristic overhang of the upper stories
making the viewing situation even worse.

By Roosing Oolvaya standards, the building housing

the Bilious Gnome was unremarkable. A chipped sign-
board hanging out over the Boulevard showed the
portrait of a yellowish gnome, his pointy ears wilting.
Shaa gave it a nod, pushed open the door beneath the
sign, and went in.

Circles and ovals of light from the street lit up the
walls. Shaa planted himself in a corner on a long
bench with a view of the door and rested his elbows on
the wood slab table. The bar behind him divided the
customers from the kegs. A staircase led upward from
the other end of the common room, disappearing out
of sight behind an alcove. A half-dozen other early
patrons drank or talked quietly, while a kettle slurped
over the low flame of the hearth.

The innkeeper appeared and supplied a mug. Shaa
traced figures in the wet circles on the table, wondering if the world really would give him a hand and toss
him something useful. It had happened before; he had
a reputation for luck. He stared absently through one
of the front windows and onto the street. Yellowish
streaks and a formation of large bubbles in the glass
rippled in the declining sunlight. Glassmaking, Shaa
recalled, was a highly profitable industry in Roosing
Oolvaya, but not because the glassmakers were very
good at what they did. The technical processes of
making glass were pretty much frozen at their current
level, bubbles and all, but somehow the glassmakers
had managed to turn flaws and pockmarks and irregular colors into something approaching an art form. It
was one of the best solutions to working within the
god-mandated limits on technology Shaa had ever seen.

During his tenure in Waterfront Health, Shaa had
somehow ended up as part owner of a glass shop. He
tried to remember what had become of it. On this
visit, perhaps he would hunt up his former business
manager and figure out just how much of the city was
really his. Across the Boulevard, a trio of itinerant
musicians had planted themselves in a clear spot against
the wall of a spice merchant. They finished unpacking

their equipment, a set of hides stretched taut around nested helices of wood and bone, and prepared to rhythmically strike the hides with bone paddles. Over the noise of the street traffic and the insulating quality of the Bilious Gnome, Shaa could hear nothing of the trio as they tuned up. That was fine with him; he was not a fan of country music. For some reason, though, his gaze kept returning to the group.

Having arranged themselves to their mutual satisfaction, the three men raised their paddles. Out of a narrow alley just to their left ran a panting young man, a boy really, his hair wild and his manner frantic. The boy hesitated, wobbling as he checked his momentum and glanced around for a new direction to run. His gaze locked on the musicians as their paddles descended. Even through the distortion of the window glass Shaa saw a look of desperate shock appear on the boy's face as if he suddenly recognized an imminent doom. The boy spun around in a convulsive swirl. The paddles came down and began to pound, and the boy jerked to an abrupt stop in mid-turn. His arms flopped to his sides, he sagged, the energy and the animation seemed to flow out of him into the ground. In a way anyone without Shaa's understanding of how the world worked might have called blind chance, the boy's face came to rest in line with a pristine splinter of immaculately coherent glass, his eyes meeting Shaa's across the street and window and common room. The face was slack; the eyes had rolled up, showing the scleral white of oblivion.

Shaa straightened. His face lit. "Ah!" he said. He bounced to his feet, ran through the door and into the street, elbowed aside an enticingly dressed young woman and the heavily whiskered riverboat man who had his hand on her hip, and reached the boy at the mouth of the alley. The boy had started to sag limply to the ground. Shaa pinched him on the bridge of the nose, quite hard. The boy failed to react; his eyes neither moved nor blinked. "Ah," Shaa said again.

He put an arm around the boy's shoulders, lifted him partly off the ground, and started toward the Bilious Gnome.

A hand reached in from the side and closed on the front of Shaa's cloak. "Not so fast, huh," said the whiskered sailor, his voice muffled by the underbrush covering his face. "What d'yer think yer doing, shoving me around, me and my, *friend,* here?"

"My apologies," Shaa said. "*My* friend is not well."

The sailor looked suspiciously at them. "Not the plague, is it?"

"There are many plagues," Shaa said. "Who can say?"

The sailor looked at the young woman, then straightened himself and stuck out his chin. "Plague or no plague, what I should do, I should take yer face and—"

Shaa looked at the young woman and raised his eyebrow suggestively. She obligingly canted one hip and nudged the sailor. The sailor followed Shaa's look, the young woman batted her eyelashes, and the sailor's grip loosened and fell away. Shaa quickly reentered the Bilious Gnome, dragging his floppy companion. The thump-twang of the paddle trio faded as Shaa kicked the door closed. Shaa dropped his burden on a bench, resting the boy's head on the table, and resumed his own seat across the table from him.

Shaa, with some charity, estimated the kid's age as fourteen. The boy stirred, his head twitched, and then he pulled himself up and looked around, blinking his eyes.

"My name is Shaa," said Shaa. "I am a physician."

The boy's gaze focused on Shaa and turned wary. "Where are we? You better not try to bleed me."

Shaa raised an eyebrow. "Certainly not. Do you take me for a barbarian?"

"You said you were a physician." He shook his head, trying to clear it.

"Well struck," Shaa said. "Although I practice medicine, I do so with discretion. Allow me to emphasize the element of discretion, and your present degree of relative safety in having been removed from the street."

"The street—" The kid tensed, spun around to stare through the window, then spun back. "What do you want?" he said desperately.

Shaa, who had allowed his eyebrow to drop, raised it again. "You present a matter for curiosity, and potential professional interest. How far behind you do you think your pursuers actually were, by the way?"

"You're holding me for the Guard, aren't you," the boy said, his attempt at a snarl emerging as more of a whine.

Shaa spread his hands. "I understand a certain need for caution, especially with your condition, but let's not get ridiculous. If I had wanted to turn you over to the Guard, or anyone else for that matter, the difficulty would have been minimal."

"I don't know you and I don't need you. I'm getting out of here."

"Be my guest. Perhaps you actually did lose them."

The kid hesitated, then rose. "On the other hand," Shaa said, "perhaps you didn't." Shaa glared up at him. The kid plopped down. "Sir, this is getting us nowhere."

The kid leaned over the table and hissed, "All right, you. I need a sorcerer. Are you a sorcerer?"

"No," Shaa said, although "not at the moment" would have been more precise. "In any case, I doubt that's exactly what you need; magicians tend to be overrated. I have other abilities. What's your name?"

"Jurtan. Jurtan Mont." The kid suddenly sounded exhausted. He had had enough fortitude to keep it back thus far, though. Perhaps he had potential. "Are you from around here, Mr. Shaa?"

"Shaa will do. I pass through every now and then." He signaled the owner, raised two fingers. "Do you drink?" Shaa said as an afterthought, as the man scuttled back to his kegs and splashed froth.

"Uh . . . yeah, yeah sure."

"You should try it, my first prescription. It may reduce the frequency of your attacks."

"My attacks? What are you talking about? What do you know about—"

"Alcohol changes the level of irritability of the central nervous system," Shaa said. The owner dropped the drinks on the table, sloshing the contents of Shaa's over the lip of the mug. Shaa moved to the left along his bench, avoiding a runoff channel. "Drink up."

Jurtan Mont took up one mug, looking suspiciously at it. "You're sure this is healthy?"

Shaa peered over the rim of his own mug, sniffed. "You have a point. Still, you *are* on the run, and so by definition you need every possible advantage you can get."

Mont started to turn white. "I know what I'm doing, I don't need you to insult me."

Shaa looked up at the ceiling, silently asking the world if it knew what *it* was doing this time. "Look, my friend, I have much of value to offer, and I am offering it, provisionally, for free, so would you please stop trying to find—"

Jurtan Mont swung his mug and tossed the contents at Shaa's face. Shaa, demonstrating a level of agility that belied his stocky frame, flipped himself off the bench, did a backward somersault, and fetched up with his neck wedged against the bar, avoiding most of the flying ale. "I don't need you and I don't want you," Mont said again, and stalked toward the door. He kicked it open, walked two steps through it, and went slack. The trio of paddlers was still thumping away across the street.

A chorus of cries and the tumult of running feet burst from the left down the block. Shaa staggered to his feet. A small band of rapidly charging men became visible through the leftmost windows. Swearing under his breath, Shaa ran toward the collapsing Mont. The lead Guardsman shouted, "There, there he is! It's him!" pointing at Mont. Behind him were more soldiers, a whole troop in fact. Without stopping, Shaa grabbed a mug from the nearest table and hurled it. The mug flew past Mont's ear and shattered against the nose of the first soldier. Shaa skidded to a stop as the rest of the platoon converged on the doorway, snagged the back of Mont's collar, and heaved. Mont's feet left the pavement, he flew parabolically backward through the doorway into the Bilious Gnome, and as he fell to the floor Shaa let go of his collar, slammed the door, and overturned a table in front of it.

Glass splintered. Shaa looked up and saw a Guardsman climbing through the remains of one of the oval front windows. The door heaved with a sound of creaking wood as it was hit by the weight of four strong men. Shaa looked around, then put his foot on the end of a bench and shoved. The bench slid across the floor and into the knee of the window-climbing Guardsman, who had just jumped to the floor. The knee folded sideways and the man fell against the wall. Shaa hoisted the semiconscious Mont by his shirt and headed for the stairs.

"My window!" the tapster yelled. Then, "My other window, oh, gods, what next?"

"What indeed?" Shaa murmured. Mont took on his own weight and reeled up the stairs as three windows disgorged Guardsmen behind them. Shaa ran after him, hearing the front door disintegrate. Mont stopped at the top of the staircase and turned to look back. His mouth dropped open. Shaa swung an elbow at him, knocking him through the door leading off the landing, and then with his other hand withdrew a small membranous bladder from beneath his cloak. The bladder bulged and churned, its shimmering silver surface dancing with rainbow highlights like the skin of a fish. Shaa paused in the doorway, looking back at the five soldiers starting after him up the stairs, and grinned at them. He worked a fleshy valve on the bladder and carefully squirted a small stream of liquid onto the two beams holding the staircase to the wall. The liquid foamed, sizzled, and dug through the wood with astonishing speed. The staircase leaned over with a horrendous grinding screech, and then, with an even louder *crack,* it broke off, pivoted over, and hit the floor in one long thud that shook the building, not to mention the soldiers who had been climbing it. A small noxious cloud hung in the air. Shaa bowed, stamped on the clutching fingers of the lead soldier, clinging desperately to the now stairless sill, listened for the thump, and closed the door. "Fortunately they have yet to bring archers," he said, clapping the dazed Mont on a shoulder and sprinting down the hall.

Mont staggered after him. "What was that stuff you just used there?" he said.

The hall jogged off at an angle, and just beyond the bend was the continuation of the staircase leading up to the third floor. "That 'stuff,' " Shaa said, bounding up the steps, "was obtained at great cost and no little risk from a small amphibian resident in certain southern swamps."

" 'Obtained?' By you?"

"In fact, no." Shaa reached the small landing at the top and saw the opening to a trap door in the ceiling above him. A beam slipped through a set of iron brackets held the trap closed. Shaa knelt, made a basket of his hands, caught Mont's foot as he came off the last step, and pushed him into the air.

"Wha?" Mont said.

"The beam, my young acquaintance. Push the beam."

"Oh." Mont heaved, dislodging the beam from the runners. The beam hit the floor on its end, narrowly missing Shaa's foot, then teetered and crashed over. Mont pushed up, Shaa pushed Mont, and the trap door lifted slowly on wailing hinges. Suddenly they heard pounding footsteps and renewed cries, but now from the second floor just below them.

"Grab hold," Shaa shouted. He threw Mont upward through the opening, hearing a strangled yelp, bent, and seized the locking beam. A group of soldiers turned the corner below and trampled onto the steps. Shaa grunted and shoved the beam. It left the floor at the top of the stairs and flew downward, things were quiet for half a second, and then the air filled with wails and the sound of a vast crashing and bashing.

Shaa looked up. Mont had one leg over the trap door's sill, and both arms. "I'm stuck," he said.

"No, you're not," Shaa said. "It's all a matter of attitude." Mont strained and rolled over the edge onto the roof. "That's much better," Shaa continued approvingly. Mont's face reappeared, and an outstretched arm next to it. Shaa jumped, caught the hand, and boosted himself out.

"Now what?" said Mont, panting.

Shaa let the trap door drop and surveyed the terrain. They were on the roof of the Bilious Gnome's building, a flat roof that sloped sharply down at the edges in a plane of shingles and rose here and there in a checkerboard of boxy rooms and platforms; the exit from the trap door was in the middle of one of the elevated platforms. The surrounding buildings were similar. "This way," Shaa said. He broadjumped across the gap to the next platform, took two running steps, and jumped again. Another leap brought him to the Bilious Gnome's rear, overlooking an alley. The top floor of a four-story building confronted him across the alley, an unleapable gap up and away.

Mont joined him, much more cautiously. "If you don't stop gritting your teeth," Shaa told him, "your jaw will freeze up, making speech uncomfortable." Shaa had produced a rope and small grapnel. He whirled it twice around his head and slung it across the alley.

"No," Mont said, turning even whiter.

"The choice is yours," said Shaa, irritated. Behind them, the trap door swung open with a clunk. The clamor of voices was again clearly audible, and did not sound at all pleased. Mont tugged on the rope. It was solid. Shaa braced his hold on the free end and gestured. Mont took a deep breath and a double hand-hold and swung out.

The Guard erupted on to the roof, spotting Shaa immediately. Mont was halfway across. Shaa surveyed the distances, calculated rates of motion—a man with a bow appeared at the front of the soldiers. "Hold on!" Shaa yelled. He slapped a coil of rope around his waist, ran at the edge of the building, and dropped. An arrow streaked over his head, narrowly missing the tightening rope. Shaa swung out over the alley and hit the wall of the four-story building with both feet. The alley beneath was filling with troops. Pausing only to dislodge a large flowerpot from a convenient third-floor ledge, Shaa streaked up the rope, reached the roof, and flopped over the eave just ahead of a flight of arrows aimed fortuitously low. The roof was flat, and lacked Mont.

"Over here!" Mont yelled. Shaa spotted a waving arm on the next roof over, pulled the grapnel free as he passed it on the run, and vaulted over the edge. Mont caught him. "Why are you doing this?" Mont said.

Shaa found his feet and looked around. The next set of roofs went up and down, each a half-story different in height, like a long row of square sawteeth. "I need an adventure," he said, launching himself at the next building.

"What?"

"There's a curse," Shaa said absently. "Come on." He vanished over the edge.

5
SHOP TALK

Max slept poorly. Karlini had neglected to mention that even when the castle wasn't executing a major move from place to place, it wasn't exactly quiet. The castle spent the night in the manner of a person with indigestion from a meal involving onions and too many beans, shifting restlessly and rumbling with an occasional burp. At half past six, Max gave up and headed for the kitchen. Ronibet and Karlini were already present, looking equally haggard.

"Nice neighborhood you've got here," Max said, squinting down at the table and trying to butter a roll.

"Some nights are worse than others," Ronibet said. She had her nose balanced on the edge of a mug of coffee, breathing in the fumes.

A crackling and snapping sound came from one wall, up near the roof. They looked up as a green tracer of ball lightning burst through the wall, leaving it singed, and swooped through the air like a dying comet. It dove into a cauldron in a splash of green sparking water and disappeared. The water in the cauldron glowed a fluorescent forest green that slowly faded. They returned their attention to the table.

"All night," Max said, "all night with the green glowing balls and the spectral voices in the ears and the cold spots in the bed." The cook brought his eggs. "This place could drive you batty. I understand why you want to get out."

"I don't know where it's all coming from," Karlini said. He was already on his second cup of coffee but was only beginning to look alive. "All these manifestations just reek of energy, but I've been looking for weeks and damned if I can find the source."

"This place was set up by a god," Max said with his mouth full," and gods operate on the second quantum energy state, that's why they're gods. It's easier to set up stable power reservoirs on the second quantum level, that's one reason gods usually have so much power to burn."

Karlini had stopped eating and was staring at Max with his mouth hanging open. "Max," he said carefully, "how did you find that out?—That's more new knowledge than anybody's been able to learn about the gods in fifty years."

"Good eggs," Max said. "Can I have another roll?" Roni passed him the basket.

"Thank you." He carefully selected a fluffy butter twist with a flaky crust.

Karlini was still staring. "Max," Roni said, "I'm afraid my husband is having some sort of attack."

"Shaa's never around when you need him, is he?" Max commented. "These are good rolls."

"At least Shaa usually answers a straight question."

"Yeah," Max said, "but the answer usually goes with a different question."

"You've had run-ins with the gods before, I know you have," Karlini said. "They don't like you, and you're still alive. I've never figured out how you manage that, either."

Max looked up, gazing at Karlini with a very thoughtful expression. "Not all of the gods don't like me,' he said eventually. "Most of them don't like each other very much, that's probably the key point." He was silent for another moment. "Not that it's much use in any given situation."

"But how—"

"I think maybe you're better off not knowing too much about it," Max said, "don't you think?" He took a bite from his roll.

"You made that remark about quantum energy states, not me," Karlini said. "If you didn't think we should know about it, why did you bring it up in the first place? It couldn't be that you were just showing off, now could it?"

Max opened his mouth, then closed it and chewed his roll with a meditative expression. "Your point is well taken. I do have certain tendencies, as you know, and as you also know, I try to resist them, not always with success." He swallowed the roll and wiped his mouth with a napkin. "As it happens, I've been doing a lot of research, and some of it has turned out to involve the gods. I will show you some of it later, as long as you're so eager to know. That way, at least somebody may be able to use it, just in·case this damned fool errand of yours turns out to be as nasty as it probably will. Are you satisfied?"

Karlini looked across at the cook, somewhat embarrassed. After a moment, a tremor ran through the room, rattling the table and breaking the silence. Max sighed and shook his head, looking around in hopes of spotting a pastry. "What a place you've got here," he said. "The crowning touch last night was the seagull. I could swear there was a seagull flying around outside my room, screeching like crazy. Now, really, you know how far this place is from the coast? No seagull could survive the trip. Any seagull that tried to fly here would be on its grandchildren by now."

Karlini held out his arm. A seagull flapped down from the ceiling and perched. It screeched once. "It was sitting on the bed this morning," Roni said. "I don't think it's anyone we know."

Max sighed again and climbed to his feet. "I'm going to have to stop trying to guess what's coming next. Well, we'd better get started."

*   *   *

Max flopped back on the rug and panted. "Every time—I forget—how *exhausting*—this nonsense is," he gasped. Symbols faded from the air around him.

"Well?" Karlini said.

"Didn't you—see it?"

"I saw *something*," Karlini said, "but I don't exactly know what it really was. It looked like . . ."

Max lifted himself on an elbow and accepted a mug from Ronibet. He appeared to have lost about three pounds. "You saw a sort of matrix outline of the castle, right? Like you were looking at it from three directions at the same time, only the views were superimposed?"

"Yes, that's what I thought it was. What was it?"

"That was the field spell on the walls of the castle. That's what you triggered, and that's what holds the place together when it shifts."

"But why was the geometry so distorted?" Ronibet asked.

"Well," Max said, swallowing a chunk of hard candy from a large bowl placed next to him on the floor, "that's the second quantum level for you. Things are pretty strange there. Did you see that big glowing mass at the base of the castle matrix?"

"The thing that looked like a jewel with tendrils coming out of the facets?" Roni said.

"Yeah. That's the power reservoir. It permeates the rock foundation at the base of the castle."

"I looked in the rock," Karlini said, "and I didn't find a thing."

"You need different techniques." Max selected another candy, a blue one, popped it in his mouth, and started to suck on it. "There's a lot going on in the reservoir, but I couldn't figure out most of it. One thing I did see was that the thing's on a deadman trigger. The rock is unstable and the field holds it together. If the reservoir runs down enough, the rock falls apart."

"And if the rock falls apart—"

"Right," Max said. "The castle falls in." The seagull strolled over to Max, dipped its head into the candy bowl, selected a green piece of crystal, tossed it into the air, and caught it neatly on the downswing. Its beak made crunching noises.

"Uh, Max," Karlini said, "how close is this reservoir to the danger point?"

"I don't know. I can barely even tell the thing is there. But it's anybody's guess how many more jumps this castle can take without coming apart. Did you see that little pulsing dot about three-quarters of the way up?"

"I wondered about that. What was it?"

"You."

Karlini buried his head in his hands and mumbled something unpleasant.

"One thing I don't understand," Roni said quickly. "If operating on this second quantum level is so hard, how do the gods do it? I've heard some of them aren't too smart."

Max watched patterns form and dissolve in his mug. "I think it's something in their auras. Somehow the auras give them a leg up, maybe filter their perceptions for all I know, probably pump their energy up, too. There has to be a stabilizing factor in there that gives a god easy access to the second level, but damned if I know how it works."

"Does it have something to do with the coupling problem?"

"Maybe," Max said, "I don't think so, but it's hard to tell. There's more than one way to deal with coupling."

Karlini snorted. "Of course, there's more than one way, that's what—"

Roni looked at him. "That's not what Max is saying. I know Max. Max is saying that he's thought of a new approach to coupling. He thinks he's invented a process that's pretty hot. Isn't that right, Max?"

"I wish I didn't like you, Roni. Yeah, I thought of something new, but it isn't all worked out yet." He climbed to his feet and glared at Karlini. "Why don't you tell me about this setup in Roosing Oolvaya?"

The seagull screeched. "All right, Max," Karlini said. "This is the way things look." He rose and went over to a bookcase. The shelves had books stuffed in at every angle, each book leaning on the others around it for mutual support. Karlini ran his finger along the spines of several volumes of bound vellum notepaper. "Maybe this is it," he said, wrenching out a folio from the bottom of a stack of ten and watching the stack collapse down into the space. The rows the stack had been supporting folded in from both sides. "No, I guess this isn't the one," Karlini said, paging through the book.

"Do you remember the time he left his hat right in front of him on the table in a restaurant?" Max said to Roni. "That big sombrero-type thing with the tasseled fringes, and bright pink to boot? It was right under his chin, and he still forgot it."

"That was our first anniversary," Roni said, smiling at Karlini. "I think he's gotten worse, if that's possible. Try the book on the lectern, dear."

"Huh?" Karlini said. "Oh, okay . . . yes, that's certainly it. How do you do it, Roni?"

"It's a concept known as 'order,' " Max said.

"Yes, you've always liked that sort of thing, haven't you, Max?" Karlini replied with an air of distraction, ruffling pages. He stopped, leafed back two pages, set the book back on the lectern, and started sketching in the air. A series of symbolic equations took shape, winding around each other.

Max squinted. "Have I seen that one before?"

Karlini paused and made a small twirly gesture. The equations halted. He reached carefully around them and pointed to one term. "You see that statement, Max? That's the root. It's a corollary to your lousy Discontinuity Proposition."

With lips pursed, Max tilted his head to one side. "Hmm." Then he grabbed a tablet and began scribbling.

"You know, Max," Roni said, "Karlini's never forgiven you for that Discontinuity work. He'd finally gotten comfortable with the Doctrines of Conversation, and then you suddenly popped up and said it was fine to dig holes through them."

Karlini's equations had resumed their winding, and were beginning to flow into a structure. "They're not inconsistent," Max responded, his attention still on his scribbling. "Conservation works whether you're there or not. Establishment of a discontinuity requires the input of energy and imposition of a degree of control, but the control uses chaos terms. If you—"

A snapping sound came from Karlini's work. The floating figure had become a rough meshwork sphere, indentations and holes drifting across the surface. Mesh lines glowed a cycling orange-yellow, brighter sparks flaring where the lines intersected. The construct rotated slowly, wobbling in two axes, making a low whirr in the air. A prominent hump on the globe's northern hemisphere jumped in and out, the sound of snapping coming in synchronization with it. Max looked down at his tablet, nodding distractedly, quickly scribbled another line at the bottom, closed his eyes, and drew his finger in a curlicue pattern along the writing. His final line of equations glowed blue, rose off the paper into the air, and shot over into the floating globe, weaving itself into the surface. The hump evened out.

"I never thought of that," Karlini said, surprised.

"Go ahead, try it."

Karlini concentrated and gestured. The ball's equator waffled wildly and started to spike. "No," Max said, "it's a modulator." He sketched in the air, leaving hanging figures. "*This* is the command string, *this* is the modifier. The modifier has nine matrix terms and . . ." The equator settled down. "There, you've got it now."

Karlini smoothed the other transients. "Thanks, Max, I've been wondering what to do about that. Now, we aim it." Six depressions appeared at equidistant spots, top, bottom, and four compass corners, holding position as the surface swept over them. "Coordinate axes."

"Right."

The hollows tilted as a unit, forward, to one side, spun slowly, reached inward. The structure shuddered, collapsed into itself, and faded from sight, leaving the air slightly curdled. Max clasped his hands behind his back and paced slowly around the space, examining it closely. He gestured again. The spot of curdled air churned and then smoothed. There was no sign of the construct. "Nice," Max said. "No visual manifestation at all. Good for a spy probe."

"That's the idea." A yellow point glowed suddenly in the center of the empty space. Karlini made twirling passes. The point stretched itself into a line, rotated out of the void, and became a flat ring. The cabinet of alembics and other glassware on the wall behind it faded from sight. Within the ring, an aerial view of a walled city appeared. Karlini sank into a chair and stretched out his legs. "This is Roosing Oolvaya from about ten thousand feet. We're looking primarily at the old section, within the walls."

The walls themselves were not visible, but sharp straight edges divided the overgrown and tangled confusion of the original city from the fields and the more open confusion of the suburbs. "How about the overview first," Max said.

"Roosing Oolvaya sits on the west bank of the River Oolvaan," Roni told him. "The river takes a long curve out to the east in this area and then loops back to the west; the city's right at the easternmost edge of this bulge. After fifteen miles downstream to the south the Oolvaan splits into its three primary tributaries: the Greater, Lesser, and Equivocal Oolvaans."

"It's Equivocal because it floods, right?"

"Right."

"Do you want to see the picture, Max?" Karlini asked.

"No, no, the words are fine." Max was carefully studying the view of the city as he listened.

Roni went on. "The east bank of the Oolvaan is the start of the mountains: the Rondingian Uplift and the Rondingian Steeps. We're on the other side of the Steeps now, in this desert. These foothills are actually the backside of the mountains. On the west bank, the ground is much flatter, rising slowly for some leagues. That means that Oolvaan attracts runoff from a considerable distance on both banks—mountain runoff from the east side and plains and farms from the west. As you go north the terrain on the west bank gradually becomes steeper and more mountainous until it's pretty much the same as the east; that whole range is the Rondingian Heights. The Oolvaan starts somewhere up in there.

"Back to Roosing Oolvaya itself. As I said, the city is on the west bank of the Oolvaan at the eastern end of one of its turns. The river widens and slows a bit at this spot. The city has a natural harbor shielded from the current by a small cape at the north end and a chain of islands in the middle of the river, basically a perfect location for the domination of river traffic. Of the five major islands, one has extra port and warehousing facilities, one's being developed for fancy residential use, two are private estates, and the last has an old imperial garrison fort that's being used as the palace of the Venerance."

"Venerance, eh?" Max said.

"It's some kind of traditional title newly dug up. He's addressed as 'Your Venerance' or 'Venerable Sir.' "

"Wonderful. Will I have to meet him?"

"The situation's fairly confused. It's not impossible. Dear, give Max a closer look at the view."

The scene expanded as the field zoomed in. Irregular blocks and streets became visible, then individual buildings within the blocks. Then the picture shimmered, a rash of mottled blotches appeared scattered across the surface, and the edge of the flat viewing disc began to smoke.

"What—" Max said.

"I don't know!" Karlini said. The blotches bulged out into the room, the images around them stretching like paintings on taffy. A horrendous high-pitched whine built. One by one in a rapidfire barrage the bubbling spots abruptly popped like pricked balloons, the view around each one fracturing into kaleidoscope shards, and an intense silver light burst in pulsing rays through the holes. Streamers of lightning spread out and reached for Karlini. Karlini's fingers were a blur, smoke and sparks coming from them as well as from the ruptured disc. "Max!" he yelled, "I can't hold it!"

The image in the ring was gone and the plate of silver light shone through like a sun. Max, who had been gesturing, too, reeled off a string of figures. The figures spun into formation and darted into the ring. The surface of the silver plate heaved, the center swelled up, and then Karlini's original meshwork ball pushed itself through, the orange mesh framework trailing interwoven threads of burning silver. Karlini's construct was no longer a ball but rather a writhing amoeboid blob, its neat grid lines shooting off in wild hyperbolic sprays, irregular fragments curling back to pierce the structure and coil through its walls. A shudder ran through the blob as Max's second barrage danced along its surface. The roaring whine intensified. Max's amulet, which had been quivering on his chest, jumped out of his shirt, lights playing in the tiny sapphires and larger stones. A tendril of lightning grazed the seagull and one of its tail feathers burst into flame. Roni, who had been deflecting the lightning, was visibly tiring. The center of the silver disc opened and drew back. Behind it was a giant eye.

"Enough of this nonsense," Max said. He thrust his left hand into the bowl of hard candies, closed his eyes, gritted his teeth, and concentrated. A small concave plate, the concave surface covered with fuzz and the back side festooned with multicolored lumps and tubes and strange waving appendages, appeared in the air over the bowl. Almost faster than the eye could discriminate, the plate split into four much smaller but otherwise identical versions of itself, each of the four split into four, those split and split again, how many times the eye could not possibly tell, and then this cloud of spinning motes dove down Max's arm and into his hand.

The bowl heaved and blew apart, fragments of bowl and pulverized candy spraying around the room like tiny, brightly colored missiles. Max's fist, though, had clenched around a handful of the candies, and a swirling haze had appeared around his hand. Strong red light leaked from between his fingers, leaked directly into the haze, and the haze seemed to be vacuuming the light up into itself. Bands of light ran up his arm like small animals through a boa constrictor. Max lifted his arm, the hand still clenched, raised it over his head, turned it behind his body—and then, with one convulsive hurling swing, whipped his arm around. A ball of sizzling plasma hurtled out of Max's hand at the head of a solid beam that started at his shoulder and ran rippling down his arm like a tubular stiletto. The plasma ball went through the center of the ring into the questing eye and the beam hit the silver disc. The disc flew into shreds. The silver congealed like clotting blood as the disc dropped to the floor, wobbled on one edge, toppled over, and exploded. Globs of sizzling silver goo rained down. Low sizzles and plops from the molten silver echoed in the sudden silence.

Karlini and Roni pulled themselves to their feet. The seagull peeped tentatively out from under an overturned armchair. Max raised himself to a sitting position propped up against the far wall, where the recoil had thrown him. "You wanted to know about coupling?" Max said, still gritting his teeth. "*That* was coupling."

"It's not very neat, is it?" Karlini said. He surveyed the room. The air was thick with smoke, and plumes rose from the evaporating puddles of silver. All the furniture was scattered around, forced back against the walls.

Max's left sleeve had been shredded completely off, and his arm was bright red and oozing fluid. He gingerly raised his arm, rotated it slowly around his shoulder, clenched and unclenched his fist. With his other hand he eased his amulet back inside his shirt. The amulet had a disconcerting habit of popping out at unexpected times; Max didn't know exactly what its powers were, but since it had taken plenty of trouble to steal it had to do *something* useful. "I told you I don't have that new method of coupling quite worked out yet," he said. "This is the first time I've tried to use it like this. You wouldn't happen to have anything like a medicine kit handy, would you?"

Karlini dug under the bookcase and came up with a small singed satchel. He withdrew a coil of linen and began wrapping it around Max's arm. "Yeow!" Max said. "I feel like I've been sunbathing for about a week."

"Just what kind of stunt was that, exactly?" Roni said.

"Nothing too fancy. I liberated a pile of energy from those candy things and threw it at that eye. Unfortunately, I don't quite have the fine control down yet. Instead of just *liberating* energy, I'd like to incorporate it into other stuff. Thanks, Karlini, that's a lot better."

"You want to lie down for awhile?" Karlini said.

"I'd rather just get on with it. Do *you* want to lie down? You took a beating from those lightning bolts."

Karlini squatted back on his haunches and crossed his arms. "If you can go on, I can go on. You know, Max, this kind of thing didn't happen the last time I looked at Roosing Oolvaya."

"I'm not blaming you. I'm sure it didn't."

"Oskin Yahlei evidently decided he doesn't want anybody checking up on him," Roni said.

"Oskin Yahlei?" Max said.

"That's who has the ring," Roni said. "That's who you're going after. I think that's whose eye was in that disk."

"Never heard of him. How are you so sure he's the one?"

"That dream I told you about," Karlini said. "The one I had upstairs in the tower. It left me with a sense for this thing. That's how I found him in the first place."

"Hmm. Well, that's consistent, anyway. I hope he didn't get a good look at me."

"You threw him quite a punch," Roni said. "He's probably not in any condition to fight with anyone for a while."

Max looked at her and grimaced. "Maybe. That anti-spy field had a hell of a lot of power in it, plus it was shielded against backlash. I don't know how much of my bolt really got through. I'm kind of sorry I had to try that powerblast thing in the first place, but it was all I could think of at the moment."

Karlini asked, "You think that blast may have only put him more on his guard?"

Max raised an eyebrow. "If it was me, *I'd* take it as a warning. That's not the real problem; this coupling thing is obviously new technology, and I'd just as soon it doesn't get out yet. Well, maybe he'll think it was another god, and he'll at least have the tact to be surprised when *I* show up instead." Max sighed. "There's nothing to do for it now: you might as well give me the rest of the story. I'd like to know what else I'm letting myself in for."

"You don't want to try another probe?" Karlini said. "A fine-beam needle probe?"

Max stared at him, then ostentatiously crossed his bandaged arm over the good one.

"Ahem," Karlini said. "Well, perhaps the story might

be best, at that." He absentmindedly righted his chair
and plopped into it. "Frankly, Max, it's not the best
time to be visiting Roosing Oolvaya. You'll see troops
in the streets. The former Venerance died a week or
so ago under suspicious circumstances. His son occupied the office and turned out the local troops, that is,
the Guard, plus a horde of mercenaries who conveniently happened to be around."

Max had been testing his arm. He'd have to keep
exercising it, he decided, or it would stiffen up. "Do
we know anything about this son?"

"From what I was able to pick up before, he was a
well-known fop with a vicious streak. Perfect puppet
material."

"Whose puppet?"

"You tell me. Big powerful magician, wants to be a
new force in town . . ."

"I had a feeling you were going to say that. So this
mess may have politics in it, too." Max sighed again.
"What about old cabinet members, other people loyal
to the old Venerance?"

"It looks like the dungeons under the palace. A lot
of people seem to be winding up there."

"Curfew?"

"Sunset to sunrise. I doubt it's been doing much
good, though."

"I'm sure. Probably be more people out at night
than during the day. Could be camouflage, if I can
keep from running into traffic jams on the rooftops.
What about this Oskin Yahlei?"

"He has a place near the north wall, I'll show you
on the map. He's passing himself off as a necromancer."

Max groaned. "You're going out of your way to
keep this from having anything fun in it at all, aren't
you?"

"I already warned you. I mentioned there might be
undead when you brought it up before."

· "I hoped you were joking."

"He may not be a real necromancer, it could just be
a disguise," Karlini said. "You shouldn't get so—"

Max jumped to his feet and stamped furiously around the room. "Disguise or not, you know as well as I do that playing around with the dead is filthy stuff. After something's been in the ground you don't want to see it in the air again. I don't know if you've ever been chased by a gang of zombies? No?" Max ground his teeth. "Well, by the time they've managed to claw their way out of the earth they're not much more than a heap of glowing mold and squirming maggots, scum, basically, with clods of stuff falling off whenever they move. They've also got an uncanny habit of showing up upwind." He paused in front of Karlini and glowered at him. "You think *that's* disgusting? We're not even talking about the *real* undead yet. As magical esthetics go, necromancy is pretty close to the bottom of the pits. Disguise, hah! Anybody who would deliberately disguise himself as a necromancer is stranger than I want to hear about. He probably really *is* a necromancer, worse luck."

"You're not backing out, are you?" Roni said.

Karlini had turned pink. "Of course he's pulling out. He's afraid he's going to blow it."

"Dear," Roni said.

"All right, all right, Max, I apologize," said Karlini. "I know you don't like zombies, I should have put it a different way. You haven't blown anything significant in years, I know that, that's why you've got to take care of this one."

"Max?" Roni said.

"Of course I'll do it," Max said. "I said I would, now let's stop beating the point to death. You should know me by now. Sometimes I just need to complain. Just answer one thing for me, and then we can start on the real preparations. Who is he, really?"

"Who is who?" Karlini said.

"Don't play around. You've been sitting around in this castle for weeks, all you've been doing is thinking about this mess. You've got to have come up with at least a good guess. Who owns this place? Who is it I'm going out to rescue? And while we're at it, who is this Oskin Yahlei?"

"Uh," Karlini said, "well, I really don't know. I wish I did, but—"

"It's the one major point you've been avoiding ever since I got here. Now, talk, or the deal's really off."

"I, uh, I'm not sure."

"I'm sure you're not. I want your best guess."

"You must have your own guess by now, Max," Roni said. She wouldn't quite meet Max's eyes.

"Yeah," Max said, "I do. I sure do. That's why I want to hear Karlini's." He fixed Karlini with his sharpest gaze. "Well? Who is it? Is it somebody I know?"

Karlini slowly let out his breath. ". . . Death. It's one of the Deaths."

Max's glower had brought most of his face into shadow, his eye sockets casting gloom down past his nose and chin. Something glittered on his chest—the filigreed amulet. "Which one is the Death," he said, "Oskin Yahlei or the castle master?"

"Both of them. I think they're both Deaths."

6
THE CREEPING SWORD
STALKS AGAIN

The Skargool ransom money was enough to let me live comfortably for years, but I was still sitting out in front at the office the next morning. I'm not sure I could tell you why. You work and you work until you get to a point where you don't have to work for a while, and then when you get to that point you keep working anyway. Damned if I understand it. I didn't think I had anything of the free-lance do-gooder in me, I didn't think I was the kind of guy who'd keep doing what I should get paid for for free, but I'd been surprised before. Of course, as things turned out, the first business through the door made me wish I'd caught the first available passage out of town.

I had my feet up, just leaning back and feeling good about things for a change, when there was a knock on the door. There was something surprising about that, and even my mood of contentment wasn't enough to make me ignore it. It wasn't the fact that it was six-thirty in the morning, when the butchers and farmers had been at work for hours and most everyone else was still dragging themselves out of bed; when you do the jobs I do you get to expect people barging in on you at all hours. With all the skulduggery going on in the city during the night an early-morning visitor

wouldn't have startled me one bit. So it wasn't the
visitor that surprised me. What surprised me was hearing the knock on the door, and nothing else.

I've got my office on the second floor of an old
building for a good reason. The stairs creak. I went
and loosened them more myself so they'd creak even
louder. I like to know people are coming before they
get up here. The neighbors hate the sound, but they
hate fights in my office even more. Me, I didn't think
anything larger than a cat could make it up the stairs
without warning me.

And then there was a knock on the door.

That was the strangest thing about it. If anyone was
going to take the trouble to get up the staircase without the slightest sound, however they did it, I would
have figured the reason was to take me by surprise. So
why would they knock?

There was only one thing to do. I rested a hand near
the hilt of my sword, tried to remember if I'd made
my last good-luck payment to Phlinn Arol, the Adven-
turer's God, and said, "Come in."

When he walked in, I knew all bets were off. Too
late, I remembered that my coverage with Phlinn Arol
had lapsed a week ago. Typical, I thought. The guy in
the doorway was the man from the Skargool case, the
one from the insurance company.

The one I'd figured was probably a god.

"Hello," I said carefully. "Have a seat."

"Thank you," he said. He rested his walking stick
next to the door, removed his brown-and-gray tweed
cape and draped it over the back of the chair, flicked
his gaze quickly over the seat, apparently decided the
brown splotches were defects in the wood and not the
remains of a recent spill, and lowered himself deliberately onto the chair, his hands grasping the armrests.
His hair was combed over a bald spot and he was a bit
too stocky to bet on in timed sprints, but his mouth
was pursed enough to make the whole face look grim.
His eyes shifted around in pale sockets, gaze darting

at the few significant features of the room—the desk, the window, the bookcase with its smattering of books and my two large creeping plants, the dented Valtubian shield, me—and it occurred to me that perhaps, just maybe, he was worried about something. I tried to look patient, and to keep my mind as far away from the ransom money as I could, just in case stray thoughts were what he was after.

His eyes settled on me again, then slid away. "I find myself in an uncharacteristic situation," he said. "I need your help. Someone is trying to kill me."

I tried to stop it, but I think my jaw dropped anyway. "You're a god. How can someone be trying to kill you?"

"Oh," he said in a flat voice. "A god. You noticed that bit with the wife and the balls of fire."

"Yeah. It's my job to notice little things like that."

"You are quite observant; I commend you. That is one reason I have chosen you to assist me."

I wished I had gone blind while I'd had the chance; that way I would have stopped noticing unhealthy things, like the fact that he was a god. The damage would have been a lot better in the long run than what he probably had in mind for me. As long as I was at it, I wished I'd lost my tongue, too, to keep me from making any more dumb remarks such as actually telling him what I'd seen. But if I couldn't see new problems to get myself into and couldn't open my mouth to make them worse, I wouldn't be myself, then, would I? "You really are a god?" I said. "You're not going to try to deny it?"

"What would be the point? Would you treat me differently if you thought me a mere sorcerer?"

"Yeah, I would. I've got a lot of experience dealing with people. I feel comfortable around them, even when they're trying to kill me."

"All the more reason, then," he said. "There is no reason for you to feel comfortable around me. We are not peers. You will work for me in this problem, but I am not your client. I am your master."

Fear or no fear, imminent painful death or not, those were fighting words, whoever he was. "You got some kind of nerve," I said. "I work for whom I choose, when I choose. I'll take your little problem if I want to, after you've told me about it, but you can't just come in here and take over my life. I may let you hire me, but you're not going to own me. I gave up the whole vassal bit years ago."

"I am not bargaining with you. This is a matter of some urgency. I have been cut off from my primary power source."

"Magic—that's another thing. I hate magic. I hate cases that hinge on magic. I hate the idea of magic. In fact, I think I'm starting to hate *you*, too. I don't think your case is going to interest me at all. Now why don't you pick up your cape and your cane and go out the same way you came in?"

He seemed to be enjoying the situation too much, like a boy with a small insect and a growing collection of tiny legs, and that should have warned me. "I thought you might take that attitude," he said. That's why I took certain precautions."

". . . What precautions?"

"Your metabolism. I've linked it to mine."

"What are you talking about?"

"I'll show you. Hit me. Go ahead."

I had been thinking about doing just that for some time. I was sure it was a bad idea, but that had never stopped me before. My left took him under the jaw. I felt it in the usual place, in my fist, but that wasn't all. A sharp pounding pain flashed out of my own chin and up into my head.

He got to his feet while I was still resting on the floor, trying to look out of crossed eyes. "Metabolism," he said. "Linked. Anything that affects me affects you. If I run out of power, you will most probably die."

I wondered how I was getting myself into this. Maybe he'd been doing something to me that screwed up my better judgment. My head was certainly screwed up, and it was only seven o'clock in the morning. It looked like my left had as much punch as I'd always given it credit for. I reached for a random thought. "This power stuff," I said. "I thought you guys had so much power you could do anything. Why do you need me?"

"Why do you have so many questions? Just follow my orders. That is the only valid choice for you."

I squinted up at the two of him and took a deep breath. "Like I said, I hate magic. I've always hated magic. This situation isn't likely to make me reconsider, but it looks like I'm stuck with it. I may be tough but I'm not an idiot. I can tell when I've been outplayed. I think surviving the experience is good for a first goal, and I'll go back to hating it later. If I'm going to get out of this, I'm going to have to do what you want, and do it *right*. I'm a professional, I assume that's why you're here. If I'm going to do a professional job, I'm going to have to know what's going on."

He sat down in my chair behind my desk, reached into my drawer, and pulled out my flask. "It has been a long time since anyone like you treated me like this," he said, pouring a long shot down his throat. He smacked his lips, and maybe I felt some of it, too, deep down in my chest. "One side of me wants to dismantle you organ by organ and part by part, and have oxen run wild over the remains." Something crackled between his hands, and it wasn't the flask. I set my jaw from my recumbent position on the floor and tried to look as tough as I'd been talking, not an easy concept when you *do* happen to be lying on the floor.

"But I'm not going to do that," he said after a minute. "I'm not going to do that because you happen to be right. If I could do your job I would be doing it myself, but I cannot, so I need your expertise. I will caution you, though. I do know *my* job. You had better not go too far, or I will show you some of its fine points."

He stared at me. Suddenly I had the feeling of something large and terrible looming at my back, waiting to
tear me apart for starters. I made myself not swallow
and stared back at him. "Right," I said. "I've got
some questions."

He took another swig from the flask. "Very well."

I hoisted myself gingerly off the floor and into the
visitor's chair. "Let's start with who's trying to kill
you."

"I don't know."

"Yeah, right. Then how about, what kind of attempts have they been making on your, uh, life?"

"There has been no direct attempt to discorporate
me."

"Okay," I said. "So how do you know somebody's
trying to kill you?"

"When I tried to leave the city earlier this morning,
I discovered a barrier surrounding it."

"Tell me about this barrier."

He paused and looked disparagingly at me. "The
explanation is highly technical."

"I'm a professional, right? Try me, I can take it."

He was right, it was technical. What he didn't know,
and what I didn't want to mention, was that over the
years I'd picked up a fair amount of magic theory,
purely out of self-defense. Just because I didn't like it
didn't mean I couldn't know something about it. I'd
been up against magicians before, and it was always a
good idea to have some grasp on their capabilities,
and whether they could really carry out the threats
they always seemed to enjoy making. So when he
started off by saying it was a type of coupling problem,
and looked at me to see if I had the slightest idea of
what he was talking about, I could raise an eyebrow
and nod back with some level of confidence.

Coupling was always a big subject on the mind of a
magician, like caravan drivers crossing the desert and
their obsession with the location of the next watering
hole. Magic took a lot of power, and most of it came

out of the magician's hide, out of his or her own life energy, or aura, or whatever they were calling it this year. This drain was usually through a loss of body mass, but not always. Part of being a magician was learning not only to produce spells, but how to cope with the aftermath.

Well, fine, walking takes energy, too. The problem with magic was the quantity involved. Major-league conjuring—something like a duel, say—could take off fifty pounds of weight in a matter of minutes and leave you incapacitated for weeks, and that was if you won. You could create a spell ahead of time and store it, but that was only good when you knew in advance what you were going to need. It still incapacitated you, but at least you were in a position where you could rest up afterward; that was some help, but not really enough. That's why magicians were always looking for ways to store up power in other forms, and new ways to get the power in the first place.

That's where coupling came in. Most things in the world were potential power sources. Living things were best, but theoretically you could use rocks, wind, water, just about anything. The amount of energy a thing had was supposed to be related to the amount of order that had gone into making it and keeping it running, at least that's what the texts said. Unfortunately there was a technical hitch. There was all this energy out there, but nobody could really get at it.

To get energy out of a rock, say, you had to couple your own energy field to the rock, do something to the rock that would release its energy, and syphon the energy into your own field or directly into your spell. In practice, it turned out the efficiency of transfer was low. Real low. Draining your object all the way down to a husk might give you one percent of the energy you could calculate was there. *Maybe* one percent, if you were lucky and really knew what you were doing. There were all kinds of tricks and wrinkles, and different classes of objects give different types of energy, so magicians tend to specialize in order to at least learn one set of techniques really well. Necromancers, for example, got their energy from the dead; along the way they learned how to fiddle with the dead in other ways, too—it wasn't all a question of energy. The bottom line, though, was that there was all this energy just sitting around, and nobody could figure out how to get it out.

That much was common knowledge in magical circles. What I hadn't known, and what I doubted anybody who wasn't a god really knew, was that the gods had coupling problems, too. Gods don't like to discuss economics, it takes away from their image. According to this one, though, keeping up a god's basic life-style took a lot of power. That's why gods tried to diversify, storing up energy from as many different sources as they could, but they ran into efficiency tradeoffs just like people. For some reason the rules didn't work quite the same for gods—he said their efficiency curves were different, and they could tap other sources that weren't open to regular people, like donated energy through prayers—but that didn't get around the fact that the rules were still there.

There was another related problem. Magicians wanted to store up as much power as they could, of course, but it turned out there was a limit to the amount you could wear. A single person or aura could only absorb a certain amount of energy at any one time—and gods had the same problem. Gods could hold more, a lot more, in fact, but they normally used it up at a higher rate, too. What they *could* do, though, was store the excess, ending up with a network of power reservoirs that they could couple into and recharge from, even at a distance, like banks full of energy.

Also like banks, these energy stores could be robbed. A lot of a god's time went into hiding, guarding, or booby-trapping his reservoirs, and especially trying to keep anyone else from finding out their locations in the first place.

"So let me see if I've got this straight," I said, interrupting the exposition. "You're in Roosing Oolvaya running an errand, away from your power reserves. When you try to leave, you run into this barrier. Not only does it keep you from getting out of the city, but if you couple through it you reveal the location of the reservoir you're coupling into."

He eyed me thoughtfully. "Yes," he said.

"Is this barrier thing some standard ploy, then?"

"I have seen barriers used before. This barrier is not typical. It seems optimized for surveillance neutralization and quarantine."

"You mean keeping magic users out of the city, and not letting them look in?"

"Essentially."

"So why do you think they're after you?"

"This is not a very big city. Who else would they be after?"

This guy might have big power, but he also had an ego to match. Roosing Oolvaya wasn't the largest city around, but it still had its share of stories; who knew what else was going on out there today? He also had a certain weakness in logical arguments. "Maybe they don't realize you're here," I said. "Maybe they don't know the field has this effect on you. It sounds like this barrier's aimed at mortals, regular magicians. Not gods at all. You could be caught up in a side-effect."

He was silent for a moment. "That could explain a certain thing. This barrier appears to be a first-level field."

"First level?" That was a term I'd never heard before.

"Human magicians operate on the first quantum level. A god generally does not."

"Whatever you say. So maybe it's just some mortal slob out there who's put up this barrier for reasons of his own, and accidentally trapped you."

"That . . . is possible."

"So you could just blast this field and crush this guy and take off."

He glanced at me. I thought I was starting to get good at picking up his moods, and this time he was actually a bit amused. "That was a good try," he said. "I have not tested the barrier yet, merely examined it. I wish to know exactly what I face before committing myself. I could probably do what you are suggesting, but perhaps not. It would certainly drain me further."

"Even if you wait, you still said you were running out of power pretty fast."

"That is true. That is why you had best plan on working quickly."

To hell with humanity. I was in a jam, and I came first. "If you need to recharge in the meantime, why don't you just sacrifice a few dozen people and chew up their souls?"

"That, unfortunately, is not an option."

"Huh?" I said. "I thought all gods—"

"You thought wrongly," he said, a little testily (I thought) this time. "That energy would be tainted, would destabilize my matrix structure." He looked at the plants. "I am not a Death."

Suddenly, I was not only out of my depth, I was overboard in the middle of the ocean with a small rock quarry tied to my leg. "Uh," I said, "who are you? *What* are you?"

His head turned slowly to face me, and his eyes gazed sharply through mine. "You may not know what I am. As for who I am . . . you may call me Gashanatantra."

What the heck, I would see how far I'd come. "Okay, sure. That's a fine name unless I need to call you in a hurry. Since you say this mess is so urgent, I'd rather call you something I don't have to figure out how to pronounce every time I try to say it. How about Gash?"

"Gash. Indeed." He paused again, and I prepared to die. Then, instead, he took another swallow from my flask, and said, "Very well. Are you prepared to begin yet?"

"Yeah, I think so. Where can I get in touch with you?"

"I will be around."

"You said that once before."

"As with the insurance investigation, I wish my role to remain as minimal as possible."

"You mean I'm bait. You want to wave me around and have this barrier-marker shoot at me."

"If you like to view it that way."

"That's fine," I said. "I understand the situation, and that's my job. There's just one thing you might want to remember. You might want to remember that it'll be more difficult for me to do what you need me to do if I'm dead. That means it's also in your own interest that I don't get that way."

"Do not push your luck. I have selected you so that you can accomplish this on your own, by yourself." He paused, his eyes momentarily wandering over to look at the shield hanging over the desk. It had a large ragged hole in the middle where a javelin had once gone through it. The javelin was still embedded behind it in the wall. "Do you think you can handle it?"

Every client I've ever had ended up asking that, sooner or later. I hadn't answered honestly yet; I usually needed the business. "I'm not dumb enough to say no, but I'm not dumb enough to say yes. You're a big-time player. So is whoever's out there, even if he isn't a god. He's probably going to be a nasty nut to crack. That may need the kind of firepower that you've got and I don't. That means if I get in trouble that's too deep I'm going to have to count on you to back me up."

He didn't say anything; he just eyed me again and then got up and left. I had the nasty feeling I might just find out how expendable I really was. One thing that he carefully hadn't said, though, and that I hadn't wanted him to know I'd thought of, was this metabolic linkage bit. I'd die if he died, he had said, but maybe it would work the other way, too. It was just possible that he'd *have* to bail me out, for the sake of his own skin, or else cut me loose. I wasn't planning to die, but I *was* planning to get out of this thing without him running the rest of my life. It would be trickier than just about anything I'd done before, but for some reason I thought I might actually be able to pull it off.

Don't ask me why I was so optimistic. There sure hadn't been much in the morning so far to justify it. And of course, like everything else, it was about to get worse.

Like I said before, I hate magic, it makes me nervous. I'm sure that kind of feeling was an old story. Back thousands of years ago, when technology ruled the world, I'm sure some people hated that, too. When the gods moved in and shut technology down, the big thing that changed was the emphasis. These days technology had acquired a mystique among the few people who knew it had ever existed, a nostalgia that I shared. Nostalgia was all it would ever be. Every time some new mechanical genius showed up, trying to introduce a new innovation or reintroduce an old one he or she'd dug up, the gods would squash the poor mortal. They kept an eye out for things like that, and they didn't miss much.

More to the point, though, just because I didn't like the idea of magic didn't mean I couldn't know something about it, or know some of the people who did it. In my business, every friend is a blessing, and every contact an asset. When I'd pulled myself together, then, deciding not to actually *finish* off the flask at that time, I headed off to see a guy I knew. He sure wasn't a blessing, but in the past he had been an asset, and in my present jam I hoped I could convince him to be one again.

Carl Lake took one look at me, after his manservant had ushered me into his comfortable second-floor solarium atop a silversmith's shop on the fashionable Street of Fresh Breeze, and said, "What has happened to you?"

I seated myself in his down-stuffed armchair in the shade of a tropical young-palm. Gash hadn't told me I shouldn't tell anybody else the real situation, but I figured I'd better be discreet. "I got a client," I said.

He pushed aside some scrolls on his desk, the polished surface gleaming with rare hardwoods, and leaned over it to peer more closely at me. "You have also picked up a curse." He scrutinized the air around me. "I've never seen a curse quite like this—beautiful work, beautiful work. Unregistered, hmm, yes."

"Unregistered?" I said. "What the hell does that mean? And what's this curse thing?"

"Surely you know of the curse registry?" he said, steepling his fingers. "Curses are often registered with an agency of the gods. Like insurance, hmm? A god is contracted to administer the application of the curse. Supervision by a god, a very valuable function, yes, but quite expensive." He clucked to himself and rubbed his eyebrows. His eyebrows, possibly because of the attention, stuck wildly up and down like ragged bottle-brushes. "The curse is woven in your aura, like this—" His hand made swooshing darting movements around his own body. "What are the details, what its purpose—without a full study I cannot tell." He spread his arms, hands open and palms up.

Well, I guess I could have told him what the curse was, but I didn't. We'd met after Carl had gone on a picnic a short way up the river. Three thugs had thrown him off a rock ledge and left him for dead, and had stolen the scrolls he'd taken with him to read in the sun. I'd tracked down the goons and recovered his stuff. Carl would never walk right again, since the ledge had been fairly high up, but he still had his solarium and a good basic stay-at-home fee-for-spell magical consulting business, so he was doing all right. Sometimes he let himself feel some obligation to me. "Well," I said, "so I've got a curse. I guess I'll just have to live with it. What's going on in town?"

"Aside from the martial law and the curfew and the troops, yes, anything going on you say?"

"Aside from them, yeah. Any strange magic around?"

"You," Carl said, "I know. You are testing me. You have some particular thing in mind you are really asking me. Yes, hmm?"

"Yes."

"Something magical, then. Hmm." He rang for tea, and I remembered what time it really was. He was still in his dressing gown, but of course magicians had their own reputation to keep up, conjurations past midnight and all that. The tea was hot and its taste alive with the tingle of exotic spices, one of the benefits of living in a major inland commercial port. "Good tea," I said.

"Yes, thank you. You are not interested in simple gossip, but then these are not simple times, hmm? As you know, I am not often political, but perhaps you have come for speculation on political trends?"

I decided to stop playing games; maybe then he'd stop, too. "Look, Carl," I said, "maybe it's political and maybe it's not. I wouldn't be surprised if it was. Somebody's put a barrier around the city, and I don't mean a line of troops. Quarantine and neutralization of surveillance."

"Hmm," he said. "That is news. A barrier of sorcery, that is news indeed. How do you know of this thing?"

"I get around."

"Indeed. Yes, well, a question costs nothing." He raked his eyebrows. "A barrier. I must examine this for myself."

"The big question is 'who.'"

"Oh, my, indeed, yes. Who indeed? A good barrier takes much power, much skill. This is a good barrier?"

"The way I hear it, yeah. Real good."

He stood and hobbled furiously around the room, rubbing one hand across his eyebrows and using the other for support. "Political, it must be political. It must be connected with . . ."

"You're the best magician in town. Could you have done it?"

"Me?" He looked at me for a second, caught between ego and the needs of honesty. "No, not I, certainly not. Such a barrier requires too much power. Not my specialty either. And myself as the most powerful in Roosing Oolvaya? At times, perhaps. Currently, perhaps not." He stopped suddenly, staring out through the milky surface of the riverbeast bladder that covered the solarium dome. "Such a barrier is employed by a sorcerer against other sorcerers. It is a sign that says, 'Beware! Enter this area at your own risk! Secret work in progress!' "

"To me, that sounds like more of an invitation for anybody who's curious to come take a look."

"You don't understand. This is a serious affair. Such a barrier is usually a preliminary when one expects an attack. Or a duel. It says, 'Bystanders get back!' "

I was starting to get the idea. "If it isn't yours, whose is it? I know the local talent, and I'd say if you couldn't do it, none of them could either."

"It could be Rounga, perhaps, but that is most unlikely. I must make inquiries, gather the magicians of the city. We will meet. Perhaps we may need to take joint action. This is a serious warning."

I went to the door. "Let me know. I want to be there."

"Certainly."

The door was large and brass and highly polished. I began to push it open and then said, "What about strangers? Is there anybody new in town?" In the reflection of his image in the door I thought I saw him stiffen, just barely.

"If so, we must find it out," Carl said.

I strode off down Fresh Breeze, turned a corner, and then quickly took an alley back through the center of the block. I was just in time to see Carl Lake, fully dressed now and leaning on a cane made from the large straight tusk of a moose-slasher wolf, hobble out of the door of his home and set out for the north. The manservant had appeared just behind him. Locking the door, he hurried off in the opposite direction. I made a quick decision and slid after Carl.

Carl stopped every minute or two to look around, but there were plenty of doorways and stalls for me to slip into. For someone who had a crippled leg, he was acting remarkably agile. With the usual crowds in the narrow streets, each person bustling back and forth with their purchases, haggling with the open-air merchants, and just generally following their own errands and missions, and with the need to stay back so he couldn't actually see me each time he abruptly turned, it was all I could do to keep him in sight. I thought I'd lost him twice in the first ten minutes. Those times I had no excuse; tailing was supposed to be part of my job. When I really *did* lose him, of course, there were other more urgent things going on.

It wasn't more than fifteen minutes since Carl had left his house. We hadn't come that far, especially for the trouble I'd been having. I was following him north on Mosk Field, where it straightens out for a quarter-mile and gets wide enough for two carts to pass at the same time. One of the ubiquitous Guard outfits, a squad of about ten guys, was working its way south toward us. Carl gave them a glance and then moved around to pass on the right. A solid stone wall about twice my height ran down that side of the block, several sharp-eyed beggars reclining in the gutter at its foot, and Carl was forced to edge right up to it, his shoulder on the rock and his tusk-cane forcing the beggars to scuttle out of the way. I waited a few seconds and headed after him.

The street and the gutter were surfaced with uneven flagstones, but the gutter was also covered on top of the stones by the standard sheath of trash and mud. Carl had moved the beggars back, at least, but I still needed to keep an eye on my footing and one on Carl at the same time. Just at the second, the footing was first in my mind—I always hate to slip in the goop.

The approaching Guard squad forced me up a bit closer to the wall, my foot hit a slick spot and began to slide, and so I raised my right hand to steady myself against the wall. I'm righthanded, and that's the hand I like to use for my sword; I use a cross-body draw with the sword slung on my left hip. Just at that second a trooper from the Guard squad moved against the wall in front of me with his sword out and pointing in my direction. Simultaneously, another man had done the same thing right behind me, and still others had filled the space between the first two, all with their swords out, and the swords of their backups behind them as well. It had to be luck, and certainly not my own, that precisely when this happened my sword hand was splayed out on the surface of the tall rock wall with the rest of me leaning against it, several feet and a shift of body weight away from actually getting my own sword free and available for use.

Points poked my back and another one poked my side. A hand reached in, pulled my sword out from my belt, and withdrew. By the time one of them said, "You're under arrest. Violation of curfew. Contempt for martial law," it was almost anticlimactic.

"That was one of the slickest moves I've seen in a long time," I said.

"Shut up," said the corporal.

The whole thing had taken about six seconds. Up ahead, Carl Lake was still disappearing around the next corner. Just as he did, I thought I saw something impossible. I put it down to overwork. Unfortunately, the enforced vacation I now had coming up was not the sort that promised much chance of rest and recuperation. I was headed for the dungeons.

7
SHAA CONVERSES

The afternoon was creeping on. Roosing Oolvaya would shortly begin to come alive with the pad of muffled footfalls, the slink of stealthy passages, and the whisper of watchwords. Knives would flash and men would fall, while decent folk would stay indoors. Overall, it would be a typical night.

Actually, though, it probably wouldn't, at least if Zalzyn Shaa had anything to say about it, and it looked increasingly like he would. Shaa considered himself a decent person (as, he had discovered, most persons felt about themselves), but nonetheless he would be out in the streets. That is, he would *start* by being out in the streets. Shaa collapsed his spyglass, stowed it away under his cloak, and turned back to Jurtan Mont. Mont was barely visible to him, in the thick shadow behind a dark chimney, but would be totally concealed from anyone on the ground or even on the surrounding rooftops, which were lower. "Let me get this straight," Shaa said. "Four days ago the Venerance clutches his throat and dies. This twerp Kaar proclaims himself Venerance, locks up his father's government as a precautionary move, and starts rounding up everybody he's had his eyes on under the cover of martial law. That is the outline, and it certainly is not remarkably unique."

Mont shifted irritably and said, "So it's not unique. Who cares if it's not unique? It doesn't have to be unique to be bad."

"Well put," Shaa said. "There are few situations these days that are truly unique, if indeed there ever were. What gives any situation its individual character are the personalities involved and the nature of one's own personal stake. Thus it is that we come to the matter at hand, in which the major issue *is* your personal stake. Yes?"

"I guess so. It's gotta be my stake, I'm the only one left. They're my family. I can't just let them rot." Jurtan mumbled something else beneath his breath.

"What was that?" Shaa said.

Mont's voice wasn't much louder the second time. ". . . I said I wish I was more of the rescuing type."

"You may not be that type, yet, whatever it is, but you do have the markings of another, more useful type."

"What's that?"

"The intelligent type. Which is to say that you're apparently smart enough to know when to get help."

"Yeah, but, I don't know. I feel like I should have been doing it myself, instead of going out and—"

"There's nothing dishonorable about bringing in a consultant," Shaa said. "You tend to behave rationally, at least some of the time, and you made the rational decision. Shall we go on?"

Mont looked at Shaa, stared at him for a moment, then looked away. His head bobbed once in an uncertain nod.

Yet a nod it had been. "Your father, you said, was one of the first to be picked up, along with the rest of Kaar's immediate family and other potential claimants to the throne, the members of the Cabinet, and similar assorted threats. Your father is a grain merchant who's doing rather well for himself; suffice it to say that is not the reason he's in the dungeon. The reason he's in the clink is that he was a military adviser to the former Venerance."

"That's not exactly what I said."

"The sort of adviser who specializes in pulling one out of nasty scrapes, hmm?" Shaa said. "By the strength of his own sword, if need be? That kind of relationship with someone like an ex-Venerance would certainly make him dangerous now. On the other hand, if Kaar could make your father go over to *him*, that would be something of a public relations coup, now wouldn't it?"

"My father hates Kaar."

"Yes, but what about torture?"

Mont gave a small snort. "You don't know my father. I think he *likes* torture."

"I suspected as much, but that's not quite what I had in mind. Not of himself, no, but what about other members of your immediate family? Siblings, perhaps?"

"I've got a sister."

"Ah, how nice. Do you get along?"

"Well, yeah, I guess so."

"I, too, have a sister. Unfortunately our relationship has certain problems."

"Uh, I'm sorry to hear that."

"As am I. But the point relevant to your situation has been made, that is, there are others available whose suffering could be used, in principle, to sway your father's loyalty. Even, one may venture to say, *you* could be used as a pawn."

"They'd have to catch me first."

"Yes, indeed," Shaa said. "Hence the scene this afternoon. Or was the Guard after you because you'd stolen an apple? So. You'd like to get all your family out before the Guard gets you, too. That is not an insignificant task."

"Are you saying you can't do it? I *thought* you were just—"

"Keep your composure. The task is not insignificant, true, but it doesn't seem insurmountable either. These old dungeons usually have some tricky way to get in."

Jurtan Mont looked down past their dangling feet and the vast slab of the warehouse wall toward the rolling black surface of the River Oolvaan, slapping the pilings under the wharf far below. "I guess I'm going to have to trust you," he said.

Eventually, Shaa said to himself, he may stop saying that and actually begin to do it. After a moment for contemplation, Shaa spoke. "Leaving aside your own personal stake in the matter for a moment, let us move on to the question of the relevant personalities. Specifically, to the issue of Kaar himself.

"As you so aptly pointed out, the whole city knows Kaar. That's part of the problem. He's the kind of person you spit at when you see him in the street, just before you run for your life so he won't slash you to death with his whip."

Mont spat over the side of the building. "Kaar's a drunk, a gambler, a—"

"A most thoroughly reprehensible creature," Shaa said, "especially given that he now seems to be in charge." Under other circumstances, Shaa thought to himself, perhaps not that bad a fellow, except for what sounded like a cruel streak. Still . . . "Given the suspicious background, and the fact that Kaar would be rather low on any candidate list of rulers likely to prove competent, I suspect there's more to this than merely Kaar himself."

"Yeah, you're right," Mont said. "There's a few things about that I don't understand."

"There are things I don't understand either, but I will venture certain educated guesses. If Kaar is the wonderful spirit and all-around great guy you describe, where is his backing coming from? After all, he not only managed to pull off the initial coup, he's also been able to make it stick, at least so far. There's more to that than just locking people up."

"What about all the extra Guard? They must cost real money."

"Ah," Shaa said, "yes indeed. That is a point of great significance. This vast body of troops, marching as one indivisible body to the tune of Kaar the Magnificent."

"Kaar the Magnificent? What are you talking about?"

"Only a small exaggeration at this stage, a bit of advertising hyperbole, but teapot tyrants have a tendency to move into the grandiloquent regions reasonably quickly. He'll be calling himself 'Magnificent' or 'Transcendent' or some such inside of a month, if he's still around."

"He'd better not be around. I pray the gods will not permit such a terrible—"

Shaa raised an eyebrow and glowered at Mont. "The gods," he said, "are another subject entirely. The current crop of gods does not deserve your prayers."

Mont dropped his jaw and looked scandalized. "But—but if we pray hard enough, maybe we could get a blessing, maybe even get a god to help us."

"The gods are a mixed blessing at best," Shaa said, "especially the little ones who muck around with people. They rather *like* creatures like Kaar. Simple, pliable, vicious, not too smart—Kaar couldn't have been a better tool if a god had designed him from scratch. The last thing we want is some god noticing the situation and deciding it could further his latest plan. Please retract your prayer, and hope the gods are busy at the moment. That's much safer all around. Now, about the Guard."

Mont closed his mouth but the expression of moral pain remained on his face. "The Guard. Right. Yes?"

"Yes. There are many more Guard troops around than one would expect for a city of this size. They have not been raised by levy, yet their faces are not familiar. Correct?"

"I, uh, I don't know. I don't spend much time on the streets. I didn't spend time on the streets," he corrected quickly.

Shaa sent a sardonic smile out over the river. "Right.

The faces are not familiar; Kaar had been importing foreign help for some time. Now what is suspicious about that?"

". . . Are you asking me?"

"Certainly I'm asking you. I'm trying to stimulate discussion, sharpen your appreciation for the nuances. Think of it as a useful form of education—relatively painless but highly relevant. Again, now, the suspicious factor."

While Mont thought it over, Shaa looked behind them, rechecking the flat roof. The city was becoming a sheaf of paper cutouts silhouetted against the declining sun, outlines starting to flicker in the glow of firelight. "How could Kaar know in advance he'd need troops?" Mont said. "His father dropped dead all of a sudden. They said it was something natural, so how could Kaar have planned for it?"

"Very good," Shaa said. "That is the point I was after. What you should remember is that they always *say* it's natural causes, but it very rarely *is*. Whenever you hear about someone dropping dead under questionable circumstances like this, certain things should run through your mind. Natural causes will run through just long enough to escape out the back. They will only creep again into consideration when absolutely everything else has been excluded, and even then they will creep very tentatively."

"How can you be sure?"

"One can never be sure. The important thing is to keep the various possibilities in mind."

"What's next then, murder?"

"Inevitably. The mediums of murder are many, but they can be categorized. There is murder by normal physical means, murder by straightforward magic, and what one might call murder by loophole."

"I think I understand the first two, but what's the last one?"

"When I say murder by loophole, I mean that some unusual illusion or subterfuge is involved." Shaa rested his elbows on his knees and leaned forward. Far off on the water, beyond the moored lines of boats gently rocking on the swell, lights twinkled on the hulking masses of the three major islands. The parapets of the palace traced out their serrated edges against the dusk of the evening sky. The walls and island shore Shaa had examined earlier with his spyglass were now deeply in shadow. "Suppose the Venerance had actually expired sometime previous to the current events. It's not impossible, you know; his corpse could have been temporarily reanimated while someone waited for other preparations to come due. Another possibility—suppose the person who died wasn't the Venerance at all. It could have been a projection, a wraith, a transmogrificant—"

"A what?"

"Somebody else spiffed up to look like him. You get the idea?"

"Uh, yeah. But then how can you know who anybody really is? How do you know anything you see is really the truth? Who can you trust?"

"Those questions are at the core of the unsettling implications of magic. Magic is a tool like any other tool, sword or hoe or ship or book, and as such can be used for good or ill. Also like most other tools, it complicates life, making many people wish it had never been invented. On a less philosophical level, the questions you raise are a major reason there are court magicians and professional aura readers. Their prime purpose is to see through appearances. For every untruth, there usually is a way to expose the underlying actuality.

"Anyway," Shaa said, stretching, "these things are not usually a problem. Magic may be destabilizing, but it's also expensive, especially the fancy stuff."

Mont was sucking on his lip. "I think I thought of something else. What if Kaar had somebody who could see the future tell him when his father was going to die?"

"I believe you have begun to achieve the proper perspective," Shaa said approvingly. "It is time to advance to the next topic."

"What's that?"

One side of Shaa's mouth curled up and pulled the rest of his face into a sardonic grin. "I thought you wanted to *act*. You did give that impression."

"Sure, I want to act."

"Well, then, what is your plan?"

"I thought *you* were going to do the plans," Mont said. Shaa raised an eyebrow. "Oh, I get it, more education. Well, we have to storm the dungeons, release the prisoners, and overthrow Kaar. That sort of thing."

"That sort of thing," Shaa said. "The two of us."

"You don't have to sound so sarcastic about it. You've got a better plan? Then tell me about it."

"I'm not being sarcastic, at least no more than usual. That basic plan happens to be the one I had in mind myself. It is, after all, a classic of its kind and, anyway, an adventure is an adventure."

"You're a pretty strange guy, you know that?"

"I have been told so. Still, I am not alone in strangeness."

Mont squinted across at Shaa. Shaa was sinking into an air of impenetrability. "You're about to ask me something I'm not going to like," Mont said. "I can tell."

Shaa made a noise midway between a snort and a growl. One of the things he hated most was being predictable, especially while he was doing his impenetrability number. "Yes," he said. "That is true. I need to know something more about your seizure disorder."

Mont looked away from Shaa, off across the river. "I don't like to talk about it."

"Nevertheless you must."

"You don't like to talk either. Let's trade. You ask me a question, I ask you one. Why are you doing this for me?"

Why, indeed? Shaa thought. I don't have to put up with this, I only put up with what I choose. He started to rise. "On reflection, Mont, I recall that you don't have the only adventure in town."

"Stay where you are," Mont said. The glint of metal appeared in his hand, its edge glittering orange in the last light of the sun.

Shaa stared at him. "You have possibilities, but you are still an idiot."

"What's the matter with a few questions?" Mont said, waving the knife. "It's only fair. Okay, I need your help, but you must want something out of me, too. I think I'd better know what it is."

"This is ridiculous," Shaa said, and this time there was no doubt about his tone. "At this rate you'll have to get a license from the Chamber of Commerce before you help an old lady across the street. Just what do you expect to do with that fly-slicer?"

"I'm going to get some answers."

Shaa sighed, then whistled a few bars of a sprightly popular tune. Mont's form sagged. The orange reflections poured from his hand, went dark as they vanished over the edge, glinted once more as the knife entered the water. Shaa seated himself again, leaned back, and draped one leg over the other, ending his tune with the flourish of a chirping bird.

After a moment Mont stirred. "That was a dirty trick," he said.

"Thank you. Think of it as another educational supplement." Shaa crossed his hands behind his head, letting one leg swing idly. "I submit that our relationship thus far has not been optimally genial. I propose we make a new start, to preserve our mutual sanity."

"What kind of new start?" Mont said warily.

I've really come down in life, Shaa thought, to be reduced to bargaining with a truculent kid. "Since your curiosity seems to be the primary sticking point, I will answer your questions, up to a limit."

"You will? Really?"

"Yes, really. I did say so. You, in return, will try to keep in mind that it's your city and your family in danger, not mine, that I am offering essentially for free a level of expert advice and assistance that you would have trouble finding at any price on the open market, and that, finally, I might actually have some idea of what I'm talking about and some reason for the things I do. You will also do what I say and argue later. Agreed?"

"Yeah, okay. I agree. But I'll be watching you— you'd better help me good!"

"I have every intention," Shaa said dryly, "hence this whole drawn-out exercise. As a token of my intent, in fact, you may even ask the first question. Try a simple one for a start."

Mont was taken aback, but not rendered speechless. "Okay," he said, "that's easy. You carry a sword. Can you handle it?"

"Although such actions speak louder than words, in a word, yes. I once took a comprehensive advanced course with one of the better blade-persons it has been my fortune to encounter."

"Who's that?"

"Maximillian," Shaa said, "the Vaguely Disreputable."

"I've never heard of him."

"Max doesn't generally go in for the popular press." Shaa paused. Mont had spoken with some authority, as though he had expected to recognize the name. "Do you try to stay abreast of the major sword-swinging talent out of basic principles, or do you have aspirations along those lines yourself?

Mont looked away. "It's not me, it's my father. He has these guys over to the house all the time and I hear who they talk about, so I know lots of the big names." He sighed, his shoulders drooping. "My father was the Lion of the Oolvaan Plain. I guess he thinks I'm a disgrace to him. I don't want to be a fighter, not really, but he thinks it's the only acceptable thing to do."

Ah, Shaa thought, you want to rescue your father and thus prove your worth; a truly honorable motive. "Indeed," Shaa said aloud. "I daresay your father's opinion of you may never be the same again following this experience."

Mont shifted nervously, perhaps a bit flustered. He cleared his throat. "Uh, I, uh—why do you talk like that all the time?" he blurted.

Shaa had the feeling that what had just emerged from his mouth was not quite what Mont had really started to say. Still, whatever it was supposed to have been would no doubt come out in due course. "The tendency toward a somewhat baroque sentence structure runs in my family. And now, if you're quite finished with your first question, it is my turn. Your attacks are related to music, yes?"

Shaa watched Mont mull, then looked back at the deepening violet of the sky. All it needs is a little of that pink phosphorescent rain, he thought, like they have around that swamp—what was that place called? I should find a way to export that rain; it certainly had character.

"My problem's not just music, it's anything rhythmic, really," Mont said. "Cartwheels going over a bridge, horses trotting, that kind of thing. Those are the easy ones; I can usually fight them off by concentrating hard, but my thinking gets sort of fuzzy and sometimes I can't see. Music is the worst. Anything that has a beat. If the music's out of tune I can maybe concentrate around it, too, only most of the time it's no use. Any music with a regular part makes me go . . . it's like my mind starts pounding along with it and pushes away everything else. The next thing I know I'm lying on the ground somewhere." Jurtan paused, cutting off the rush of words. Though his head was turned, Shaa had the feeling he was setting his jaw and gritting his teeth. "You, ah, you don't think I'm a—a freak, do you?"

"Certainly not. Your ailment may be unusual but I wouldn't categorize it as freakish. It might be a curse;

however, I very much doubt that. My snap diagnosis would be some interesting oddity in your organic nervous system. None of your fault, obviously, but a significant handicap nonetheless. Hmm . . . I must think. There may be something we can do about the condition."

"You, ah, you know I've been to lots of doctors."

"The revelation does not shock me."

"None of them did anything that helped. They kept bleeding me, or waving their arms around and giving me horrible things to drink. None of them would ever talk so I could understand, either."

"Yes, well, the state of the medical profession is not what it should be," Shaa said superciliously.

"Are you sure you're really a doctor? I mean, you're not like any of the other ones."

"Few of the other ones are like me. Sadly, the scientific method is not currently in repute."

"The what?"

"Just my point." Shaa had been thinking while he talked, and the most singular symptom was intriguing him more and more. "Music, you say."

"Music," Mont groaned. "Yeah, music. Sometimes it feels like my life's run by music. I—oh, I don't care if you think I'm crazy, but I'd might as well tell you this, too. The, uh, seizures aren't all. I, uh, I hear music all the time."

"Please elaborate." Shaa, his fingers interlaced on his chest, his eyes closed, was beaming beatifically up at the sky. Finally, he thought, a decent diagnostic challenge. "This is quite fascinating," he added.

"Uh, thanks," Mont said. "Whatever I do, there's always a little bit of music playing along in the back of my head. It matches my mood, sort of matches what I'm doing. Other times it matches what's going on around me, picks up if there's action or excitement or stuff like that. There's all different kinds of sounds, all kinds of instruments, every instrument I've ever heard and lots more. Of course, I can only hear an instrument—for real, I mean, like when a live musician's playing on the street—I only hear it when it's out of tune, or when it's not being played right, but I've still heard enough to know what they sound like. Trumpets, birds, thompers, you name it, I hear it in my head."

"One's own private orchestra," Shaa murmured. "Swelling with the crescendos of life. Playing marches at weddings, off-key polkas at wakes, soft strings for candlelit dinners, the slink of slide-horns for menace. That is quite an affliction, my friend. Have you yourself tried to play an instrument? Have you tried to write this music down?"

"I've—I've never tried. I, uh, I didn't know what might happen."

Feedback? Shaa wondered. Resonant effects? "We will see. There is much in you to study. You are unique, yes, but certainly not a freak." He sighed. "Much as I would like to begin the investigation now, there are other pressing matters afoot. It is time for our plan of action."

"Just a second. You asked your big question, I get to ask you mine."

Like most people, Shaa thought, Mont is sharpest where his self-interest is concerned. "I try never to do business with a sea-lawyer," he said, "but I suppose sometimes it is a necessary evil. Very well, ask away."

"You know my question. Why are you helping me?"

"That one again? There is a prophecy."

"What do you mean, a prophecy? That's no answer."

"That's not much of a question." Shaa's eyes, if Mont could have seen them, were not focusing on anything in particular. "There is a prophecy that I would meet the major love of my life while on an adventure. I don't seem to have met whomever it is yet, so I am forced to continue to dredge up new escapades. There are also certain penalty clauses involved, making it unproductive for me to swear off the idea of love and merely retire on a permanent basis."

Those were not the only other clauses, but Mont probably didn't know enough to ask and Shaa certainly didn't intend to volunteer them.

"What about that curse you mentioned before?"

"This prophecy isn't a curse? It doesn't guarantee anything about the condition I'll be in at the time. It won't be too exciting to fall in love with someone just after I've been run through with a pike."

"If you say so," Mont said, apparently failing to detect Shaa's evasion. For a change, Shaa thought, Mont had managed to do something helpful. "Well," Mont continued wistfully, "at least there's a nice girl out there waiting for you, whatever shape you're in."

"The prophecy unfortunately neglected to mention details of personality. It also neglected to mention such particulars as sex."

"Uh . . . do you mean . . ."

"Who can say?" Shaa said gloomily. "All I can hope is that the escape clause will not be too offensive." He eyed Mont. "I do tend to think twice before introducing myself to people."

Even in the gloom, Shaa could see Mont turn white. Mont gulped. "Can't you fight it? Maybe the prophecy could be wrong."

"The circumstances of its origin made things quite clear. Unfortunately. Now, if you're quite satisfied for the moment?"

"Uh, yeah, I guess I am."

"Then we can get on with it," Shaa said. "I have some skill with boats."

"Huh? But we don't *have* a boat."

"Acquiring the boat is one of my skills." Shaa rose to go.

8
SCIENTIFIC INTERLUDE

"Well, that's all of it," Max said, wrenching closed the top flap of his knapsack and snapping the fastener in place. "Now do I finally get to see these marvelous research results of Roni's before I go out to have my head chewed off?"

Absently, Karlini rubbed the back of one hand across his eyes, making them even redder. "Max," he said, "I'm exhausted. Let's do it later."

"I'm *leaving* later."

"Oh, yeah. Right." Karlini fought back a yawn, then gave in and let it envelope his face. "Where's Roni?"

"Probably in the lab, where else?"

"But it's *late,* she must have gone to bed hours ago."

"Yeah, she did go to bed when it was late, but it's not late anymore, it's early." Max pulled back a curtain. "See, sun."

Karlini yawned again. "All right, you torturer, all right. This way." Max left his gear on the floor and followed Karlini through the door, down the hall, and up a flight of circular stairs. Karlini removed a key on a large ring from a hook on the wall and unlocked a door at the top landing. "Roni?" he said. "Dear?"

The room was empty. "Must still be asleep," Max said. "Why don't I just poke around myself and let you go to bed. I'm sure I can figure things out."

"I'm sure you can," Karlini grunted. "Most of it was your idea in the first place. Lock up when you're finished." He retreated back through the door and clumped off down the stairs.

The room occupied almost the whole top of one of the lower towers, the walls admitting a blaze of early sunlight through windows set all the way around. Roni and Karlini had set up a substantial array of equipment. Beakers, bottles, dishes, and flasks were stacked neatly against the walls, enclosed in a variety of field preservation spells. Two stacks of books sat next to the door. On top of the books were a set of three matching ledgers bound in hide and spotted with multicolored stains and spills. A fourth ledger was on the table in the center of the room, open to a page in the middle. To the left of the ledger was a low wooden box with a latched cover and thin tendrils of steam issuing from the joints. In front of the box was the microscope.

Max seated himself on the stool next to the table and ran his hand fondly over the ancient scope. He carefully rotated the compound lens mount, ran the viewing lens up and down, adjusted the reflecting light-source mirror, then rested his elbows on the table and his chin on his hands.

Roni was keeping things up nicely. The microscope had been the finest thing he'd ever owned, and he'd come close to dying over it more than once, but a scope was made to be used and Max was away too often to give it the attention it deserved. It had made quite a wedding present.

And now, if Roni was correct, it had helped her make a remarkable discovery.

Max, as was his nature, spent a lot of time thinking. One of the things he liked to think about was magic and the way it worked. After hearing from Roni about her research into animalcules and her resulting theory of cells as the building blocks for larger living creatures, a year or two earlier, something had connected. He had been looking down the scope at a bulging whitish ball of sliding tendrils and protruding blobs easing through the thin film of water. "Where does magic come from?" Max had said suddenly.

"I don't know," Roni said. "Where *does* it come from?"

"There," Max had said, staring at the amoeba. "Somewhere in there." The amoeba had sidled over to a smaller spinning oval, surrounded it, and sucked it in. "That thing eats food and turns it into energy. We eat food and turn it into energy, except we can also turn it into magic." Max looked up at Roni. "Somewhere in one of your cell things, something turns that food into magical energy. You want a new research topic? Find that interface. Figure out that step."

Max lifted his head and drew the ledger over. The book held Roni's latest lab records. Before flipping back through the pages, Max's attention was drawn to the most recent entry by the heading "MAX:" printed in large letters above it. It was a short paragraph containing setup instructions and the activation words for the filter spell. Max read it again to make sure he had things straight, then unlatched the cover of the wooden box, eased it open, and removed a round glass dish with a flat top. With a fine-blown pipette he found in a vase of water, Max sucked up a small quantity of liquid from the dish, transferred it to the center of a slide, added a touch of dye from a vial capped with a dropper, and positioned the slide on the microscope's lower stage. A thick stubby candle, half burned-out, sat next to the microscope in a holder with a curved, highly polished back. Max lit the candle. The light from the candle, focused and intensified by the reflective holder, shone onto the mirror of the scope and up through the slide. Max applied his eye to the viewing lens.

A few adjustments of the knurled knob on the body brought the image into focus: several motes of dark debris floated through a clear orange landscape, flickering with the spits and puffs of the candle. Max switched to the highest-power lens. Off in one corner he saw a flutter of motion, and steered the field toward it. An oval shape with a slightly fuzzy border spun into view. Its interior held the pigmented forms of mysterious structures—a major round one, lines and squiggles and balls and tubes implying others, all swimming in and out of sight at the limit of visibility under the uncertain candlelight.

Now for the *really* interesting part, Max thought. He glanced over at the book, found the sentence he wanted, and spoke the three activation words there. A sizzling sound began. At the base of the scope a silvery nimbus formed, circulating around the stage holding the slide and the lower part of the compound lens mount. Max returned his gaze to the lens and adjusted the slide to return the animacule fully to view. Sparks and crackles of miniature lightning jumped around the field, each flash of energy illuminating the scene more sharply, then letting it fade again into orange shadow. Inside the cytoplasm of the animalcule, though, something else was going on.

At one side of the larger round spot, in an area of overlapping squiggles so tiny that Max could barely pick it out, there was a sudden sparkle of green. Max focused in on it. Yes, it was there, it was definitely there—a twinkling of infinitesimal pinpoints, each the barest flash of green.

Max straightened up and scanned back through the ledger book. Roni had also seen this phenomenon—a microscopic constellation, she had called it. After fine-tuning the filter spell to weed out any significant artifacts, she had concluded that the effect was real. Those green pinpoints each marked a release of magical energy.

Max pursed his lips, took another look through the

scope, sat up again. Uncapping the inkwell on the table, he dipped a pen and wrote below Roni's last line in the ledger: "Incredible! You've found it! Fabulous work! Of course, now the real fun begins—first to understand exactly how this conversion works, then how to harness it, then how to control it."

He sat back and stared off through the windows at the landscape revealed by the light of the dawning sun. Plans, Max thought, more plans, always plans. But this one is different. If we control the roots of power we can finally take on the gods.

"So what do you think?"

Max jumped, startled out of his reverie. Roni was leaning in the doorway, wrapped in a robe, her hair tucked into the robe's hood. "I didn't hear you come in," he said.

"You were concentrating, I didn't want to disturb you. I always like to watch you when you're thinking at the walls, you get the most wonderful dreamer's expression."

"Hah," Max said, "don't give me that. It's beside the point." He turned his head away and looked out the window at the colors of the rising sun. "What do I think? You've done landmark work, that's what I think. It was worth getting dragged here to see what you've accomplished."

"Thank you, Max. Max, I just wanted to tell you, I'm sorry about the situation, what we're asking you to do for us."

"It's not your fault. That still doesn't mean I'm looking forward to it, because I'm not. This thing could be pretty goddamn unpleasant, you know," Max said.

"I told you I'm sorry, Max, I really am."

Max leaned back in the chair and stared up at the ceiling. "Sometimes I think friends are more trouble than they're worth; all I seem to do some years is bail them out of problems. They don't want to die. Well, I don't want to die either, but somehow it's always *my* life getting risked out in front."

"You do it because you like to do it."

"That's true up to a point. Beyond that point, I do it because I don't have any choice."

"You've chosen not to have any choice," Roni said. "You chose to live up to certain ideals. You're the one who wanted to take on the gods. You didn't have to do that. Lots of people have been living with the gods for a long time. You *chose* to make that your problem."

"The problem was there, I only inherited it. Why are you getting so worked up about it?"

"Because I'm tired of you complaining. You decided to let yourself inherit the problem. Now it's an obsession with you. You wanted to demonstrate you have free will? Well, okay, you've done it. You've got free will. Why not use it for yourself for a change? Why not find someone and fall in love? It would do you good, you're getting too sour."

Max raised one eyebrow and looked sideways up at Roni. Was *that* why she was worked up? Give me a break, Max thought. "I've *been* in love," he said.

Roni turned slightly red. "You know it would have never worked out."

"You know it might have," Max said. "But it's all right. You chose Karlini instead, probably a better choice in any case—Karlini's a lot easier to get along with than I am—and that was that. I think of you as a good friend, and I like you, but I don't love you."

"Max, I—"

"I don't want to talk about it. Anyway, that's not the only time I've been in love, and things didn't work out the other times either."

"You should still find someone new."

"I'm not in the mood," Max snapped.

"Max, that's—"

"You think I should show free will? You think I should settle down? I *can't* settle down. I wouldn't mind it for a change, but I *can't*. The last time I tried, a fireball dropped out of the sky and blew up the house. I managed to get out. The problem was I wasn't the only one inside. And you say I should fall in love? You say I should show free will? Forget it. That's the dream. I stay on the road because I don't have a choice. I won't have a choice until I can turn and fight back." Max stabbed a finger toward the microscope. "And with this stuff you're doing here, along with what I'm putting together myself, I'm finally going to be able to do it."

9
WHAT I DIDN'T KNOW

Even after they dumped me in the closest jail I was still thinking it over. The way the Guard had arrested me had been as slick as a training lesson. I couldn't see anyone bothering to learn my habits well enough to trap me that neatly, with me not even able to draw my sword, much less fight or run, so it had to have been just good luck for them or bad luck for me. Either way, it didn't make me optimistic about getting any benefits from my metabolic association with Gashanatantra, my erstwhile client. Any luck *he* had sure hadn't rubbed off.

That wasn't the only thing about the operation that bothered me, though. That squad had been ready for me. They knew I was someone they were after, they'd recognized me immediately, and they'd acted in perfect coordination and without hesitation. Reviewing my activities for the last few weeks, I couldn't think of anything I'd done that would make me that important a target. In fact, their recognition of me was just a little *too* perfect; I don't have that distinctive a face, but they hadn't even checked me against a description. They'd just jumped.

That left a couple of possibilities. I ruled out mistaken identity—with all the crazy stuff I had been

mixed up in lately, it didn't surprise me at all that
something else weird had happened. Of course, being
picked up by the Guard because I'd been confused
with somebody else would have been the most ridiculous thing of all. I didn't think I had to reach that far.
No, I had the feeling I'd been pegged. A person out
there in the city wanted me out of circulation, and had
managed it very nicely. One side of martial law is a
tendency to arrest everyone handy and sort things out
later. With all the confusion in the city, and the number of people being grabbed, I could just disappear
into the shuffle for a week or two and no one would
think twice about it. With Gash and his damned metabolic link hanging over me, though, on ice was exactly
where I couldn't afford to be.

I didn't have to think too hard to get a prime candidate for wanting me out of the way. The barrier-
maker was the obvious one. Oh, sure, some person
who had his own grudge against me could have chosen
this time to get even, but I thought I'd piled up enough
coincidences for one morning. It was improbable enough
to think that the barrier-maker already knew I was out
looking for him. I had no reason to think he knew
who I was, except for the clear fact that I was sitting in jail, and I didn't think I knew who *he* was. I
didn't *think* I knew who he was, but I sure had a
candidate; after all, the list of people I'd talked to
since this new mess had started was real short. Carl
Lake. My thoughts kept coming back to Carl Lake.

You could say Carl had led me right into that Guard
troop. He could have left his house, assuming I'd
follow him, and sent his manservant off to arrange
things with the Guard. He didn't necessarily even have
to arrange anything—for all I knew he could have just
plain taken control of the soldiers' minds and walked
them through it directly. Following a magician is tricky,
anyway, and like a sap I'd let myself ignore it. When
magicians are around, you never know what things
just happen by themselves and what's really their doing.

The final misstep that had put my hand out of reach of my sword—was that chance, or did magic make my foot slip? The perfect coordination of the Guardsmen— was it practice and drill and luck, or was somebody else running them? That's why I hate magic. Things are usually complicated enough without having to worry about whether a given thing was random or not, whether a hidden puppet master was calling the shots in a way I'd never detect, or whether a piece of evidence was real or had materialized out of a puff of colored smoke.

Carl had acted a little strangely during our talk, too. He'd taken things a little too calmly, like maybe this barrier wasn't really news to him after all. And then at the end, when I was leaving, he'd jumped when I'd asked about anyone new in town. I'd seen enough to make me think that if he didn't put up the barrier himself, he had a pretty good idea who did. I had to assume that since Carl didn't tell me about it, he didn't want me to know. If he didn't want me to know what was going on, or to mess in with it, the next step was to see that I didn't find it out on my own.

We'd been friendly enough in the past, but of course cordiality didn't necessarily mean anything when you got down to serious business. Still, if he was up to something tricky now and knew I was after him, he might choose to merely stash me out of the way rather than do me in. That might even have advantages for him. In case whatever he was doing was out-and-out dangerous, it wouldn't have been stretching the point too much to imagine him giving himself an insurance policy; if things got desperate enough he could get me out. For that matter, he'd always thought I was pretty competent. If he'd really arranged to get me in the clink, he might think I wouldn't let myself stay there long, and that when I got out, the first place I'd come asking questions was wherever he was. If he was in trouble, I'd be there to help him out of it. That idea was nice for my ego, in a backhanded sort of way. Looking around the jail, though, I had the unpleasant feeling that that concept might just overestimate my abilities by a little too much.

The jail was small. The main cell was about the size of my office, and if you added the room where the guy with the keys sat you could tack on the landing at the top of my staircase—space for a chair and a front door and not much else. I thought it was pretty poor planning, myself. If you're going to hold a coup, you'd better arrange enough accommodations for the loyalists you're planning to pull off the streets. They were probably just using the jails in the city itself as holding areas, shipping the prisoners off to the dungeons underneath the island palace whenever they got around to it. I hoped they would think of that soon for the jail I was in. The place was small, but it was real crowded.

The cell was basically a cage of thick iron bars built into the side of the building. The bars ran horizontally as well as up and down, and were attached to each other where they crossed by heavy bands of metal and an occasional messy weld. Whoever had built it hadn't wanted anyone getting out, ever—the cage had a ceiling of the same crosshatched bar, and a floor. I still had the small knife in my boot, but I sure wasn't going to saw my way out with that. Forget the lock, too. It wasn't big and it wasn't heavy, but its outlines had the kind of vague fuzz that charged-up magic gives. I thought that was a pretty flagrant example of overkill, but maybe it had its point. The only key that would open that lock was the one that had been in the hole when the spell was cast. It couldn't be picked.

I had the chance to examine the details of the jail's construction so closely for a simple reason. When they threw me in, I couldn't go very far. In fact, they had to lean on the door to close it, like trying to get the lid down on a trunk you've just packed for a three-year vacation. The cell wasn't filled, it was stuffed. There must have been forty people in there already. I'd never tried to get forty people into my office, but I think the back wall would have come off well before thirty. The troopers shoved me in backward, and the first thing I heard were the growls and "oofs" from my nearest new neighbors as my momentum elbowed them aside. My own mother could have been in that cell, somewhere in the back, and I never would have known it. After I got finished studying the way the bars in front of my nose were put together and gradually squirmed my vantage point around, though, I was somehow not surprised to recognize the second face at my back.

"Gag," I said, "you don't look so hot. You need some air?"

The face of Gag the Hairless was almost beatific in its look of peace. It was the face of a man who had just had his fondest dreams come true, and to whom such details as incarceration in an iron box were now so much insignificant confetti. He slowly noticed me, his expression lost in dreams. "Nah," he said blissfully.

Even his mustache had gone tranquilly limp. "Hey, Gag, talk to me. What were you smoking?"

With the noise in the cell, I could only hear him because his mouth was almost embedded in my ear. "The payroll," he said. "The payroll for the Black Legion."

I said, "You were smoking a payroll?" not because I thought his answer was in direct response to my question, but because I thought he might get irritated enough to bounce back down to the human plane for a few lines. To my surprise, it worked. His eyebrows furrowed and his eyes focused.

"Eh," he said, "what?"

"The payroll for the Black Legion?"

His mouth resumed its town-wide smile and his eyebrows relaxed. "You wouldn't have believed it. The most amazing thing you'd ever see in your life. Like heaven, that's what it was like. The Black Legion, you know, one of that bunch of mercenaries this Kaar guy brought in? They wanted their loot up front. Two months' worth of down payment, retainer, yeah, that's what *they* got—a whole safe full of nothing but gold."

Gag giggled. "You told me I better not push my luck. I never had so much luck in my whole life. Everybody wants a hideout, right? I had one, this great little inn place, up an alley out of the way where nobody'd even think of looking for an inn. It was perfect. I'd go back after a job, rest up, relax— perfect."

His smile widened, a feat I hadn't thought was possible. "I wasn't the only one who loved it. The Black Legion stumbled over it, too, decided it was the perfect spot for their own hideout. The place to sit on their loot." Gag chuckled. "Sure they threw me out, but the same time they were rolling me down the stairs they were dragging this safe up."

"You got the *whole safe?*"

"You should have been there. Everybody should have been there. It was great. The room was in the back, so I just hung down off the roof, sawed through the wall, and blew out the back of the safe. Just between you and me, it wasn't that much of a safe," he said, lowering his voice even more.

"If an outfit like that isn't smart enough to protect its own payroll, they deserve what they get," I said.

"That's exactly like what I said, too. Course, I'm here, so they had to do *some* protecting."

"Ah. Did they get the stuff back?"

"Nah. Why do you think I'm here, and not floating around in some sewer?"

"You got a point there," I said. "The Guard found you instead of the Black Legion?"

"How'd you know?"

"If you stole the Legion's whole two-month stash and they had *you* but they didn't have *it,* I think they'd spend as long as it took to convince you to give it back. They have a lot of ways to convince people to do things like that. Most of them are hard and blunt or cold and sharp."

For the first time Gag glanced around with a nervous look. "Uh, yeah. Hey, uh, you know something? The Guard heard the Black Legion was after me, and since they spotted me first they picked me up, but I kind of think they don't know what I did. If they knew, maybe I wouldn't be in here, huh?"

"I think you've hit it right on the head," I said. "And here you are, just sitting around, just waiting for somebody to remember you and find out what you've done. Who knows—maybe the Black Legion will decide to check out the jails themselves. They could walk in the front door there any second."

"Don't say it," Gag said with a note of resignation. "You're a right guy, don't do this to me. I gotta get out of here, I know I gotta get out of here, only I can't. I ain't got none of my stuff. I can't blow out of here without my stuff."

Well, there went *that* hope. "Why don't you think about it for a while. You're a smart guy, Gag, maybe you'll come up with something."

"Well, okay." He didn't sound too convinced, which meant he was being realistic. Realistic or not, we had to think of something. If nothing else, we'd suffocate if we stayed in that place. I stood on my toes and scanned the crowd, but Gag was the only person I recognized.

I turned and studied the lock again. There was something about it that puzzled me, but I couldn't quite figure out what it was. It was a normal round lock, about six inches across and painted black. Its outlines were slightly indistinct and slowly swimming—

Wait a minute. I'd never seen fuzzy edges before on anything but a cat or after anything but a binge. My eyes were still good so I figured it couldn't be them. I'd only *heard* that some sorcerers were able to pick out magic-loaded items by that woolly radiation. Some of them had *described* the manifestation as a little bit of haze around whatever it was. I'd only *heard* about it, I'd never been able to *do* it—but there that lock was, sure enough, fuzzing away like mad. Maybe, I thought with a sudden surge of hope, I was getting a little inadvertent help from Gash and his metabolism thing after all.

I stared at the lock. Well, what did I do now? The way popular tale-tellers liked to describe it, when you worked magic you reached out with your mind and then something impressive happened. I knew better. Magic was work, hard work, and the hardest parts were in the theory. Another reason I didn't like magic was that I could never handle the math.

On the other hand, what did I have to lose? Maybe gods didn't have to do things the same way regular magicians did. So I tried reaching out with my mind. Have you ever tried reaching out with your mind? Right. All I had to do was actually think about how to do it, and I realized I didn't have the slightest idea what it meant.

I scowled at the lock. I want you open, I thought. The lock just sat there, ignoring me. I tried to fight down my growing frustration. I'd heard at another time that frustration was the quickest way to magical paralysis. Even if you felt you couldn't do something, you had better not pay too much attention to the feeling or it would dominate you, and the feedback would make sure that you really *couldn't* do it. I can do it, I told myself, really I can.

The lock still sat there. I decided to try another approach. I concentrated on the lock, I visualized the lock, I visualized the lock open. I tried to fill my mind with lock, lock, nothing but lock. Nothing but *open* lock. I wrapped my hand around the lock, willing power to flow across and blast it open. I even thought about *tasting* the lock.

The obstinate nasty son-of-a-bitch lock didn't even twitch.

Against all my attempts at control, I was getting frustrated after all, but what I really was getting was mad. I hit the lock with the side of my hand. All thoughts of the lock vanished. "Yeaow!" I said, clutching my hand, wondering if I was dumb enough to have broken it.

Suddenly we heard the tramp of lots of feet outside, and then the rattle as they stamped onto the uneven boards that made up the floor of the jail under the bars of the cage. A Guard lieutenant and half-a-dozen very large troopers crowded in, their swords drawn. I could see a whole bunch of other soldiers behind them, and through the window I spotted more of them spreading out around the building. "All right, you men," the lieutenant said, "you're getting out of this rathole."

Nobody spoke. We all knew that wasn't the bottom line. I closed my eyes and thought, "Open!"

I heard a rattle of chains and more stamping and opened one eye enough to peek. Another half-dozen soldiers were dragging in a long length of heavy chain studded with manacles; that lobby was getting really packed. The lieutenant said, "Time to move out to the palace," but when I'd seen that chain I'd already figured it out. I was annoyed and frustrated and mad, and the pain from my hand was like the time a ruby-eyed marmovore tried to chew my finger off. The last thing I wanted to add to my mood was the pleasure of being shackled in irons and dumped in a dungeon, and so I screwed my eyes shut and thought "OPEN!" as hard as I could, trying to push all of the anger and pent-up frustration into it, sweeping everything else out of my mind until it was only OPEN, my entire world was *OPEN*, I felt myself hitting my hand once again against the lock for good measure, all the muscles and veins were standing out on my forehead, and then all at once my head spun, I lost my balance and fell hard against the bars. That's all I need, I thought fuzzily, I gave myself a stroke. But something, I didn't quite know what, *something* had happened.

My nose was mashed up next to the lock. I squinted at the lock. It was still closed, locked tight. I snarled at it. "Gods damn—" I said.

The floor rumbled. I opened my eyes wide and looked around. Everyone else, Guard included, was doing the same thing. The floorboards creaked and rippled, and one of the troopers lost his balance and pitched over, taking his neighbor with him. Another man fell backward through the door. "Earthqua—" somebody shouted, and then the rumbling stopped.

The quiet in the jail was striking. The Guardsmen picked themselves up, gazing nervously at the floor. Most everyone was nervously aware of the floor. "Right," said the lieutenant. "*Now* I want you all to—"

And then the rumbling was back. Boards groaned, metal screeched, Guardsmen fell down, and the cage that was the cell lurched backward and dropped a foot. Beneath the cage, the wood floor rippled and puckered down, then tore open and began to rip back toward its edges. The bars at the bottom of the cell, in the middle where the weight on them from the standing people was heaviest, slowly started to bend downward into the widening hole underneath. Even over the rumble and the creaking and the squeaking, I could hear the snap and clang as the bands and welds holding the bars together started to go. All at once, a man in the center of the cell dropped out of sight with a wail like he'd fallen straight through a trapdoor, which, in a way, was exactly what had happened. The cell lurched again and tilted more.

People were sliding and dropping in numbers now, as the bars peeled away in earnest. A few men had managed to jump up in the air and grab hold of the bars enclosing the ceiling, and their dangling forms were increasingly visible as the rest of the crowd lessened. I had one hand wrapped around Gag's collar and the other arm looped through a bar in the door. "When the avalanche is over, we go!" I yelled at him as he, too, grabbed a bar.

"But that hole!" Gag said. "It's deep! We fall in and we keep going forever!"

"It's not that deep," I said, loosing my grip on him.

"Listen to the screams. They don't gradually fade away like they're falling out of range, they just go on a little and stop. You can even hear guys moving around down there."

Gag listened. On the other side of the door, the lieutenant was fumbling with the key, trying to fit it into the lock. The other troopers and the jailers were staring blankly at the scene. Boards that had fallen from the ceiling were scattered on the floor, and the floor itself was covered with small dark holes and splintered floorboards that waved their jagged edges in the air. I reached through the bars, grabbed the front of the lieutenant's tunic, and jerked sharply toward me. His head swung forward and hit two bars, one on either cheek, he started to slide to the floor, and the key dropped out of his hand, bounced once on the floor and once in the cell, and then spun with a single reflected flash over the edge into the pit and disappeared.

"Nice move," Gag said approvingly.

"Thanks," I said. "Time to go." The cell had tilted back at an angle, resting partly on the wooden back wall of the jail building. The wall had bowed outward and was creaking ominously. The handful of remaining prisoners were clinging desperately to the bars as far away from the center of the cell as they could get. One man who had still been hanging from the roof of the cell looked down, sighted carefully, swung once, and dropped into the hole. A second later we heard a low thud and an "oof" over the shouts and clatter.

Gag and I edged gingerly out toward the hole and looked down. The cell floor meshwork of iron bars that remained actually extended out over the rim of the pit before the bars came apart from each other and began to curve down. The entire center section had torn completely off, but certain other parts of dangling mesh were still attached to the rest of the floor structure. Right below us, two twisted bars reached down five feet below the level of the floor. Enough cross-bars were still attached to these to make a kind of crude ladder leading into the gloom of the pit. Below the bottom-most rung, perhaps ten or fifteen feet farther down, was a flat floor. This level was now covered with mounds of dirt and rock and former prisoners. "A room," Gag said. "That's a room down there."

"Somebody's basement, I bet," I said. The wood frames and braces that had supported the room's ceiling still stuck up through the rubble. It was certainly a convenient time for a cave-in, if that was really what it had been. Something went "zzftt!" through my hair and clanged off a bar across from me—an arrow! It was less than half a minute since the first rumble, but the Guard was sorting itself out. I pushed off, slid down the curve of the twisted ladder, grabbed the bottom rung with both hands as I passed it, paused, swinging back and forth, sighted an open spot, and let go.

The prisoners in the basement were sorting themselves out, too, with many of them already on their feet and the rest either still unconscious or deciding whether their limbs were actually broken or just battered and strained. Gag arrived next to me, looked around, and said, "Where's the exit?"

"Behind this," a brawny man said from one side. He was straining at a section of slate covered two thirds of the way up by a rockslide, snapped timbers protruding from the sides of the pile. Another two men were using lengths of broken cell bar to sweep dirt and rocks off the slate. With a crack, another timber splintered and the rock settled further.

"Forget that," Gag told me with a professional air. A loud clanging came from above as someone set to work on the cage. Gag cocked his head, listened, and then said, "The Guard's gonna get through those bars inside of ten minutes."

I had spent a moment orienting myself, and I thought what I had in mind might work. I turned Gag around and led him back, stepping over a groaning form. "The street runs back here," I said.

"So?" Gag said.

"So I spotted a manhole cover down the block when they dragged me in. There's a sewer under that street."

I could scarcely see Gag at all in the darkness, but I caught a glint from his teeth as he grinned. He was running his hands over the surface of the wall, and I joined him. Then, down at the bottom, I felt rock. "Over here!" I yelled. "Another way!"

Men immediately surrounded me, dragging away a stack of crates that blocked part of the wall, kneeling to scrape away at the base, pushing and yanking at the stones. With a low grinding shudder one of the big stones moved. "Here!" someone said. "Push!" We scrambled for a hold, drew our breath, and leaned. The stone rumbled and moved into the wall, one inch, two, and caught up.

Behind us, with a clang and a new crash, more of the cage and a shower of rocks and floor fell into the basement. "Now!" the man said again, and we all strained against the stone. It caught, jerked, caught again, abruptly rattled away from us with a dull bass groan, and then there was no resistance at all. The stone slid out of touch, we fell against the wall with all our force suddenly released, and a great crash and plop and splash sent a shower of water up through the hole and into our faces.

Below us now was the gurgle of running water. One man squirmed headfirst through the hole and slid free with another splash, a second man followed, and all of a sudden a pileup had formed. "Let's do this orderly or we'll never do it at all!" I shouted, the crowd eased up, and I took advantage of the small gap in front to swing my legs through the opening, grab a handhold on the rocks on either side, and lower myself carefully through.

This sewer was square-shaped instead of the usual cylinder, and only about five feet across. The rock we'd pushed out had formed the upper part of one side of the wall just above the surface of the water, and it now sat there on the bottom breaking the current at a crazy angle. The first man through lay limply over the stone, unconscious from the bash he'd taken when he'd rashly plunged headfirst. I took a second to prop his head out of the water and then headed off downstream.

The only light came obliquely through the slats of the manholes and the collection tubes leading up to the streets and buildings. I didn't need light, though, to tell me I wanted out of there fast. Scuttling and paddling along bent over like a hunchback through what was frankly some pretty disgusting water while breathing putrid air was nowhere near my favorite part of the job. As a matter of fact, the lack of light was probably good. I didn't really want to know exactly what kind of junk was floating along and brushing up against me. It was better to have the trash down here than up in the streets, I knew, but that observation paled a little when you weren't actually *in* the streets, appreciating their relative cleanliness. Sounds of flailing and splashing behind me were suddenly joined by shouts and crashes, and I figured that the Guard had gotten wise and opened a manhole. An intersection appeared, I turned right into a larger tube, and the sounds behind me faded.

I hoped Gag had gotten clear, not to mention the rest of the poor souls who'd been swept up in the dragnet, but I wasn't going to spend all my time worrying about them. I had other things on my mind. There was still Carl Lake, and Gashanatantra, and whether that little earthquake or cave-in had really had something to do with me, and other matters like that. I jumped up to catch the ladder hanging from the next manhole I passed and climbed up through the shaft to the surface. Levering up the edge of the heavy wooden manhole cover, I peeked out. I didn't recognize the street, but that didn't matter. The important point was that the street was deserted.

I pulled myself through and let the cover drop. The street was narrow and short and dull, not much more than a block-long alley, which made it perfect for the kind of entrance I was making. I turned left at the corner and then left again, and then I knew where I was—about ten blocks in from the waterfront and a few blocks north of the south wall.

The sun was casting the shadows of early afternoon. A lot could have happened while I was having my dealings with the Guard, and I figured I'd better get back in touch with events pretty quickly. On the other hand, my sojourn in the sewers had left me thoroughly unfit for any decent human contact. The street I'd entered had a horsetrough a block or so down, but it was going to take more than a simple trough to deal with me. One idea was a fast jump in the nearby river. That would get me wet but not necessarily clean; the sewers had to empty someplace. A public bath was another idea, and I was about to go looking for one when my mind unexpectedly lit on the third and best idea of all.

I took off at a jog. People wrinkled their noses and tossed rotten things at me as I passed, and the lucky few who saw me coming had enough time to move out of nasal range. I didn't blame them a bit. I lost a small pack of dogs that had showed up out of nowhere, rounded one final corner, and pounded on a neat oval door next to the open-front stall of a glassmaker. A window opened on the third floor high above my head. "Who is it?" said a woman's voice.

I stepped back and looked up.

"Hey, who are you?" she said.

"Look under the scum," I said.

"I don't believe it."

"I'm having a little trouble with it myself," I said. "How about coming down and letting me in?"

"Are you crazy? Let you in? After what happened

last time you were here, you think I'd even open my door for you?"

Maybe this wasn't such a good idea after all. "Flora, be reasonable. I was under a goddamn spell, you know that. I was more embarrassed than you were."

She sniffed at me. "Maybe that's true. I don't care. Even if it is true, you shouldn't be in my neighborhood at the moment, let alone my house, looking like you look and smelling like you—"

"If you don't come down here I'm going to start smearing myself on the walls. *Then* you try dealing with the neighbors."

"If I let you in, what next?"

"What do you mean, what next?"

"Are you planning to tell me later you were under another spell?"

I considered telling her I *was* under another spell, only not the kind she was thinking of, but under the circumstances I thought she might not take it the right way. "You're safe from me, Flora, I promise I'm not going to pull anything."

"We'll see about that. Where's your sword? I've never seen you without a sword."

"The Guard took it," I said. "I'll tell you about it when I'm clean."

"I'm sure I'm not interested," she said haughtily. "But all right, then, suppose you're telling the truth for a change. What do I get out of this?"

"The story's got more in it than just the sword. It'll tell you something useful."

"Useful? Hah! What could you tell me that would be any use at all?"

"The information I've got could keep you from getting dead. Is that good enough?"

Her head withdrew and the window slammed. A moment later there was a stamping on the stairs inside and the door swung open. Flora stood back from the doorway and folded her arms. "Okay, the door's open, big detective. Now what do you want?"

"The first thing you can do is get me cleaned off."

She reached out for the door and started to slam it. "Carl Lake been around lately?" I said quickly.

The door paused. "Why?" she said.

"He called you to a meeting, right?"

Slowly the door swung open. "How do you know about it? And what's it to you?"

"Clean up first."

She sniffed again, gagged, and turned a light shade of green. "If I want to stand close enough to hear what you're saying, I guess you'll have to get cleaned up. Go around the back."

The front door closed, and I went around the side of the building to another pair of larger cross-timbered doors, like the doors to a barn. One of them creaked as the bar inside was pushed back. With a louder creak, the door slid open just enough for me to ease through it and into Flora's workroom.

The workroom was a two-story chamber with a loft, filled with several hulking barrels and tanks, two bookcases, a workbench, and a blackboard. Windows around the second floor let in the light. "Stand on that grate," Flora said, indicating a square mesh inset in the floor with open space underneath. As I walked over to it, she threw a lever and manipulated a crank on the wall. Belts attached to the crank stretched up to the ceiling and ran off into a complicated maze of pulleys and gears. A tube and spout attached to one of the tanks swung over until it was suspended over my head. She drew a figure in the air, a figure that trailed like blue smoke behind her finger and then drifted across the room to spin slowly around my head. Through the slight haze of dancing blue motes, I saw Flora throw another lever. A valve squeaked, up on the tank, liquid gurgled, and then a rush of water cascaded through the tube and out of the spout and down over me. Bits of blue from the hanging ring came off in the water and washed over my clothes in a glittering rain, spreading and scouring away the slime and refuse with remarkable efficiency.

"I'm sure I won't be flattered," Flora said over the patter of the water, "but why did you decide to come here?"

I rinsed my mouth, gargled, and spit. "You're a magician, your specialty is water, and you were close. I needed to talk to another magician, I needed to get washed off, and I needed to do both of them pretty quickly. That may not be flattering, but it's unfortunately the truth."

She cranked the lever back and the stream of water slowed to a trickle and stopped. "So that's the truth," she said. "There wasn't anything in that little talk about friendship."

"These days I don't know who's a friend and who isn't," I said, brushing water out of my hair. "Besides, if I'd said I was coming to see you because you were a friend, I sort of thought you might take it the wrong way, judging from the other part of our conversation outside."

She threw her head back and laughed.

"What's funny?" I said.

"You!" she whooped. "You've got a timid streak as wide as the Oolvaan!"

"I call it tact. Throw me a towel."

She found one and threw it, still laughing. Flora was in her fifties and in good physical shape; magicians usually had to be because of the physical demands. She had put on a few pounds, though, which probably meant that business was slow; Flora was on retainer to the Venerance for maintenance of the flood-abatement defenses, but the weather had been quiet lately and I guess she didn't have too much else going on. Remember coupling? When a magician was running a lot of spell-work, he or she had trouble keeping body weight up; the power expenditures kept burning up tissue. Between jobs, the thoughtful magician tried to gain some body mass, in order to have an extra cushion to draw on when things picked up again.

Flora wasn't really my type, not that I'd ever figured out exactly what that was, but events had thrown us together a few times before this and we'd found that we could be pleasant with each other. It wasn't automatic, pleasantness never was, but it did happen on occasion, and so every so often we'd been friends.

At the moment, though, it remained to be seen. "All right, big detective, you're clean now," she said. "Now it's the turn for your mouth."

I decided to stay where I was and drip over the drain for the time being. Under the circumstances, I didn't want to take off my clothes and wring them out. "I got a client this morning," I said. "He was some magician I'd never seen before who'd been in the city on business and now was having a problem in leaving. According to him, it wasn't the Guard. There was some kind of magical barrier around the city that hadn't been there before. He wanted me to find out who'd put it up and get them to take it down."

"You're not a magician. You hate magic. Why would you get involved in something like that?"

"The guy was amazingly persuasive," I said. "I didn't like the idea of him turning me into a toad. I took the job and went to see Carl. When I asked him about the barrier he tried to act surprised, but it sounded like it wasn't big news to him."

"What kind of barrier?"

"Magical quarantine, supposedly, also to keep people from looking in across it. Magicians, I mean, not regular people."

"Carl couldn't establish that kind of barrier. Nobody in Roosing Oolvaya can . . . except maybe for this new guy."

"New guy? What new guy?"

She had seated herself in a chair pulled out from the desk. I followed her lead and lowered myself to a more comfortable position on the floor next to the grate. "I've only heard rumors," Flora said. "Some new guy in a rented house near the north wall, supposedly very powerful."

"Hmm," I said, "a *real* big-leaguer, and new in town. That's interesting. I didn't think Carl had built this barrier thing himself, either, but I thought he might have known who did. He was acting like he knew more than he was telling. Carl usually does, but this was different, I had a feeling something was up. Anyway, he said he might call a magicians' meeting and check things out himself. Maybe, I thought, and maybe not. I left his house, went around the block, and came back just in time to see Carl leaving. He was going north. I followed him and walked into a Guard ambush."

"You, an ambush?"

"Yeah, me. The situation was a little peculiar, but I was still sloppy. They threw me in a cell, I managed to get out, and I headed over here to see you."

Flora's earlier nastiness had faded. "So," she said thoughtfully, "what do you think now?"

"What I know and what I suspect are different. I've got a feeling that Carl's up to something that's not healthy. He has called a meeting, obviously, but I'm suspicious about what's really going to happen there. Maybe Carl's got some new friends, like maybe this new guy by the north wall, and maybe this guy's telling Carl what to do; and maybe what he's telling Carl to do isn't real positive for the rest of us. I don't know if this has anything to do with the larger situation in Roosing Oolvaya, but I wouldn't be too surprised if it did.

"So why did I come to see you? I've got a lot of suspicions and real few facts. I do know enough about these things to know that by the time you have hard facts it's usually too late. I thought you'd be interested in the suspicions, and I wanted to warn you about this meeting."

"You're right, it's interesting," Flora said, "but I

still want to know what's on Carl's mind. I can take care of myself. I'm going to that meeting, and I'd better leave soon, too."

"I wasn't suggesting you shouldn't go. I just wanted you to be as suspicious as me. And I wanted to know when and where it's going to take place."

"All right, you warned me. The meeting is at Carl's place, in about an hour, seven o'clock. Carl's boy said everybody of any magical consequence in town would be there." She got to her feet. "I'm not going to ask you what you're going to do now," she said pointedly, staring sharply at me, "because I don't want to know and you wouldn't tell me, anyway. I think we're even on this one. But you might think about being careful, for a change."

I stood up and brushed the last water off my pants. I knew I'd gotten one thing out of the visit, at least; I wouldn't have to throw out my clothes. "You want me to ruin my reputation, do you?" I said. "Well, I'll do what I have to do, and you'll do what you have to do. We'll all do what we have to do. That's how the world's supposed to work, isn't it?" Hopefully we'd all be doing whatever it was we were doing for a long time to come. There wasn't much more to say, so Flora let me out the large barn door in the back and I went off down the street. She hadn't had a spare sword sitting around, either, so I was trying to figure out where I could come up with one in the time remaining before I had to be at Carl's when I passed the opening to an alley.

Nothing about the alley was distinctive, but for some reason I pulled to a halt a half-dozen paces beyond it, turned around, and went back to have a look. The alley ran back from the street between two leaning buildings, its only apparent features a few piles of assorted trash. I eased carefully down it, whatever had drawn me back in the first place pulling me on. All I saw was trash. Then I got to the end, saw how the alley turned there at an angle to proceed behind one of the leaning buildings, and spotted a figure with a human shape resting in the shadows against the wall. "Hi there," I said. "I'd been wondering when you'd show up again."

Gashanatantra got to his feet, leaning on his walking stick, and brushed off the back of his tweed cape. "You have not discovered information of use to me," he said, rather ominously.

"You don't like what I'm doing? Then fire me, and take your retainer back, too. I've found out plenty. I've been in and out of jail once today already on account of you, the Guard confiscated a perfectly good sword, and if nobody's tried to beat me into the ground yet it's probably because they were waiting in line for their turn to come up."

"Your outrage at having your professional competency questioned is not of concern to me," Gash said dryly. "Results are."

"I know," I said, "I know. You told me as much before. Give me some more time. I've got a good lead."

"This Carl Lake person?"

"Yeah, him, that's right. He may or may not be the one you're after, but either way he knows who is. If you really wanted to be helpful, you could go over and drag it out of him yourself."

He chuckled. " 'Front man,' I believe the term is? That is you."

"That's what you said before. Let's get serious, really. Tracking this barrier person down isn't going to be the problem. The problem's going to be what to do when I find them. Just what do you expect me to do? Capture them? Kill them? Have a nice talk with them and convince them to raise the barrier because I've got a client who doesn't like it?"

"I don't know how much guidance I can give you," he said musingly. "You will be there, so you must use your own instincts."

"Great. My instincts tell me *not* to be there. But

suppose I am, suppose I do what looks right to me and then you decide that isn't what you wanted. It'll be a lot harder to go back and try again."

"I want the barrier raised," Gash said. "I want to know who established it, and why. I want to know if they were aware of my presence and whether this is an attack directed at me, and, if so, the perpetrator must die. That is all. The details are your business. Now, you must go or you will miss your appointment."

"Thanks for the help," I said, and turned to go.

"There is one more thing." I felt something strange happen just behind me, something that pulled at my back and gently tried to twist it in a couple of directions at once like a silent baby tornado. I peeked cautiously over my shoulder.

In Gash's hand, where the walking stick had just been, a small sparkling whirlwind the length and shape of the stick had sprung up and was now fading. The form it was leaving behind was long and sharp with the colors of pure-minted metal and glistened with the sinuous lines of complicated etchings and mysterious runes. "I believe you said you needed something like this," Gash said. It was a sword.

My jaw was open to my chest, but I didn't care. Slowly, I turned to face it. I didn't want to reach out for the thing. The sword was like every last one of the most beautiful things I'd ever imagined had suddenly been wrapped up all in a single material object, the gold at the end of dreams, and here I was, being confronted with it without warning in a lousy alley, concrete and solid and genuinely real. Jewels shone on the hilt and sparkled like lenses on the flat of the blade, flush with the metal. Hues and bright waves washed along the surface of what looked like steel but couldn't possibly be; no steel was that perfect. "Take it," Gash said. "You were looking for one, and you're going to be late."

"Ulp," I said, but somehow I managed to stick my hand out.

"Grasp it here, like this," Gash said, moving his hand back on the hilt and leaving room for my fingers. As my skin neared it, sparks leaped between my palm and the hilt. A force took hold of my hand and inverted it, trying to contort it into a small flat ball. I gritted my teeth and gave a short lunge, my fingers wrapped around the hilt, and with a last audible spark and a sharp sting the sword settled into my grip.

"From the matching of auras, my metabolism to yours, it will know you." Gash released his hold. The sword was alive in my hand, trying to flip me over and bash me against the wall. I set my feet and concentrated on keeping my balance.

"Thanks," I said, for once meaning it. At the moment, the problem of what Gash was making me do and being thrown in jail and me probably finding some nasty way to get myself killed before the evening was out seemed not to matter. As I stood there, though, fighting that stunning sword, I realized that, dazzling though it was, I wouldn't be able to keep hold of it and even walk at the same time. "Is there any convenient way of putting this thing away?" I asked him.

"Remember this word," Gash said, and spoke something in one of the tongue twisting ancient languages. The sword seemed to writhe in my hand, waves of radiating power trying to mash my arm down to bone pulp, and then it was a walking stick again. The emanations were gone.

I tried the word. Nothing happened.

Gash pronounced it again, slowly, emphasizing each syllable. I tried it again, and this time I was rewarded by a biting shock that numbed my arm halfway to the elbow.

"Don't insult it," Gash said. "Monoch is fairly intelligent for a sword."

"Sorry," I muttered, climbing back to my feet. I closed my eyes and concentrated, then said the word. My hand holding the walking stick vibrated and grew hot, and with a fiery sensation as if the skin on my

fingers was being peeled back to my wrist, the outline
of the stick flowed like molten iron pouring into a
sword-shaped mold and the form of the sword was
back. I quickly said the word again. The condensing
sword paused, almost exasperated it seemed, heaved a
metallic sigh, and again subsided into its traveling
form.

"It is not necessary to fully vocalize the word,"
Gash told me. "You can mouth it silently and Monoch
will hear. Now go."

"Right," I said. I turned and I made my way back
to the street, leaving him there behind the building,
and headed off toward Carl Lake's place. I would
certainly be called to account for anything that happened to his sword, so I was treating the walking stick
gingerly; who knew how strong the thing was when it
was in disguise. Still, with a sword like this one I could
get out of some pretty tight spots. Of course, with a
sword like this one I'd have more of a tendency to get
myself into those spots in the first place. Hopefully if
the situation came to it, I'd actually be able to keep
my feet and swing Monoch at the same time. I'd deal
with it if I had to, but overall I figured my chances had
gone up. Now a decent bookie might only laugh for a
quarter-hour before taking a bet on me.

I approached Carl's house from two streets behind,
trying to make every sense I might have act alert. As I
moved in, I started to feel an odd sensation in my
stomach—or maybe it was just that I hadn't eaten all
day. The closer I got, though, the stronger the feeling
grew, like my stomach was circling the outermost currents of a whirlpool. What are you up to, Carl? I
thought.

The ends of the half-timbers stuck out from the wall
of the building just behind Carl's and one to the side. I
stuck the walking stick down the back of my tunic and
climbed up the timbers three stories to the roof. The
roof had gables and came to a shingled peak, unusual
for Roosing Oolvaya, but I found a rain gutter and

edged along it around to the back. Carl Lake's second-floor lodgings came into view, lamplight clearly shining through the translucent hides covering his streetfront solarium. Shapes moved within. From my position I had the advantage of height, but I wanted more. I dropped gently onto the rear of Carl's roof and moved closer in a slow crouch. The entrance I'd used in my visit that morning opened on the Street of Fresh Breeze, and it was from this street that I now heard the approach of a small party of people, and then the rapping of a fist on the door. The shadow in the solarium moved again and vanished. I had taken cover behind a double-barreled chimney and withdrawn the small knife from my boot, and now I crawled quickly up to the solarium roof, slashed a small hole in the hide at a spot screened by the shadow of a palm tree within the room, and stretched myself out flat. I applied my eye to the hole.

The solarium proper occupied the floor below me, so I was looking down on it from a position above the heads of any standing occupants. The fronds of the palm spread out in front of my eyehole, but I could see around their edges into most of the corners of the room. At the moment, the room was empty. I got the walking stick out of my shirt and arranged it next to me, with one hand on the handle just in case. A clumping of boots on stairs grew, and a small party filed into the solarium from the staircase at the far end.

Carl Lake led the pack, followed by a half-dozen or so magicians. I knew Flora, of course, and I'd dealt with Rounga and Italio Ignachi from time to time, but I recognized some of the others as well. They settled themselves around the furniture and Carl's servant entered with a tray of tea and finger refreshments: small cakes and smoked fish on crackers. I could have used some of them myself. I told my stomach to shut up; we were on a case. There was another knock from the street, the servant descended the stairs and re-

turned with another small group, they took their share
of the tea and cakes, and then Carl got back to his feet
and started to talk.

"You are wondering why this meeting, yes, why
have I asked you here. Surely nothing of much import
could happen here in our small, peaceful city of Roosing
Oolvaya, hmm?

"Sadly this is not the case."

He clasped his hands behind his back and started to
pace. There was something strange about that, but I
couldn't immediately identify what it was. "All of you
are certainly aware of Kaar and the, hmm, related
political developments, and may have speculated upon
them. What may still be news is that the maneuverings
of politics have been joined by similar activities in our
own field. Perhaps the developments in *our* field were
indeed the primary, and Kaar himself merely a manifestation. Shall I be concrete, hmm? Have any one of
you had need to leave the city in the past day? No?
Then, yes, you do not know. There is now a barrier
around our city."

A hum of conversation arose, then quickly quieted
as Carl waited. My stomach had begun to lurch again,
but now it didn't feel like I was hungry. That whirlpool sensation I'd gotten as I approached was back,
and getting worse.

"This barrier," Carl continued, "represents the application of extreme power; I have examined it myself.
It is similar to one described by Iskendarian in his text
on intruder protection, some of you may be familiar
with it. Certain other unusual emanations have appeared as well, clustered around the north city wall. It
seems a new power has appeared in our midst."

I blinked. A dark mist, so thin it was all but invisible, was creeping along the walls of the room below.
When I looked at it, my stomach rang alarm bells. The
haze was perfectly transparent, lending just a hint of
black to whatever was behind it, but it wasn't my

imagination. It was really there, and it was spreading out to surround everyone in the room.

"When confronted with a new order, what should we do, each of us? Could we resist, hmm? Perhaps flee? Or perhaps be passive, patient, yes, waiting to see, and with the potential of absorbing for ourselves whatever benefits may accrue?. Or perhaps . . ." Carl glanced around. "Perhaps we understand the implications, and establish the appropriate allegiance."

Now no one was saying anything. In fact, Carl was the only person who was even moving. They were all covered, every last one of them except Carl and his servant, with that sinister black mist. I tightened my grip on the walking stick.

"You have no discussion, hmm? Later, perhaps, we will discuss. For now," Carl said, in a new forceful note, "you are present to hear the way things are, yes, the ways things are. Then perhaps you will have a choice to make. Of course, hmm, perhaps you will not.

"I would ask you to rise, but as you will now surely be aware, yes, you are indeed immobilized, hmm? We will thus sadly omit the formalities." He stood up straight, straight as a training sergeant, and his previously gimpy leg was now straight and true as an arrowed bull's-eye. That's what I'd missed, and what I thought I'd seen when I'd followed him before. The limp was gone.

"These manifestations, yes, every one, have in common the association with a particular individual. Fellow colleagues, I now give you the new, true master of Roosing Oolvaya."

Right below my vantage point, a door opened. A form stepped through it into the room. His head was below mine and he wore a dark cloak, but at the mere sight of him my stomach spun over into the heart of the whirlpool and my balance reeled. The dark mist clung to him, too, but more than that, it *wheeled* about him in gleeful billowing gales. That was his aura, I realized suddenly, and I didn't know how I knew it but I'd hopefully be able to worry about that later. The aura was feeding off the magicians in the room, probably off me, too. That wasn't all. From the same depth of perception that let me see these sights and understand them, at least in part, came another dreadful fact.

There's an old saying, 'What you don't know can't hurt you.' Well, I'd always known it was wrong, I had a nasty habit of ending up in situations where exactly the opposite applied, but I hadn't until that moment appreciated just how bad it could get. Not knowing something existed, not knowing it *could* exist, was not going to protect me one bit. I hadn't known what I'd have to face, hadn't even known it was a physical possibility, but now that was so much crying in the wind. That wasn't just some magician down there. The black figure in the room below was a Death.

The figure spoke. "I am Oskin Yahlei," it said.

10
SHAA AND MONT GO BOATING

"I don't know about this," Mont said.

"The amount of preparation goes in direct proportion to the length of the boat desired."

"The length of the boat."

"Yes," Shaa said, "at the waterline. Now, be quiet. This is perfectly straightforward."

Jurtan Mont looked at the new knife in his hand, and the iron bar in Shaa's. A muscle in his neck sent lancing pains up toward his ear whenever he moved; they'd been hunched over behind the crate on a quiet stretch of wharf for the last half-hour. Waiting for the Guard. This guy is crazy, Mont thought.

Shaa, for his part, was right at home, having spent a large part of his life hunched over under similar circumstances. In this kind of operation he would have preferred to drop unexpectedly from above, but taking into account the limited experience of his new colleague a simpler and less flashy plan had seemed appropriate. Suddenly Shaa felt a nudge in his side. Mont, barely visible in the dim splashes of light from a lantern gently swaying from its bracket on the wall of a nearby warehouse, pointed down the wharf. Shaa held up two fingers and waggled them interrogatively. Mont nodded. Shaa produced three largish pebbles, took aim, and tossed. The rocks landed some yards to the side along the wharf, one-two-three, sounding to the suspicious ear just like three hurried, somewhat stealthy footsteps.

Mont grasped his knife gingerly around the guard and reversed it, presenting the hilt. The familiar rattle of cuirasses and running men became audible over the splat of river swells. Two Guardsmen burst into sight around the corner of the crate. They paused, looking away toward the source of the spectral footsteps. Shaa swung his bar. The second Guardsman heard a muffled "clunk" mixed with the clang of ringing metal, wheeled, saw a glinting streak as Mont's knife hurtled hilt-first past his nose, blinked, opened his mouth, and went for his sword. Shaa let the bar continue its follow-through, using its angular momentum to help throw himself forward, half leaped, half-fell over the subsiding form of the first Guardsman, and slammed fist-first into the second. The man exhaled forcefully as Shaa compressed his chest, fell roughly to the deck, quivered briefly, and relaxed. Shaa bashed the man's head on the planks once more for good measure, stood up, dusted off his hands, and retrieved the bar. "Good heft," he said. "One must never overlook a promising rubbish heap. You wouldn't believe some of the useful things people just toss away."

"Why are we doing this?" Mont said. "We could easily have avoided these guys."

"When we hit the palace," Shaa said, fastidiously wiping off the bar, "we're going to want a disguise. Since nobody knows all of these Guardsmen anyway— you get the idea?"

"Uh, yeah, but why waste the time now? We could have been in the palace by now. I'm sure they've got plenty of Guards in there."

Shaa raised an eyebrow. "Indeed. However, when we get there, I imagine we'll be rather busy—here, give me a hand. The cuirasses buckle at the shoulder and under the arms."

"How much of this stuff do we need?" Mont said, fumbling in the gloom.

"Cuirass, sword-belt, and jerkin. The rest isn't standard; it's more or less what they were wearing when they signed up. You've got the same kind of leggings anyway, so you'll do fine."

They worked in silence, punctuated by grunts from Mont. "This thing doesn't fit," he said finally.

"They never do.",Shaa, however, due to his previous experience, had had the foresight to choose the Guardsman closest to his own size. One of the men groaned and stirred.

"Aren't we going to do something to them?" Mont said, looking around.

"You're welcome to roll them into the river if you want," Shaa said, his voice some distance away. "I tend to choose the path of forbearance, on the grounds that we live in a world full of enough casual violence as it is. One should remember that these men are not necessarily evil, just Guards. Ah, here we are." His shape rematerialized at Mont's side. Mont jumped, his new cuirass rattling. "This, I believe, is yours?" A shard of light became Mont's knife, balancing neatly on its point in the center of Shaa's palm.

"Thanks," Mont said. He grabbed the knife and slid it into his belt on the opposite hip from his sword. "If we don't throw them in the river, what's the alternative?"

Clang. Clang. Shaa replaced the bar in his belt. "By the time they wake up we'll be on the island. Come on."

The wharves occupied most of the long east-facing curve of Roosing Oolvaya's riverfront, jutting out into the slack current, pulling back, winding around artificial pools and coves. Hundreds of vessels rocked at their moorings against the wharves or in the confusion of cheaper spots just offshore, vessels ranging in size from dinghies up to the massive cargo-hauling river barges. Here and there a light twinkled in a cabin or a lantern picked out the dim spiderspins of rigging. The air was quiet, though, lacking the usual floating strains of river melodies and the lilt of harsh voices raised in strife. "This one," Shaa announced, staring over the edge of the wharf.

"Why that one?"

"Are you going to be difficult again?"

"But—it's tiny!"

"You were perhaps expecting the Venerable Yacht? We don't want to attract attention. On the other hand, we don't want to get swamped. Observe the relatively high gunwales." Actually, Shaa had considered stowing away on the Venerable Yacht as a possibility, but the scheduling had proved inconvenient.

The twin uprights of a ladder poked skyward at the edge of the wharf. Shaa indicated the ladder with a hand. Mont descended and Shaa picked his way carefully after him. The bottom rungs were coated with slime, and led to a small platform floating at the base and a boat moored to the platform. The swells went slap-slap-slap against the side of the boat. "Go ahead," said Shaa. "Get in."

The boat in question was apparently used for local net fishing and the tending of crustacean pots. Its length was three fathoms, or a little less, but it was narrow enough in beam for one person to handle the pair of oars amidships. The gunwales were indeed high, matching Shaa's requirements; the state of the river was somewhat agitated. "Shaa," Mont said, "there's some very scummy water in the bottom of this thing."

"It's called 'bilge,' " Shaa said, casting off the stern line and proceeding along the wharf toward the bow. "Everything has a name." He released the bow line, tossed it into the boat, and stepped gingerly after it. "In fact, scummy bilge is a good sign; that means the water has been sitting there for a long time."

"So?"

"No, don't sit there, sit in the bow. The front." Shaa arranged himself between the oars, facing aft.

The boat lurched as Mont tumbled forward. "If the water has been there stagnating for weeks, that means the boat has not been leaking."

"Oh," Mont said. "That's good."

"Indeed. Now, I will row, and you're going to guide and fend. Push off."

Mont leaned over, shoving at the nearest piling. The prow spun slowly toward the river. Shaa craned his neck around, sighted down past the end of the wharf, and began to paddle. The boat moved tentatively ahead and nosed out into the current.

"I think there's something up ahead, big," Mont said.

Shaa looked around again. "I see it," he said. "Now keep your voice down." Shaa backed water with the starboard oar, then stroked carefully. The boat proceeded along a hulking wall festooned with freshwater barnacles, edged around an anchor chain leading silently off into the darkness, and regained course.

"Uh—I think it's open now."

"Good." Shaa checked; Mont was right. "Do you see the palace? The second island from the left?"

"Yes, I see it. I know where the palace is."

"We will steer thirty degrees to port, to compensate for the current. That's the left."

"I knew that."

"Indeed," Shaa said. He rowed, grunting occasionally. Between the swells and the current the outing was fairly strenuous. Probably a storm upriver someplace, Shaa thought. Things could be worse.

Mont looked back toward the shore. The ground level rose gently as one retreated through the city away from the river, so rank after rank of rooftops and protruding upper stories ascended into the distance, lit by the patchy orange glow of torchlights. The black shadows of barges swayed uneasily in the foreground. Their boat was swaying, too, not only side-to-side but forward and back as well. Mont began to hear, faintly, the nasal honk of a distant foghorn. "Uh, Shaa?" Mont said. "I'm not feeling too good."

"Are you seasick, or—"

"Do you hear a foghorn?"

"No, indeed."

"Then I'm starting to synchronize. I think it's the way these waves are hitting the boat." Clouds of fluffy white were moving in from the corners of his vision.

"Don't fade now," Shaa said. "Here. You row for a while; it will give you something else to concentrate on."

"If we had a sorcerer," Mont said weakly, "we wouldn't have to row."

"If we had a sorcerer, you would have much more serious things to worry about." Shaa shipped oars and moved to the bow. Mont eased reluctantly past him.

"Stroke," Shaa said.

Mont's learning curve was steep. They spent several minutes moving up it before they straightened out, again on course. The island of the palace of the Venerance slowly approached. The river gurgled around them.

"We're—getting there," Mont panted. "What do we—do when we—get there?"

"As we have done to date—improvise. More starboard oar, please. See, isn't that better? I'll take over in a moment. How well do you know the palace? The island, too, for that matter."

"I know—how to get—to the dungeons—if I start—in the right place."

"And the secret passages?"

"What—secret passages?"

"Every palace has secret passages. Especially those with dungeons."

"I thought—you said—you'd find them."

"I had thought you might be able to help."

"If you—can find them—I'll be glad—to use them." Mont fell silent, except for the sound of loud gasping.

Shaa glowered back at him. "Perhaps I'd best take

over now," he said. "I'd hate to have to stop right in the midst of everything because my aide-de-camp had gone into heart failure." Mont gratefully released the oars and fell over. The boat twisted in the current and began to move south. Shaa clambered over Mont onto the oar bench, dipped a hand over the side, and splashed water in Mont's face. Mont sputtered; Shaa rowed.

Mont gradually recovered his breath and struggled back to the bow. He looked ahead at the approaching island. "Where are we going to land? This is the side with the docks and the beaches, but it'll probably be loaded with guards."

"There is little 'probably' involved. You forget, however, that we are also guards." Shaa rattled his cuirass.

"Yes, but landing from the river in a snapper-boat?"

"That is a very good point," Shaa said, pleased. "You are acquiring a sense for details. If we cannot land on this most convenient side, what about the others?"

"Well, there's rock, cliffs, walls, that kind of thing."

"Indeed," Shaa said. "How climbable are they?"

"They're not *supposed* to be climbable at all."

"Umm." Shaa thought about it, steering against the current to the north of the island in the meantime. Finally he said, "Let's have a look at the north wall."

The island was still ahead, but it was beginning to slip around to their right. Atop the rocks and curtain walls were the lights of torches and watchfires, casting splashes of red and yellow across the towers and crenelations. The building was a palace primarily by convention, having started life as the local Imperial garrison keep centuries before, in the time of a greater empire. The fortifications had been designed to resist a large-scale assault, and had successfully done this several times over the years. Still, Mont thought, a few hand-picked, highly trained, supremely motivated men might . . . Mont stopped himself. It wouldn't help to treat this thing like it was just another adventure story.

While Mont daydreamed, Shaa considered logistics. First, they would have to land the boat. Second, climb the wall and get into the palace complex. Third, act unobtrusive long enough to sidle undiscovered into the dungeons. Fourth, free the prisoners. The *right* prisoners, Shaa amended sourly, remembering an annoying exploit that had come to involve an ax-murderer some years before. Fifth and subsequent, no doubt, overpower the troops, overthrow Kaar, and overcome the inevitable apathy of the populace. By then, it should at least be time for breakfast.

"We're getting pretty close," Mont said.

Shaa glanced to his left as he faced the stern of the boat, at the long sweep of shadowed wall now immediately downstream. The shadows were surmounted sixty or seventy feet above the water by an abrupt line of twinkling torchlights and the shifting forms of men, the line broken by silhouettes of catapults and troughs for boiling oil. At the base of the rock, water foamed a faint glowing blue. "Look there," Shaa said.

Just ahead of their position, a narrow bar of sediment protruded from the tip of the island, built up by the current behind a lee in the rocks. "That?" Mont squeaked. "You've got to be—"

"Quiet," Shaa said. "Please." The spot would be barely big enough for the boat but only if the boat could be made to arrive there. Shaa angled the prow and dipped with one oar, and the current propelled the boat in roughly the right direction. The noise of the water increased; waves crashed against the rocks on both sides. The boat bounced, then leaped. Something grated under Mont's feet, the wood vibrating angrily. The bow rose up and came down on a rock, timbers boomed and splintered, and then another wave lifted the keel cleanly and set the boat down on the beach. Mont fell over the side and clutched weakly at the cracked prow. It came away in his hand.

"Augh," Mont said in a thin voice. "You—you— how lucky can you expect to—"

"Skill, my friend," Shaa said distractedly. He was standing on a log protruding from the packed gravel, looking up at the rocks and the wall.

"But the boat—it'll never sail again. How are we going to get—"

"You did plan to free prisoners, yes? Perhaps deal with Kaar in the bargain? Obviously the route of our departure will be different."

"Ah," Mont said, "ah, obviously, of course. Ah, what now, then?" He tilted his head back, too; the rocks went upward at an angle that approximated the vertical. Water splashed around his ankles.

Shaa brushed spray from his eyes and squinted. "There, look there. Halfway up and somewhat to the right."

Then Mont saw it, too—a small area of the cliff face splashed with a gentle orange glow. The glow did not come from the battlements above.

"A window," Shaa said, "of some type." From under his cloak, shrugging off a shoulder strap, Shaa produced a leather bag the length of his arm. He undid the thong at one end and withdrew a squared-off cylinder of wood bound with metal bands and other attachments. Several smaller parts followed. Shaa swung two supports out from the sides of the cylinder, and its form became apparent.

"A crossbow?" Mont said.

"Indeed." Shaa placed the butt end against the log embedded in the ground, snapped out a small pedal on the underside of the body, now several feet in the air, positioned his foot on the pedal, and stood up on it. With a smooth metallic whine, barely audible over the crash of the river swells, the pedal sank slowly down. "The mechanism works, I believe, on an armature of nested springs." Shaa again consulted the leather bag, which now yielded a lumpy arrow and a reel of thin cord. "Observe," he said. He clipped a fastener from the cord to the arrow's trailing end, held the arrow just in front of the fletching, and struck its blunt point sharply against the remains of the boat. With a sharp "sproing," half-a-dozen rods snapped outward from the front half of the arrow to stick out radially from the tip, like spokes. Shaa displayed the grapnel, then folded the hinged arms back against the shaft and engaged the locking device.

"That's the most improbable thing I've ever seen," Mont said incredulously, "but it's never going to hold our weight. We're both gonna die."

"Prepare to be surprised," Shaa said dryly. "The fabricator specializes in such devices. He has a remarkable obsession with the mechanical."

"What friend is this one?"

"Max," Shaa said, "the same Max."

The same one who'd taught Shaa his fencing? That sounded pretty farfetched, but so did most everything Shaa said. Mont decided Shaa must be testing him again in some weird way. He figured he'd better be noncommittal. "This Max guy sure must get around."

"Yes, he does at that." Shaa had now attached the reel of line to a socket at the butt end of the crossbow and carefully seated the arrow within its guides. He backed out along the log to the edge of the lapping water, raised the crossbow, sighted down the mark at the brighter spot in the cliff, and sprang the catch. The arrow lunged out, the reel of cord humming busily behind it, and disappeared into the rocks. Shaa had cocked his head to listen, and now he nodded with satisfaction. "I will go first," he said.

"Where? How do you know where it is? How do you know the thing's even holding?"

"All I ask is some modicum of trust," Shaa said testily. He collapsed the crossbow and stowed it in its bag, slung the bag back under his cloak, and put his weight on the cord.

The cord held. Rocks reared their jagged edges invisibly in the darkness. Shaa, wary of fraying, kept the rope high. Several person-heights above the river the jagged rocks became large stones set more neatly together, and the climb evened out. Shaa pulled up with his arms and walked up the stones with his feet. The glow, its location and distance uncertain in the dark, drew closer, and then he was suddenly abreast of it.

The arrow had gone through the interlaced iron bars protecting a small square ventilation hole, springing the grapnel against the wall of the shaft within. Torchlight flickered up the shaft. Shaa, looking through it, saw that it slanted down to meet a corridor. It would be a squeeze, but it should be passable. He found a piton, wedged it into a space between the stones above the hole, and belayed the cord around it, removing his weight from the grapnel. The grapnel was well-made and he certainly trusted Max, but it was better all around not to push things to their limit. Again fumbling beneath his cloak, Shaa, with a small grunt of satisfaction, produced the bladder of the small southern amphibian he had employed to such effect earlier, in their escape from the Bilious Gnome, and squirted foaming liquid on the iron bars. Shaa held his breath. The liquid hissed. Then the grating sagged, tilted, and swung free to dangle from Shaa's cord, caught at the end of the grapnel.

Shaa lowered the grating into the shaft, then followed it. The squeeze was indeed tight, but not nearly as bad as such things sometimes were. The incline was fortunately not steep. Mont appeared at the window and flopped headfirst over the edge. "You do this sort of stuff for fun?" he whispered.

"Why, don't you like it?" Shaa said distractedly. "Quiet." He pushed himself down to the shaft's outlet. The corridor below was silent. Shaa eased his head out of the shaft and glanced quickly around.

The corridor ran parallel to the outer wall, then angled back into the interior of the castle. Dust was thick on the narrow floor. The torchlight they had glimpsed outside was still little more than an orange glow, though it was much brighter at the turning on the left. Shaa dropped to the floor and came up in a crouch, his hand on his rapier. Nothing stirred. "Well, you know this palace," Shaa whispered back into the shaft. "Which direction do we take?"

Mont, who had been getting tired of being scrunched uncomfortably up the shaft behind Shaa, appeared in the opening, then lost his balance and slid free. Shaa caught him and managed to lower him soundlessly to the floor. Mont shook his head, cocked it to one side, closed his eyes, and appeared to listen. It occurred to Shaa that Mont had probably been doing the same thing in the shaft, thus distracting himself enough to make him lose his hold. Still, it was entirely possible that whatever inner tunes he was hearing might make his distraction worthwhile. Mont chewed his lip and opened his eyes: they were unfocused.

"I think it's better on the right, away from the light," Jurtan Mont said. "Let's go right."

Shaa finished stowing the grapnel, loosened the iron bar in his belt, and headed to the right down the corridor.

11
THE CURSE OF THE CREEPING SWORD

"I am Oskin Yahlei," he said. The dark figure in the dark cloak, hood thrown back across his shoulders, looked slowly and deliberately around the room, fixing each person there with his glare. The currents of the black aura pulsed and wove in the air like spun smoke. He didn't look up through the palm tree at me, in fact, seemed not to recognize my presence, and I kept very still, wishing I could even stop breathing. A heavy gold ring glittered on the middle finger of his left hand. The ring made me think of the eye of a hurricane: the eddies and twirls of the mist seemed to circle around it, looping, streaming, billowing about in swirling coils. Somehow, in a strange way I didn't understand, the aura seemed more bound to the ring than to the rest of Oskin Yahlei himself.

I didn't care how this information had gotten into my memory, whether I was tapping the outskirts of Gash's mind or what, I was just trying to ransack whatever I did seem to know as quickly as I could. Me, I couldn't see an aura if it smashed me in the nose, and even if I could see it I wouldn't know what it was, but since Gash had pushed me into this mess in the first place I had no qualms about using his knowledge to help get me out of it. Get me out of it alive, that is, an idea that all of a sudden had a lot more gut meaning than it had ever had before.

Even in a time and place where the gods are real personages, and they show up on earth in the flesh to give people trouble directly, without intermediaries, you've got to make a distinction between the actual and the mythic. Not everything you can think of is real, even if a lot of weird things happen to be. I'd always thought Death was a concept and a state, not an independent entity. Unfortunately, based on the information my mind was now finding hidden in its files, that impression had been seriously wrong.

I mentioned before that human magicians aren't all the same. They're differentiated by specialty, the way they handle energy, their ethical orientation toward the use of magic, all kinds of distinctions. Gods specialized, too. I'd picked that up before, but I hadn't realized how far the differences went. The answer was, pretty far, and the Deaths were a perfect case in point.

Something there was never a shortage of were deaths, and nobody ever liked to waste a ready source of power. That was really the key. When something died, its decay to the state of death released energy. The gods who were Deaths could tap and absorb this death-power. Pain, injury, slow dying or fast, they all gave off this energy, and some Death was usually around to take advantage of it.

If passive absorption was all it was, who really cared; lots of things are more ghoulish than that. Unfortunately, that wasn't all, of course. It was only a small step from taking advantage of death to causing death, and just a little bit farther to having some control over it, too, and once you could control death, well, you could control a lot of life, too, couldn't you.

The upshot was that even the rest of the community of gods treated the Deaths with respect, or if not respect, at least caution.

Nobody I'd heard of knew exactly how many gods

there were; estimates tended to range from twenty or thirty up to a few hundred. If Gash knew, his aura wasn't telling, and the number probably varied anyway. That didn't matter. What might be important to me was the number of Deaths, maybe a dozen. They weren't all equal. What the pecking order was, 'Gash didn't know, except that there was one big boss over the rest.

I doubted if this Yahlei was the Death Supreme himself. I couldn't quite see the Death's Death slumming around with a bunch of pipsqueak mortals, but frankly I didn't think it would matter much whether this really was The Man or just an underling. Either way, we were talking serious big-time trouble, and there I lay on the roof over his head without the slightest idea of what to do about it.

Oskin Yahlei finally fixed his gaze on Carl Lake. Yahlei looked male enough in aspect, although for all I knew that was just a matter of affectation. "These are the best ones in your city?" Oskin Yahlei said.

"These are the *only* ones in the city," Carl said. "You said you—"

"I know what I said." Yahlei walked out into the room, and as the angle changed I saw that he was wearing a black eyepatch over his left eye. He fingered it with his hand, the hand with the ring. When the ring passed near the patch, the covering over his eye seemed to grow slightly transparent, with the ghostly shadow of skin and eye socket and swollen tissue seen dimly behind it. He lowered the hand and the image faded.

My own right hand was quivering. I glanced down at it. The walking stick had begun to vibrate, and if I listened closely I could hear a low whine. A shock stabbed up through my palm. "Shut up," I hissed at it, trying not to vocalize. "You'll give us away." The nebulous image of the sword was now visible around the stick twirling and churning. "I'll call you when I need you," I added. Reluctantly the shape faded and the whine died, but my hand still felt like it was clutching something alive, like maybe the tail of a large, impatient jungle cat.

Carl Lake had turned to follow the Death as he'd moved. Oskin Yahlei scrutinized him. "Your friend, Lake, has assured me you are all reasonably intelligent," he said, still eyeing Carl but speaking now to the frozen crowd. "If that is true, you will have realized that resistance would be impractical. It will also not have escaped your notice that your active collaboration with me can have significant benefits. Observe Lake, now considering a new career in gymnastics and contortions."

"Indeed, yes, Master," Carl Lake said, "my leg." He flexed it, raising it to his chest, then did a knee bend.

Oskin Yahlei frowned. "The demonstration is appropriate, that 'Master' business is not. I told you I'm looking for responsible assistants, not toadies."

Carl gave a quick nod and bowed, probably to disguise how white his face had suddenly gone. "As you wish it."

"Indeed," Yahlei said, "yes. As you will also have suspected, this Roosing Oolvaya is the first in a series of steps I intend to take. I will need deputies of power and knowledge to stand with me. Their power will increase and they will grow in stature, becoming aides, viceroys, governors. Perhaps—" He paused, turned, and looked around the faces again. "Perhaps even more."

Huh? I thought. (It really was my own mind thinking, for a change.) The whole world had heard legends about people who became gods, long ago and on some other continent, but it had never happened to anybody anyone knew. If what Oskin Yahlei was implying was true, though, it *was* possible, and he could arrange it. Even if they didn't know he was a god, they might think he was powerful enough to do it. On the other hand, he could just be using the hint as sucker bait.

But I knew his audience, and I knew that with that one tantalizing insinuation he'd caught some of them.

My options were shrinking, not that they'd been wonderful to begin with. I could burst through the roof with the temperamental sword whirling and try to cut Oskin Yahlei down before he had a chance to blast me. If I was going to try that, I'd have to hope for a hand from the crowd, and at the moment I thought some of them would rather side with him than me. The best I could hope for there would be the magicians fighting among themselves. It was also possible that even a distracted Yahlei wouldn't drop his hold on them, and might even decide to drain one or two magicians for a quick energy fix. I could throw the sword and maybe manage to skewer him. I could also just keep on watching. If he left, I might be able to trail him home and take him by surprise, away from potential allies. "Don't *worry*," I told the sword, suddenly restive again, "I'll feed you, I'll feed you. Be patient."

"On the other hand," Oskin Yahlei went on, "there is another side to this. I can simply crush and absorb you. Any one of you." His one-eyed gaze settled on a small man on the settee. I didn't know him. "You, perhaps." The black aura intensified around the guy, seemed to settle into his skin. His eyes opened wide and the eyeballs rolled up behind his lids, cords stood out in his exposed throat, and without making a sound, he began to shrink inward like a collapsing wineskin. He turned sideways and slid to the floor, his muscles limp and diminishing. The colors of his own aura appeared, flowing out of his skin like shattering shards of glass, colors glinting and gone as they disappeared into the black.

At the right limit of my vision, half hidden behind a palm frond, there was a sudden quiver of motion. One of the other magicians in back of Oskin Yahlei was raising an arm. I couldn't see who it was, only the slowly lifting arm, but I did abruptly see that the misty black coating on that side of the room had decreased, probably with Oskin Yahlei's diversion of effort. The walking stick started to hum. "No!" I thought at it, and then another idea I hadn't considered popped into my mind. "Let's try this one, Monoch."

How had I done whatever I'd done before, when I'd seemed to open the floor of the jail cell instead of the door? COLLAPSE, I thought, concentrating at the floor of the solarium. The guy next to the settee now resembled a rotten gourd with the insides being sucked out of it. COLLAPSE! "Come on here," I muttered at the sword, "give me a hand."

The arm of the magician behind the palm tree was gradually coming into line with Oskin Yahlei's back. I didn't know if the sword understood what I was trying and I had my doubts whether it could help even if it did, but for some reason my projected concentration began to sharpen and gain force, like an image through a spyglass brought suddenly into focus. *COLLAPSE!* I thought, my whole mind wrapped around the reality of the boards peeling back beneath Yahlei's feet to fling him deep down into the earth. Oskin Yahlei's black aura had intensified with the transfusion of energy, and the ring on his hand was glowing. He smacked his lips, then kicked the shrunken heap on the floor. "That is the alternative," he said in a conversational tone. "I give you all your own free choice. Join me or—"

Green lines had begun to form around the outstretched hand of the magician behind Oskin Yahlei. Still talking, Oskin Yahlei, had started to turn. Abruptly he froze, his brow furrowed. He looked up to scrutinize the ceiling, his gaze tracking across the solarium hides toward my eyehole behind the palm tree. The tracers of green in the magician's hand grew together, I thought *COLLAPSE, GODDAMMIT!* as vividly as I could, and—

The building shuddered. In the solarium, an oil lamp on an ornate pedestal tipped over, spraying burn-

ing oil over the far wall. Oskin Yahlei took one step,
the floor snapped up and hit his descending foot, and
he dropped to one knee. Part of the roof just behind
me fell in. A fiery green construct that looked like a
set of flying meathooks with smoke coming out the
back shot out of the upraised arm of that other magician, zoomed over Oskin Yahlei's head, banked just
shy of the wall, and headed around for another pass.
The building was groaning with the sound of grinding
wood and disintegrating joints, but the crowd in the
room was still silent. Then the roof bounced again as
though someone had walloped the house with part of a
small mountain, and I looked quickly back over my
shoulder. I was just in time to see the back of the
building behind me, the one a floor taller than Carl
Lake's, detach itself from the rest of the structure,
pause in midair, and surge toward me to collapse with
full force against the house I was on.

A chimney hurtled over my head and plowed through
the solarium's hide roof. The hide ripped, one section
of canvas burning from the spilt oil fell away over the
side of the wall, and the whole building started to reel
out over the Street of Fresh Breeze. I spread myself
flat and clutched at the surface. Cries and pandemonium arose abruptly from the wreckage of the solarium; Oskin Yahlei had finally been distracted enough
to relinquish his hold. The green meathook again rose
into view, looking tattered, started to dive back through
the gaping hole in the roof, then halted indecisively.
All at once, it turned and headed straight for me. I
rolled on my side, brought up the walking stick, trying
to say Gash's magic word the right way, and swung at
the diving construct. The stick, refusing to change,
waved past it. I threw myself onto my back and the
hooks zoomed past my belly, gnashing angrily.

I was pretty angry myself. The roof just beyond my
feet abruptly caved in. I started sliding down the folding roof toward the hole as the green meathook finished its turn and pointed itself at me again. I snapped

at the disguised sword yet again, but this time it listened. The walking stick melted its shape and burst into flame, my arm holding it tried to turn itself inside out. I flopped awkwardly to my left, propelled by the sword's strange momentum, and at the last possible instant the blade of the sword danced out and passed straight through the twin green shafts holding the sharp meatcleaver spikes. The severed points shot off out of my sight like miniature javelins, the rear section, trailing lime-colored smoke, passed over my head and buried itself in a pile of broken boards, and the sword, now unleashed and hunting for more trouble, flung me away from the widening hole in the roof and toward the edge of the solarium.

Carl Lake's house, in the deliberate process of turning itself into a pile of scrap lumber, lurched again and staggered farther toward the street. One whole wall was now on fire. Ahead of me, in the wreckage of the solarium, roars, hisses, small explosions in the air, and sprays of multicolored light indicated that the local magicians were squaring off against someone, and probably against each other, too. In the second I had before hurtling over the edge of the roof to join them, straining to wrestle the sword down and say the word to deactivate it, I did manage to catch a glimpse of a neat rain shower condensing out of the air over the fire; Flora was okay, anyway. "Ki'tonk'ta-ah'," I gasped. The sword, which seemed to be getting crabbier every time we did this, began to change back, and I hit the lip of the roof on a line running across my lower ribs. My arm flailing the walking stick came around in a fast arc under the force of my fall. Chest and arms and head were sticking out over the wrecked solarium. Looking down at the dented palm tree leaning against the wall, I scrabbled with my free hand and fended off with the stick, and then, just as I had decided I'd actually managed to retain my balance, I spotted a crumpled form, its hands clasped over its head, huddled in the space underneath the tree.

I cast a quick glance around the room. The husklike body of the magician Oskin Yahlei had used for his demonstration had rolled against the burning wall and was starting to char. The front wall was largely gone. The last of the other magicians were lowering themselves through the splintered holes, down the rubble and onto the street. I spotted Flora helping a man with a bloody head and a twisted arm, decided not to bother her, and instead carefully swung the rest of my body over the edge of the roof and dropped past the palm tree to the floor. I bent down to examine the huddled figure.

As I'd expected, he was pretty much undamaged; he'd only been hiding. "Hi, Carl," I said.

He lifted one arm and rolled his eye up. "You," he said. "You're probably wondering why I did what I did."

"No," I said, "I'm not." I grabbed him by the back of the collar and pulled him to his feet, the new bruises across my ribs and along my side sending out sharp throbs of disapproval. "I think I understand real well why you did what you did. You did real good for yourself, getting your leg fixed, and everybody has to look out for himself first, right? How could you have known you wouldn't end up running the city, and anyway you didn't actually get me killed yet even if I did lose a perfectly good sword."

"You don't hate me?"

"Just because you were on a different side than me? Nah. How could I hate you when you're about to help me out?"

He rubbed his bottlebrush eyebrows. "Hmm, indeed," he said. "Hah."

"Hah," I said. "Hah." The building shook again. The floor, which already had about a fifteen-degree tilt toward the street, settled some more. "Where's your friend Yahlei?"

"He has left."

"I figured that out. I want to know where he went."

We were next to the door Oskin Yahlei had originally entered through, under my former observation spot. The door was closed, but the frame had partially fallen in around it and the top panel of the door was mostly splintered board. I kicked at the doorknob with the heel of my foot. On the second try the doorknob tore through and the door smashed open, the hinges came loose from the jamb, and the whole door crashed noisily into the next room.

I still had Carl by the neck, and now I dragged him with me through the empty doorframe. We clambered over a fall of rubble, the section of roof that had fallen in next to me moments before, and then just behind us the ceiling creaked, the creak grew into a rumble, and the rest of the roof came down as well; the door I'd removed must have been all that was holding it up. At the end of the room the side wall had fallen into the alley. The largest drop from one major clump of rubble to the next was now no more than a few feet, so when I pushed Carl through the wall ahead of me I figured he couldn't hurt himself that badly, especially not with his new leg and all.

I made it down faster than him, gritting my teeth against my assortment of aches, so I had plenty of time to get him by the neck again before he decided to take off. I may not have hated him, but I sure didn't trust him either. I figured he might not be too happy about leading me to Oskin Yahlei's hideout. Me, I could hardly even believe I was considering what I was considering. Unless Gashanatantra showed up unexpectedly, though, the ball was still in my court, and the only way I might get it out was to keep moving.

It was so dark I couldn't see his face, but I didn't have to. "You must be insane," he said, when I told him what he was going to do. "To go deliberately to seek out Oskin Yahlei? Insane, certainly insane."

"You're probably right," I said, "but don't let that part concern you. If you have to, think about the terrible things crazy people are apt to do."

"What, you will kill me? How could that be more terrible that the wrath of Oskin Yahlei?"

"Oskin Yahlei'd have to catch you. Me, I've already got you."

"Hah," Carl said. "With what you will kill me? You said you have no sword."

"My bare hands will do if they have to, but I've something easier. You see this?" I waved the walking stick in front of his face.

"Indeed, yes, a basic staff." Carl sounded less than impressed, but the chuckle he was starting didn't last more than half a second.

The stick began to whine. As Carl looked around for the source, it added a pulsing glow, too, picking up its cue to the hilt. I still didn't know how smart the sword was, but it did show a sharp instinct for betting on where a meal could come from.

"Ah, hmm," Carl said.

"Yeah, you should see it when it's not in disguise. I think it likes you. Of course, it's been getting pretty hungry." A spark leaped across and hit Carl on the nose. "So, are you ready?"

"Um, hmm, yes, I believe so. You can calm that entity down?"

"Sure," I said, "no problem. Now let's go."

A buzzing crowd had gathered in the Street of Fresh Breeze in front of the demolished building and its neighbors, which weren't in much better shape. I had a feeling the crowd wouldn't be too pleased to greet either one of us at the moment, so I led Carl down through the alleys and out the other side of the block, still feeling an occasional crash and shudder emanating from behind us. We gained the street and Carl led me north.

'What happened in there?" I said. I was finally taking the chance to catch my breath; that had been an intense couple of minutes there.

"For how long did you watch?"

"From the beginning of the meeting. You did say I'd be invited, after all."

"Hmm, yes. Then you must have witnessed the attack on Oskin Yahlei."

"The guy with the green meathook, yeah."

"Not him alone." Carl rubbed his eyebrow. "The earthquake, the devastation, the ruination of my house, this, too, was an attack. But by whom?"

"You mean you don't know? I thought you knew everybody you'd invited."

"None of the people in attendance has this class of manifestation among their known skills. It is most curious . . . You have not recently taken to magic, have you?"

"Me!" I said, with what I hoped was not a guilty start. "Hah, what a thought."

"Hmm, no, no, of course not. Indeed, the emanations were . . . very peculiar, unlike most anything I have encountered."

Those emanations were unlike those of anyone in the vicinity except Oskin Yahlei, I bet, unless there was another god lurking around I hadn't met yet. We were still winding our way north. The curfew was up, so we were whispering and sticking to the shadows, not that there had been any hint of trouble. Maybe the Guard had picked up Oskin Yahlei on his way home, hah hah. I was keeping a close eye on Carl's hands, but it was just as well his magic wasn't heavy on anti-personnel skills; that's how the muggers had been able to get him the first time we'd met. "How much farther is it?" I said.

A faint shriek rang in the air from somewhere up ahead, maybe ten blocks. Suddenly it stopped.

Carl had listened carefully. "Approximately that distance," he told me.

"Thanks a lot. That'll put us almost at the north wall."

"That is correct."

The area were were heading into wasn't particularly

fashionable. The houses leaned out over the street on their own here, the pavement was more irregular when it wasn't completely dirt, and the streets were growing into narrow alleys. The streets also wove around more, pointing north, then northwest, then east. It wasn't the kind of neighborhood where big-time magicians usually like to hang out. "Just what's so great about this Yahlei person, anyway?" I asked Carl.

"He is a necromancer. This means something to you, yes?"

"All right, yeah. Necromancers are supposed to be hot stuff."

"Indeed, yes. So consider this. Even among necromancers, Oskin Yahlei is very, very powerful."

"Okay, so he's very, very powerful. What else?"

"That is not enough for you? Give up this silly quest."

"I've got a client who's even more insistent than your Oskin Yahlei," I said. "That's why I can't."

He had been trying to lag for awhile, and now he stopped in his tracks. "But why? Why, yes? What is one more client for you? Will the client kill you, hmm, drain from you the aura and crush you to a husk? But Oskin Yahlei—both of us will only die. He will think the attack on him was my fault, that I have been false to him, and he will . . . indeed, both of us will be lucky to merely die."

I decided not to tell Carl that Oskin Yahlei wasn't just a regular person-type necromancer, either, at least not yet; he seemed upset enough as it was. "No he won't, you'll convince him it wasn't you. Now come on, already, or I'll let you try pleading to the stick."

He looked around at the walking stick, remembering what it had shown about itself, and started moving again. "Very well, I shall be fatalistic." A few moments later we drew up to another corner, and he put his hand up for me to stop. "Carefully," he said. "Look here."

I eased past him and poked an eye around the edge.

The street we were now hidden in was definitely an alley, about four feet wide and filled with trash; the cross-street was much wider, say fifteen feet or so across. It ran east and west, roughly, with a gradual turn north at each end. A few aimless lamps behind barred windows pushed back little clumps of night. The lamps were like twisted drunks in the dark, shrugging off the black like blows off ravaged shoulders; it was that sort of place. Across from me was a large vacant lot, overgrown with trees and shrubs and surrounded by a weathered block wall. Carl had pointed down the street to the right, so I looked in that direction. Next to the lot was a two-story building of the same stone as the wall. In fact, the wall continued around the building, too, its top glistening with spikes and jagged glass and sharp iron rods. The building was surrounded by pillars and ornate cornices. It sure hadn't started life as a house; those walls were pretty thick. It looked more like a fortress.

"A former temple," Carl whispered behind me. "The god whose tract it was fell from prominence some years ago."

And now it was Oskin Yahlei's headquarters. Going over the wall and in through an upper-story window, one of my favorite techniques, looked doubtful in this case. I was being forced into a decision I really didn't want to make.

A quiet clattering off to my right turned into a small party of Guard troopers. They approached the temple and stopped. The soldiers were looking around nervously and starting at nothing; I had the feeling they didn't like the neighborhood. A door opened, spreading a quick fan of light across the street, and a man leaned out to hold a brief exchange with the Guard leader. The new man was visible to me only in profile, except for a sigil on his tunic that caught the light. It was new to me—a twisty purple blob with fire coming out of it. The conversation ended, and the party went through into the temple. Two of them had swords at their backs, and hands that seemed bound. Two prisoners who wouldn't be coming out again anytime soon, I was sure.

Something bothered me about that vacant lot next door. It was obviously part of the temple property, because of the wall, but even in the darkness it didn't feel like a simple overgrown garden. I asked Carl.

"Certainly you realize that is the cemetery, yes?"

The cemetery, of course. Raw material for a necromancer. I wanted to be somewhere else. Unfortunately, I wasn't. "Carl, tell me about him."

"Oskin Yahlei?" He sighed. "He is very powerful, but already you realize that. He approached me first two, no, three days ago, demanding my allegiance. I knew little about him, excepting only his power, until your visit to me this morning. I told him your story of this barrier. He was surprised; he did not anticipate his work would become apparent at this time. Since this was evidently what was happening, he elected to strike against those who might spread the word."

"He doesn't want publicity."

"Manifestly so. Indeed . . . yes, this I will say. He is powerful, but often uncertain, insecure, indecisive, as though his power is in some ways new to him. As before, at my unfortunate lodgings. The energies at his command could have devastated the block and all within it, yet at the crucial moment he elected to flee. He is a dangerous foe, and the more dangerous for his unpredictability."

I glanced around the corner again. The old temple was still there, and there wasn't a sign of Gash in sight. He wasn't going to bail me out. I faded back from the edge. "Okay," I said to Carl. "Thanks. That's very—"

I had been planning it, I'd had to. Carl was still turning his head when I laid the walking stick hard across the back of it. He sank to the ground. I ripped pieces from his shirt and tied him before rolling him under one of the less offensive piles of garbage. Then

I straightened, adjusted my clothing, forced my body
to assume a confident upright air I didn't feel at all,
and crossed into the street.

The wall around Yahlei's temple had a new door in
it, barred and thick as the wall and ribbed with iron. I
approached, looking neither to the right or the left,
raised my arm, and struck the door with the stick.

The door gave off a rolling hollow boom. After a
moment, the small panel in the upper half slid back
and an eye appeared. "I am here to see Oskin Yahlei,"
I said. I was trying to make it sound like I had legiti-
mate business every day with folks like Oskin Yahlei,
but I don't know how successful I was. I felt, in fact,
like I was doing the dumbest thing I had ever come up
with.

The eye looked down my body, then back up. "Now
who is calling?" the voice of the lackey asked.

This was it. I rolled my own eyes up and hoped for a
reprieve. None descended. There was no way out. I
steadied my voice and said, "It is I, Gashanatantra."

12
SHAA AND MONT GO TO JAIL

Shaa and Mont dropped silently off the tail of the Guard troop and let the soldiers they had attached themselves to clatter off into the gloom. "I don't like this," Mont said.

"It's called protective coloration," Shaa said. "Most intelligent creatures use it." They had progressed toward the center of the island, deep into the catacombs. Shaa glanced around, his eyebrows slightly knitted. "There must be a dungeon around here somewhere, this place feels too much like dungeon to be anything else."

From the layout of the halls they had passed through, Mont had a fairly good idea where the dungeon was, but he decided there was something he'd better get cleared up first. "When we find the dungeon . . ."

"Yes?"

"When we find the dungeon there's sure to be some kind of guardroom—"

"Unquestionably."

"—unquestionably, and that'll probably be full of guards."

"No doubt."

"Right, no doubt. What are we going to do about them?"

"What do you think we should do about them?"

"Oh, knock it off already," Mont said. "You're the expert, tell me an expert plan."

Shaa considered reminding him that his basic plan was founded on improvisation, but chose against it. "We will reconnoiter first. Then we will attempt to gain unalerted entry using our—" he rattled his cuirass, "—disguises. When we are in position, we will attempt an ambush."

"Do you have any idea how many places that plan could go wrong?"

"Yes," Shaa said, "I do. Now, where is that dungeon?"

"I, ah, hmm . . ."

"What are you listening for?"

Mont was rotating his head slowly. He raised his hand. After a moment, he opened his eyes and pointed down the hall in the direction taken by the troops. "The music sounds best in that direction, sort of low and creepy. Dungeon sounds."

"Very well." They moved quietly off in Mont's chosen direction.

"I've been thinking . . ." Mont whispered.

"Yes?"

"When we get to the dungeon, why couldn't you say you're an interrogator come to torture the prisoners? Like, uh, with that cloak and all the stuff you're carrying around you'd be a natural."

Shaa stopped short, then resumed his pace. "That my friend, is a first-rate idea. It is exactly what we will try."

"Uh, ah," Mont said. The concept that Shaa might have actually said something nice to him had taken him by surprise. The corridor forked, Mont sniffed the air and led them down the left-hand passage. That passage soon forked as well, and they descended a tight coil of steps. Lights were visible at the base, and the sound of voices. "Ulp," Mont said, hesitating.

Shaa drew him back. "Are you afraid?" he whispered.

"Ah, uh, I . . ."

"It is a simple and human thing to feel fear," Shaa said. "Strength of character comes when you feel fear and nevertheless go on."

"Are *you* afraid?"

"Of course. I always am, in a situation like this."

"But you don't seem—"

"That is a different matter, called style. Each person must evolve that for himself. Or herself. Now, listen closely." Shaa whispered a few additional instructions to Mont, Mont nodded, and again they descended the stairs. At the bottom of the staircase was a pointed archway, and beyond it an open rectangular room.

Across from their entrance was a heavy wood-beam door embedded in an iron frame and manacled securely to the wall. Two other doors on the facing walls stood open, but those revealed merely further corridors. Aside from the usual array of guttering torches, a plank table and two matching benches, a firepit, several swords and cudgels hanging from hooks on the wall, and an antique torture cage rusting pleasantly to one side, the only furnishings were four guards. They put their hands on their swords and turned toward the entrance.

Mont put up his chin and strode into the room. "This is the interrogator," he announced, indicating Shaa with an outstretched arm.

Shaa, standing in a dramatic position framed in the center of the archway, his legs planted and one hand on his hip, removed the iron bar from under his cloak. He lowered his eyebrows suggestively, twirling the bar like a baton. "It's about time," one of the guards said. "You want us to bring 'em out, or you want to go in?"

"The interrogator will go in," Mont said.

The guard corporal looked around, said, "You! Come with me!" to one of the other troopers, and moved to the bolted door, producing a brass ring with large keys from his belt. "Better let the two of us go in first," he said over his shoulder to Mont, as he unlocked the door. Shaa looked guilelessly at the ceiling. The door creaked open, the weight of the two guards behind it, and Shaa and Mont followed the two into a dim corridor lit by widely spaced torches. The walls of the hall were thick brooding stone hewn from the rock of the island, broken occasionally by gates of iron grill and tasteful patches of moss. "You want the roundup from the first day, I imagine," the corporal said, stopping at the first cell.

Shaa leaned against the wooden door to the cell block, swinging it partially closed, then nodded to Mont. Mont, standing just behind the corporal, shielded himself from view with his body and brought the knobbed hilt of his knife down hard against the man's head. Shaa took two quick steps and swung his bar. Both guards sank to the floor together. Shaa nodded appreciatively. In a passable imitation of the corporal's voice, he called back, "Can you guys give us a hand in here?"

The heavy door creaked open. Shaa, now standing behind it, swung his bar again, hearing the swish of Mont's thrown knife. Mont's second throw was better than his first, on the wharves earlier in the evening. The guards grunted and collapsed.

Shaa left the guards where they'd fallen and trotted toward Mont, who had already fumbled the correct key into the lock. The door rasped and opened. Mont stepped into the cell and looked anxiously around. Shaa drew his sword and moved to the entrance behind Mont.

The cell extended some distance back into the rock. The only light was a meager trace of orange that leaked in from the torches in the passage, leaving the depths of the cell still totally black. Shadows moved in the dark. The half-dozen forms closest to the door were illuminated enough to see that they were dressed in civilian clothes, now besmirched. One of the prisoners gaped sullenly at Mont, while the others ostentatiously ignored him behind turned backs. Mont examined them, stopped, took a nervous half-step forward, and said, "Father?"

The man at the center of the small group wheeled and stared. The light caught lean hollows in his face and made slashes across sharp eyes, and his silvering hair glowed orange in the torchlight. "Jurtan! What do you think you're doing here?"

"Uh, rescuing you. All of you."

Jurtan's father drew back his arm and swept his hand into Mont's face. Mont reeled backward into the door. "You little *twerp!* You couldn't rescue a flea! They've taken you prisoner, too, haven't they, and you come in and *lie* to—"

"Father, just give me a second to—"

"Rescued by *you?*" The man moved menacingly toward Jurtan. Jurtan was still clutching the barred door, trying to regain his feet. "Of all the ridiculous—"

"Sir," Shaa said, "we would be pleased to let you remain here, when we leave with the others."

"And who do you think *you* are?"

"Opinion has little to do with it. I am Zalzyn Shaa." Shaa extended the arm with the bar to one side, crossed the other forearm over his waist, and executed a neat bow. "Whether I am at your service obviously remains to be seen."

"What are you doing here?"

"As my esteemed companion aptly explained, we are rescuing you. Or not, as you prefer."

The former Lion of the Oolvaan Plain stared at Shaa, speechless.

"We are unwelcome here," Shaa said sadly. "Jurtan, if you please—the key. We will leave these gentles to their own contemplations."

"You wouldn't *dare!*" Mont's father roared.

"Yes," Shaa said, "I would."

"You *rodent!* You *flea!* You unspeakable heap of—"

"Dad," said a female voice, "shut up." Another shape appeared in the gloom.

"Oof!" This was yet another voice, a reedy high-pitched one belonging to an elder of some sort. "Yeaouch!"

"Oh!" said the woman. "I beg your pardon, Your Grace." She pushed forward, revealing the same sharp eyes and confident manner as her father. "Jurtan, good. What's your plan?"

"Into the hall, quickly," Shaa said. "Everyone!" He was already moving, Mont after him, the girl next. Shaa strode over one of the prostrate guardsmen, put his foot under the hilt of the man's sword and kicked up, causing the sword to spring into the air, and ran ahead, not breaking his motion. The sword wheeled twice in the air and the hilt thudded solidly into Mont's hand. Mont closed his hand out of reflex, gaping at the sword. His sister ran around him past the thicker door and into the outer room.

Shaa charged across the guardroom, started up the stairs, and paused. The sound of marching feet was audible from above. It was also growing louder.

"Uh, Shaa?" Jurtan said, just behind him.

"What?"

"Did I mention that sometimes the music warns me when something's about to happen?"

"Oh, great," Shaa said sarcastically.

"Over here, everybody!" Mont's sister yelled from across the room. Shaa turned to see her waving people through one of the other doorways. Mont's father, a disgusted expression on his face and a sword in his hand, plunged past her, snarling, "Let me to the front!", and was gone.

The marching feet-tramp reached the staircase and began to descend in their direction. Shaa would have loved to lock them out; unfortunately the staircase was the one entrance to the room that didn't have a door. Mont lent a shoulder and they shoved the guardroom table across the floor. Upended, it might block the archway—a soldier clattered around the bend from above and saw them. Shaa leaped to the top of the table and displayed his sword. The guardsman jumped forward two steps, drawing his own sword, and engaged. Shaa swept his other arm around from behind and hit him with the iron bar.

The clang of the bar faded and new footsteps clattered on the stairs as the soldier rolled limply beneath the table. Mont, holding his sword, began to climb up next to Shaa.

"No," Shaa said. "I will hold them here. You must safeguard the prisoners."

"But—"

"You will fight later. Action, wherever taken, is nonetheless character," Shaa said. "Go."

Mont chewed his lip, leaned in the direction of the exit, bobbed uncertainly on one foot, looked at Shaa, and then took off down the tunnel.

Another voice spoke from Shaa's shoulder. "You can't hold this room alone," Mont's sister said. "There're too many doorways."

Shaa glanced across and down at her, where she stood next to the table. "I appreciate your encouragement," he said dryly.

"Look *out!*" she said.

With a sardonic twist to his mouth, Shaa leaned and thrust at the second soldier without bothering to look, and felt his sword fenestrate a chest. He bowed slightly in the direction of Mont's sister. "Your name?" he said.

"Ah, Tildamire," she said. She was quickly discovering the same thing her brother had found out earlier, that Shaa's attitude had a remarkable capacity for disconcerting its target. "There's another one coming!"

"If you're going to stay, you might as well try to lock the other doors." Shaa had turned more serious attention back to the staircase. The squads he had seen so far generally ran to ten men apiece. Two were already under the table—no, *three*, he thought, as the iron bar unchivalrously claimed another victim. The fourth and fifth rushed together, side-by-side, the one on Shaa's left fractionally closer; Shaa had his sword in his right hand and was presenting his right side to them, almost within reach. He stepped back, moving to their left, the trooper on the far side lunged just a little farther, Shaa's blade nicked out at the soldier lagging behind, and the man lost his balance on the slick step, fell across the length of his partner's sword, and carried them both forehead-first into the heavy slab edge of the table.

Two sets of legs now stretched upward along the lower stairs. Shaa quickly knelt, rummaged under the table with one hand, temporarily sticking the iron bar in his belt, and came up with another sword. Six, seven, and eight rattled around the corner. Shaa hefted the new sword, drew it back, and launched it hilt-first over the heads of the first two guardsmen. It hit the third man in the shoulder. The impact of the heavy hilt spun him slightly, making him flail about for balance with both arms, and suddenly another multi-person tangle was crashing down the stairs. Shaa performed detail work with his iron bar.

The table creaked behind him. "I could only lock one, and it isn't going to hold for long," Tildamire told Shaa.

"Quiet," Shaa said. The footsteps of new fodder on the steps had stopped. Shaa jumped down from the table, landing silently, and backed across the floor, holding his sword warily in front of him. A reddish glow appeared at the top of the circular staircase.

"What is it?" the girl whispered.

The glow intensified, as something drew around the stairs and came closer to them. "I suggest flight," Shaa told her.

"But what about you?"

"I will delay it," Shaa said, "I hope." The glare from the staircase was painfully bright, and was now casting a sharp-edged fan of pink across the floor and table and ceiling. The fan swept along the room, spreading out. Shaa twisted a small stud on the hilt of his rapier, breaking the integrity of its inhibition spell, and bands of flaming blue wearing hard jagged spikes danced down the blade. He looked at Tildamire. "Thank you for your solicitude. I am, however, not suicidal. Now go."

She took a last glance, her mouth hanging slightly open, and ran out the remaining open door after the other prisoners. Shaa backed to the doorway and kicked the door shut after her as the thing from the staircase floated into the room. It figured there had to be a sorcerer hanging around somewhere, Shaa thought, his habitual air of smugness somewhat dented by the circumstances.

The light burst into the room, skimming down the last stairs and over the table. Shaa squinted against the glare. The construct was tall, Shaa's height, a spinning pillar of intermeshing helices, interference patterns traveling slowly across its face. Waving tentaclelike protrusions flowed from irregular nodes on the surface. The thing leaned into a turn and scudded toward Shaa, its screeching whine mounting. Shaa struck an *en garde* and cut at the nearest tentacle, felt a brief catch as the blue blade bit the air, and saw a severed tentacle end twirl to the floor in a wisp of shooting sparks. He let the momentum of the sword swing it through another tentacle and went for the body.

The bands of fiery blue ground into the construct like a sharp saw. Then the sword caught again and turned in Shaa's grip. He fought for control, seeing his shadow ahead of him on the floor. In the instant he noticed the shadow and realized that one of the glowing tentacles had snuck around behind him, a pain as of flames flayed his back and lanced through to his chest. He hacked frantically at the tentacle behind him, nicked it, and fell to his knees as yet another flailing arm swept over his head. The whirling body drew nearer; his earlier thrust had bashed in one side and the thing was wobbling erratically, but it was not yet near its end. The functional tentacles reached for him. Sweat ran down Shaa's face into his gritted teeth. His spine contorted and he threw himself back, swinging his rapier in front of him for a stop thrust. A shower of sparks cascaded over his face, and Shaa felt a lightning shock run down his sword-arm and into his shoulder.

13
MAX DROPS IN

Over the mountains they ran into a storm; under rational conditions they should have let it ground them. Thunder crashed on all sides, lightning lit the giant billows of heaving clouds, and downdrafts threatened to rip the bird's wings off and smash them all into the ground. Haddo's skill and the buzzard's native cussedness drove them on; Max wanted to hoard as much of his strength as he could. The sky was merely overcast when they reached the river.

The bird turned south, the scattered lights of ships making cryptic beacons below them in the night. Ten miles north of Roosing Oolvaya they went into a long glide. The city was only a mile or two downstream when the bird leveled out, twenty feet over the long swells. Max adjusted his face-mask, checked the pack straps, and slid into the river. Haddo and the bird banked east and faded out of sight in the darkness. Max turned on his back. The current floated him downstream.

Roosing Oolvaya approached. With a little luck he'd be in and out quickly, Max thought. His arm still hurt. He'd made liberal use of some healing gunk or another Karlini had had sitting around or he wouldn't have been able to move it at all. Not that partial incapacitation surprised him—it was the typical kind of problem for a mess like this. A broad eddy swept him closer to the west bank. The moon was just rising, low in the east and mostly waned away, and behind the clouds to boot. The walls blocked the light from the city. Max picked out his secondary landmarks as faint silhouettes, sighted on the north-point lighthouse, and struck out for the northeast corner tower.

Crosscurrents and whirlpools caught him as he neared the wall. He had expected them, too, and had made allowances for an irregular passage. A final riptide dragged him into the lee south of the tower. Max put out a hand and rested it against the piling supporting a rotting wharf, taking a moment's rest. The suit of treated hides Karlini had dug out of a storeroom was supposedly waterproof. A trickle was running in down the back of Max's neck, though, and several other small leaks were accumulating water in the attached booties; just enough to be thoroughly annoying. Max scratched between his shoulder blades, glowered at the suit, and then started measuring his way to the left along the bulge of the city.

He soon came to the end of a wharf, saw a twenty-foot gap before the next, sighted up at a spire rising just beyond the wall, and nodded with gloomy satisfaction. Max felt out with his hand. Three feet from the wharf the stone of the wall ended in an arch. Water smacked against the stone lip, and against the iron grating spanning the outlet. Max took a deep breath, put his head down, and dived.

The grating was solid in the rock. The center section, however, was hinged, and the lock had not surprisingly rusted out. Max secured the gate behind him with a twist of rope. As he'd expected, the magical barrier around the city was short-circuited by the flowing water; he'd felt nothing more than a sensation like a fine-tooth comb being dragged backward through his aura. The culvert proceeded under the wall before turning up, but the ceiling height was more than ade-

quate to allow walking. He slogged inward. The real
reason he had bothered with the water-repellent suit
was that it also repelled whatever was in the water;
Max was notoriously fastidious, and sewers after all
were sewers. He kept the bone-and-hide face-mask
firmly planted over his nose, inhaling as infrequently
as possible.

At an intersection he stopped to verify his bearings.
Stretching away from him toward the west was a round
tunnel, awash to mid-thigh level, its lower roof broken
by periodic shafts leading up to gratings in the street.
Other feeder tubes entered high up on the side surfaces, some spilling runnels of dark fluid. Dim light
came down some of the vertical shafts and made strange
glittering patterns on the moving water. Max sloshed
forward, passing one major turnoff, then another. A
clatter ahead caught his attention. The illumination
down one shaft abruptly intensified as the manhole
cover above was lifted, twisted and elongated shadows
writhed on the wall, Max heard a cry begin only to be
abruptly stifled, and then one of the shadows separated from the other and came sweeping down. A
figure dropped from the shaft into the water. The slow
current pushed the man past Max, his throat cut. Max
crouched and entered a tunnel to the side.

He threaded his way through the maze. It was difficult to appear completely transparent to sorcerous
search, because of the radiative characteristics of auras;
to make an aura totally disappear was nearly impossible. Making an aura look like it belonged to somebody
else, on the other hand, was much less complex and
generally more successful, camouflage being a basic
principle of nature. So it was that Max appeared, to
even a probing search, as a large and fairly bedraggled
muskrat. The disguise was helpful in more ways than
one. Some large species lived in the river, but they
tended to find the taste of muskrat unappealing. Eventually the tunnel Max was following ended at a massive stone block.

Max stopped to consider. By his calculations the large block was part of the foundation for the north wall. The house of Oskin Yahlei should be a few hundred feet west, just south of the wall or perhaps immediately next to it. The neighborhood had been outside the original city. During the reconstruction after a large flood half a century or so earlier, in the same spurt of civic zeal that had seen the sewer system go in, the wall had been extended north to encompass what was then a thriving district built on a series of low hills. Also encompassed were a number of Roosing Oolvaya's original cemeteries. With the periodic floods, putting graves above the water level had looked like a good idea. As far as public health went, the plan had worked out fine; flood waters left the bodies alone. On the other hand, floods weren't the only things that were interested in them.

The first thing a necromancer did when moving into a new domain was chart the locations of all the local graves. Corpses, after all, were the necromancer's basic stock in trade and source of raw material. A necromancer's dream house was next to his or her own private reserve. This was what Oskin Yahlei had managed. Max had serious questions about parts of the situation, but about one thing there were no doubts. Oskin Yahlei had the potential to be very dangerous.

Max decided to remain with the underground route for the time being. He backtracked to the nearest intersection and went right. The culvert tilted gently up, the current grew faster and gained bite in its force. Max leaned into it; the incline meant he was ascending the underside of a hill. Passing beneath another vertical shaft, he heard the rattle of a small group of men on patrol passing overhead. The clinking faded off into the night. Another opening approached on his right, and Max approached it cautiously.

The water swirled at the intersection, making a small foaming whirlpool with dim blue highlights. Down the side passage the blue glow was stronger. Max peeked around the arch. Beyond the junction the secondary passage widened, increasing in height and continuing slightly uphill. Thirty feet ahead and five feet over the water level he saw a boat landing recessed into the wall, the blue glow emanating from somewhere at its back. Humanoid shapes moved on the landing, their shadows dancing madly on the water.

There were two—no, *three* of them, virtually reeking of necromantic conjuration; the anticipated zombies, no doubt. Max smiled a not particularly pleasant smile. He reached over his shoulder and removed the top item from his pack. Submerging himself to the neck in the water, he unwrapped the article he had selected, revealing two lead balls connected by five feet of thick cord. A second item fell free into his hand—a hollow reed about a foot long and two inches in diameter. Max glanced around the corner again and checked the clearances. With a little luck it would work, and he wouldn't even need his injured arm.

Max moaned loudly across the end of the reed. The mournful drone resonated down the passage, hanging in the air with the echo of a wailing hum. He waited a minute, then moaned again. This time Max was rewarded with a chorus of splashes from the direction of the landing. Footsteps sloshed in the tunnel. The creatures were coming, Max thought, and why not? After all, what self-respecting undead could resist the famous Zombie Love Call? Max said a final word to the cord; it, too, began to glow. Then he popped the end of the reed in his mouth, sank down, and watched the shaft, the top of his faceplate just out of the water, bracing himself against the current. Another splash sounded, very close now, the blue glow strengthened, a twisted shadow fell upon the water and the far wall, and then a hand appeared around the corner. A web of faint sparks knit the greenish tissue together around its gaps and tears, tendons sliding in plain sight over the stark white bones. Clutched in its grip was a tarnished brass handle.

Suspended from the handle was a globular mass of writhing blue coils—a zombie glowworm, for all Max knew. The rest of the body attached to the hand shambled wetly into sight. Internal organs shifted restlessly within the zombie's chest cavity, a trail of intestine leading back around one leg and up the tunnel. It looked around, searching eagerly for the source of the call. A second zombie elbowed its way into view, followed by a third; the smell was mounting well above the normal odor of the sewer, penetrating to Max's nose even within the face-mask. He raised his hand, twirled the weighted cord twice around his head, and let it go. The cord spun around the torso of the first zombie, snapping through the rotten humerus in its right upper arm and flinging it off-balance to its rear. Sparks of white crackling along its length, the cord continued to spin, chewing its way through bone and flesh alike. One iron ball smashed through the second zombie's ribs as the first creature slammed into it. The cord snapped tight, the momentum grinding the two together; one torso suddenly imploded under the pressure, and bits of tissue splattered against the walls. The third zombie tottered and fell as its feet were swept out from under it. With a paroxysm of splashing, the tangled mass of zombie floated quickly around Max and headed downstream. The current had taken the lamp, too—it bobbed behind them, spun in an eddy, dwindled, and went out of sight around a corner. Max allowed himself a quick smirk, then went around the arch into the side passage. He climbed a short ladder to the landing.

The landing was little more than an alcove in the side of the sewer tunnel. Max stowed his face-mask in the pack as he glanced around. The area was now almost totally dark, the only break in the blackness being provided by a wiggling blue wormlet that had snagged on the sharp edge of a rock. A small rowboat was pulled up into one corner of the alcove and secured with a cable through an eyebolt in the prow.

Another ladder led up to a trap door in the landing's roof. Max examined the ladder carefully, then gingerly climbed it, pausing at the top to ease open the trap-door just enough to peek in over the edge. The trap-door occupied the corner of a cellar otherwise filled with crates. The yellow-red light of candles showed in the jamb of a door in the wall above. Nothing was moving. Max pulled himself through the door onto the cellar floor, eased the trap down, felt his way to the stairs, and paused, one foot poised over the first riser. Something felt strange about the stairs.

Max lowered his foot back to the floor. Bracing himself with one hand against the rock-and-dirt wall, he closed his eyes, reached gently out with his other arm, and made a flowing gesture with his hand. He concentrated, letting the orientation of his senses precess slightly out of their normal alignment. Max opened his eyes. A swimming haze surrounded him, small oval paddles like disembodied hummingbird wings spinning through it. He focused past his aura, up onto the staircase. A nebulous pink haze hung over the steps. It faded as he watched, still churning silently.

So much for the stairs. Max didn't know exactly what the thing was, but that was fine with him; he wasn't interested in research at the moment. It was Max's firm philosophy to avoid the frontal assault wherever possible. To his great regret it wasn't always possible. In this case, though, there were other options.

Max spotted a thick bearing beam holding up the ceiling in front of the door at the top of the staircase. Climbing over a crate, he reached a spot below the beam and raised his left arm. His sleeve fell back, revealing the wrist appliance he had last used back in the bar at the desert oasis. The spring-loaded mechanism in which Max usually kept a knife was good for other things as well; he removed the knife and inserted a dart. He steadied the appliance with his other hand and released the catch. Springs pinged, the dart lanced up, trailing a thin cord, and with a low "choonk" the dart embedded itself in the beam. Max leaned on the cord; the hold was solid. He went up hand-over-hand, fending off from the wall with his feet, taking care not to touch the staircase.

Max quickly drew abreast of the door, dangling just below the ceiling and at the outside of the landing at the top of the stairs. He put his eye to the crack at the door jamb. The stairs continued upward beyond the door, ending flush with the floor of the next story in a closet that looked like a pantry. That door was standing open, admitting light from another room; Max's door unfortunately was locked. He reached inside his suit and slid out a set of lockpicks. Max took a firm grip on the cord, taking the dead weight off his left forearm, lowered himself to the level of the lock, and inserted one of the picks.

Ten seconds later the lock clicked. Max pulled the door open, swung himself over the banister and through the doorframe, and steadied himself with a foot up on the handrail and his free arm over the lip at the edge of the floor just above his head; the current section of staircase looked fine, but he wasn't quite ready to trust it more than the other. As he had spied through the crack, the stairs went steeply upward to an open door leading onto a plain whitewashed hall. The well for the stairs would ordinarily be covered by a wooden slab; this cover was currently raised on its hinged back and secured overhead. Stacks of dry goods in sacks and boxes covered the rest of the closet floor and were heaped against the walls around the open stairwell. There was no one in sight.

Max pulled himself up to the door sill at the floor level and took a quick glance around the door into the hall. It was still empty. Crouching, he let go of the climbing cord, reinserted his knife into the wrist appliance, turned the recessed crank that wound the springs, spent a quick moment stretching out his injured arm, which had been holding up remarkably well under the exertion, and eased out into the hall, closing the door behind him.

Across the hall he could see the entranceway to a darkened kitchen and a thick candle in a wooden holder next to it on the wall. To the right of the kitchen the back hall intersected another hall, this one much fancier, leading away toward the front of the building. Max slid across to the kitchen, blew out the candle, then leaned sideways to see around the corner into the front hall.

The front hall was cluttered with gilt mirrors and footed end tables. Max's section of the hall was now in deep shadow, but the light was much better toward the front, where the left side of the hall opened onto a large space lit by the glow of many candles. The hall's ceiling also opened, becoming a series of free arches casting strange patterns under the flickering light. A set of double doors broke the wall on the right. At the end of the hall was a small enclosed entryway leading to the front door.

Unfortunately these were not the only features. Two men-at-arms were visible in the corridor where it faced the larger open room, one positioned at each side of the double doors, another was planted next to the half-closed door to the entry, and the shapes of two more were visible at either side of the door to the street. They each bore a strange device of purple bands with a column of coiling flames ascending from it. So Oskin Yahlei had his own private militia; that was a detail Karlini had neglected to mention.

Max glided silently back out of sight. A climbing staircase beckoned across from him, down the continuation of the back hall. The problem was that the man at the entry door was looking straight back along the cross-corridor. If Max tried to sneak across, even in the deep shadows at the rear, the guy just had to spot him. Max had an advantage in that no one knew he was around; if he tried to direct the man's eyes away or use some other distraction he might make it to the staircase, but he'd have a bigger chance of alerting another element of Oskin Yahlei's forces. Or a trap. A staircase wasn't worth that much. He decided to check out the kitchen.

The kitchen was located in a rear corner of the building, with two outside walls and a small window. Max hoisted himself atop an upturned washtub and looked out. In the dim light outside he made out a small field, with perhaps a hint of the city wall at its back. Directly outside the window was a skeletal tree. He closed his eyes and felt quickly around. The window didn't seem trapped, but Max didn't like the feel of the tree, or of the grounds, for that matter. The window was constructed around wooden cross pieces set in an elliptical frame and hinged to swing outward; when Max tentatively tried to ease it open, though, the window stuck. A convenient canister of kitchen grease later, it moved silently open, the barest start of a shriek yielding to another glob on the hinge.

Max stuck his head out through the open frame. Another roundish window on the second story was a few feet to one side. By standing on the sill he could almost reach its frame. He crouched, then sprang, grabbed the lower jamb of the second-story window, and chinned himself on it. Inside the window was a bedroom, dark and quiet. The window opened at his touch. He lowered himself silently to the floor.

Max tiptoed toward the door. Behind a screen concealed from the window was a bed, containing a sleeping girl covered only by a small rug. He paused and raised an eyebrow, wondering briefly at the tastes of gods. There were certain things in the story of Oskin Yahlei, the mobile castle and its kidnapped occupant, Karlini and Roosing Oolvaya that made less than total sense when accepted at face value. Max was especially suspicious about Oskin Yahlei. Hopefully, though, Max thought, moving to the door, the moment of resolution was approaching. The corridor beyond the door was bare.

The corridor ran directly over the back hall Max had scouted downstairs, and in the same direction.

Where the cross-corridor on the first floor had led to
the front of the house, though, there was nothing here
on the second floor but a blank wall. On the other side
of the blank wall, Max assumed, was the second-story
extension of the large open room off the front hallway
on the ground level. The architecture was unusual for
a house. Max had already taken into account the cemetery on the lot and concluded that the place was
probably a converted temple, with the big room on the
first story being the temple proper. One thing he was
still wondering about was what god the temple had
originally been dedicated to.

Across the hall from the bedroom he saw another
door standing ajar. The room behind it was empty.
Max crossed and entered. On the wall to the left of
the door were three large open windows overlooking
the expanse of the sanctuary. A tightly wound circular
staircase in the back left corner led down to the ground
floor, probably to the room that had been on the other
side of the double doors flanked by guards. Empty
bookcases lined the remaining walls. A blackboard on
a tripod stand, recently erased, leaned against the
bookcase behind the stairs. A large desk with a matching armchair and the carved lectern next to it dominated the center of the room. The desk bore a stack of
cryptic papers, a scattering of glassware, candles, and
chalk, and a set of unlabeled canisters with tightly
sealed lids. This was apparently Oskin Yahlei's workroom; he would have to show up there sooner or later.

Why a god needed a workroom was another question that was fueling one of Max's pet suspicions. He
crept to the top of the circular staircase and paused.
Voices were audible from the room below, but their
meaning was lost. Rising, Max crossed to the nearest
window for a view of the temple interior. Scattered
candles and a few torches smoldered below. Whatever
altars, tapestries, fonts, or other furnishings had originally filled the chamber were long gone, leaving only
bare walls and long trails of soot. In the typically dim

light, Max could make out a half-dozen of the men
with the purple badges, and another group of perhaps
eight or ten clustered to themselves near one wall—
regular Guard troops, most likely. The Guard soldiers
were watching a small number of prisoners; the light-
ing made it difficult to tell exactly what was going on.
No one was being given the level of attention and
respect that Oskin Yahlei would command, so if he
was in the building he was probably in the room just
below. Max stepped back from the window and eyed
the workroom. The only hiding place that would be
concealed from both the door and the staircase was
behind the desk, so Max moved around the desk and
lowered himself to the floor.

The voices downstairs were still engaged in conversation. Max rummaged inside his backpack, pulled out
a flat rectangular case, and snapped it open. Inside
was a blowgun and several darts with finned ends.
Their needle points glistened with a sticky dark brown
substance; a scratch would cause immediate stupor
lasting hours in most any living thing smaller than
Haddo's buzzard. A larger dose—two darts' worth,
say—would not only turn down the conscious mind
but the vegetative as well, thereby arresting the victim's breathing. Fitting the tubular halves of the blowgun together, Max slid a dart inside and placed the
weapon next to him on the floor. For good measure,
he also loosened the stiletto in its leather sheath strapped
to the outside of his boot, and then set to work with
his other preparations.

Max didn't know exactly what he was going to need
to do. That is, he knew what he had to do—deal with
the ring, the ring that was holding the owner of Karlini's
castle a prisoner, the ring that Oskin Yahlei was no
doubt wearing—he just didn't know exactly what he'd
have to go through to accomplish that. To deal with
the ring he'd presumably have to deal with Oskin
Yahlei first. He wasn't sure how much dealing-with
Oskin Yahlei would take, but Max figured he'd better

be prepared. From all accounts, the ring had been designed to trap and encapsulate the owner of the castle, allowing the ring's wearer to utilize the power of the being penned up in it. It was this occupant that Max would have to let out. Any magician in his right mind would only take on a task like that when the conditions would allow patience and fine control; there were a lot of nasty things that could go wrong. For one thing, recorporating a disembodied entity was a major job usually done in several stages. When the entity was presumed to be a Death, and when one could reliably assume he would emerge in a state of no little annoyance, that only made things worse.

Max didn't have the luxury of choosing his time and place, but he'd prepared as well as he could. He and Karlini had designed a set of nested confinement spells that Max now had with him. The plan was to incapacitate Oskin Yahlei, by sneak attack or subterfuge if possible, and then encase him in the big confinement field with the ring still on his finger. The ring itself would be wrapped in the other restriction spells within the larger cage matrix. Max was hoping that would give him enough protection to probe the nature of the ring's defenses while containing anything that started to leak out; the probes that would enable this were ready, too. The whole sequence was linked and programmed, in fact—the confinement layers would crystallize simultaneously in a self-supporting array, automatically activating the probes in quick graduated sequence. A battery of quiescence/somnolence thrall-routines firing with the probes would hopefully calm the ring's occupant to a decent level of sedation. If he had to, Max would try to release the ring's prisoner at that point, when the results of the probes were in, but he was hoping that wouldn't be necessary. With a little luck he'd have stabilized the ring enough to get it off Oskin Yahlei and take it away with him without setting things loose.

Max lay his rapier on the floor within easy reach.

He had begun to think that swords were too convenient a solution for many problems, and one that lacked finesse, but they certainly did have their uses. No regular sword would bother Oskin Yahlei, of course, but with the number of soldiers around it still might come in handy. It could be a serious enough business that Max wanted all the backup he could get.

Even with all the preparations, his luck at penetrating the city and Oskin Yahlei's headquarters without discovery and without serious opposition, and his ability to react well and think on his feet, Max was still hoping he'd make it through the experience alive and in one piece. It wasn't a question of whether something would go wrong. Of course something would go wrong, something always went wrong. The only question was how disastrous it would be.

Boots tramped and armor clattered in the room below. A heavy tread started up the circular staircase. Another lighter set of footsteps followed it, uncertain steps, falling one-two, one-two-three, as though the walker wasn't quite sure what he was doing. The voice of a man began to separate itself out from the muffling walls. ". . . mumble, mumble of this ring?" Max put the blowgun to his lips and sank down behind the desk, peeking out from the side around the chair: A man's hand appeared on the banister, the middle finger wearing a gold ring, then behind the hand a head. A black eyepatch covered the left eye, and the black aura of the ring covered the flesh.

Oskin Yahlei, the man who might be Death, came up through the floor.

14
MONT SOLOS

Jurtan Mont vaulted the body of a Guardsman his father had speared as his sister, running faster, caught up with him. "Just who was that guy?" she panted, glancing back over her shoulder.

"His name's Shaa, he says he's a doctor." Another strangled yelp came from the head of the column. The prisoners were straggling out into a long line, Jurtan bringing up the rear, as the less physically fit among them lost their first wind. Some of the people from the original cell had had the foresight to open other doors up and down the dungeon hall. As a result, the fleeing crowd was now quite a rabble of merchants, local royalty, government advisers and officials, various family members, priests and clerics, and representatives of the general public swept up into the hand of Kaar. The yelp from the front was followed by a thud of body hitting floor and a muted berserker battle cry. Jurtan's mind, which had been projecting a soft traveling string motif at him, insistent in its runs of rapid notes and propulsive rhythm, gave a quick skip at the barely melodic barbarian yodel, which had sounded suspiciously like the voice of his father. He blinked, grabbed mentally at the stabilizing sound of the strings, regained control, and plunged ahead with only a momentary hesitation. "Where is Shaa, anyway?" he asked.

"He stayed behind. A magician showed up. It didn't look too good."

"He stayed to fight a *magician?*" Jurtan said. That didn't make much sense; Shaa had said he wasn't a magician himself, and if he wasn't he couldn't possibly last long. "I hope he's okay."

"You sound worried about him."

"Yeah, well, he's a pretty strange guy, but I'd have been really sunk if he hadn't popped up."

"What about you?" his sister said. "I never thought *you'd* really show up."

"I didn't think I would either." Jurtan was still scared to death, but beneath that was a low thrill of accomplishment. Whatever Dad had said, he'd been doing pretty well so far. "Dad didn't seem too happy about it. Is it just him being the way he usually is, or has he got some extra problem this time?"

"Oh, you know Dad." Another prostrate trooper rolled past beneath their feet. "They caught him in an ambush, one of them held a sword across his neck while another one pounded him over the head. He's mad he didn't go down fighting, taking ten or twenty of them with him."

"It looks like he's sure trying to make up for it now."

"Well," Tildy said, "you know Dad."

The corridor forked ahead and widened to the right. The line of staggering people made the turn like a single creature, a giant tunnel-traveling worm maybe. Jurtan and Tildy followed. "You know this place," she said. "Where are we going?"

"If Dad wasn't so mad, he'd head for the armory and clean it out, hang a dozen swords and maces and stuff over his back, then hit the barracks or the docks or someplace like that. But he's pretty mad—how does he feel about Kaar right now?"

"He was talking about Kaar a lot in the cell, wanting

to tear his arms off first and make him eat them, that kind of thing."

"I kind of figured that. I think he's probably going after Kaar directly, no matter who's in the way."

"He's going to get to Kaar through here?" They had entered an area of storerooms, with wooden doors opening from a central sorting floor. Corridors and staircases snaked off in various directions.

"Yeah, I think I remember—" The music in Jurtan's head abruptly shifted mode, the strings grew harsh, and a transformation to harmonic sevenths gave an air of urgent danger. "Watch out!" he yelled. "Something's gonna—oof!" The large woman just in front of him had stopped short, craning her head at something up ahead, and Mont had barreled into her going full speed. He spun back and fell to the floor.

The line of moving people ground to a halt at the renewed sound of metal ringing on metal up ahead. Boots pounded behind them, too. Tildy whirled as Jurtan struggled back to his feet. The lead elements of a new bunch of troopers charged around the fork in the hallway, bellowed, and thundered in their direction. "Everybody scatter!" Tildy yelled, grabbing Jurtan's arm and yanking him toward the closest door next to them at the side of the room. The door had been almost completely shut, but not quite, since it was slightly warped in its frame. As Tildy's shoulder and the hurtling front of Jurtan's reeling body plowed into it, it opened quite definitively, launching them both headfirst into the room beyond to sprawl amid the room's contents.

Jurtan plowed through a rack of shelves, bounced off a wall, pushed off the wall, and slammed back against the door just in time to fling it shut. He fumbled for a lock, a bar, something to block the door; the darkness in the closet was broken only by the irregular frame of the door and the rays of light that tickled through it from the room outside, along with the pandemonium of sudden cries and bashings and running footsteps. "Tildy?" he said. "Are you okay?"

"I—*Jurtan, watch—*"

Jurtan spun around. Through the gloom and clatter, he saw a rush of motion—a large hulking shape was rocking down toward him. He threw himself sideways. The massive shape teetered through one of the rays of errant light from the doorframe, revealing itself to be the case of shelves he had fallen into and upset. Jurtan buried his head against the wall as the giant case slid in a collapsing mess against the front door.

"Tildy?"

"Jurtan?"

Whomm! The door shuddered under an impact from the other side. The shelves merely creaked and collapsed further. Jurtan was lying on a mass of crunching wood and small delicate objects where he had landed in his mad leap out of the way; they only cracked and snapped more as he struggled up. Fortunately, the mass of falling stuff had mostly missed him, inflicting nothing more than bruises and scratches. "We've got to get out of here," he said.

With a groan and a loud rattle, the outline of light around the door flashed again. "I don't think getting out is going to be the problem," Tildy said. "I think I'd rather stay in."

"You're okay, aren't you?" Jurtan said. He had been fumbling in his belt, looking for his carrying-pouch.

Tildy giggled a weak giggle. "Okay? Sure, I'm okay. We're only penned up here like pigeons in a coop, waiting for the foxes to break through the—"

Then Mont found the pouch, and what he was after inside it—a lighter flint. He struck the flint. The momentary spark that flashed out showed a fairly small closet, now filled with wreckage, a dust-covered sister, and the former contents of the fractured shelves. Mandolins. Lutes, fiddles, a twisted harp. Underlining the point, a string snapped with an quivering twang somewhere deep within the pile. Other cabinets stacked against the walls of the closet held other instruments.

As Shaa might say, Jurtan thought, there is a certain air of inevitability about this. The door shuddered again under the weight of energetic bodies, and one of the panels in the top half began to give way. A new jagged slash of light spilled on the far wall. Through the crack in the door parts of shoulders could be seen. "Do you have any ideas?" Jurtan said.

"I'm looking for a sword or a good club or something—you'd better do the same thing."

"Okay, so you don't have any helpful ideas either. In that case, there's something I want to try." He pulled the lid off one of the crates and rummaged inside.

"Will it help?"

One board in the door panel snapped cleanly away and sailed across the room. A brawny hand reached through, flailing ineffectually. "It might," Jurtan said. He held up a flute and squinted at it.

"The other way," Tildy said.

"Huh?"

"You hold it the other way round."

"Oh." Jurtan reversed the flute and put it to his lips. More hands were madly ripping apart the upper door; it was a matter of seconds till they broke through completely.

"I hope this is good, Jurtan," Tildy said.

"Me, too," he mumbled. The music in Jurtan's head, which had been holding at an expectant quiver, added a sudden snarl of trumpets and the rolling patter of a snare drum. He put his fingers over the holes on the body of the flute, blew into the mouthpiece, and froze. His body froze, his arms in their raised position and his eyes staring downward at the flute. A high clear sound had appeared in the air, and his ears were locked around the sound, hearing it to the exclusion of all other senses, his mind stuck on the single thought of the sound and the breath coming almost on its own from his chest. And as his breath whistled through the flute, his mind realized slowly, very slowly, that it was actually working, it had not after all gone blank, his thoughts were forming and circulating like leaden snails but they were indeed alive, he was awake, and there was music not only in his head but also, for the very first time, outside of it as well.

Jurtan Mont took another breath and blew again, and this time, even more amazingly, his fingers began to dance on the body of the flute. Music, true music burst out, harmonizing and rounding with the music in Jurtan's head, a midrange fluid running melody against the insistent scales of the strings and the exulting blaze of trumpets. He wondered how it sounded to the listeners—probably weird, because most of the music was really in his mind; the flute sound would be tantalizingly incomplete without the rest. He concentrated on his eyes. Haltingly, with a deliberately leisurely pace, they began to roll up. His fingers, unconcerned with any irrelevant actions elsewhere in the body, seemingly plugged directly into some hidden musical control center, kept up their flying leaps back and forth along the flute. Then the doorway came into view, the splintered upper door, the large gaping hole where the whole wooden panel was smashed through, the two Guardsmen halfway through the opening—the two Guardsmen! The two Guardsmen, draped across the lower lip of the opening, their arms trailing downward, their heads lolling, their faces blank.

Jurtan's suspicion was growing stronger. He managed to turn his head slightly, just enough to spot his sister. Tildy, too, had slumped backward to the floor, a dazed expression on her face, her fingers curled limp and loose around a club-shaped piece of wood. Jurtan gradually closed his eyes and concentrated on listening. Over the magnetic rush of the music, like a whirlpool of sound still trying to suck him back in, was—nothing! No running feet, no bashing swords, no cries, no moans, nothing!

Wow! Jurtan thought. *That's pretty good!* It looked like everybody in earshot was paralyzed, knocked out, shut off, just the way he usually reacted when music hit him. Right behind that realization came another that he didn't like nearly as much—his fingers were really starting to hurt. And the flute was heating up.

Whatever this ability was, its power was beginning to take a toll; Jurtan didn't know how much longer he could keep the playing up. If the effect on the people around him was anything like it was on him, though, they might start to wake up as soon as the music stopped, but if they did they'd be pretty groggy. They wouldn't be used to the situation, either. That would give him a bit of time. Maybe he could buy a little more time than that, too.

Jurtan focused on the music, willing it to go faster. His fingers, already racing, began to fly. A repetitive pattern in the strings moved a tone higher, then higher than that, picking up an element of added insistency. He began to note the approach of a crescendo. A wisp of smoke curled up from the flute. Then, suddenly but with an air of finality, in a paroxysm of muscle-wrenching glee, a blast of virtually concrete pandemonium shot out from under Jurtan's hands and across the room and out around the hall. The flute burst apart, shattering into tiny shards. A surprising silence echoed.

Then the silence was broken by the crash of Jurtan sagging backward into the shelf of twisted mandolins. He was *exhausted.* His fingers were swelling; in the light from the hall he could see the red and purple colors of developing bruises on the tips. They hurt, too. Jurtan put out a hand to support himself and jerked it back after only the barest touch, wincing at the tenderness. An electric tingling he'd been vaguely aware of was fading, making itself known by its absence. There was also the sharper pain from the flute splinters driven into his fingers and his face around the lips.

Jurtan's catalog of woe was abruptly interrupted by a groan from the doorway. One of the Guard was stirring. Jurtan gritted his teeth, shook a few protruding splinters loose from his hands, and staggered to his feet. Tildy was breathing but seemed deeply unconscious. He eyed her wood club, chewing his lip. The club had been the supporting upright from one of the shelves, not much of a weapon really, but on one end of it was a heavy iron fitting. *Okay,* he thought, *but I sure wish somebody was around to see this.* He knelt and wrapped his hand around the club.

Yeow! It felt like he'd rested his fingers on an active griddle. Jurtan yanked his hand back, then heard another gurgle from the trooper in the door. He forced himself to reach out again, settled the club into the crease of his palm, as far away from his fingertips as he could get, and lifted the shaft of wood into the air.

I can do it, he thought, *really I can.* The soldiers in the door were stirring, but that was about it. Jurtan looked down at them for a moment, set his jaw, and swung the club, then swung it again. He tried to tell himself it actually wasn't that bad the second time.

The door was so battered that Jurtan was able to kick it off its hinges and out into the hall without using his hands for leverage. He spent another minute bashing the remaining dozen troopers in the hall over the head. Then he returned to the instrument closet, gingerly selected a new flute from the crate, and slipped it into his belt.

More than anything else, Jurtan wanted to tear off looking for Kaar himself. His father was not one of the groggy people scattered around on the floor; Kaar was undoubtedly where *he'd* gone, and who knew what kind of trouble he'd gotten himself into. Jurtan figured that if his new-found ability was going to be good for anything, it could at least show Dad he could be useful to have around. Maybe Dad would even accept that you didn't necessarily need to know how to hack people up with a sword to be a productive member of society.

But he couldn't go, not now, not yet. It wasn't just his hands, he could force himself to use them if he had to—in fact, he already had. The problem was something else. It looked like it would be at least ten or fifteen minutes before Tildy and the other former prisoners were back on their feet, and when they woke up they'd still have to deal with the soldiers. That would have been okay, if only Tildy or the prisoners could be relied upon to wake up first, but, of course, they couldn't. Jurtan didn't want to out-and-out kill the troopers and he couldn't use his hands well enough to tie them up, so there was only one alternative. He'd have to wait and keep an eye on things himself. With a sigh, he cleared a space with one foot, settled to the floor, and leaned back against the wall.

Kaar wasn't the only major thing nagging at Jurtan's mind, though. Where was Shaa?

15
BIG TROUBLE

Shaa awoke. The surface upon which he was propped was heaving irregularly; another boat. His hands were manacled together on the other side of a thick post, and the post ran up through the low ceiling of the deck above his head. Frothy water splashed outside the low window to Shaa's right, glowing softly against the night as it fell back. Shaa took stock, glowering in the darkness. His chest hurt when he breathed. Various other locations around his body throbbed. His cloak and all the equipment beneath it were gone.

Laddered steps led steeply downward to the deck from a hatch just forward of Shaa's post. The hatch was suddenly thrown back, introducing the face of a soldier and a hand with a sea-lantern. Shaa scowled up at him. The man grimaced back at him, and said, "Time to say your prayers, spy."

Shaa raised an eyebrow. "Indeed. Where are we going?"

A dark cloud seemed to settle down over the guard's face. "Oskin Yahlei," he muttered, and slammed the hatch.

"Huh," Shaa said. Maybe it was a suburb.

"Uuoaah," said a new voice, rather hoarsely, behind him. Shaa craned his gaze back over his shoulder.

Another man, also manacled, but to an eyebolt at the stern of the chamber, was raising his head gingerly off the deck.

"Good evening," Shaa said.

"Cheerful one, aren't you, eh?" the man said. He groaned again. "Didn't you hear where they're taking us?"

"Indeed. Perhaps I lack the appropriate referents. I take it Oskin Yahlei is a name designed to strike fear into knowledgeable hearts?"

"He's some kind of sorcerer, one of those, eh—what 'cha callum?—works with dead guys?"

"Necromancer?"

"Yeah, that's the one, that's Oskin Yahlei." The man had pulled himself up against the aft wall, his legs sprawled across the floor and his chained arms contorted behind him. In the dim light from the open windows caked blood could be glimpsed all along one side of his face. His clothes were little more than tatters; they had apparently not been much to start with. "I knows the name, I've never met him, not me, not yet, but every day they comes into the cell and picks some guy and takes him out to Oskin Yahlei and the guy never comes—"

"The cell? Which cell? You are not, I take it, a political prisoner?"

"Me, politics? Eh, hah, never touch politics, not me. Whadda you take me for?"

"A thief," Shaa said, "hopefully."

"Nah, not me. Me, I burn down buildings. Why you asking?"

This is not helpful, Shaa thought. "If you were a thief, you could have picked these locks and gotten us out of here."

"Oh. Hey, that's a good idea! Uh . . . you're not a—"

"No." *Yet again the problem of extrication devolves on me*, Shaa thought, *so what else is new.*

"Oh," said the arsonist. "Eh, so like I was telling

you, every day they takes some guy to Oskin Yahlei and we never sees him again. This time it's me, and you, too.''

Raw material for a necromancer, what a delightful conclusion to the day. Let this be a lesson, Shaa thought; the next time early retirement is offered, I should take it. Enough with these crummy adventures.

The slap of the waves changed as the boat pulled up to a pier, the deck rolling more erratically as the hull responded to the reflections of water against the dock pilings. Shaa and his companion were dragged through the hatch and up a series of ladders to the street, and were hurried off, hands still chained, under ever-watchful guard. The men on the boat had handed them over to an escort that had been waiting for them at the dock. This new party was made up of a dozen or so men from the regular militia, and one other man who seemed to be in charge. Under this man's cloak, his jacket bore the same unfamiliar device Shaa had spotted earlier in the day, the purple pretzel; possibly it was the sign of Oskin Yahlei's own personal retainers. As near as Shaa could figure it, they were heading north and west, toward the hills around the north wall.

Shaa's chest still hurt, in a dull deep ache with sharper patches on the surface, and that was starting to worry him. The electric blasts he had taken from the tentacled thing conjured up by that magician might have done him lasting damage. Because of the nature of his curse—one of his curses—Shaa was forced to be especially protective of the structures in his chest; what he needed now was a rest cure, but that was an unattainable luxury. He would have to be very careful, and very lucky, and hope that he didn't have to deal with too much magic in the near future.

The procession turned left onto an empty street that ran parallel to the north wall and just south of it. Through the overgrown shrubbery on a vacant lot, Shaa could see the massive blocks of the city wall. A rundown building came after the empty lot, and then a stone wall crowned with spikes. They approached the tall door in the wall.

The man wearing the sigil of the pretzel rapped on the door. A panel in the top part slid open, another servitor peered out, a few whispered words passed back and forth, and then the door swung heavily inward. A short path led across a narrow courtyard to an ornate stone-front building. The gate behind them closed, and then one of the large double doors to the building ahead of them rotated open, its top lintel at twice Shaa's height. Yet another door, equally as tall, blocked the inner exit of a small entry hall or vestibule.

Once beyond the inner door, the function of the building suddenly became clear. An auditorium opening ahead and to the right, its ceiling stretching the long two stories to the building's roof, had once been the worship-room of a temple. It didn't appear to have been a major temple, as such things went, but the signs of altars and hangings and other similar apparatus were still unmistakably visible as lighter shapes against the soot-worn walls. The place certainly hadn't been a house, especially considering the neighborhood; that area of the city had never been the place people went to build their mansions. The left edge of the auditorium, more of an aisle really, became an actual hallway ahead leading toward the rear of the building. On its left wall were a set of smaller but equally ornate double doors, now closed, but flanked on either side by pretzel-wearing guards. Another half-dozen guards were scattered around the temple. The Yahlei man who had accompanied Shaa's party from the waterfront spoke to the sergeant of the Guard escort. The sergeant did not seem pleased.

"You will *remain* here with the prisoners," the Yahlei man said, his voice rising. "Do you *understand?*"

The sergeant glared back at him, rather sullenly, Shaa thought. He opened his mouth to speak, bit off a word instead, wheeled, and said, "All right, you men, let's go, bring them into the big room."

A sword jabbed Shaa's back. The troop turned right and proceeded to the far wall of the former temple. Against the wall was a shiny new line of iron eyebolts driven into the stone at head-top height. "Chain up the prisoners," the sergeant growled.

From behind them came a sudden collective intake of breath. The double doors at the side of the aisle crashed open, the echoes booming through the large open space into the shocked silence. The party turned, all eyes in the room swiveling toward the doors. A new figure stood there, in a cloak so black it seemed to eat the light, dramatically framed by the lines of the doorway. An active fire in an iron grate behind him etched his shape in a writhing bed of red. The hood of the cloak was thrown back; the left eye was covered by a patch of black leather stark against the pale gray of his face, and his right eye was blue and deep with a hardness like slate.

The figure clasped his hands behind his back as the pretzel man from the waterfront approached and whispered to him in a deferential murmur. Against the intense hush, the only other sound was the soft crackle of the fire. The pretzel man gestured across the room at the Guard troop, then specifically indicated Shaa. The one-eyed gaze of the dark figure focused on Shaa. Shaa grew cold, and felt like his will was flowing out onto the bare floor and back across the temple. It was *not* his imagination, Shaa relized; the dark figure was projecting some leechlike force. The pretzel man, who was perhaps more of a chamberlain, said something else, the figure nodded, and the two of them approached.

The members of the Guard began to sidle unobtrusively away. The chamberlain, who was lagging discreetly behind his boss, snapped out, "Stay where you are! Hold them securely!" Then the dark figure put his arm out, palm down, and the chamberlain shut up with an abrupt rattle in his voice.

The figure spoke. His voice was like the dull clang

of a cold gong. "You are the one called Shaa? Could that be Doctor Shaa? The famous Zalzyn Shaa?"

Acting on instinct, his conscious faculties in collapse as the room swam before his eyes, Shaa said, "Indeed, yes. Have we met?"

Another mass inhalation of breath swept around the room. The chamberlain leaped forward, roughly elbowing a Guard trooper out of the way, and smashed his hand as hard as he could against the side of Shaa's head. Shaa let his head and body rock to the opposite side and back, absorbing the blow but keeping his feet. The pain was still deep and sharp, but served to partially clear his head. The chamberlain drew his hand around for another swipe.

"Forbear," said the figure.

"Yes, master." The chamberlain shrank back, glaring ominously and somewhat petulantly at Shaa.

"Toadies," the figure said to Shaa, in a more conversational tone. "I look for responsible assistants, viceroys, aides, and all I find are toadies."

"Sycophancy is, sadly, a pervasive problem," Shaa agreed, the pall of stupefaction beginning to lift. "I take it you are Oskin Yahlei?"

"Indeed," said the voice, with an explicit shudder of doom.

The man who burned down buildings let out a high shrieking wail, dropped to his knees, paused there, and then fell deliberately over on his face. Oskin Yahlei had turned to watch, displaying a look of some bemusement, Shaa thought. Then he turned back.

"I also take it," Shaa said, with more of his usual sardonic drawl, "that you are really the one running things around here, which things naturally include the activities of Kaar, the Less-Than-Totally-Competent."

"An apt turn of phrase," said Oskin Yahlei.

"Thank you."

The chamberlain could no longer contain himself. He flung himself at Shaa, yelling, "Shut up, you, you and your sniveling mouth, no one talks to Oskin Yahlei in that tone of—OOUP!"

"Please excuse me," Shaa told the suddenly prostrate chamberlain, removing his foot from the man's midsection. He straightened up and gave a pleasant bow in the direction of Oskin Yahlei, restrained somewhat by the pull of the chains around his arms. "My apologies, Mr. Yahlei. Toadies, as you said."

Oskin Yahlei again clasped his hands behind his back. "I have heard reports of your activities in the past. Perhaps these accounts were in error. Are you merely a jester, sporting with the good will of those more powerful than yourself?"

"I think of it, rather, as a question of attitude," Shaa said. "Ultimately, if one dies, one dies; if one lives, one lives. If one lives, one must adopt a certain attitude toward things. I prefer that which you see."

Oskin Yahlei eyed Shaa. "I can see that you have the potential of being quite insufferable to have around. Still, if word of mouth is accurate, you have your uses, and your capabilities. This unfortunate affair at Kaar's palace, which I will most likely have to handle myself, is it all your fault?"

"I wouldn't go quite that far," Shaa said. "Yet, in all honesty, I must claim some responsibility." The fact that Oskin Yahlei hadn't rushed right off to the palace to manage things raised a couple of possibilities in Shaa's mind. Either things weren't that serious there, or were indeed already under control, or Oskin Yahlei didn't care that much what happened to his puppet, Kaar. If that was the case, he might have decided that Kaar had already served his purpose. Perhaps Yahlei felt it was time for him to take charge of Roosing Oolvaya in a more personal and visible form. On the other hand, he might have other, more substantial problems to worry about at the moment.

"Hmm," said Oskin Yahlei musingly. "Then you couldn't have been the one at Lake's." He stared up at the ceiling. Indeed, this was a man with a lot on his mind, Shaa thought, and one with his own set of complexities. Shaa was willing to bet he wasn't a simple necromancer, but what else could he be? He radiated like a god, but he certainly didn't project the personality of one; gods were usually more decisive, more forceful, more impressed with their own attitude of arrogant superiority. And who was Lake? As usual, Shaa thought sardonically, it looks like I've wandered into somebody else's ongoing plot. Oskin Yahlei looked back down. "Why are you here, Shaa? What interested you in Roosing Oolvaya, at this moment, at this particular stage of events?"

"I'm here in Roosing Oolvaya because I had to leave Drest Klaaver in some haste and decided to head east," Shaa said. "I am standing here with you largely because of a curse and my own unfortunately theatrical personality."

"What chance has there been of . . . manipulation?"

Shaa had been asking himself the same question. There had been no particular reason for a coup in Drest Klaaver at that specific time. Some of his luck, one way or the other, could also have been stage-managed. "I try to resist the concept of predestination," he said. "Still, like everyone else, I'm always open to the possibility, though I'm sure you know how difficult it is to tell."

"Quite so. Do you have companions?"

"I do indeed. Which ones are around at the moment is, I regret, something you will have to find out for yourself."

"Be still," Oskin Yahlei said to his suddenly restive troops. The members of the Guard escort who were in Shaa's line of sight had the expressions of those making longer and longer lists of other things they had to do and other places they had to be. "He is mine to deal with as I wish."

Oskin Yahlei stretched out his arm, pointing at Shaa with a middle finger that bore a gold ring alive with tiny lights and dark vortices of force, the full emotive power that had first hit Shaa from across the room again building. "Shaa!" he thundered. "My patience ebbs! I will grant you a choice! You know this choice! You will join me, or face a terrible doom!"

So he needs a quick ally, eh? Shaa thought weakly under the renewed onslaught. "Whether I've got friends around at the moment or not," he said aloud, his voice less rickety than the rest of him felt, and loaded in fact with his most ominous air of serious menace, "if I get hit with that terrible a doom they'll come after you. For every one you inflict on me, you will receive back ten. A terrible doom for me will yield you a ruin of such appalling devastation as to pale the sane imagination." How's *that*, buster? he thought.

Their eyes were locked, Shaa's two with Oskin Yahlei's crushing one. Oskin Yahlei moved his out-stretched arm around to the side, aiming it now at the man who burned down buildings, who was still quiver-ing on the floor. "See the merest hint of your doom," Oskin Yahlei said.

The man on the floor froze in mid-quiver; it was as if he had been set upon by a taxidermist between one breath and the next. A black gauze seemed to flow over his body. Then—

From the gate in the wall outside came a sudden pounding, a hollow rolling boom. Oskin Yahlei, an expression of extreme irritation on his face, looked up from the arsonist and then down at his prostrate cham-berlain. The chamberlain sprang to his feet and dashed across the auditorium to the outside door. Shaa noted with dim satisfaction that the man was holding his side and running with a lurch, rather than a steady stride. He disappeared through the door, then quickly re-turned, now wringing his hands.

"Oh, master," he said in a low mumble, barely audible to Shaa, "a man outside, with a staff. He demands to see you."

"Someone from Kaar?" said Oskin Yahlei.

"No, he, ah, he says his name is Gasha-something, Gashalarahra, Gashana—"

"Gashanatantra."

"Yes, master, that was it."

Oskin Yahlei lowered his arm, his mouth pursed, his eyebrows raised, lost for a moment in rumination. "So he has come. I will see him," he said thoughtfully. The chamberlain took off again toward the door. Oskin Yahlei started to stride after him, then paused, sparing a glance over his shoulder, first at Shaa and then at the Guard sergeant. "Secure them to the wall," he said to the sergeant. "I will be back." He stalked through the double doors at the side of the hall and vanished from sight. The door to the vestibule swung open again and the chamberlain reappeared, leading a new man, dark-haired and of medium height, several inches shorter than Shaa, wearing a dark-gray leather outfit that looked considerably the worse for recent wear. The man was hefting a polished hardwood walking stick. The chamberlain indicated the double door, the man sauntered through, and the guards at either side swung the doors closed.

Shaa let the soldiers drag him back against the wall and rattle the chains. He was thinking earnestly. That man was Gashanatantra? *The* Gashanatantra? Not Gashanatantra the Devious, surely not the mad plotter himself? But indeed, how many Gashanatantras could there be? And certainly no one in his right mind would knowingly impersonate Gashanatantra, *Gashanatantra*, of all possible entities. If I was looking for yet another doom, Shaa thought, that one would assuredly be quite low on my list. Gods, this was really much more in Max's line. If he were around, he would surely understand what was going on.

They were taking their time in there. Shaa scanned the room. Above the double doors at the far side of the temple, cantilevered out over the aisle and supported at the free edge by three small pillars, was another room with three large open windows overlooking the auditorium space. As Shaa glanced up at it, a shape flickered in back of one of the windows, just at the corner, as if someone had taken a quick peek out at the temple below. A new complicating factor? Well, at this point it probably couldn't hurt.

The temple held nothing else of immediate interest. Under the circumstances, escape looked like a good idea, but with all the guards around and the manacles on his hands now holding him to the wall, simple escape would be difficult. He did have an ace-in-the-hole. Unfortunately, the ace was booby-trapped, courtesy of his ever-popular curse, and with the treatment he'd already received it was liable to leave him in much worse shape than if he merely tried to roll with events. Shaa looked around again, hoping for new inspiration.

"What's that?" one of the Guardsmen said suddenly. A faint shriek, a clatter—a rapid sparking, snapping ts'k-ts'k-ts'k sound—a blinding flash of white light from the windows of the mezzanine room!

"My eyes!" wailed somebody close by. Afterimages began to fade, images returning to their normal colors after the sudden white-for-black and black-for-white, but then from the upper windows came more lights, multicolored lights, expanding spheres like bursting bubbles of orange and blue, another stark lightning flash! The building rattled. A giant groaning sound built, rising out of the very ground, mounting to a roar like an avalanche, like mountains being ripped from the earth. A plane of arctic cold settled down through the room, leaving behind it on the walls sheets of condensing ice. As though surging ponderously into sight from a great depth, *something* began to take shape in the room on the next floor, the force of its vexation slicing through the building like a flayed nerve. The mezzanine windows pulsed red and the wall around them flew apart, the pillars buckled, the roof of the aisle cracked along its length and began to drop toward the floor, and several men around the room were

thrown tumbling by fragments of smashed wall propelled like hurled cudgels by the force of the superheated gas.

Shaa squinted, trying to protect his eyes; all around
the auditorium the guards and troops were crouching,
covering their heads, glancing frantically around. Ripped
beams and fragments of flaming floor dropped in a
sudden rain. From beneath his screwed eyelids, Shaa
unexpectedly caught sight of the shape of a man in the
middle of the falling wreckage, cascading with the
beams and fiery brands, and not just any man, but a
strangely familiar figure. The figure twisted in midair
and landed on one knee in a crouch, shaking its head.
Another massive roar came from the floor above,
from behind the remains of the mezzanine windows,
amplified by the fact that most of the wall that had
muffled it before was no longer there. The figure had
dropped to the floor right next to a cluster of Oskin
Yahlei's troops; they started toward him, drawing their
swords and trying to shield their heads at the same
time. Shaa was still surrounded by the soldiers of the
Guard, several of them now motionless or squirming
on the floor, the others trying desperately to spot a
way out. None of them were paying any attention to
him. He lashed out with a leg. The nearest man ran
into it, folding his knee backward, and lost his grip on
his sword; and guard and sword fell to the floor. Shaa
shoved the guard away, got his foot under the sword,
took aim, and kicked up. The sword arched through
the air. "Max!" he yelled over the din.

The dazed figure had disappeared from sight behind
the five remaining guards and their twirling swords,
although the guards seemed to be having some trouble
actually reaching the spot where he had been. As the
sword flew overhead, an arm suddenly stuck up from
the pile, neatly grabbed the hilt, and converted the
sword's tumbling flight into a smoothly churning downward spiral. Arm and sword disappeared behind the
guards, Shaa heard the high-pitched "whoo-whoo-whoo"

of rapidly spinning metal within the rest of the din, the guards paused in their motions, and then, one-two-three-four-five, all of them seemed to fling and jumble themselves to the floor.

It was indeed, Shaa realized with only the barest surprise (being long accustomed to similar entrances by his friends), Maximillian the Vaguely Disreputable. Max, apparently still in the same motion, was letting the momentum of the sword throw him into a twirling leap over the falling guards, when a giant ball of orange flame materialized in the hole in the wall near the ceiling. The ball roiled, the skeletal beams around it bursting into flame, and then a pair of glowering eyes and a snarling mouth began to appear in red outlines against the licking glare of orange and yellow. The mouth opened. Max, still in midair, started to curl into a ball, hiding his head, when the mouth spoke. A pressure wave of superheated air shot through with slashes of driven flame slammed across the temple. The floor collapsed. All the furnishings in the room, the dead or injured guards, the wall hangings, and the airborne Max blew down with the floor and were gone. Giant stones and flaming timbers flew. The walls splintered and crashed out. The scene spun, and then Shaa discovered himself sprawled in a pile of smoldering rubble, with his wrists scraped raw and his shoulders half-pulled from their sockets. But the manacles on his wrists now ended in loose dangling ends of chain.

The hovering creature outlined by the flames gathered itself, rearing back, beginning a dive toward the gaping hole in the floor, the shockwaves of its unleashed power pulsing through the air like ripples in a pond. The time for reflection was past. Shaa staggered to one knee and raised his arms.

16
THE DEN OF OSKIN YAHLEI

"It is I, Gashanatantra," I said. The eye behind the viewing panel in the gate of Oskin Yahlei's complex blinked, screwed itself shut, then slightly as it opened and fixed itself on me again.

"Ah, who was that?" the lackey said.

"Gashanatantra," I said, affecting a note of testiness.

"Just a moment." The panel slid shut with a rasp. I glanced up the street and then down the street in the other direction. Still no Gash, and the trickle of information in the back of my brain was silent. At the moment it looked like I was on my own.

The gate clanked from the other side and swung away from me. "This way," the lackey said. He was wearing the same insignia I'd seen before, the twisty purple rope braid against a background of flames. I followed him across a small courtyard, through the open door in the front of the stone building I'd examined from the street, and through yet another open door at the other side of an enclosed entry hall. More guys with the purple badge on their clothes closed the doors after us. On my right was a large open room, no doubt the main worship-center of the original temple. A bunch of Oskin Yahlei's troops and a squad of regular Guards spread out around the place were eying me with a collective look of surprise. The regular Guardsmen were holding the two chained prisoners I'd seen them bring into the building awhile before. Maybe the fact that the two guys were still alive and in apparently good shape meant that Oskin Yahlei had shaken off the bloodthirsty mood I'd seen earlier in the evening at Carl's, when he'd sucked that magician down to a mummy. If he had, I wouldn't complain. The lackey was pointing to the wall on my left, where another set of double doors were standing open. I strolled up to them and went through, and the doors were closed behind me.

A fire burned in the far wall, roaring its way out of a massive walk-in grate. Hardwood panels lined the walls and wood of a slightly lighter grain ran in pegs and grooves on the floor. To my left, in the corner of the room, a circular staircase wound upward. Several leather-bound chairs with high backs and fluted arm-rests were grouped around an area rug in front of the fire. Standing in the midst of the chairs with his back to the fire and his arms crossed on his chest was Oskin Yahlei.

"Gashanatantra," he said. His voice had the same chilling boom, but he wasn't trying that trick with the black aura, not yet anyway.

"Oskin Yahlei," I said. I stared at him for a beat, then lifted one eyebrow and moved toward the chairs. He fell back one step as I approached, watched me sink into the most comfortable-looking chair, his mouth slightly open, and then reached behind him to lower himself into another chair across the rug from me. I set the iron-shod tip of the walking stick on the floor between my feet and rested my hands on the handle, the fingers interlaced. Oskin Yahlei and I scrutinized each other.

"At last we meet," he said.

"Indeed," I said.

"Your aura is an aura of power, yet you have not

chosen a very inspiring aspect, if I may be allowed the boldness."

"You may," I said, "for the time being. Later on we shall see."

I wouldn't have believed it if I hadn't seen it myself— Oskin Yahlei swallowed nervously. *Oskin Yahlei*. Maybe my instincts hadn't been totally bonkers after all; maybe Gashanatantra really *was* bigger fry than him. And he thought *I* was Gashanatantra. One of my early mentors had once told me, "When you can't think of anything else to try, go for the most audacious thing in sight. Then don't give up. You wouldn't believe some of the things you can get away with when you're on the move."

In fact, I'd already made it past one of my biggest fears. It had occurred to me that I might walk through the door and find Gash himself sitting there, having a pleasant conversation with Oskin Yahlei.

"So," I continued. "You are trying to set up a little operation for yourself."

"It is as you see. We must all have our little operations."

"So they say," I said. "Yet an operation can be a delicate thing, with many factors to consider. For one thing, there is the question of turf, of setting up one's operation in territory that belongs to another."

"I need no lesson in etiquette from you," Oskin Yahlei said. He was trying to project a note of bravado, but frankly I thought it sounded a bit hollow.

"Perhaps you do," I said, "judging by your situation." For myself, I was trying to make my speech patterns match what I thought Gash's might be like in the present situation. It was turning out not to be as hard as I'd expected, and that worried me. I had a suspicion that the metabolic link thing might be warping my personality, too, by contaminating it with Gash's own. "One must be wary of irritating others," I went on, "unless one is particularly looking for a confrontation."

"This city is free ground. I have irritated no one."

"Have you not? Your ambition is vast, your plots spreading, yet your coverage of details remains faulty and weak. You have no idea who you have antagonized. You," I said, going with my hunch, "you are improvising, without the slightest idea of what you are really doing."

"I owe you no explanations."

"Success is its own best explanation. Unfortunately, even that is not an option in your case. Your position here is becoming very shaky. Jackals gather at your feet—do you not hear them?"

Now the gray of his face went two shades paler. It looked like I was hitting home, but I wasn't even sure what I was talking about. "There is still an explanation," Oskin Yahlei said, "the incompetence of Kaar notwithstanding. A god must have a power base."

"A god."

"Yes. A god. You, Gashanatantra, are certainly a god, but I, Oskin Yahlei, am equally so a god."

I thought the way he put that was pretty interesting, like perhaps he'd only recently stepped up to being a god himself. That was right along the lines of the theory I had been starting to develop. It was time for another part hunch and two parts bluff.

"Indeed," I said. "Yet it is interesting that you should set up your headquarters in such a place, a temple once devoted to *another* god. It is interesting. Indeed, no, *disquieting* may be a better word. To appropriate the fruits of the labors of one of your betters in such a fashion hints of poor taste. Especially so—" (here it came, my next big salvo) "—when done by one such as yourself, one so new to the brotherhood."

Oskin Yahlei frowned. "It is said that those worthy enough to take power are worthy enough to hold power. One holds power as one desires; this is a tenet of the—brotherhood."

I leaned back and crossed my legs. He'd gone for it, at least I thought he had. "Yet do you know who you have aggrieved by the taking of this temple? Power is held by worth, yes, indeed, but also by the sufferance of one's peers. It is never good to seek their wrath."

"Whose temple?" Oskin Yahlei said. "And whose wrath?"

"The temple and the wrath are one and the same. And the bodies in the convenient storage area next door, the cemetery of the temple, that you are even now hoping to use to further your pitiful plans, they are the same as well. They belong to this same someone. They are a reserve of material for such as you, for such as you but not for you, yourself. You are," I said, now really warming to my role, "you are a clever upstart, clever but not wise, not wise with the cunning of years and the knowledge of your place." I tried to put a boom and the roll of dark thunder into my own voice. "You wish to know whose ground this is? Then know you for a certainty that this ground is *mine*."

His jaw dropped, it actually dropped. "But you— but this—"

"Mine. And you use it by my sufferance, a commodity now growing increasingly scarce." I shot a stare at him. Out of the corner of my vision something else caught my attention—the gold ring on the middle finger of his left hand. The black aura that clung to his form like a faint mist still seemed tied to the ring; in fact, now that I looked, Oskin Yahlei seemed to be *wearing* the aura in the same way he was wearing the ring. Wearing it, not making it himself. The ring glinted in the firelight as I started to shift my gaze back away from it. Glinted—wait a minute. That wasn't all. The ring was *moving*. The ring was twisting on Oskin Yahlei's finger, by itself, turning slowly one way, then the other, trying to gradually slide its way up the finger toward its first joint, screwing itself deliberately off his hand.

Oskin Yahlei reached across with his other hand and absentmindedly pushed the ring back down his finger. I raised an eyebrow, and then he suddenly realized where I'd been looking. He closed his good eye, the skin of his face wrinkling around it in a grimace of pain. "The ring," he said.

"Yes, the ring," I said. "Indeed, yes, the ring. Tell me now tales of this ring."

"Why do you toy with me?" Oskin Yahlei said, his eye still closed. "Issue your judgment and let us be done with it."

"I toy with you as it is my pleasure. Tell me of this ring."

He wet his lips. If he was operating out of his depth, like I'd figured, then by pretending to be one of the big boys I'd suspected I might be able to intimidate him into going belly-up. By now I was pretty sure he wasn't really a god, he was just an imposter. He wasn't a god, he was a necromancer, a human necromancer, how competent I didn't know, but he sure wasn't fast enough on his feet to be too hot an operator; he hadn't run his game well enough before, and he was folding too easily now. He'd gotten by so far through bluster and flinging his power around when he knew there wasn't anybody else there who could fight him, and by cowing people into doing his work for him. Well, now I'd managed to intimidate *him*. I'd badgered him into the defensive, and as long as he stayed there it looked like I might get out of this thing in one piece. I might be okay, that is, as long as he didn't force me to prove I was who I said I was.

"This ring," Oskin Yahlei said slowly, "is mine."

"You may wear the ring, but that does not make it yours. And do not tell me it was a birthday present either. I have heard that one before."

He paused again, thinking. I was thinking, too, or I'd have kept the pressure on him. If he wasn't a god, the big question at the moment was where he'd gotten the *power* of a god. It looked to me like the ring was the key. If somebody's power was in their aura, and the black aura that seemed to be the manifestation of Oskin Yahlei's godlike abilities was tied to the ring, then it was only logical to conclude the ring was the source of that power. The problem was, I didn't know anything about the abilities of the ring itself, and only a little about the capabilities of Oskin Yahlei wearing it. Eventually I was going to have to try to take Oskin Yahlei out, me with only Gashan-atantra's crotchety sword and my own wits to fall back on, and I wanted to have a better idea of what I'd have to face.

"The ring passed to me only recently," Oskin Yahlei said reluctantly. "It was part of a deal, and now it is mine. The ring fits only one wearer, its first wearer, and its power becomes the power of the owner. The power of the ring is now my power. I am one to be reckoned with."

"You are not the one to decide that," I said. "You would match my power, *my* power, against the power of a *ring?* Not enough to be a fool, you must have lost your reason as well."

"I meant no provocation. I seek your pardon."

"We will see about that, too, when I have heard the truth. You mention a deal. There is more to this deal than you wish me to suspect. Such a ring is a greater reward than your cunning would deserve. It must have been intended for another, yes?"

"What are you talking about?"

"You know exactly what I'm talking about." At least I hoped he did; *I* still wasn't sure I did. I was still pushing the hunch and the bluff, but as I did, something was starting to click. And then I thought I had it.

Oskin Yahlei mumbled something to himself. Then he said, "I cannot speak of it."

"You mean you do not *wish* to speak of it. You do not wish to speak, because to speak you would have to tell of your treason, your doublecross against the one whose creature you are."

He looked at me, wheels turning in his brain, and then suddenly his face went even whiter and his eye snapped open in shock and sweat burst out on his skin. "You," he said. "It was you all along. You were the one I never saw."

"The ring is not yours," I said in my tone of ruin. "The ring is mine. This is why I know you. That is why I have been here in Roosing Oolvaya, watching you, seeing your plans, learning your failures, assembling your doom." Inside I'd gone cold. I was reacting to him, making things up as I went along, following his hints and his lead, but what I'd stumbled onto had the taste of truth. Even if it wasn't true, at the moment it was enough that Oskin Yahlei believed it. This thing with the ring had been a real god's plot in the first place, and Oskin Yahlei the necromancer had been working for him. He'd been working for him, but he hadn't known the identity of his boss. Whatever the plan had been, the ring was the thing the god was supposed to get out of it, to help him increase his own power no doubt, except Oskin Yahlei had pulled a fast one and kept the ring for himself. That much I felt pretty sure of now. The leap I'd made was in saying that this god Yahlei had been working for was really Gashanatantra.

But it made sense. Yahlei had doublecrossed Gash, and now Gash was using me as his surrogate to track down Yahlei. I was supposed to dispose of Oskin Yahlei, and then Gash would show up and pocket the ring, only I didn't think it would be quite that simple. I couldn't see someone like Gash giving up the chance for a real meaty revenge against an upstart menial like Yahlei. And I didn't think the real Gash was going to be too pleased if he found out I'd gone imposter myself, and that I'd compounded the insult by figuring out what was going on.

Even if I was wrong about Gash's role, it only made things worse. Oskin Yahlei could have been working for somebody else entirely, and Gash had merely stumbled onto the setup himself. In that case, whoever Yahlei had doublecrossed was still out there, and I'd have not one very powerful and very nasty customer to contend with, but two.

The one thing that looked certain was the ring. Whoever was out there, they'd want the ring. Oskin Yahlei had said that the ring would only work for the original wearer, but that was the kind of restriction a smart technician could usually get around; yeah, they'd want the ring, all right. Everybody would want the ring. At the moment, though, Oskin Yahlei had the ring, and I had Oskin Yahlei.

But I didn't want him to panic. If he tried anything at all, anything desperate, the chance that I wouldn't be able to handle it was excellent. I tightened my glare on him. "Yet you still may have your uses," I said. "Your doom is not immutable. I can avert the harsh decree."

"You are still toying with me."

"No. I will give you your chance. You will take it if you have the sense."

"What must I do?"

"What do you think? First, the ring."

He sighed. "Yes. Very well." He grasped the arms of his chair and rose reluctantly to his feet. "Will you have me just yank it off, or will you allow us more prudent precautions?"

"Since we are at our leisure here, precautions are a reasonable step. Make no rash assumptions, though—remember that I know your perfidy. You are on parole, and I will be vigilant."

Oskin Yahlei looked at me, his expression of sudden hope shadowed by the cast of fear. He gave a stiff nod. "My workroom is up the stairs."

I rose from my own chair, taking the grip of the walking stick in my right hand. Oskin Yahlei moved ahead of me toward the circular staircase in the corner of the room. I took a breath and followed him.

My foot was on the first riser and I was beginning to allow myself tentative congratulations for actually pulling this thing off when the skin under my collar began to squirm. Faintly, very faintly, I caught the hint of a larger, different space being perceived through other senses than my own. A new awareness stirred in the back of my mind. I'd had a feeling a little like this once in a jungle, when something that had been watching me had looked away, and then had suddenly turned in my direction again. Maybe my senses were sharper now than they'd been earlier in the day or maybe I'd just been expecting this; either way, I'd been afraid of this. I didn't know how great my chance was of explaining to Gash why I was running around impersonating him, let alone telling him what I'd found out, but I wouldn't have bet more than an ool on me, myself. I'd been hoping I wouldn't have to find out. Unfortunately, all of a sudden it looked like I wouldn't have the luxury of the choice. The presence hovered there in the back of my mind, watching, listening, waiting. The bit of awareness that was trickling through reeked of surprise. It couldn't believe what it was sensing. It couldn't believe what I was up to.

The wheel had just advanced, and I had the unpleasant feeling I knew who was rolling under the tread. I may have had Oskin Yahlei, but now it looked like Gashanatantra had me. The handle of the walking stick started to vibrate in my hand.

My body was still mine, but who knew how long that would last; I thought I was already feeling some resistance in my limbs. I hurried my next steps on the stairs. Oskin Yahlei was almost a half-turn above me, approaching the exit to the room on the next story. "You wanted me to get him, well, I'm getting him," I muttered desperately to myself.

"Do you have any idea of the full power of this ring?" Oskin Yahlei said.

I mumbled something in response. Oskin Yahlei paused and turned on the steps, but by the time he could see me I had managed to put on a stern face, and the walking stick yanking my arm in a spasmodic dance was on the other side of my body from him. He

stared down at me, I stared up at him, and then he
turned back and headed up. I went after him. I was
five or six steps behind when the sword decided to
flame on.

The fact that I'd thought Gash might try to talk
directly to the sword didn't help me at all. Sparks
spraying on the risers as the sword condensed out of
its cloud, the sword whipped my arm up and around
and threw me forward in a lurch; I would have dropped
the sword, but my fingers were locked in a rictus
around the hilt. Oskin Yahlei's head was already
through the entrance in the ceiling, his hand ahead of
him on the railing, not nearly far enough ahead of me
to get out of the way. His head started to spin and
incline downward in my direction as he heard the
sudden whine of the sword, and then my shoulder
went into the back of his knee. The sword cut through
his arm and into his side with a spray of shooting fire,
like hot metal being beaten on a forge, and Oskin
Yahlei began to fold toward the floor. His head snapped
hard against the solid wood railing, flipping him over,
and the sword pulled free with a wet slurp.

Something flashed against the corner of my vision
just overhead, making a quick *szoop/sproing* sound,
but I was busy with other things. The sword was
moving in again. Oskin Yahlei's body had fallen half
on the floor of the second-story room, half stretched
downward on the stairs, and I was sprawled along the
upper steps across his legs. I got my left hand braced
against my right forearm, trying to drag the sword off
its trajectory and embed it in the floor, but it was no
longer bothering with distractions from the likes of
me. Ahead of my face, I could see Oskin Yahlei's
drooping eyelid, the eye behind lolling low in its socket.
It focused on me as the tip of the sword began to
scrape toward him through the wood of the floor. His
flesh seemed to flow toward the blade in slow liquid
waves.

"You are not Gashanatantra," Oskin Yahlei said.

"No," I said around my clenched teeth, "and you weren't Death, either, so maybe that makes us even."

The ring on his hand was spinning frantically now, a wisp of friction-raised smoke rising from the finger around it, and vague blue figures were forming in the air above us. The black aura was alive with shimmering highlights and eager snapping sparks. In fact, tendrils of aura seemed to have wrapped themselves around the sword blade, pulling it closer. I threw my weight against the sword one last time to force it back. Then all at once, as I had known it would, the sword tore clear of the floor, threw me to the side, and dove deep into the torso of Oskin Yahlei. He made a horrible gurgling sound and went rigid.

"I'm sorry," I started to say, but beyond us in the room was a flash of motion and another unexpected voice yelling over mine, "Don't touch that ring!"

My thought and my action came in the same instant. My thought was, "Gashanatantra! He's here!" My action was plain. I wrapped my hand around the gold ring and yanked it clear of Oskin Yahlei's finger.

17
COUNTERPLOTS AND
AND COUNTERSPELLS

Max had figured something would go wrong and had wondered what it would be, but this was the quickest answer he'd ever been hit with. Blowgun and dart at the ready, he watched Oskin Yahlei's head rise up through the floor at the top of the staircase, taking his aim on the emerging neck. Another rapid footstep sounded behind Yahlei on the stairs. Without warning, the whine of magical energies suddenly released burst up into the workroom. Oskin Yahlei started to spin. A fan of sparks spouted up the stairs toward him like a fountain of pink lightning, arching over his head and out across the room, and a nimbus of flame pulsing with the beat of the whine swung up from behind, cut through his right arm and into his back, and hurled him toward the floor. Max hesitated, then tracked the falling Yahlei downward with the blowgun and puffed. Just as the dart left the barrel, Oskin Yahlei's head caromed off the heavy banister and flipped him to one side; the dart shot through the space where he should have been and embedded itself in a beam.

So that was the way it was going to be. Yahlei's attacker had now appeared through the floor himself, the sword in his hand wearing its power like a blaze of fiery pearls. Max popped the next dart into the blowgun. He was deciding whether to go after Yahlei again or switch to the new complication when it abruptly became apparent that the new guy and his sword were not in agreement on what they were doing. The sword was straining toward Oskin Yahlei, but the man had gotten his left arm braced under it and was trying to force it out of the way and into the floor. Through the rain of sparks, Max could see the muscles standing out on the guy's arm and neck. His teeth were clenched and his face was turning red with blood, but the sword was going to win.

It was one of those lousy over-muscled enchanted swords with half a mind of its own, and all of that mind was bent on drinking blood and devouring flesh. It was going to get it, too, Max thought disgustedly, so good-bye Oskin Yahlei. That wasn't the only good-bye. Max was sure this was just the kind of situation the Death in the ring loved: hacking, pain, destruction. He would be coming awake. As long as the ring stayed on Yahlei's finger, though, he couldn't get out, and with a little luck the confinement spells Max had ready could calm him back to quiescence. Max dropped the blowgun and made a pass with his hand, fluttering his thumb painfully over his wrist. The blue spirals of the first spell took shape over Oskin Yahlei's head.

Yahlei spoke, his voice little more than a wet rattle. "You are not Gashanatantra," Max heard.

The other guy's response was even fainter, but Yahlei was facing away while the guy was pointed straight in Max's direction so the words carried toward him. "No," the man said, "and you weren't Death, either, so maybe that makes us even."

Oh, no, Max thought, not Gashanatantra. Is he around, too? If this guy was tied up with *him*, there was no telling what he might do. In fact, Max realized suddenly, there *was* telling what he might do, the idiot. The sword pulled free from the floor panel that had caught it up and dug deep into Oskin Yahlei. Oskin Yahlei stiffened, the black aura rising off his skin like a hardening shroud. The man leaned forward over him.

Max was on his feet and around the desk, yelling desperately, "Don't touch that ring!", his hands making frenzied passes and the blue confinement framework dropping toward the floor. The guy didn't hesitate. He lurched forward, grabbed Yahlei's finger, seized the ring, and pulled.

The ring came free in his hand. A long yellow filament of lightning jumped from Oskin Yahlei's finger to the ring and squirmed for an instant in the air, smoke curling up from both the finger and the ring. A ripple washed through the black aura, starting at the finger and spreading in a quick expanding circle across the surface of Yahlei's body, as though the aura was shaking itself loose from the skin in an accelerated molt. The blue confinement grid locked into place around Oskin Yahlei. The grid had assumed a lozenge shape formed of small faceted planes, each flat surface circulating with whirlpool whorls, one face now folding outward to encompass the ring; tiny fuzzy marbles glowing with blues and greens separated themselves from the inside surface of the grid and began to bounce around the interior. The matrix closed on the guy's arm.

The man still had the sword in one hand and the ring in the other. Neither object was quiet. A web of silver electricity centered on the ring had enveloped his left hand, illuminating the bones with each coiling flash, and the sword held the other hand tight in its spell as it fed on the flesh of Yahlei. Max ground to a halt and started madly throwing power into the grid, trying to stabilize it, pushing the next spell in the series to release. The reaching appendage of matrix touched the other man's skin. Then—at the circle of contact—a sudden ZZZZ-NAPP!, a powerful on-and-off flash of incendiary blue! A backlash surge quivered across the matrix, caught Max in its force, and threw him away from the stairs into the desk; the edge of the field at the surface of the guy's arm swelled, turned white, and shattered. Tumbling white shards cascaded down.

Max reeled back up and gestured again. What the hell had happened there? He sent a quick probe at the guy, at the guy's aura. The aura was—*huh?* It was *multiplexed.* The man's own aura was overlaid and interwoven with the master wave and a set of locklines and some other stuff he couldn't immediately recognize from the aura of somebody else, from a somebody else he did indeed recognize. So *that's* where Gashanatantra comes into it, Max thought, new possibilities flickering through his mind.

But the end of the matrix field was still open and the black aura was up to something. From a look at the guy's aura, the matrix would never be able to lock together in its strongest configuration, through his skin— the aural lines were too strong. Max hurled a modifier string, hoping the matrix would hold long enough to encase Oskin Yahlei and the ring and the other guy, too. The black aura was a peeling sheath of smoky vellum seen through the surface of the blue lozenge, gathering itself for a move. A new shaft of lightning ripped from Yahlei's finger toward the ring, and then the sheet of aura flowed off his body and down the thunderbolt in a smooth wave. The lightning darkened, the aura drew itself in, condensing and growing more solid as it arched out, and the force of the leading edge of the aura slammed dead center down the bore of the golden ring.

WHOOOOMM!! A blaze of electric white winked out from the ring. The floor shook, things fell off the shelves, even the heavy desk jumped up and hopped a foot back as the light fogged out vision like a sudden thick cloud. Max dimly saw the guy fling out his arms and hurtle backward down the staircase, all the color washed from his body and his front stained boiling white. The sword pulled free from Oskin Yahlei and flew after him, beginning to spin end over end as it left the guy's hand, but the ring held stationary in the air, its spinning glow visible even through the haze of Max's flash-blindness. Max staggered back against the desk, fighting to stay on his feet amid the pounding shock waves. The confinement matrix was in shreds. His second and third order vise-clamp spells were fighting their way toward the ring but were already losing force; they'd never make it on their own.

A black funnel spun out of the other side of the ring. It was the black aura, passing into the ring as a solid tube and fanning into a vortex as it left. Tracers of force leaped from the walls toward the vortex, each giant spark making the cloud pulse red or yellow or green from its interior radiating out, and sending lines of light whipping around the surface like barrel hoops. Max grabbed control of the third confinement spell, fed it a new shot of power from his metabolic reserve, and squeezed. The spell turned a brighter blue and tightened on the ring. The tube of inflowing black began to narrow. Max gritted his teeth and fed again, blue flashed, and a corkscrew kink grew in the tube as the spell dug in further, fragments of black flaking off like spray from an ocean breaker. The vortex was now the height of the room, surrounded by expanding shockspheres bursting like bubbles, silver and orange and blue, but in the midst of it something physical was taking shape. There was little doubt what that was, or rather, who. The form of the trapped Death was coming through.

Max held the confinement field steady and began to concentrate on the link-phrases that would call up his new coupling spell, the one he'd used to fight the eye of Oskin Yahlei with Karlini back at the castle; if he swung out with that kind of hyperenergetic slug, it should be good enough to knock even a Death into a manageable state. The coupling intermediary unfolded itself, a concave burgundy-colored plate with moving tendrils on its back floating in the air over the desk; the plate split into its four smaller replicas, and—

Lightning flashed again in the depths of the roiling cloud. The cloud now filled the room, and in its core was a mounting fire condensing in a roughly human shape. Out of the constant shaking, seemingly out of the earth beneath the temple, an immense moan grew, swelling into thunder. A beam cracked loose from the ceiling, began to pivot down into the vortex, and burst spontaneously into flame. Ice had been congealing on the walls; one roof-hanging icicle growing with incredible speed directly out of the air exploded in a billow of steam. A feeling of dread filled the room.

In the heart of the fire, a Presence began to form.

Max abruptly decided he'd better change tack. He'd never be able to actually get the Death back in the ring, not at this stage, not the way things were going; the only thing he might be able to do was control the damage. The Death was manifesting in an attitude of extreme vexation, a very, very dangerous condition indeed. The coupling spell split again into its swarm of tiny modules and descended toward an ornamental skull on the desk as Max reached out for the quiescence sequence of his programmed spell-chain; maybe that could calm the Death down, help him instantiate normally, instead of—

A fireball pulsed through the vortex, the outer layers of cloud and all the ice on the walls vaporized in a sudden fog of dark steam, pieces of roof hurtled upward into the night, coils of force gathered, and the Presence reached out. Max, caught in the force of the vortex, once again flew through the air, hit the wall, bounced off, hit another wall, and fell to the floor. Something burned on his chest—his amulet! Silver lights were racing across its surface. The tiny sapphires and the few larger stones and the big ruby had come ablaze with color and were blasting twining shafts of energy back out at the vortex. Now, that's interesting, Max thought. And then the Presence noticed him.

Max felt the flail of its attention shift in his direction. This manifestation of the Death had become an essence consumed with frenzied rage and moderated by only the barest trace of sentience. As Max opened his mouth for a last-ditch word of power, the thing lashed out at him with fire. The flame struck the energy shaft from Max's amulet. A crack of massive thunder!—a titanic flash of red!—the flame broke against the field of the amulet and curled off to the sides (like a water wave crashing around the prow of a boat) and the impact of colliding fields smashed Max backward as the wall disintegrated around him. Impossibly, Max was unscathed, well, quite a bit singed actually yet certainly alive; he twisted (now in midair), saw a split-second image of onrushing floor and cowering guards. The floor came up as it spun down to its proper place, and Max collided with it on one foot and fell to the other knee in a crouch. A pile of smoldering wreckage dropped on his back. He shook his head and forced himself back to his feet, fragments of wood panel cascading off him onto the floor. The rubble had also fallen on the Guardsmen he noticed next to him, but true to form they had already spotted him, decided he was someone worthwhile to attack, and were converging on him with their swords. And, also true to form, his own rapier was buried somewhere in the ruin of the upper room.

"Max!" said the voice of Zalzyn Shaa.

Max whipped his gaze up and saw a sword spinning toward him above the heads of the soldiers. He ducked under the lunge of the first man, straightened up with his left shoulder in the guy's stomach, lifting him off his feet and throwing him backward into the man just behind him, jabbed the elbow of his other arm into the breastbone of another soldier behind him on the opposite side, got his left hand on top of the head of a fourth soldier, and used that as a grip to help fling himself into the air. The flying sword slapped into his right hand outstretched above the clamor.

His other hand was still on the head of the soldier he'd used as a vaulting pole. Max pushed off clockwise as he reached the top of his leap and began to descend. His new sword traced a downward spiral path, looping gracefully but with remarkable speed around the lunges and guards and attempted slashes of the troopers, leaving a neat trail of red outlined across their torsos. The troopers fell, Max began another leap over their declining heads in the direction of Shaa's voice, and—

A large fireball burst out of the mezzanine workroom and paused overhead, trailing orange jets like the tail of a comet. Waves of terrible heat slammed out, the beams and the wall and the ceiling around it exploding into flaming ash. Within the blaze of plasma, crude features appeared, a pair of jagged eyes and a savage red mouth. Max whipped his head in and wrapped himself into a ball as the mouth curled into a sneer. The lips parted.

A scorching wind smashed into Max with the force of a lead hammer and drove him into the floor, except the floor itself had already blown through from the pressure and was tumbling into the basement. Something caught at Max's side, debris pelted him and scraped him loose. He plunged again, and just as he opened one eye and got a glance off under his arm (still in his tucked position with his head sunk onto his chest and his arms wrapped around his head) he hit bottom, slid two feet along an embankment, rolled over an edge sharp with jagged stones, and plopped into a steam of steaming water. *Disgusting* water—the blast had broken all the way into the sewer under the temple. Flaming pieces of the temple floor were striking all around, raising a constant fountain of water that vaporized in the hot air. Max got his nose out of the water to breathe, trying to assess his health and collect his thoughts, but then with another massive rumble a new mound of debris appeared overhead, silhouetted against the yellow storm of flames in the building above, the pile of debris (surely an entire wall at least) expanded in his vision and grew huge, and dropped full along the line of the open sewer.

Max's personal protection field had done pretty well for him so far—it couldn't ward off everything, but it did mean he was only bruised and bloody and in moderate pain rather than totally pulped. How it would fare against the equivalent of a major avalanche, though . . . As fast as he could, Max spoke a preconjured word reserved for a significant emergency. Energy drained from his body and slammed into his shield as the rubble descended. The flaming avalanche caught him and threw him into the sewer wall, crushing him into the stones. Then the weight and the force were dragging him down, down beneath the level of the water, down to the bottom of the sewer bed, down into the muck, mashing the air from his lungs, pinning him to the rock without a hope of movement. Dimly, through the rushing in his head, he heard the roar of the Death far above. His awareness began to ebb.

Max tried to concentrate—surely there was still some way out!—but all his mind would focus on was the mess he had left up above. The process of recorporation had gone just about as badly as it could. Instead of having all the Death's personality elements instantiate in concert, the component of wrath and rage had seized control, with all the power of a Death at its disposal. There was no intelligence there now, and the only consciousness was the desire to destroy. Such cases were occasionally mentioned in the texts; the Frozen Dunes covering a hundred square miles on the southern hemisphere continent of Zinartica where a city had once stood were supposedly the result of one of them. The situation was bad, it was very, very bad. They were dealing with a mad god. And the man upstairs on the firing line was Shaa.

Shaa raised his arms. This was exactly the kind of mess he tried to keep himself out of; it would cost him, there was no doubt about that, the only question was how much. Again, the curse, Shaa thought, that damnable curse.

But there was no help for it. That was *Max* down there.

The chains holding him to the wall had come apart but the manacles were still on his wrists. Shaa bent secondaries from the wild energy sheeting out of the temple, established a forcing function with a muttered sentence and a small sweep of his fingers, added the modifier for iron. Field lines formed over him in the air, intensified as they swung past his shoulders, glowing blue-green, and funneled like water through a ruptured dam into the manacles. His skin underneath the manacles stung, and then with a soft tentative cracking, the metal, dropped past freezing into the supercooled, split and fell past him to the pavement, crackling in the night air. It had taken an extra second he could ill afford but hopefully would be worth it; Shaa knew it would be easier to just get the cuffs off than to contain the feedback from the iron interacting with his aura.

The temple in front of him was engulfed in flame, and the street was filled with a rabble of faltering Guardsmen and men wearing purple pretzels. The arsonist who'd been brought in with Shaa sprawled on the ground nearby, hands still manacled behind his back. Through the gaping hole in the wall and past the sheet of fire, Shaa saw a churning mass of hovering flame, now sporting eyes and a ragged mouth and dark reaching talons. Either Oskin Yahlei's true form has been unleashed, thought Shaa, or something very powerful doesn't like him. The patterns of the thing's aura boiled as well with flames of the mind, blistering images rolling in insane torrents, snatches of personality jumbled with memory and intellect, all tangled together in a searing flood.

That meant the thing might react on an instinctual level. Shaa stretched out, carefully shaping the motion of his hand. The aura was rotating madly in the flames, not as any kind of neatly woven matrix but with arching loops and whorls and trailers that shot out to the sides and dangled free in the air, torn dead-end straws from a busted basket. Shaa selected a bristle patch of trailers, nudged them around toward the main mass, felt for their common frequency. With a complicated pass of his other hand, a cigar-shaped cloud of matrix symbols pulsing and rippling in a complex compound beat sprang up around the trailer patch. The cloud and the trailers began to resonate against each other. Coils of dizzy flame spun out from the oscillating surface. Shaa gritted his teeth and pushed, and the trailers and the attached cloud jammed into the main mass of the aura of the thing.

The recoil threw him clear across the street into the wall in front of the opposite house. Even without direct contact he felt the irritant grow, felt the Presence notice it and try to swat it away, and felt a titanic roar as the now-fully resonating field expanded out into the rest of the aura. Shaa pushed himself into the ground at the base of the wall. He felt a blast of heat, the leaves of the tree over his head flared and burned, and the remains of Oskin Yahlei's temple house exploded, sending chunks of flaming wreckage out across the city. He felt a dark roiling shape burst upward, writhe in upon itself, and head for the river.

He'd been lucky. The principle of economy of force had worked. If the Presence, certainly a god gone mad, had been operating on anything higher than a basal level the maneuver would never have worked; creatures with their intelligence intact were usually able to ignore a hotfoot. If that side of his luck held, the thing wouldn't remember who Shaa was when it calmed down.

On the other hand, his breathing was labored, much too labored, and the pain in his chest had the force of the weight of an elephant behind it. He coughed, and noted a fine spray of pink froth. A hand helped him to his feet.

"Wow, man, that was really something," said the man who burned down buildings with a note of professional respect.

Shaa shook off the hand and took a staggering step toward the temple. The heat singed him even from across the street. The sound of the fire matched the roaring in Shaa's own head. "I have a friend down there," he said.

The surface of the rubble heaved in the flames and settled further. "Hey, man, I'm an expert," said the arsonist, "listen to me. There ain't nobody in there no more. This is something I know."

"You don't know my friend," Shaa said. He tried to raise his arm, got his hand to the level of his chin. The arm was much heavier than it should be, and the crushing pain in his chest had moved up to include the shoulder. A fire retardant field, that's what I need first, he thought. He tried the first step, the equation for a fire-relevancy matrix. The breath froze in his chest. He fell backward into the grip of the arsonist.

"You don't look so hot," the man said. "All white and gooey."

"Let me down," Shaa said. It was worse than he had thought. It had gone beyond congestive heart failure this time. His use of magic, tied by his curse into his general metabolism and his cardiovascular system, was giving him a full-fledged heart attack.

It looked like I'd really, finally blown it. I yanked off the ring, and with a shock like knives driving straight through my skin the thing seemed to weld itself to my fingertips. The sword Monoch had my right hand and now the ring had my left, and a magical firefight like I'd never seen was breaking out directly in front of my nose. I couldn't follow it, things happened that quickly. Lights exploded, winds blew back and forth; the black aura got up off Oskin Yahlei like its own living creature, fighting its way through the strange blue cages that dropped around it, and then the blue cage was after *me*, too, flowing over my hand holding the ring. *Hello, Gash,* I thought, *are you there?*

I didn't get an answer and the sword didn't want to help either; it was too busy gorging itself on Oskin Yahlei. But then the blue cage closed on my wrist with an electric shock down to my bones, stopped by itself, and suddenly fell apart. The man who'd startled me into thinking he was Gash fell back, rallied himself, and launched another attack. I didn't take it personally, in fact I was glad of the attention; in the few seconds that had passed I'd realized a couple of important things. The black aura had been locked to the ring until I'd let it out, and it was going to cause everybody a lot of trouble unless somebody got it back in. Wherever he'd popped up from, that's what this other guy was trying to do. Probably he even knew what was going on. Hopefully I'd survive to talk to him about it, since I had a feeling the aura in the ring was going after me first.

I was trying to fight back myself, but the ring was ignoring me, the sword was ignoring me, and Gash had gone to hide under a rock someplace. Indeed, the only thing that seemed to be noticing me at all was the black aura, which was throwing itself straight through the ring toward my face. Forces tried to tear my fingers loose from the bone. That was when the world turned white, a giant blast WHAAAMED!! into me, the ring ripped loose from my hand leaving pieces of my fingers still attached, and I was tumbled backward down the stairs, trailing a column of acrid white vapor from the front of my body. I hit the banister and spun in the air. Something caught me square across my upper back, something surprisingly soft and yielding, and all of a sudden I was sprawled upside down with my feet waving over my head, tangled in the ripped fabric of one of Oskin Yahlei's overstuffed armchairs. Monoch made a cartwheel across my vision, clanged against the stone flue of the fireplace, and dropped somewhere behind my head.

I struggled to my feet, having to fall to the floor first to manage it. Helices and flaming balls and the sharp flashes of released energies were still rolling down from the top of the staircase. I was aware of the blood flowing down my left hand and the fiery mass of bruises along my front, but I wasn't going to let a little pain stop me now. The man fighting upstairs was my big hope for getting loose from Gashanatantra. If I was going to get him to do that, though, the thing he had to do first was deal with the aura I'd set loose from the ring. I grabbed up the sword Monoch with my right hand. The sword was more sluggish than usual. It tried to do its turning-my-arm-inside-out number but its heart wasn't in it; all it really wanted to do now was lay around and digest. "Shut up and cooperate," I growled at it, and I was just starting toward the stairs when the wall into the temple and that side of the ceiling fell in.

I dove to the floor and covered my head as the rest of the ceiling burst into flame from above. It occurred to me, irrelevantly under the circumstances, that the din of destruction was very faint in my ears; I wondered if one of the close blasts had blown out my eardrums. A rain of debris was falling into the temple. In the middle of it I spotted the magician from the room upstairs. He was now on the temple floor and in the process of cutting down a group of soldiers with a sword. Again I got my feet under me, favoring my hand and body, and lurched across the heaving floor toward the temple. I took two steps, a third, and then the sword abruptly leaped out to the side and jerked me toward the circular staircase. "What are you—" I yelled, but as I started to yank Monoch back my eyes ran along the line of the pointing blade and fell on the thing smoldering at the bottom of the steps, trailing a dying funnel of green magic. It was the ring.

The floor under my feet was pitching madly, and whole sections were ripping free and disappearing somewhere below. "Okay," I said to Monoch, "there's the ring. What am I supposed to do with it?"

It suddenly occurred to me that if the ring didn't actually come into contact with my flesh I probably wouldn't set it off. One of the armchairs had slid across the floor into reach and was caught up against a dangling beam torn loose from the ceiling. I gingerly grabbed a torn piece of fabric with my left hand, gritting my teeth at the raw scraping on my torn fingers, parted the remaining threads, leaped a widening chasm, and landed at the base of the stairs. Dropping the satin cloth over the ring, I held my breath, and picked the satin-wrapped ring back up.

The ring was warm and mobile in the cloth but showed no inclination to attack. I tied a quick rough knot and eased the bundle into my pocket, then turned back to the temple.

In the brief moment it had taken me to snatch up the ring, almost the entire temple floor and large sections of the walls had disappeared, and the fractures in the floor had spread almost to my feet. The magician in the temple was gone, as were the guards he had been fighting, and what seemed like half the remaining structure of the temple was cascading after them into the basement. A swooping ball of flame dominated the airspace, leaving fire behind it in the air and on the walls and dancing along all the remaining wood I could see. Peals of harsh roaring thunder were echoing through the rush of the flames.

In the smoke and heat it was becoming difficult to breathe, but every exit I could see was blocked by fire. Every possible exit except one—the basement space I could see through the holes in the floor was still dark. It looked like the fire hadn't started to really burst downward yet. I hooked my arm around a protruding bearing beam now stripped clean of its floor panels and swung myself down.

Light from the fires trickled through and I had some glow from the sword Monoch as well, certainly enough to move with. I clambered onto a long canted section of boards that had fallen and landed intact, in their original assembly, and scurried ahead. A good person-height separated my head from the level of the temple floor, but I bent low, trying to balance the need to hurry to escape incineration against the requirement of evading the notice of the flame-thing. The stone floor of the basement had fractured where I could see pieces of it beneath the rubble. The bramble of beams approaching on my left had come alight with spreading fires, so I steered right, dropping to the floor and easing myself under a groaning heap of wall listing over on the other side. My next footstep landed on an apparently solid piece of stone floor, my weight shifted, and the stone gave way. I slid after it. I fell free for a distance equal to my own height and landed up to my hips in a channel of moving water.

Another giant wail exploded from above. I looked up, and was just in time to see the flame-creature burst upward through the roof and arch away into the sky. Over me on all sides was a solid curtain of fire. It was well and truly time to get the hell out, and the sewer I'd fallen into was the best route I'd spotted so far. I hadn't seen a sign of the magician who'd confronted Yahlei, but he had to be down here somewhere, too; hopefully he was not only down here but still alive as well. Just ahead of me sticking out of the water was a large mound of wreckage with small tufts of fire at its top. I moved toward it.

18
REPERCUSSIONS

At last, thought the Lion of the Oolvaan Plain as he bounded up another flight of stairs, leaving behind him yet another trio of guards sinking slowly to the floor, *the blood of dripping swords.* The business had started as a pain in the neck, but now he was into the good part; he hadn't had so much fun since the last time he'd knocked heads in a bar fight on a trade mission to Drest Klaaver. The Lion had come around to the admission that his runt son Jurtan had not done badly. Of course, it had taken the satisfaction of killing or maiming a dozen or two of Kaar's guardsmen to put him in the proper frame of mind, but what else were guardsmen for anyway? And ahead of him now at the top of the stairs was the door to Kaar's private apartments.

Jurtan's father leaped powerfully up the steps, taking them two and three at a time, twirling his nicked and dented sword in absent spirals at his side. He reached the top, landing on both feet with a powerful THUD that shook the short balcony. In front of him was the door. At the other end of the balcony, cowering intelligently against the wall, were four guards. The Lion bared his teeth at them and growled. One of the guards grinned weakly back at him and tossed something across the floor. It was a key—the key to Kaar's door. The Lion's snarl widened. He strode across to the door, kicking the key contemptuously out of the way, planted one booted foot on the floor, and raised the other sole-first. His mighty thews, though slightly stiffened these days through lack of use, nonetheless strained, his whole body contracting forcefully. His foot exploded against the door, and with a giant CRASH-RIIPP!! the lock tore completely loose from the heavy wood panels, part of the stone door frame disappeared in a sudden cloud of gritty dust, and the door smashed open. The Lion sprang after it into the room.

The antechamber was the receiving room of the Venerance. The far wall held a wide expansive window looking west across the river and over the city; the curtains were open. In front of the window was a large desk. At the desk, with his back to the door, gazing out at the city, sat the slight, rather sallow form of Kaar, his head propped on his hands. "It was Oskin Yahlei," Kaar said quietly. "Oskin Yahlei made me do it."

"Then he's dead meat, too," snarled Jurtan's father. "Who the hell is he?"

"I think you're going to be a little late for him."

The Lion looked up, following the direction of Kaar's gaze. With the curfew and the late hour, Roosing Oolvaya was quiet, the dark broken across most of the city only by the glow of the occasional street lamps. Near the north wall the situation was different. A low hill and the surrounding neighborhood stood out in powerful reds, bright as the light of day, in the heat of a fountain of flame twisting high into the air. "That's Yahlei's place down there," Kaar said. "I don't know what he is, not really, but from the way he killed my father and trapped me I know he's just oozing with power. Anybody who could hit him like that—" Kaar nodded out at the scene "—is bound to be even worse."

A ball of fire rolled upward from the tower of

flames and arched out over the city. The ball was leaving a dying trail behind it in swooping, looping curls, and the trail only emphasized its path: toward the river, toward the Palace of the Venerance, toward the Lion and the watching Kaar. The ball swelled in their vision and took on added detail.

"Sorcery, damn it," snapped the Lion. "There's always sorcery. I *hate*—"

"Look," Kaar said, "if it's all the same to you, I'd just as soon you kill me before that thing gets here. I'd rather face a sword."

Jurtan's father scowled down at him. Kaar didn't seem half the oaf he remembered. If he was telling the truth, it sounded like he'd learned something from his experiences. The old Venerance was gone now, and the place still needed somebody in charge. Maybe Kaar wouldn't be a bad choice after all.

On the other hand, he'd kept the Lion penned up in the dungeon for days. The Lion raised his sword.

"That's strange," Kaar said. "It seems to be stopping."

The Lion looked back up. Kaar was right. The ball of flame, now over the river channel between the docks and their position, had bent around in a tight circle low above the surface of the water. It cast a sullen red light across the river swells. The window glass rattled in its frame. A low wind began to rise.

"Look, fellow," said the man who burned down buildings, "you've got to get away from here. This whole neighborhood could go up."

Shaa, lying full-length on the ground with one hand pressed to his chest, his head propped up against the base of a wall, was breathing with difficulty through his open mouth. He opened one eye, looked up at the arsonist, and nodded. He reached up an arm and the arsonist pulled him to his feet. The entrance to an alley was visible just to the west along the street. They began to stumble toward it.

"What's the matter with you, anyway?" the arsonist said.

"We receive the dooms we know," Shaa said testily. His ankles felt boggy.

"What dooms? What are you talking about?"

"When I conjure." Three words, Shaa thought, and I'm out of breath. What a mortifying condition. He started again. "When I conjure, I am afflicted . . . with a backlash. Proportional to the . . . magnitude . . . of the work." He put a hand against the building wall at the entrance to the alley, leaned over, and panted. "Unfortunately," he managed, "that isn't . . . the whole curse."

The arsonist was already almost lost in the shadows deeper in the alley, but Shaa could see him pause and turn his head. "What do you mean, that's not the whole curse?"

"There's a part . . . that involves . . . my sister."

"ZALZYN SHAA!!"

The voice came out of the empty air over the arsonist's head in a powerful hollow echo. The arsonist clapped his arms over his head and fell over into a pile of trash. A flight of pigeons behind Shaa in the street flapped into the air. *Aargh*, Shaa thought. *What timing, what wonderful timing.*

"What is that?" wailed the arsonist.

Shaa sagged to the ground, propping his back up against the corner of the building. "Eden. My sister."

"ZALZYN SHAA!!" A cornice cracked and dropped to the cobblestones, shattering into dust and shards of chunky plaster.

"Uh, thanks for getting us out of there and everything," muttered the man who burned down buildings, struggling to his feet, "but I'm gonna take off now." He broke into a run and vanished down the alley.

"WAS THAT A FRIEND OF YOURS?"

"Purely a matter of . . . circumstance," Shaa gasped. "How's the family?"

"THEY ASK ABOUT YOU," Eden said, *"WHEN*

THEY WANT TO ANNOY ME." A row of windows overhead exploded out in a liquid cloud of twinkling firepoints.

Shaa waited for the crashing and tinkling to settle out against the roar of the spreading fire down the block. He took a deep breath, let it out slowly around the giant hand in his chest. "If you keep this up . . . Roosing Oolvaya may sue you . . . for renovation costs."

"THEY'RE WELCOME TO TRY. BY THE LOOKS OF THINGS, YOU'RE DOING PRETTY WELL IN THAT LINE YOURSELF."

"There's no need . . . to act so implacable. Why not sit down . . . have a drink . . . or a bowl of hot soup . . . or something." In a sudden gust, a flurry of leaves from the street and a cloud of ash blew past Shaa into the alley. "That's curious," Shaa mumbled. The leaves were going in the wrong direction. Things emanate out of the contact point, he thought, they don't blow into it. Then he realized that the gust was not due to Eden, it was a new, different wind starting to come up.

"FEELING RATHER POORLY, AREN'T YOU?"

"You know the curse."

"YES," said Eden, *"I DO INDEED."* The voice thundered along the narrow confined space. Houses on either side of the alley lurched against each other, sending pieces of fractured facade crashing down onto the piles of trash. The wall jerked at Shaa's back and shoved him sprawling into the street. Behind him, the wind was growing into an actual howl.

"That isn't your wind, is it?" Shaa said.

Eden paused. *". . . NO,"* she said, *"IT'S NOT. JUST WHAT IS GOING ON THERE?"*

"A mad god. I think we're about to see . . . what he's going to do next." Shaa took another breath. "Look, Eden, you'd better get on with it . . . if you still want to have a live victim to attack." Linked to the curse that incapacitated Shaa whenever he used magic was an additional kicker. Shaa and his sister were cursed to be enemies, and to mount raids on each other whenever feasible. It wasn't usually feasible. Eden could only detect Shaa when Shaa had activated his power for some conjuration, and when she couldn't detect him she generally couldn't attack. On the other hand, that also meant that Eden was able to pounce on Shaa when he was at his weakest. He had never been quite this weak before, either.

It was a fine arrangement for families who liked such things; in the society where they'd grown up, infighting and internecine discord were the glue of basic social interaction. For Eden and Zalzyn Shaa, though, there was one problem. They'd always liked each other.

"CONTACT IS SLIPPING. CRZK GRZZ INTERFERENCE! KNKK ZGRZT TAKE THSTZZ!" What was Eden trying? They had found loopholes before, but the Curse Administrator was very sticky about letting curse-parties get away with anything; he was fairly implacable himself. Lightning crashed in the direction of the river. A seagull screeched overhead, then swooped down out of the darkness and landed next to Shaa. It waddled up to his face and eyed him. Shaa eyed it back. Eden's voice at the contact zone said something completely unintelligible. Then a globule of milky white looped unexpectedly out of the contact-point, dropped toward Shaa, and burst.

"What's that?" Jurtan said suddenly.

"What's *what?*" Tildy said. She dropped her end of the final Guard trooper they were dragging into a storeroom and straightened up. The man's head fell back and thudded onto the stone floor. Jurtan had an arm out, supporting himself against the doorframe, and was staring with a blank look into space. His mouth was sagging.

"It's the music, it was going along kind of hopeful and zingy and then out of nowhere it picks up these low deep shuddery organ chords, oom, oom, oom, oom, ooom, just getting lower and lower and slower and slower. I mean—I mean the music's mostly shaking, it's too low to even hear right, more like an earthquake with rhythm than music with notes.

"It feels like something terrible's about to happen."

The sheer level of destruction was the only thing that saved Max. The roaring built in his head as the weight of the collapsed wall ground him into the rock, and the water surged over his face. He tried to move his hand in a gesture of power but the rubble held it pinned in place. Then, suddenly, with an abrupt slurping sound, the water ebbed. Max coughed, a desperate racking cough, sucking dusty air into his lungs against the pressure of the debris on his chest. The impact of the rubble on the sewer had opened a chasm in the facing stones, letting the water and sludge drain away into a cavity in the earth. And not a moment too soon, either. Max's mind began to clear.

Far overhead, he felt a terrible presence lift—the Death was taking off. Shaa must have been able to do something. That would be a great (if temporary) help to Max and the rest of the neighborhood, but implied nothing good about Shaa's own probable state. The Death was still in the vicinity, too—Max could feel him out there somewhere, radiating his mad anger—and somebody was going to have to deal with him. Unless another useful person unexpectedly showed up to take on the job, that somebody was going to have to be Max; at least he'd have to try. Of course, Max had a more immediate problem: the first thing he had to do was get out of the building before he got crushed or fried by the approaching fire. He might be able to blow the rubble off with magic. If he was able to manage that, though, it would drain his already stretched power reserves most of the way to nothing. That was not a very appealing status in which to think about facing a Death.

Wait a minute—Max thought he heard something upstream in the sewer, something that wasn't just the sound of subsiding temple. It might be a Guard—it probably *was* a guard—but he figured even that was worth a try. "Hey!" Max yelled. "Who's out there? Somebody's alive in here!"

Shadows moved through the rubble in the rough shape of a person, thrown toward him by the light of the leaping flames. "What?" Max heard vaguely.

"Get me out of here, you nincompoop!" From the direction of the person, Max saw a sparking spray of different light, the source long and solid—the form of a sword. "You with the sword!"

The wreckage settled with a groan, wiping out the reply. Max wasn't sure, but he thought the man was starting to tear at the rubble. "What?" Max yelled. "Say that again!"

"Were you the guy upstairs?"

"Yes, I was upstairs! Were you the one who ambushed Oskin Yahlei?"

"Yeah," the voice said reluctantly. It was growing stronger. A clatter, a rumble, and the wood shifted further. A beam started to bend itself across Max's right knee.

"Hurry up out there or I'm going to crack a leg!" Max said.

"I'm working as fast as I can."

"No, you're not! Use the sword, idiot."

"The sword?"

"Yeah, the sword, the sword in your hand. A sword like that thing'll slice through solid rock."

"Oh." The light swung wildly, making a full bass whining sound that turned suddenly to the screech of ripping wood.

So the guy didn't know how to use his own sword. Not that surprising, actually, considering the trouble he'd been having with it before. "Come on, already!"

"Let me concentrate, will you? There's fire coming down my neck!"

"Yeah," Max said, "mine, too." A small pile of wood chips stirred just above his head and slid onto his face. Max shook his head, eyes closed, and most of the wood fell off. When he opened his eyes again, a new hole had opened on his left, and in the hole was a hand. "Oh-kay," Max said. "This is more like it. Nice to see you. Just hold up that large beam on your left and I'll try to ease out of here."

"Not so fast," the guy said. "If I let you out, you've gotta help me, too."

"What do you mean, I've got to help you?"

"I'm in big trouble. I've got this problem with Gashanatantra— "

"I don't believe this," Max said. "Don't tell me about your big trouble! Whatever it is, your big trouble is worth about half a thought at the moment after the mess you've started."

"The mess I've—hey, do you want to get out of here or not?"

"Look, idiot, this is all your fault."

"What are you talking about? It was the gods. When gods start meddling around—"

"Don't give me that! The gods are always everybody's convenient excuse for things they've screwed up by themselves."

"Yeah, sure. The only free will I've had lately is whether to cooperate with Gash and maybe die or try to walk out on him and certainly die."

The fire was burning closer, and the beam was settling more firmly on his leg. The help Max was getting from his protection field wasn't going to last indefinitely. Max glared out at the guy, lying full-length along the twisted path he'd cleared, his form silhouetted against the fire and lit from the side by the glow of the whining sword. Max took a breath and forced himself to speak calmly. "You let him out. You know who I'm talking about, the Death in the ring. You let him out. The first thing you're going to do after you get me out is help me get *him* back under control before he pulverizes your city. Then I'll help you with whatever your problem is. Got it?"

"Okay," the guy said quickly, "that's a deal. Let me hold that beam." He reached to his left along Max's leg, got his arm under the wood, and started to strain at it. The pressure lessened. Max had freed his left arm while they were arguing; now he'd managed to squirm it down the narrow passage to grab a handhold against the rocks. He pulled with his left hand and pushed with his right, felt his legs slide, catch, slide, and hold up at the foot.

"One more heave," Max said. The man heaved, a warning rumble sounded from above, Max gave a pull and a twist and a forward scramble, and then he was free of the hole and scraping along past the guy and then out of the guy's passage entirely into the open fiery air. Behind him the debris was visibly settling. Max spun, got the guy by the foot, and yanked. The guy came free with a "Yeow!" and Max shoved him to his feet. Over their heads was a solid curtain of flames.

"This way," the guy said, "down the sewer."

The water level was climbing again, now over Max's ankles. "Downstream," Max said. "Here, look." He scrambled onto the pile of debris. Next to the wall of the sewer the pile was lower, with the flames above them and still off to the left. Favoring his right leg and fending off the wall with his right hand, Max clambered onto the rubble and looked ahead. Fifteen feet farther down, the roof of the sewer resumed, unbroken, with a clear hole underneath it for entrance. Max took a breath and charged. Flame fanned him on the left, wood and stone shifted beneath his feet, and then he was sliding through the hole into the open space of the sewer. The sewer bed was thick with mud and sludge, but only a slowly rising trickle of water was making it past the jam upstream; steam rose from the walls from the heat of the fires overhead. There were, Max was glad to see, no zombies in sight. The tunnel ran a gentle downward course as the north hill sloped down toward river level, and a hundred feet or so farther along was an access cover. Max stopped underneath it.

The guy pulled up next to him. "Who are you?" he said.

"Max," said Max. He looked back up the access shaft, then paused. There was something *else* strange about the guy. He concentrated, closed his eyes, and then suddenly he had it. Max put his hand up and touched one finger to the guy's temple.

"What are you—"

"What is *your* name?" Max said, his voice abruptly hollow and resonant with the Voice of Command.

A shudder ran up the guy's body. He made a gargling sound in his throat. "I—" he said, "I, uh, I—augh!" His head flopped to the side and started to jerk.

"All right, forget it, relax," Max said, dropping the Voice. "There's no time for this anyway. Didn't it ever occur to you that somebody'd slapped you with a spell of namelessness?"

The guy was moving his head around with a dazed look, but his acute distress had faded. "A spell of what?"

"What it sounds like. Hides your name, keeps anybody around you from noticing you don't have one and that they've never asked you about it. Here, push me up this thing."

The guy held out his hand, Max stepped on it, grabbed a handhold overhead, and went up the short flight of rungs cut into the side of the shaft. "What did you just do to me?" the guy said.

"No time," Max said. "We've got to go find my friend Shaa."

"Who's *that*?"

"Zalzyn Shaa, who saved your neck, too, back up there, and who I'm sure is now in very lousy shape as a result, and *then* we've got to take care of the Death you set loose, and we've got to do *that* before *he* gets his act together." Max reached the top of the shaft and put his hand on the cover. The cover was heavy, as usual, but unlike an ordinary cover this one was vibrating, almost shaking in its frame. Dust and a roaring whistle sifted down through the cracks in the wood. The cover drummed against Max's hand as he applied his strength to it.

"I'm gonna need a scorecard before this thing is finished," the guy below was muttering as he followed Max up the ladder. "Look, Max, why don't you just call me, ah, the Creeping Sword, at least for the—"

The cover heaved, wobbled once back and forth, then lifted itself bodily and flew off to the side out of view. A flurry of leaves rushed down over Max's head, and behind them the force of a wind growing toward a howl. Max rolled himself out of the shaft onto the street. Lightning flashed behind him in the direction of the river. In the sudden burst of light, Max could see a mass of churning clouds overhead, forming themselves into a giant wheel-shaped bank centered somewhere toward the wharves. He struggled to his feet against the kick of the wind. The head of the other guy—the Creeping Sword, aargh!—appeared at the exit to the shaft and glanced around. Max leaned into the wind, wrapped his hand around the guy's tunic, and yanked him up to the street.

"You're gonna have to find Shaa yourself!" Max yelled over the wind.

"What about the plan you were just talking about?" the Sword yelled back, coming to his own feet.

"It's out of date, damnit!" A tree branch whipped past and down the street, followed by a tumbling ovoid door. "This is what I was afraid of!" Max had his eyes slitted and one arm out, like a blind man feeling for a handrail; there were purple curlicues around his fingers. The pillar of fire that had been Oskin Yahlei's base was a block or two behind them, just beyond the crest of the hill, the fire being torn into long leaping shreds by the wind. One of the fiery streamers looped toward the ground south of the Yahlei temple. In an explosion of orange sparks, a new coil of flames erupted from someone's roof as the streamer lashed back into the air. Suddenly Max grinned.

"Eden, I love you!" he yelled into the wind.

"What?" said the Creeping Sword, his mouth next to Max's ear.

"It's Shaa!" Max said, "you can't miss him! He's got some kind of beacon on him, someplace in the street near Oskin Yahlei's!"

"Just a second! Where are you going and—"

"Wherever the center of this thing is!" Lightning flashed again; this time it was definitely over the river. Max turned to go.

The Sword caught his shoulder. "If this Shaa guy is such a good friend of yours, why aren't *you* getting him?"

Max spun, struck the man's hand back, then somehow got a full grip with his own hand around the Sword's neck, while using his other hand to force back the man's sword arm. Max lifted him several inches off the ground, and shouted up into his face. "Are you planning to be helpful, or is the only thing you're good at being difficult? You want anything left of your city? You going to tell me *you* can take care of this mess?" Lightning crackled behind Max. The Sword's eyes, drawn past Max toward the lightning, went wide. Max flung him to the side and spun again.

Visible now in the constant flicker of the lightning, spinning slowly in the air midway between the island of the Palace of the Venerance and the wharves, over the major navigable channel of the river, was the ghostly image of a towering castle.

Max ground his teeth, bent over the Sword, pulling him to his feet, and stuck an accusing finger in front of his nose. "You find Shaa and you keep him alive, you hear me? Anything happens to Shaa and you're going to feel like Gashanatantra was your best friend compared to the trouble you're going to have with me!

Wherever you go I'll find you, get the idea?" Without
pausing for a reply, Max turned again and broke into a
run, wobbling in the still-mounting wind, heading east
toward the river.

Shaa, he thought, damnit, *Shaa*. But with the power
reserves in the castle to draw on, the Death might be
unstoppable, that is if the Death managed to get to
them. The only person who might be able to stop the
Death before that was Max (even if Max hadn't done
too well against him back there in the temple). My
best friend against my goddamn sense of civic responsibility, Max thought, and the whole thing probably a
lost cause anyway; so what else is new. A funnel tube
had emerged at the hub of the wheel of cloud, the
lightning dancing up and down its walls, and the funnel was reaching downward toward the river. Max
paused at an intersection, letting a tangle of wooden
crates and a large bush blow past him down the cross
street, then staggered ahead. Just as he reached the
center of the street the wind suddenly howled an even
louder howl. The force hit Max and lifted him off his
feet, flung him ten feet to his right and into the side of
a house, and as he started to slide to the ground the
world abruptly filled with sound, the sound of a vast
hollow clang that rolled on and on like the boom of a
twenty-mile-wide sheet of hanging metal. Karlini had
not exaggerated, Max realized as the waves of sound
pummeled him from above and the ground surging in
resonance pounded him from below, the sky was indeed ringing like a solid metal dome that someone had
just struck with a rod ten miles long. At least, Max
thought, this will make Roosing Oolvaya notice that
something's going on.

The massive gong died away into head-stuffing echoes. Max struggled back to his feet. That removed one
problem, anyway. Max had been trying to decide
whether to expend a chunk of his remaining power in
warning Roosing Oolvaya that it was a reasonable idea
to take cover, but he didn't think there was much he

could add to the much more convincing demonstration of the gong. In fact, it also removed another problem— the problem of how Max was going to stop the castle from coming through. The answer was simple. He was too late, too far out of range, and the emergence cycle was too far gone with its own momentum. It couldn't be stopped. And the castle was materializing smack- dab over the middle of the river.

Screams and cries were erupting all around, with torches being lit and people flinging open windows and other people beginning to run madly into the streets. Max cut around a man wrapped only in a sheet gazing with his mouth open to his chest in the direc- tion of the river and pounded again toward the wharves. The tallest tower of the hanging castle was solidifying dramatically, color and substance filling it like paint spurted on a window from behind. The entire castle had accelerated in its counterclockwise spin and was starting to settle toward the water. Lightning flashed, then a large jagged cluster of it struck high up on another tower, the blue-white energy clinging to the surface and writhing its way down the walls like a madly creeping bramble-bush. A red glow lit the rock foundation of the castle from underneath.

A woman ran past Max in the opposite direction, yelling, "To the roofs! To the roofs!" with a great deal of good sense. In fact, Max suddenly decided, as the whole expanse of the castle curtain wall congealed and the wave of crystallization spread out across the rock, there was no longer a moment to lose. Just ahead of him along the street was a four-story building, shop on the bottom floor and residence areas above, the fourth- floor windows flaring with candles and the light of another torch sparkling on the roof. Straight behind the roofline was the center of the spinning cloudbank alive with the strobe of lightning, and the sinking mass of the castle.

The wind had now begun to ease. Max reached the building, jumped onto a shuttered windowsill, caught hold of a protruding half-timber above his head, and clambered upward toward the roof. It was really amazing, Max reflected, how after a while you stopped paying attention to injuries when things got serious, assuming, of course, that you hadn't actually broken anything critical. He'd started off the evening with a torn-up arm; as events had progressed he'd picked up more burns and fire damage, a mess of deep bruises, a badly strained leg, and maybe even a few cracked ribs and a ripped muscle or two, and yet here he was, still making it straight up the side of a wall. You do what you have to do, he thought, or at least you try.

The streets that had filled with people were now just as suddenly emptying again. Max reached the top of the wall and swung himself out around the eave. Ahead of him at the center of the sharply peaked roof was a small roof deck surrounded by a sturdy wood railing. Although his sword had disappeared somewhere in the jumble of recent events, Max had retained his climbing-cord. He slapped out his knife and snapped in a dart, stretched out his arm, and activated the mechanism on his forearm; the springs *sproinged* softly, the dart arched up along the roof, and with a rapid *woosh-woosh* the dart-end of the cable wrapped itself tightly around the roofdeck railing. Max belayed the cord around his waist and walked it up the slope of the roof.

Three adults in night clothes and a small child occupied the deck, a lantern on the floor and a trapdoor open at their feet, the harsh wind ripping at their garments. Their attention was totally focused on the river fifteen blocks ahead. Through the occasional gaps in the buildings Max could see a flickering violet haze over the sea wall and the wharves; at least somebody had energized the flood defense field. Gaps were showing in the clouds overhead and the lightning in the hub of the wheel was losing force. A last spray of glowing colors filled out a row of crenelations on the spinning castle, the rock at the castle's base (already below Max's eye level) inexorably closed on the surface of the water, a tall breaker splashed froth on the up-stream face, and as the rotation of the castle brought the dripping rock around toward the city, Roosing Oolvaya seemed to draw its breath in one giant collective gasp. Then a massive *SMACK, SMACK-SMACK-SMACK* of swells slapping along the underside of the castle became an even heavier rumble, a smooth mound of water lifted in a ring all around the castle, growing tall, huge, above the castle's rock base, above the curtain wall, above the lower battlements, the top of the mound breaking into churning foam and starting to curl; and with the greatest *THUD!!* and *THUMP!!* and screeching grind of all the castle dug itself into the riverbed and its monster wave rushed ashore in the midst of the wharves.

19
THE CASTLE
OF DEATH

The building began to quiver, the rooftop vibrating up and down underfoot in a stacatto drumming pound that grew louder and stronger with great speed. Max had wrapped his arms around the railing and had taken a firm stance on the floor, anticipating the shaking and not wanting to be distracted from the spectacle if he could help it. If he was going to die, he was going to die, but either way it was going to be quite a show. The wave hit the wharves already traveling faster than the gallop of a seasoned horse, a vast dark form alight with the glow of foam and the trapped reflection of firelight from the city, lifting far above the warehouses, higher than Max's vantage point, higher than anything else in Roosing Oolvaya, eight, nine stories tall, potentially ten or even more. It plowed through the mass of packed ships and straight across the wharves without hesitation, carrying barges and tall-masted river schooners and keelboats and dock pilings together into its thundering wall as if they were all merely sailing into a bank of thick mist. The top of the wave, now racing slightly ahead of the main body, had formed a solid mass of whipping foam cascading forward as a tube. Then the wave's leading edge swept up past the base of the wharves into the line of violet on top of the sea wall.

Roosing Oolvaya's flood barrier had locked into its full-strength configuration as a dense violet web spun like extended fishnets along the riverfront. Suspension cables woven through its matrix bound the web to pilings of a deeper glowing purple that rose up every fifteen feet out of the sea wall, making the whole assembly resemble a suspension bridge slung on its side. The pilings were buttressed from behind by long thick struts driven solidly into the foundation rock; it was a durable and resilient barrier indeed. Of course, the floods it had been designed for generally rose slowly and not in a single crashing surge, and since the highest flood tide ever recorded in Roosing Oolvaya had only reached a level of two stories, the barrier had been extended upward to a generous height of three.

The expanding circle of the wave plowed into the long barrier net ten blocks south of Max and spread immediately north and south from there in a fast rolling tower of exploding spray. Max could feel the power of the secondaries kick in as the web snapped tight against the incredible hurled force of the water. The net stiffened, strained, stretched, bowing backward to try to take up the shock; sections began to yield as the supporting columns ripped free from their underpinnings or simply snapped clear through at the roots; and at a spot twenty blocks south and then another five blocks north the overstressed web parted completely, letting the wave rush clean through the shredded breaches. The tall crest of the wave poured over the top of the barrier as spillage over a dam and rushed ahead into the streets. But the greatest mass of the wave was at its base, and its greatest force as well, and against this the barrier was doing its job—holding back, fending off, retarding the internal phase synchronization, reflecting the resonance of the water back into itself and rearward into the river—so that in the half-second of delay the wave had its bottom cut out from under it and spread out backward, converting the single towering mound of water into a surge that was indeed still tall, still mighty, still crushing, but now more elongated and dampened, with much of its grandest energies spent.

The ground lurched violently as the ground-borne shock waves passed them, jerking the rooftop perch forward and back in a continuous quaking spasm. A building a few blocks in front of Max toppled into its neighbor and both spun together out of sight. Off to the side, other buildings were falling, too, as the boom and crash of the approaching water beat against them. A repeating whoosh-WHOOOM!, whoosh-WHOOOM! sound suddenly explained itself as a manhole cover rocketed into sight at the top of a geyser spout, propelled by the pressure of the bore of water bashing through the sewer under the street. *Whoosh*—the water jetted on through the sewer channel—*WHOOM!*—the next access cover streaked up into the air at the head of another fountain column. Then the ear-filling rolling bellow seemed impossibly to double in force, and the wave burst around the corner in front of him.

Three stories tall and capped by a fierce mound of glimmering foam, its churning face thick with tumbling wood and pieces of rock and (there for an instant and just as quickly gone) the complete hull of a small boat, the wave came roaring down the street. Toward Max—its angry top just below his line of sight—around him—in a sheet of thrown spray thick as a sudden cloudburst—smashing through the building—with a giant creak and hop and stagger that knocked Max back against the railing and spun him to his knees—and miraculously past, flotsam spinning in its wake and the level of the flood water slowly subsiding. Spume made looping patterns in the slack behind the crest.

I charged back up the hill through the howling wind, looking for this Shaa person. Between Gash and Oskin Yahlei and now Max I was wishing I'd picked up something safe and simple when I was a kid, like glassblowing maybe, rather than a sword and a curious

mind. At least Max was gone for the moment, and
Oskin Yahlei seemed gone permanently, and Gash
was keeping quiet wherever *he* was. A big shock
knocked me to the ground with the sound of a giant
bell. I rolled, got up again, rounded a corner, and
found myself down the block from Oskin Yahlei's
flaming temple.

All the Guardsmen who could move had long since
scattered, leaving a few huddled shapes behind them
on the street. Flames had made the leap to a building
on the next block downwind, and to another one a
block or two beyond as well. Fires didn't bother me at
the moment; I figured that that castle dropping into
the river was going to send up a big enough splash to
put out a volcano. I was looking for a beacon, Max
had said. I trotted up the street, glancing around. Just
past the glow of the Yahlei fire I spotted it.

The buildings flanking the alley where I'd stashed
Carl Lake had partially collapsed. I didn't see Carl,
but I did see the body of a man lying on the ground in
the street just across from the alley entrance. The
form was covered by a whitish-yellow glow clinging to its
contours. More of the glow made a half-dome shape
in the air over him, starting at his head and popping
over in a low arch to end just beyond his feet. The
man inside had his eyes closed and was breathing with
some distress through his open mouth. I recognized
him. He was the same guy I'd seen being held prisoner
by Oskin Yahlei's guards when I'd bluffed my own
way through with my imitation of Gashanatantra. "Are
you Shaa?" I said to the man.

One eyelid creaked open, and the eye rolled up and
found me. "Zalzyn Shaa," he confirmed, in a low
voice that merged into a wet cough. "Though only
marginally," he managed to continue, "at your service."

"Your friend Max sent me to find you."

"Ah," Shaa said. "Then help me prop myself
against that wall."

"What about this glowing thing?" I hadn't wanted

to touch it; I'd already had enough to do with magic to last another ten years, especially magic I didn't know anything about.

"Don't worry about the field," he said, "it won't bite you. It was a gift of sorts."

"If you say so," I muttered. I stowed the sword Monoch without complaint on its part, got my better arm under Shaa's back, feeling nothing more than a mild tingling as I slid it through the glowing dome, and dragged him through the mounting tremors in the ground over to the building. When I stood up, the prickling feeling was still there in my arm. Beneath the tingle, though, my hand (which had gotten a lot of punishment in the last few hours) was feeling surprisingly better. "Is this thing some kind of healer?" I said, flexing my grip.

"Unfortunately my system is resistant to curative spells," Shaa said. He sounded a lot better sitting up. "The field seems to be more along the line of an energy transfuser, in addition to its attribute of attracting searchers to the vicinity." He coughed and spit up fluid. "Just what is going on down there where you came from?"

The wind had died away while we were talking. I couldn't see the flying castle from our location, but from the roaring and general pandemonium coming from the direction of the river and drawing closer fast I could make a pretty fair guess. "This big castle popped up over the river and dropped in. I think that's the sound of the wave coming after us now."

"Hmm," said Shaa. "Fortuitously we are on a hill. I assume the mad god summoned this castle?"

"Mad god, Death, yeah, I guess so. That's what Max figured."

"And he proposes to deal with it himself?"

"He did seem to have that idea," I said. "He was pretty testy at the time we met, or I might have been able to talk to him more about it."

"Indeed. I take it you are not actually Gashanatantra?"

"Gash?" Oh, right, he'd seen my entrance at Oskin Yahlei's. "It's a long story."

"I propose we let stories wait until after the wave," Shaa said, and he was right, because sure enough the wave was in the process of showing up. The street rumbled like a herd of giant buffalo were pounding up it, a cloud of spray and mist erupted out of the Yahlei fire and the heart of the fire withered into steam. Fountains of water shot straight up out of the sewer covers, and then around the corner and up the street came the wave itself. It looked like most of its force had already been spent on the lower sections of the city, but it still had enough momentum to spill up the hillside and wash gently over the two of us there at the top, leaving debris scattered behind it on the street. I held Shaa out of the surf as the top of the water tugged at my knees.

"Things must be pretty bad down there," I said.

"What remarkable insight," Shaa muttered. I was about to say something else when I heard a sudden spasm of coughing and splashing behind us in the alley.

"Oh!" I said. "Carl!" The water was ebbing. I dropped Shaa back against the wall and bounded over him. A shape was flopping like a long carp tangled in a mound of debris ten feet into the alley. I splashed through and fished it out. It was indeed Carl Lake.

When Carl had finished coughing up enough water to go back to breathing, he looked up at me. "Thank you," Carl said, "unless you have merely returned to finish your job?"

"I did what I had to do and you know it."

Carl coughed again, glaring up at me. "May I join you?" he said to Shaa.

"It is a long wall," Shaa said.

Carl plopped himself down next to Shaa. "My head is in extreme pain," he said to me in an accusing tone.

"Maybe we're even, then."

"Hmm," said Carl. He looked across the street, at

the wreckage of the temple. What was left of the water on the street was now mostly foam. "The reason for our conflict has passed with the passing of Oskin Yahlei, yes?"

"Yeah," I said, "I guess so. But—"

"I must interrupt," Shaa said. "I regret the necessity of my own inaction when there are important things to do, yet you who are not really Gashanatantra, on the other hand, have no such excuse."

"What?" I said.

Shaa raised one eyebrow. "Primus, for you to pass yourself off as Gashanatantra before Oskin Yahlei, you must have a high level of effective power. Secundus, your quite interesting aura supports this thesis. Tertius and higher, from my reading of the situation you probably had a fair amount to do with that same situation in the first place. You know full well where Max is going and what he will be attempting to do, and you can further figure out that he will need all the help he can get. Now, are you the man of action you appear or merely a worn-down counterfeit?"

"Max told me to stay here with you. He said if anything happened to you, he'd—"

"Your solicitude is warming," Shaa said sarcastically. "I am thankfully in better shape than Max feared; at least I am not acutely dying. Under the circumstances, your friend Carl and I can protect each other, for the time being." Shaa cocked his eyebrow at Carl; Carl nodded. "Protect, that is, considering that with a mad god on the loose Roosing Oolvaya itself may not be here much longer."

I didn't like being a pawn, but on the other hand the situation was what it was; at the moment their plot was more urgent than mine. "All right," I said, "I'm going. But if your friend Max tries to wipe me into the landscape, somebody's gonna pay."

"Don't worry," Shaa said, closing his eyes. "Whatever happens, someone *always* pays."

* * *

The mass of the castle rose sheer from the dark river deep in the heart of the current. Waves still reflected back from shore to shore, ruined wharf-front to castle stone; the waves were still tall but no longer monsters. Ice sheathed the base of the castle, sparkling strokes of flash-frozen spray cast up from the breaking river swells leaving their crisscrossing tendrils far up the walls. The castle shuddered and eased itself a few feet deeper into the muck. A large cake of frost peeled off the north wall and fell back toward the water, the high plumes from the splashes immediately freezing again against the supercooled stone. Each avalanche of tumbling icicles cast its own ghost-light streamers on the towers as it dropped, cold transparent refractions of flickering green and blue, and the crackling of the ice and the pound of the turbulent river and the massive fidgeting of the castle and the cries from the city made a huge rolling groan that rose up into the sky.

The castle had stopped its rotation as it settled into the riverbed. It rested now at a slight angle off the perfectly level, with perhaps a fifteen degree inclination out toward the wharves. Sourceless lights had appeared behind walls and deep within the towers, red and blue and purple, illuminating various details of the castle: backlighting a jagged crenelation here, the curve of a cylindrical spire there, the span of a freeflying arch high up on a downstream pinnacle. As if the mere presence of the castle was not strange enough, part of its structure was still in motion. A small cylindrical tower capped by a peaked tile roof jutted out from the side of another, taller tower, with a vantage point out over the water and down past the curtain wall. Rather than being attached firmly together after the immutable fashion of stone, though, the smaller tower was pivoting against the larger one, swinging back, down, and out to the side, swooping forward at the bottom of its arc to point downward at a dizzyingly acute angle, then barely scraping by the large tower again at the top of its path; rotating back, out, around.

In fact, as Max looked, it became apparent that the rotating tower was even stranger yet. Two windows were visible on the small tower, lit from within, and the light also cast into relief the network of stones on the surface. Once you had accepted the fact that the tower actually was moving, solid stone against solid stone with no sign of a mechanism in evidence, you would expect the lighted windows and the tracery of stone cracks to be moving along with it. Instead, the windows were maintaining their same orientation, upright with respect to the larger tower, one facing directly toward Max and the other mostly edge-on, but the rotation was making the surface of the tower and the window and the stone stretch and flow as the shape inside swept around; it was as though the stone surface was artfully sculpted on a large flexible balloon, and this balloon was faithfully matching the excursions of a rigid framework turning within.

The tallest tower of all sprang out of the central cluster of spires and halls and coiled roofs and shot straight up into the night sky. That tower, if Max remembered correctly, was the one where Karlini had experienced his second visitation, when he had stumbled on the office of the Death and had seen a vision of the Death being attacked. A glowing red smoke-ring surrounded the tower just below its pointed roof. Within the ring, a ball of more intense and churning red was following a slow orbit above the stone. On each pass, it left behind it a crackling red trail that hung in the air and slowly decayed, almost fading to a wisp before the ball of flame came around on its next trip and brought it to life again. The fireball was just sitting there, tracking its way deliberately around, and that was more worrying than almost anything else. It could mean that the Death was getting itself together and quieting down. On the other hand, it could also mean that the Death was gathering its strength for a

supreme gasp of nastiness. Either way, the safe thing
to do was to encapsulate the Death and reason with it
later, but for that to be possible, the thing that had to
be done first was to bleed off the Death's power
reserves. And *that*, Max thought disgustedly to himself, was going to demand proximity.

The flood water had dropped below the two-story
mark and was still falling as it ebbed back toward the
river. A body spun past in a tangle of brush, its staring
face pointed upward. Hopefully the citywide toll was
low. With the warning given by the flamboyant nature
of the manifestation, people should have had time to
get to upper floors. Even so, buildings had collapsed
and other people had undoubtedly been caught in the
streets, not to mention the destruction of the ships and
boats; the result was sure to be grievous if not totally
catastrophic. If the castle stayed where it was, though,
river transit might ultimately be ruined and the economy of the city destroyed. It was certainly time for
Max to get going.

The most feasible route was the water. Leaving the
other occupants of the roof still staring open-mouthed
at the spectacle that surrounded them, Max slid down
his cord toward the water, then balanced himself temporarily against a beam. The ebbing tide was choked
with fractured wood, chairs and assorted small furniture, pots, shrubs, and, yes, here and there a body.
Quite surprisingly, though, Max had managed to retain his backpack, due no doubt to the reinforced
construction of the straps, and in the pack was his
face-mask and breathing tube; most of his water-
resistant outfit had been shredded, but at this stage
that was beside the point. Max fitted the mask into
place, shook loose the cable, eased himself into the
water, pointed himself toward the river, and began a
careful crawl stroke.

He swam with the current. Landmarks were difficult to make out, but the most important landmarks
would be the river and the castle; those would be

difficult to miss. People were beginning to rouse themselves in the buildings around him—relighting lamps,
pulling other people out of the water. Max rounded a
corner. The street ahead of him was covered by mounds
of floating lumber, from pieces the size of matchsticks
all the way up to full structural beams and intact
fragments of floor, twirling and shifting together on
the water. One wall of a building protruded above the
surface, a jagged platform of floor still attached to it
five feet up. Several people had gathered there and
were shining a lantern on the water below. Beyond the
wall and the tangled wood fragments, looming like a
square-edged leviathan with its back barely awash, sat
a riverfront warehouse, pushed off its foundation and
carried as a battering ram through several blocks of
buildings. Max made his way past its crushed front and
along a side wall that was fairly unbroken. Behind the
warehouse, swept clean by its plowing mass, a channel
stretched clear and straight to the river.

The current was more definite here, although the
swells and smaller waves washing back from the river
into the city were becoming more pronounced. Max
swam ahead along the channel. A flickering source of
purple light approached on his right; then, lifted by a
wave, Max saw a crackling shaft of lacy violet about
ten feet long hanging just above the water, rolling
absently with the swells—a piece of the flood barrier
matrix. He passed it with a deliberate distance to
spare. The shredded remains of the rest of the flood barrier web slipped by underneath, then a ragged section
of wharf. Max pulled up, treading water, raised his
head above the surface, and pursed his lips in thought,
for ahead of him in the river, the half-moon rising now
in silhouette beyond it, was the castle of the Death.

The rock groundwork and most of the outer walls
had sunk beneath the water, and, of course, the main
entrance as well. Since the side of the castle facing
Roosing Oolvaya was the one canted over at an angle,
the crenelated top of the curtain wall was only ten feet

above the water level, low enough for the larger waves
to ride completely over it. Max lifted his hand into the
air and tentatively sketched a string of compact characters. He hadn't tried this before, but the principle
was well-founded; there was no reason it shouldn't
work. The characters flowed together, melting and
merging, and wound into an open circlet of soft silver,
a smaller solid disk hanging from it; Max lowered the
circlet over his head, resting it above his brow, and
positioned the solid disk in front of his left eye.

While the disk appeared solid, it was still massless
and immaterial, and so passed smoothly through the
truly solid form of the face-mask that was also in front
of Max's eye. Through the viewing disk the castle
appeared brighter and the water less distinct. The
foundation and the submerged walls were clearly dis-
cernible ahead and below, and at their heart the dark
pool of energy interwoven with the matrix of the rock.
Fine black tendrils ran up through the castle, infiltrat-
ing the walls and internal airspace like nerves or branch-
ing capillaries. The image had the pulse of a heartbeat
rhythm, shifting proportion and perspective amor-
phously with each regular surge: *beat*—the castle went
depth-negative, reversing its dimensions, so that the side
curving toward Max seemed to suddenly embed itself in
space and curve away—*beat*—side and front structures
superimposed themselves, crowding each other in an
irregular mapping—*beat*—shift, change—*beat*—shift,
change. Unfortunately this wasn't the information Max
was looking for, since at the moment he was more
interested in traps, and viewing things from the perspective of the second quantum level was quickly giving him a headache to boot. The near point of the
castle was only fifty yards away, but that was apparently too far for such details as trap nodes. He could
see one area of reasonable detail, though—the red
smoke-ring circling the topmost tower. Through the
quantum lens, the red fireball was a spray of hot
anthropomorphic shapes and mad field lines wound

about with arching helices. Max didn't know whether that meant the Death was calming down or getting ready to run amok, but the image sure didn't look serene. Another thing he was seeking, which he hadn't been able to see either, was the location of Roni and Karlini and the rest.

Max flipped the lens up on its circlet and nosed over into the water. A wave came up behind him, lifting him as he paddled. Would it be high enough? It was. The wave broke against the curtain wall of the castle, but Max was riding it toward its peak; he slipped with the crest between two square crenelation stones, across a small lagoon covering an underwater courtyard, and washed up next to the interior wall facing the yard, just below a window. He pulled himself up on the sill, saw nothing inside, and rolled through.

The floor was awash to ankle-depth but the room was empty. Max crossed it quickly, trying not to splash, positioned his lens again in front of his eye, eased open the door, and peeked out onto a flat landing off a circular staircase. The same sheet of shallow water covered the landing. A deeper pool hooded the descending stairs, large bubbles bursting on its surface. A low orange glow suffused up through the water from some unseen source below. In the dim light, Max's right eye made out the features of stair and stone resting quietly and apparently inert. His left eye could see the scene more distinctly through the lens, but the lens revealed no sign of greater activity. He moved up the stairs.

Through the lens, the stairs rippled and revolved, seeming to suddenly point down when he was still obviously going up, abruptly receding to a distance of miles and then popping back to sit atop his nose. He passed a room on his right; his right eye saw it as a simple sitting chamber but his left added a churning blue disk hanging in the air at neck-level. Additional rooms passed by on the left, the staircase coiled tighter and steepened its pitch, and then the wall opened on

the right into a level corridor. Max took a step toward
the corridor and froze. The corridor was constricting
about thirty feet ahead, drawing together from all four
sides like a soft tube pinched around by fingers; his
left eye saw it and his right eye saw it, too. In the
center of the constriction zone dangled a small kalei-
doscopic vortex. Max spun back to the staircase and
froze again. Something from below was following him
rapidly up the steps.

Max backed warily upward. *Give me a break already*,
he thought, *I don't have time to waste like this; I've got
to find Karlini.* An orange glow spread up the stairs,
strobing with the heartbeat rhythm of the castle. A
distant tremor ran through the floor. Max glanced
around, behind him, down—*DOWN!* He flung himself
back, scrabbling convulsively upward, as a twisted mass
festooned with pincers and shining with a sick orange
glare sprang up *through* the stone floor itself and spun
toward him. Max flung a destabilizer at it, followed by
a barrier disk; the disk folded twice along sudden
orange creases and toppled melting to the floor while
the destabilizer dart degraded into a pile of tiny leaves
that hung fluttering in the air; the orange thing pulsed
again and changed, gaining several long-stalked eyes
with multiple pupils and a set of mobile jaws; and Max
turned and ran full-tilt away from it up the stairs. A
turn and a half above, the staircase ended at a dead-
wall landing. A single doorway opened on the side.

The construct was right behind him, now sporting a
dragging tail and ventral fins. The walls around Max
as seen through the lens were squirming with life, the
veins of black energy in them throbbing with knots of
slipping silver. Half-a-dozen veins had leaped out from
the walls and were embedded in the orange construct,
feeding it silver globs—that gave Max an idea. He
backed through the door, trading maneuvering room
for time while his fingers wove in the air. He had
entered a circular chamber twenty feet across with a
peaked ceiling and several open windows, an observa-

tion turret slapped onto the side of the major tower. The orange creature shot after him, its pincers gnashing, but missed the doorway and plowed into the wall. That didn't stop it; with a grinding growl, a five-foot section of stone wall next to the door exploded into gravel and smoky dust, and the creature pushed its way into the room. The thing's half-dozen eyes turned to face him.

It had been a long time since Max had worked this particular kind of transformation and it was a complicated one to boot, but the technique was coming back. He pumped activation potential into the transmutation bridge. There, he had it! The air curdled behind the creature. A foot-long section of each dancing feeding tube turned gold, then yellow, then gray. The construct paused, three of the eyes whirling to peer around behind it, and the tubes of energy began to stretch and fall toward the floor like wisps of smoke suddenly possessed of solid weight. That was, in fact, close to the truth; Max had gotten them with a solidification bridge that was warping mass into their immaterial matrix structure. Two of the veins cracked in midair and splintered. The creature was waving its pincers around, lights and refractive effects sparkling around them as it zapped off its own wards and counterfields, but the bridges had their contacts firmly bound and with its power rapidly declining the creature couldn't shake them. Its orange color faded toward a translucent yellow. Then the eyes wobbled up to peer at Max and one of the hanging mouths broke into a nasty grin. The construct grabbed at the solidification bands, reversed its own polarity, and *yanked*. A wave of accretion poured along the feeding veins and burst through the construct in a surge of gray.

The statue that had been the construct dropped toward the floor, the snarling mouth lagging in the air for an instant behind it, the whole assembly still gaining mass at an accelerated rate. Max began to lunge around it toward the door. The mass hit the stone floor weighing a ton or more. The floor cracked around it, a giant shudder shook the room as the cracks ran up into the walls, the floor canted abruptly outward, and with a final lurch and rumble, the entire room pulled free from the tower wall and started to fall. The doorway slid up and away just short of Max's fingers. He turned and vaulted across the room, hit the floor and leaped again, sprang headfirst in a clean plunge through the window space opposite the doorway, and arched over in a long swan dive toward the water far below.

20
THE DANCE
OF DEATH

The falling turret entered the water thirty feet to Max's right and a second ahead of him; the splash had barely begun to reach him when he sliced into the river. The blow drove the air from his lungs. He let his momentum carry him deep, felt his ears pop as the pressure wave from the turret radiated past overhead, turned, stroked back to the surface, shook the water out of his eyes, took a deep gasping breath, and looked around. He had shrugged out of his backpack in midair so the impact wouldn't rip his shoulders off; now in the river swells starting to carry him downstream there was no sign of it. A flash caught his attention out of the corner of his vision. Upstream and high in the air, a moving pinpoint slid down against the stars, no, more than a pinpoint, a dot, not a dot at all but a disk, a disk with sprouting lines on both sides, *flapping* lines. Then abruptly the moving dot was a large swooping bird, claws down and open and grasping, painted dim white by the light of the moon, gliding toward Max over the surface of the water. The bird flapped once more, Max raised his arms, the claws swelled, and with a thud to his chest and a lurch in his stomach he was jerked into the air. In two powerful wing thrusts the bird gained altitude and banked toward the castle. The river tilted crazily below. Max looked up instead.

A hood with two bright sparks at about the right place for eyes peered back at him around the neck of the bird. "Fortunate are you waited I around," Haddo said.

Another wing flap, and the bird cleared a battlement with no more than five feet to spare. "Thanks, Haddo, you're a handy guy!" Max yelled up. Haddo had been planning to loiter in the vicinity of Roosing Oolvaya to see what happened there before heading back to the castle. Of course, it had ended up saving him a trip, since the castle had come to him instead. "What's the situation?"

"Karlini, must help. Progressing is evacuation—" Haddo broke off and squawked angrily at the bird. The bird banked sharply right, skimmed a wall, flapped once more, cleared the ridge of a slate roof, and brought its wings up, cupping them underneath; the three of them paused abruptly in midair and then dropped. Below the bird and rushing up at them was the landing field. Ten feet above the field the bird opened its claws; Max, who'd been anticipating this, curled free and rolled down onto the grass. The bird glided across the field, grabbed a bundle of books and other packages wrapped in a net, stuck its left wing in the air and snapped to the right, and passed out of sight just above another wall and a line of chimneys. Max came to his feet and trotted across the field. A man with sacks over both shoulders came out of a door in front of him.

"Oh, good," said the Great Karlini, swinging the sacks to the ground, "you've showed up."

"You can thank Haddo," Max said, "yet another time. Things downstairs in this place are getting pretty hairy; I don't know how long it would have taken me to get up here on my own. What's the situation?"

Karlini began stuffing sacks and loose books into another net. "We'd gotten ready to evacuate like you suggested, so we're almost finished now. This is the end of the stuff from up here, and Wroclaw's got a boat downstairs. Roni and the cook are with him."

A rolling tremor ran through the castle, followed by the rumble of stone collapsing somewhere out of sight. "Yeah," Max said, "and what about you?"

Karlini swallowed and gnawed on his lip. "I still can't leave. Whatever it is that's locked into me hasn't turned itself off."

"I was afraid of that," Max muttered. "The Death may have a manual override on your hook-line, but he's got to be sentient to use it, all of which means we've got to get you loose ourselves, unless, of course, we can think of some way to get the Death calmed down and make him friendly at the same time."

"It does look that way. You have any ideas?"

Max had flipped down his lens and was studying Karlini through it. Karlini's form was suffused with a vague skeleton of wispy black, but unlike the construct Max had just fought, the streamers inside Karlini were self-contained, with no apparent connection to the rest of the castle's energy matrix. "I think there's some resonant effect going between you and the castle," Max said. "Maybe if we can destabilize the castle field we can pry you loose. If we destabilize the field, we may also be able to bleed off energy from the Death, which may make him more tractable if we hit him with something like a confinement shell."

"Okay. How?"

"What did you find out from your probes after I left?"

"Well," Karlini said, "I couldn't get past the defenses on the power reservoir, but I did manage to sneak a tap into the energy transmission system; I think I can run a shunt if we need it. Oh! I also found the castle's jump engine, figured out part of the activation mechanism, too. That thing takes a *lot* of power. Unfortunately, all of these contraptions are embedded in the foundation, and the foundation's under thirty feet of water."

"That's going to be a problem," Max said. "I don't think we have the extra time to set up a dive-bubble, so we'll have to work it remote. The way I see it, we've got to handle these things in unison: we have to get the Death under control, move this castle out of the river, and pry you loose, keeping ourselves alive at the same time." A large shape rose into the air beyond the wall at the end of the field, becoming Haddo and the bird. They glided over the yard, snatched the last net off the ground, and swooped off into the night.

Max and Karlini straightened. "That's it for the airlift," Karlini said, "so I guess that means we have to get to work."

"Right. Where's the tower with our friend the mad god?"

"This way." Karlini took off across the field and through a doorway, Max right behind him. "I know a route that'll get us around the worst of the trouble."

"The god will be pulling a lot of power himself," Max said. "We can bleed off some of that energy to fuel a beat resonance wave and try to overload the stability focus points. The castle will have to feed more power into the stabilizers, and that'll make them stand out against the matrix background; we superimpose a shunt surge on top of the resonance wave, tell it to home in on the stabilization loci, change the beat frequency, and maybe we can blow the stabilizers out. With all that going on the god should be weakened enough for the confinement shell to work."

"Did you bring the ring?" Karlini said, heading up a long flight of stairs. The castle was quieter in this section, and the space-warping effects and perceptual illusions that had hit Max lower down were much less flagrant. A wall rippled and changed texture on the left, but the stairs were stable.

"No, damnit; it disappeared in the mess when the

Death got out. You were wrong, you know—there was only one Death, not two. Just the Death from this castle, and Oskin Yahlei using his power."

"But you don't have the ring."

"I did the best I could. It'll make the confinement more difficult, but I think we can still pull it off. While I'm doing the incarceration, you'll set the jump engines to trigger off a time-decay fuse—"

"Where are we going to send the castle?"

"We don't want to drop it on another populated area; what it's done to Roosing Oolvaya's been enough. I'm sure there isn't enough power around to throw it into space . . . probably the safest place is the middle of the ocean."

"It may be simpler to return it to wherever it started from in the first place," Karlini said, coming out the top of the stairs and charging to the right along a hallway; the ceiling of the hall was shifting between gray stone and a translucent gauzelike substance that glowed bright yellow. "I think that location's programmed into the mechanism."

"Fine," said Max. "You set the jump engine to activate however you want, as long as we have enough time to get out of here first, and while we're getting out I'll deal with your hook-field; the power flux should be low enough by then to be able to shake you loose. Well, what do you think, is it all going to work?"

Karlini paused at the foot of a new circular stair leading up into a tower opening off their current hall and glanced back over his shoulder at Max. "You're the expert in gods, not me. What do *you* think?"

". . . Iffy," Max said. "I don't really understand all the guts of this second-level stuff yet, and we'll be trying some pretty complicated things. I don't know if we'll have enough power to make up for the inexperience."

"Are there any alternatives?"

"I do have one other idea, but I don't even want to try it unless we absolutely have to."

"One of those."

"Yeah," Max said, "it's one of those."

Karlini had cocked his head and closed his eyes, apparently listening to something somewhere else. He opened his eyes, straightened again, and squared his shoulders. "Roni and Wroclaw are pulling away," he said. "This is it, then."

"Right." Max had been sketching in the air, and now another headband with vision-disk settled over Karlini's brow. Through the lenses, they could see giant cables of winding black coming together from all parts of the surrounding structure and funneling upward through the tower walls, coiling around each other to merge as they rose toward the tower's peak and the mad Death. Max dragged an armchair away from an end table in the hall, plopped it down at the base of the stairs, and began making passes over it. One of his coupling intermediary disk formations took shape above the seat cushion.

Static charge crackled—another of the heartbeat change-pulses. The stone walls heaved in a long rippling wave like the snap of a whip; behind them, the hall they'd just used as an entrance folded in on itself ceiling-first in a cloud of billowing dust. "That was our exit!" Karlini yelled over the noise.

"We'll blast through the outside wall and jump if we have to!" Max yelled back.

Karlini's reply was drowned out by another massive rumble. The floor rocked forward, back, then subsided into a low shudder, several degrees of new tilt added onto its previous downhill slant. The armchair had become enveloped in a swarm of darting blue mites as the disc split and split again, and Max could feel its energy beginning to flow through the transformer coupling into his own body. Max leaned in through the tower entry and glanced up; through his lens he could see red waves of pulsatile light spilling down from above, the staircase seeming to writhe and snap like a plucked string. He reached gingerly upward with a passive probe—yes, the mad god was still there, still gathering strength through the black cables, but also apparently still unaware of their presence below. With a muscle-wrenching pass over the chair, he started to formulize the framework for the first confinement shell.

Karlini had one palm pressed flat against the stone of the wall, his teeth clenched in concentration; his other hand was carefully sketching figures in the air. The figures oozed from magenta to silver, losing their separate forms and breaking into small round plates like scales. The scales spun away from Karlini in the shape of a miniature tornado and began to fill in the surface of a large glistening teardrop-shaped glob suspended next to him. A ripple ran through the glob and it started to oscillate, its form sliding from long and thin to short and plump and back again like a pool of hanging quicksilver, its colors reversing figure-for-ground at each pulse; then all at once the glob surged forward and flowed into the wall. Just as it entered the wall the pool fractured into a sudden cloud of smaller droplets. Each droplet darted toward one of the coiling black cables and sank into it, and began to spiral down along the cable toward the heart of the castle. "Are you ready, Max?" Karlini said.

A nestled series of counterrotating meshwork spheres hung over the remains of the chair, apparently forming one continuous surface communicating along twisted shifting bore holes. "Yeah, almost," Max said, "but I'm still a little out of range. I want to get closer."

"Better move it, then; we should see something from the stability points in under a minute . . . what's *that*?"

The sphere-construct had moved ahead of Max and was floating up the stairs to the tower. A rolling blue cloud finished condensing around Max's hand; he made a final pass above the cloud with his other hand and the cloud heaved and took off, trailing a line of knotted blue behind it like a fishing line. The cloud banked

for a quick turn once around Karlini and then dove
straight into his chest. Blue smoke puffed out around
his torso. The blue line had stretched out across the
room, growing wispy and almost invisible against the
stone, but it became distinct again where it terminated
in a solid blue bracelet locked hard around Max's
wrist. "If we have to bail out before I get back down, I
might have to crack you loose by remote," Max yelled
down to Karlini, as he followed the sphere up the
stairs, "and I think we'll have enough going on without having to run a fresh spell-guide, too!"

"Okay!" Karlini said, his voice ringing in along the
blue line. "Be careful!"

"Yeah," Max muttered. His whole body was tingling from the slug of energy he'd absorbed from the
chair; he'd have to use that energy soon or blow it off,
or he'd go unstable himself. Another turn up the stairs,
and the red glow from the top was becoming harsh in
its glare. Black coils of power surged up around him
through the walls. Max stretched out, felt around—
yeah, there was the Death, all right, still orbiting the
tower and sucking in power from the castle. Max
tugged at the confinement sphere, adjusting control
parameters. The sphere broke apart, segment by segment and layer by layer in a quick radial stream, the
fragments shot toward the walls and dove through
them to merge with the black current, and the disas-
sembled pieces shot upward toward the mad Death.

"Here it goes!" came Karlini's voice, and at the
same moment the stairs lurched underfoot. A rending
groan so low in pitch that Max felt rather than heard it
vibrated through the stone. Riding on top of the groan
was a throbbing whine, pulsating out of time and out
of rhythm against the heartbeat pattern of the castle as
a whole. A wave ran up the black energy coils; their
progression speeded up, slowed, reversed, surged forward, stopped, and went into a pattern of quick jerks
back and forth. Max felt out again and snarled—the
Death had gulped up part of his confinement matrix

along with his power feed, but not enough of it for full activation. Max bled power into the confinement framework, trying to force more matrix elements toward the Death along the guide of the black carrier beams. The now stalled current heaved sluggishly. The Death inhaled again, more forcefully, like a man trying to draw in oxygen through a clogged air-line, the current lunged ahead—

Through his control-link with the matrix framework Max felt a CLICK, a SNAP, a swirl of agglomeration! The Death had sucked up the pieces of the matrix! Embedded in the substance of the mad god, spread around him and through him, binding him in coils of constricting power, the confinement spheres were locking together! A trailing barrage of solidification fronts ran up the black feeder tendrils, leaving crystallization in their wake. On the side of the outer sphere a boil rose, swelled, and popped, ejecting the matrix's keel-string. The keel-string shot out and embedded itself deep in the castle stone; the confinement field, still gaining strength, began to constrict; then, all at once, a gout of heat and flame and raw heaving power came bursting through the not-yet-closed interstices in the overlapping matrix spheres, as the Death recognized suddenly that it was being trapped, and was not pleased, no, not pleased at all.

Max threw power, power into the matrix grid, power into the feeder cutoffs, power into the keel-string. The mad god was definitely weaker than an instant before, wilder, disoriented by the gyrations of the castle's internal mechanisms as they tried to compensate for the destabilizing forces beating at it. From his infusion of energy and his level of preparation, Max was stronger than he'd been earlier, back at Oskin Yahlei's, but that didn't mean the Death was weak enough yet to surrender or that Max was strong enough to make him. A section of tower wall half a turn below Max crumbled and fell away. The stairs writhed beneath his feet. Max refused to be distracted by more antics of stairs; he was concentrating instead on using his last power to hold on. It wasn't until the section of circular stair above him whipped flexibly back over his head and wound itself twice around his body that Max caught on, too late, to the fact that the entire tower was folding and writhing, shattering rocks were flying off to the sides, and the tower was sliding off the face of the castle toward the river.

"Not *again*," Max thought, as his stomach knotted with the abrupt downward acceleration. He pulled his left arm loose; then, with a THUD that threw his head straight back into one of the dancing stones above him, the remains of the tower hung up against a lower battlement and began to rotate outward, the tower toppling over onto its side; and then, with a *THOOMP!* like the tail of a mile-long beaver slapping a pond, the tower sank flat and full-length into the river.

Max's thoughts were gooey and his lungs (the air blown out of them by the impact) were filling with water, his head throbbed with waves of agony, but the one principle he had programmed down to the depths of his personality was Do Not Die Until You're Ready! He made the pain goad him. He slid, he clawed, he wrenched, he shoved, he pulverized a stone slab with the last gasp of his transfused power. He fended off another section of wall tumbling more slowly toward the riverbed, and at last there was nothing above him but water, but there seemed to be an awful lot of water and no surface he could find. . . .

Then something had him by the shirt, a hand, pulling him upward—air!—and over a low gunwale of raw wood onto a pile of rope in some kind of small boat. Max retched up water and desperately sucked in air, his eyes still closed and his mind sloshing in the bottom of his skull like melted gelatin. "Roni?" he croaked.

"What are you talking about?" It wasn't Roni's voice, it wasn't even the voice of a woman, but it was familiar. Max's mind staggered up and began to put itself in gear. "I'm—"

"The Creeping Sword," Max gasped, coughing over the side.

"Yeah, right, I found your friend Shaa, he's safe back in the city, and—"

Max spit once more, then turned to gaze upward, still drawing in loud gulps of air through his open mouth but now making himself take notice of the scene above, forcing himself not to close his eyes under the pain. The tower had taken a wide section of lower wall with it as it fell; smoke and vapor hung behind in the sky. A spray of multicolored curlicues and shooting fireworks was erupting out from the high gash where the tower had been attached, casting bursts of sharp light through the billowing clouds of dust; hopefully that meant Karlini was alive and still working in the rubble. Above the castle and winding through the spires, a compact red sun swooped and darted in swift arcs like a tailless kite bound down by the keel-line. Pieces of stone flowed like putty toward it as it passed; in fact, the castle's entire upper works had begun to sag and melt. The castle's heartbeat rhythm of pulsing change was visibly accelerating. One of the rotating towers detached itself and slid toward the water, then abruptly changed its mind and tumbled upward into the sky. The red fireball swept down again toward the river, close enough for Max to make a quick check on the confinement field. It was holding most of the way around, but the last critical tie-points were starting to decay. "What a mess," Max muttered across a thick tongue. "If I only had that damned ring I could—"

"What ring?" said the Creeping Sword, suddenly hearing Max through his own running commentary and interrupting himself in mid-remark. "You mean Oskin Yahlei's ring? I've got it."

Max whirled his head. It was a mistake. It almost made him pass out, but— "You *WHAT?*"

"Yeah, I've got it here, I spotted it—"

"Where is it? Quick! Give it to—no, wait a minute, yeah—you hold it."

"What are—"

"Shut up and hold still, you've just gone from contingency plan to center stage."

"Now wait a second—"

"Look up there and then give me another cute remark," Max snapped. He was gesturing furiously with both hands, digging down past the bottom of his energy store, the corner of his lower lip clenched intently between his teeth. A blue coupling-disk formed itself reluctantly in front of the Creeping Sword's chest. The disk wobbled, and the concave surface facing the Sword turned yellow and purple in a checkerboard pattern. In the maze of fine structures on the back of the disk, new connections were growing.

Something large landed near them in the water, splattering molten gravel around the boat. The Creeping Sword opened his mouth.

"You wanted to be clear of Gashanatantra, didn't you?" Max snarled. "Well, this may do it." The disk sank onto the Sword's chest, delicate tendrils reaching out from it into his body. "I'm going to try to couple Gashanatantra's power through his link to you into the containment field in the ring. Get out the ring and hold it up, and keep that sword under control."

The walking stick that was the Sword's sword in disguise had started to whine. "Shut up," the Sword muttered at it, fumbling at his belt.

A pillar of harsh red shot out of the fireball and across the sky in a focused beam; one apex of the confinement matrix was going sour. The disk on the Creeping Sword's chest burst into sudden blue life with a vibrant hum. The Sword choked back a "Yeaow!" and held up the ring. An array of lenses and hovering silver meshwork herders had emerged from the disk and were passing through each other, jockeying for position. Max growled at them.

In the red glare that illuminated the castle and the

river and threw highlights across the city waterfront and the Palace of the Venerance, something else was forming—a bank of clouds, emanating from a point directly over the castle and blowing out radially, and starting a clockwise spin. A pinwheel of silver electricity spiraled out from behind a battlement and arched out toward the water. "Here we go," Max said, making a last gesture and folding his fingers together tip-first to let them writhe under his palm. A whiff of dust shot out of the back of his hand and curled toward the chest of the Creeping Sword. The dust spun into the coupling-disk.

The disk flashed lightning-blue and seemed to lengthen itself backward into the Sword's chest cavity, through it, *behind* it, elongating into a tunnel, stretching off in a zigzagging warp. The Creeping Sword looked down, an unsettled expression on his face, and started to say, "I don't think Gash likes—" when with a loud *WHOOOEEERLL!* something appeared in the far distance of the tunnel and hurtled back out toward them, a form of *solid* royal blue so sharp it burned the eyes. It bashed out through the disk in a thick rippling column, constricted itself into a point, and leaped toward the ring. The ring burst out in a hot burning gold as the blue column sliced down its bore and looped into the sky. Fifty feet above the river it disappeared against the night black.

Max watched the careening red fireball through slitted eyes. One second, two—where *was* that thing? It wasn't working! Forget it now, they were all doomed, and—

A round spot of blue appeared on the side of the fireball. The grid of the confinement field stood out suddenly like a glyph writ in lightning, blue lightning. The blue spot pulsed and flowed out, the ball flashed with competing forces—*WHOOOM!*—silver-white with the blinding impact of an exploding sun washed the scene with glare. The world broke into two colors— the upper face of the castle and the near face of the Palace and the wave peaks radiated a smoking flaring

silver, and the shadows and hollows behind cast the
dead black of the abyss. Waves of thunder rolled.
Then—

The air was suddenly still. The thunder faded to
mere echoes returning from the hills, the glare eased
to afterimages. Near at hand, Max heard a low sucking, slurping sound—*SLOIAYERRRULLP!*—against
the dying booms of the thunder. The space inside the
ring flashed once, red running to blue, and the colors
spun out and fell against the surface of the metal. A
nimbus of ghostly blue wafted through the ring and
dissolved slowly in the air. "Well?" said the Creeping
Sword.

"Let's put it this way," Max said. He was having
trouble putting words together, and his vision was
refusing to clear. "Don't try—don't try to wear that
ring or, or we're going to have to go through all of this
another time."

"Then you did what you were trying to do?"

"Yeah, we got lucky."

"What about Gash?"

"I don't know, don't know." The wind was coming
up again; a sheet of water blew off the crest of a river
swell and sloshed into the boat. "Now gotta get Karlini."
Overhead, the wheel of clouds was thickening. The
upper works of the castle glowed a sullen molten red,
drooping and smoldering in strange liquid forms. Max
felt out along the spell-guide. "Karlini! Karlini, you
there?"

"Max?" The sound of Karlini's voice was distant
and weak. "Glad you're back—the castle's almost ready
to go."

Max's vision was not clearing, it was getting worse,
it was closing in from the sides in a dark band. The
throb in his head filled the air. The voice of the
Creeping Sword sounded as far away as Karlini's. "Max?
Max!"

*   *   *

He was wobbling in the stern of the rowboat, looking up at the castle and talking to somebody who wasn't there, his left arm half-raised and his right knee slowly folding, and then he just settled to one side, fell over on the rope piled in the bilge, and came to rest with his head hanging out over the gunwale. He'd bled off so much weight since I'd seen him earlier that he looked like a victim of sudden starvation—his clothes were dangling on him like sheets—and the parts of him exposed to the air seemed pretty well bashed in under the nasty red glow from the castle. "Max?" I said again, but he was out. And he'd left me holding the bag.

Gash was still back there somewhere. I could feel him, but Max's little trick had taken him by surprise; he was weakened, too, so I didn't think I had to worry about him for a while. The real problem now wasn't Gash, it was Max. He'd given me a pretty rough time, treating me the way I don't let anybody treat me, using me as a convenient tool for his own schemes, not seeming to care whether he killed me in the process. And the process *had* hurt—my chest where he'd slapped his blue whatever-it-was spell felt like the riverfront of Roosing Oolvaya looked. Not only that, it had hurt Gash, too, and I'd felt that at secondhand back through the metabolic link; I'd really gotten it coming and going. I wasn't sure how I was able to be on my own feet myself, but I was, and I had to make some quick decisions because I was the one on the spot.

The simplest thing would be to forget this guy Shaa, forget the other friend Max had been talking to up in that castle, whatever *his* problem was and whatever Max had intended to do about it, and just roll Max over the side back into the river. If he came looking, I could tell Shaa I hadn't made it out here in time, and if I really had to I could blow town or lay low for a few months. Yeah, most likely somebody would come after me, but I'd had people after me before; probably still did, for that matter, it was part of the business.

The important point was that I could get rid of Max right now, and I'd never have a better shot. Not only was it the best idea for me, it had a lot to recommend it from a purely good-sense and good-of-the-community viewpoint.

I hate magic, and one reason is the mess it's made of the world; magic is more destabilizing than any other force of man or nature. Add a little magic to a situation and just watch how quickly things get out of hand. I didn't know how much of the current disaster had been caused by Max and his crew and how much of it they'd been fighting themselves, but now my favorite city was a wreck, who knew how many people were dead, river trade could be ruined for years, and what really had been solved? It was infighting among a small group, that's what it was, and all it did was trample people trying to live their lives and stay out of the way. If I took out Max, it looked like I'd be ridding the world of a prime player in a game I didn't like.

I almost made myself do it, I really almost did, and in a way, that shocked me more than anything else, because it was the kind of thing I'd promised myself I'd never ever do again. This mess had woken feelings I'd been trying to grapple with for years. They say you learn. They say you do what you have to do and after a while you get used to it, but I'd done things years before when I was nothing but a dumb hired-sword punk kid that still hung darkly in my memory, making me squirm whenever I thought of them and sending me out in the street to do something nice for some other poor dumb idiot. Maybe I just had a resistance to education. On the other hand, either we're all going to be barbarians, or somebody has to rein themselves in, decide when they're going to draw their own line, or decide when there's something they have to do because they think it's the right thing to do, even if it doesn't directly benefit themselves, even if sometimes it may be incompatible with their own survival. I'd done that, and that was the way I tried to live my life.

What is a good guy, really? Somebody who has principles and stands up for them? Somebody who does the right thing when he has a choice? Maybe. But what's the right thing? Keep the strong from taking over the world? Sometimes. Don't murder people if you can help it? Some people deserve murdering, so what then? Help out your friends? Usually. What was the answer, the real answer? Damned if I know, and anyway the situation didn't demand the whole book; on the scale of potential crucibles this one was pretty small, the whole affair was relatively minor to anyone who wasn't actually in Roosing Oolvaya at the moment. It didn't matter. I didn't know what a good guy was, but I always thought of myself as one of them. I could see Max thought of himself the same way. Both of us tried to do the right thing as we saw it, even if it wasn't necessarily the right thing for us. If I threw Max back in the water, I couldn't think of myself as the kind of person I wanted to be anymore, and that was worth a lot more to me than avoiding the trouble I'd surely inherit by keeping him alive.

So Max collapsed in the stern and I had to think of what he'd want me to do next.

The most urgent problem would be this Karlini person he'd been talking to. The water around the submerged base of the castle was foaming and churning, piles of large bubbles were boiling up around it, and the general tenor of the dancing lights on the walls and the descending cloud bank overhead seemed to imply that the castle was building up to a big event, and that event was coming real soon. Max had a link to Karlini back up in the castle and Karlini would be waiting for Max to help bail him out of some jam. Under the circumstances, my bet was that the thing Karlini needed bailing out of was the castle itself.

I could see a faint light-blue glow starting at Max's left hand and looping off toward the castle. I dropped down next to him and stuck my own hand in that beam. What had Max done? It had looked like he'd just talked. "Hello?" I said. "Anybody there? Karlini?"

Sure enough, I heard a faint voice. "Who are you?" it said. "Where's Max?"

"Max isn't doing too well, he's out cold. What kind of help did you need from him?"

I thought I heard a low "auugh!" kind of sound from the other end. Then, "If you need to ask, I'm sunk."

"Karlini!" I said. "I may be able to shoot you some more power, if that'll help."

"I don't know what he was going to try," Karlini muttered, "and this castle's going to move any second."

I still had the ring in my hand, clenched on my palm in a fist; tingling waves of heat were spreading out from it through my hand and up my arm. I still had Gash's metabolic link, too. Between the two of them they had to be good for something. I put my other hand, the one holding the ring, in the beam, and started to concentrate. "Help Karlini," I thought. *"Help Karlini."* I'd had practice with this kind of thing twice before now, even if those episodes hadn't worked quite as planned; this time it was coming easier. I got my other hand free and slapped Max across the face a few times for good measure, splashed some water in his eyes. The blue beam rippled.

"What's going on down there?" Karlini said.

I was looking straight ahead with my jaw locked and my mind wound around *"HELP KARLINI!"* and so I saw it start to happen. The disk of clouds overhead had been dropping; just as they reached the spire of the castle's tallest tower the whole castle strobed white, flickered, and began to fade. Roosing Oolvaya lights glimmered behind it. Next to me in the boat, Max was still unconscious. He was out cold, but maybe he was warming up a bit—he'd started coughing, thrashing his head against the water now splashing over him from the wind-driven waves breaking on the boat, and his hand was fluttering. His hand? I touched the ring to it. A puff of pale blue filled with snaky lines like the core of a thorn bush boiled up out of the air and shot up the beam toward Karlini. I thought I heard a voice say, "Max! I'm loose!" and then a length of blue thread tumbled out of the sky like a snapped kite string and coiled across the boat.

High up on the castle, at the ragged base of the tower Max had ridden down to the river, another dot appeared and started to fall. I could see that the dot was turning into the figure of a man, and that was too bad because it was falling outward from the castle but not out far enough, and there was a stone wall and a cluster of small buildings in its way long before the waves. Except—

Except he'd timed things better than I had, and he knew more about what was happening, too; so when he hit the uppermost roof in his path a second later the castle was by then no more than an outlined ghost drawn in spiderweb against the city, insubstantial as a cloud and still fading, and he passed straight through it without a catch and continued in the same trajectory toward the water. The water—THE WATER!

The castle had gone, and all of a sudden there was a big castle-sized hole in the river where there had been rock an instant before, and the water was starting to pour into it like a falling cliff. It was hopeless, hopeless for all of us, but I grabbed for the oars. Karlini fell. Then, suddenly, behind him in the midst of the cloud of thrown spray, behind him and coming up fast was a white shape, a large growing moving shape, the shape of a giant bird! Bird and Karlini disappeared as the rowboat rocked, the incredible pull of the cataract dragging us backward. I was thinking *"HELP!"* and *"RESCUE!"* and other such things but nothing was happening, nothing good anyway, nothing but the downhill slide of the boat; another couple of seconds maximum and that was going to be that. A flicker of motion at the side, low above the waves—the bird again!—coming toward me with labored wingbeats that barely cleared the water, Karlini no longer in the air by himself or in the river but in the dangling claws of the bird; and that was great for him but there was no way the bird could manage another person-sized passenger, let alone two. I dropped the oars, spun, yanked the boat's rope out from under Max, and hurled it into the air. The rope tangled, uncoiled, started to fall, the bird flashed by overhead, the rowboat spun down the smooth rushing surface of the torrent—the rope snapped taut! The eyebolt at the prow where the end of rope was knotted creaked and began to tear through the wood. I grabbed the rope and strained back against it as hard as I could. . . .

But the long moment passed and the rope held, and the hole behind us in the water filled, and the waves and giant ripples began to race back and forth across the surface of the river. The bird let the rope drop out of its beak and soared exhaustedly away, and I picked up the oars.

From the bottom of the boat I heard a loud groan. I looked down.

Max had one eye half-open with part of its pupil showing, and was trying to lever himself up with a hand on the side of the boat. "Karlini?" he croaked.

"Under control."

"Castle?"

"Up and gone."

Max's eye slumped closed and he sagged back into the bilge. "Well," he said faintly, "I guess that was all simple enough."

21
BACK AT THE
BILIOUS GNOME

It was finally Godsday. On Godsday in a city like Roosing Oolvaya, where no particular god held unchallenged domination, shops were usually open and people went about whatever commerce they chose; other people, of course, typically scurried from temple to temple, currying their accustomed favor. This was not a typical Godsday, though, and so three activities were the most popular—cleaning up and dredging out, appealing to the gods, and appealing to the spirits; the remaining bars were packed. Cleanup might take weeks, reconstruction would take even longer, and the owners of the two intact shipyards would become extremely rich, but all of that felt very long-term at the moment. Even with all the work to be done, many of the luckier inhabitants of Roosing Oolvaya (and everyone who had survived considered themselves lucky, at least in some measure) felt they deserved at least a moment's celebration.

The common-floor of the Bilious Gnome might have been mistaken for a hospital sickroom, what with the number of bruised, smashed, splinted, and wrapped people in attendance. Few people in sickrooms, though, could tear through a freshly roasted side of beef with the abandon of Maximillian the Vaguely Disreputable, who, beneath a liberal swath of bandages, looked like he had just come off a three-month stretch of dedicated dieting. Attempting to match him bite for bite from across the large table, and falling farther and farther behind, was the Great Karlini. "Watch out with that gravy, dear," said Ronibet, wiping a small brownish glob from her sleeve.

"It's all Max's fault, anyway," Karlini said, pausing in mid-chew and sliding the words out the side of his mouth.

Max pointed a knife at him. "Don't forget who wandered into a castle that didn't belong to him in the first place."

Karlini said something else around his mouthful of food that this time was totally unintelligible. "You'd better not repeat that," Max said.

Wroclaw had produced a damp cloth and was devoting his professional attention to the gravy spot. He bent to scrutinize his handiwork, lowering his mouth to the level of Roni's ear. "Master Maximillian's level of agitation is still uncommonly high," he said in a low voice.

"It's Shaa," Roni murmured. "He's worried about Shaa."

Wroclaw glanced casually toward the end of the table. "With some justification, it would appear."

Shaa was reclining in a large mud-encrusted chair that was covered by a fairly clean sheet, his legs elevated and outstretched along a bench. He had a flagon balanced on the chair's armrest. "Thank you, no," Shaa said to Jurtan Mont, who was reaching toward the flagon with the refill pitcher. "I am suspicious enough of this beverage as it is." Shaa sniffed ostentatiously at his cup, then broke into a sudden paroxysm of wet coughing.

Max looked up sharply. He gazed down the table at Shaa, his face blank. Shaa indicated the flagon. "Noxious emanations," he said. "It is possible that water has inadvertently been substituted for the requested ale. Could I interest you in a verifying taste?"

"I've had enough water in the last few days to hold me for the next five years," Max said. "Try it on your poison tester, there."

Jurtan Mont, who was of course the individual Max had alluded to, opened his mouth to try a rejoinder. His sister Tildy kicked him under the table. "A wise woman," Shaa murmured approvingly to her. "Responding to Max can often lead to complications. Would you appropriate the asparagus?"

Max's attention had already wandered. Recuperation from a bad spell-drain ordinarily left his mind part vegetable, and that part was mostly onion, garlic, and other roots known for their nasty temperament. The major thing he had focused his limited concentration on was indeed the problem of Shaa. Shaa had insisted on making it in from the street under his own power, but the effort had left him breathless and drenched in sweat; his face was still white and his breathing difficult now, almost two hours later. It was graphic confirmation of his state. Shaa had told Max earlier that in his professional opinion as a physician, he was not in terrific shape. On the other hand, medical science being as imprecise as it was, he could actually be in thoroughly lousy shape. With Shaa's resistance to magic-based cures, fixing him would be a knotty problem. Of course, Max did have some ideas. It was about time to rid Shaa of those damn curses anyway.

The only sounds for a moment were those related to eating; the man calling himself the Creeping Sword had just finished his story and everyone was digesting as much of it as they chose to. Karlini wiped his plate with a chunk of bread. "One thing I don't understand," he said, chewing thoughtfully on the crust. "I still don't know how I got decoupled from the castle. Max had something in mind but he didn't know exactly how he was going to work it. That was while he was awake. When it came to it, he wasn't even awake, he was unconscious."

"Then why did you jump?" said the Creeping Sword.

Karlini shrugged. "I felt something all of a sudden, like . . . like indigestion all over my body, maybe." Karlini glanced at the empty bowl that had held the potatoes. Karlini was quite fond of potatoes, and had figured large in the bowl's demise. "I figured that was it, Max pulling me loose, and it *was*, but anyway I didn't have a choice. I didn't want to ride the castle where it was going; it was already coming apart and I didn't know if it would survive the jump. I doubt it did, by the way. I thought I might have destabilized things enough on my own for me to pull away without stopping my heart again, and when I jumped I was betting Haddo would catch me."

"Again to rescue comes faithful servant," Haddo said, a carrot disappearing into the dark void inside his hood.

"Yes, thank you again, Haddo," Karlini said.

"Lots of us thank you," said the Creeping Sword. "Like me. You pulled me out of that whirlpool."

"Good are thanks," Haddo said, "also for faithful bird. Welcome gives bird, welcome give I. But thanks, everything is not. When extreme is danger, demonstrated is value of faithful servant, so also perhaps would not mind faithful servant particular recognition."

"What recognition?" Karlini said. "What are you talking about, Haddo? Everybody knows what you did, everybody's thanked you."

"Am talking bonus," said Haddo. Wroclaw's ears perked up.

"You want *what?*" Karlini said.

"Simple is word. Also, is pertinent other topic, of contract to renegotiate, of status to elevate."

Karlini looked at his plate, then at the dramatically shrunken carcass dominating the table's center. "Roni, how did that old heartburn recipe go?"

"Calm down, dear. Haddo, we'll discuss this later."

"Wise is mistress," Haddo said, bowing his hood demurely. "Always obedient, is faithful servant."

Karlini made a rude sound. "Quiet," Roni said. "Then maybe you'll get an answer to your question. Max?"

"Well," Max said, "magic isn't always strictly deterministic, you know. The way the Sword describes it, *something* happens when he goes into his spell-mode. What it is exactly, I don't know; some kind of resonance effect against his metabolic link, maybe. It sounds like he can say what he wants a spell to do, but he doesn't have to go through the work of actually designing the spell and setting it up. He just says, 'Do this,' and the spell-field tries to figure out something that's close to what hc wants. That sound plausible to you, Sword?"

"I guess," said the Creeping Sword. "I don't care. I'm getting rid of it as soon as I can. I don't want to cast spells. I tried it three times and it only worked right once."

"You ultimately got the results you wanted every time, didn't you?" Max said. "In my book that record's pretty good. Anyway, in this case, the Sword's spell-mode decided the best way to 'Help Karlini' was to get *me* to help Karlini, even if I wasn't conscious, so it went in and dug something out of my mind. I wish I could remember what it was it found."

"That's not a very neat answer," said Jurtan Mont. "What about—"

"In a mess like this you're lucky if you get one neat answer out of the whole thing. Results are usually more important than answers, anyway."

Shaa looked at Max; Roni and Karlini looked at Max, too, then looked at each other. "Is that the same Max we know who just said that?" Karlini whispered. "Who said answers aren't important?"

"I think so—"

Results, Jurtan Mont thought. Well, okay; I found out some new stuff about myself, stuff that doesn't look half bad, Tildy's free, Dad's square with Kaar, Kaar's getting square with the city, and it looks like Dad may even be willing to take another look at me, too. I guess when you look at it that way, it's really not bad, not bad at all.

Max, for his part, was looking over his own shoulder toward the door, where the voice of a man had opened up, bellowing, "You! Hey, you!"

"What's your problem?" Max yelled at him. "We've paid for our space, we're just trying to have a pleasant lunch here." Shaa had said the Bilious Gnome was the only half-decent place around that was halfway intact; he'd assured Max there would be no repercussions from any of his previous escapades.

"Maximillian," Shaa said across the table. The man in the door was familiar to him. He was the bartender who'd been on duty the last time Shaa had been at the Bilious Gnome, when he and Jurtan Mont had been chased by the Guard. The man's face was proceeding through shades of color heading toward purple. "YOU!" he said, pointing an accusing finger at Shaa from the end of his outstretched arm. "Get out of my place!"

"Are you the owner?" Shaa said.

"Don't start nothing with me! I said 'out,' and *out* you— "

"I happen to be rather comfortable at the moment," Shaa said, "and somewhat debilitated to boot, and as such am reluctant to leave this," he indicated the mud underfoot and the temporary ladder leading to the second floor with a wave of his own hand, "inspiring and tasteful establishment. If you must press the issue, let us discuss matters with the owner."

The man who had served the party emerged from the back room, rubbing his hands on a gray towel. "What's the excitement here, folks?"

"Are *you* the owner?" Shaa said.

"I'll do for it."

"You will do," Shaa said, "*if* you are the owner." The man squinted at him. "Are you crazy? Nobody's seen the owner in years. I just manage the place, hold part of the receipts back in case the guy shows up. I ain't never seen him myself, you understand, but he's the kind of guy you don't want to cross, if you get my drift. They made that pretty darn clear when his man bought the place."

"How would you recognize him if he does appear?" Shaa said slowly. Max looked over at him, examining his face, recognizing in his voice a certain note of growing suspicion.

"When he bought the Gnome a couple years ago he sent over this little crystal cube."

A nonplussed look appeared on Shaa's face, a once-in-several-years phenomenon. "Bring the cube," Shaa said.

The manager looked at him, opened his mouth, then closed it without a word and went out into the back room. A moment later he returned. In his hand was a small faded purple cloth tied at the top with a drawstring. he handed the bag to Shaa. Shaa loosened the string and inverted the bag over his hand, and a clear crystal cube about a thumb's-length along each edge dropped into his palm. Shaa scrutinized the cube with a contemplative expression. Then he touched the ball of his thumb to a depression in its polished face.

Deep in the heart of the cube, a strong purple glow burst out.

"I'll get your money," said the manager, and stumped off again toward the back. Shaa removed his thumb from the cube, and the glow died. Everyone at the table, all of whom had been staring at the cube, shifted their gazes upward to the face of Shaa. Shaa tilted his head back and began to examine the ceiling.

"You have anything you're interested in telling us?" Max said.

Shaa hrrumphed and cleared his throat. "Well, ah, you recall the period when I was Waterfront Health Inspector for Roosing Oolvaya? I, ah, invested some of my proceeds in local business. Actually, you see, I employed a fiscal adviser, and I was a bit behind on keeping track of things, ah, myself. Then, well, the post of Health Inspector moved abruptly to another, and I moved on, away from Roosing Oolvaya. In some haste."

The manager was returning with a hefty iron-bound chest. He dropped it with a heavy thud on the table in front of Shaa.

"My own place," Shaa said to him, glancing sadly around the room at the broken windows, smashed staircase, holes in the walls, and fractured tables still left from his own earlier visit, and at the superimposed damage from the flood, "and in such a state. Friend Manager, you should make it a point to cultivate a better class of client in the future."